SECRET DREAMS OF A FEARLESS GOVERNESS

Historical Regency Romance

THE DUKES' LADIES
BOOK 6

ABBY AYLES

This is a work of fiction.

Names, characters, organizations, places, events, and incidents are either products of the author's imagination or are used fictitiously. Any resemblance to actual person, living or dead, or actual events is purely coincidental.

Copyright © 2019 by Abby Ayles

All rights reserved.

No part of this book may be reproduced in any form or by any electronic or mechanical means, including information storage and retrieval systems, without written permission from the author, except for the use of brief quotations in a book review.

PRAISE FOR ABBY AYLES

Abby Ayles has been such an inspiration for me! I haven't missed any of her novels and she has never failed my expectations!

 -Edith Byrd

The characters in this novel have surely touched my heart.

 Linda C - "Melting a Duke's Winter Heart" 5.0 out of 5 stars Reviewed in the United States on December 21, 2019

This book kept me on the edge of my seat and I could not put it down.

 Wendy Ferreira - "The Odd Mystery of the Cursed

Duke" 5.0 out of 5 stars Reviewed in the United States on April 13, 2019

Oh this was a wonderful story and Abby has done it again! This storyline was perfect and the characters were developed and just had you reading to see if they get their happily ever after!

- Marilyn Smith - "Inconveniently Betrothed to an Earl" 5.0 out of 5 stars Reviewed in the United States on April 8, 2020

The sweetest story, with we rest abounding! I especially liked the bonus scene - totally unexpected engagements. Well written with realistic characters. Thank you!

Janet Tonole - "The Lady Of the Lighthouse" 5.0 out of 5 stars Reviewed in the United States on December 27, 2022

I just finished reading Abby Ayles' The Lady's Gamble and its bonus scene, and I wanted to tell other readers about this great story. I love regency romances and I believe Abby is one of the best regency writers out there!

Carolynn Padgett - "The Lady's Gamble" 5.0 out of 5 stars Reviewed in the United States on March 16, 2018

Such a great Book! So enjoyed the characters....they felt so " real"....and loved the " deleted" scene. Thanks Abby, for your gift of writing the best stories!

Marcia Reckard - "Entangled with the Duke" 5.0 out of 5 stars Reviewed in the United States on May 22, 2021

I loved this story. It took you through all of the exciting ups and downs. The characters were so honest. I could read it again and again.

Peggy Murphy - "The Duke's Rebellious Daughter" 5.0 out of 5 starsReviewed in the United States on December 3, 2022

I am never disappointed when reading one of Ms. Ayles stories. They have strong characters, engaging storylines, and all-around wonderful stories.

Donna L - "A Loving Duke for the Shy Duchess" 5.0 out of 5 stars Reviewed in the United States on December 23, 2019

A thoroughly enjoyable read! Love the complexity of the intelligent characters! They have the ability to feel emotions deeply! Their backstories help to explain why they behave as they do! The subplots and various interactions between characters add to the wonderful richness of the story! Well done!

Terry Rose Bailey - "A Cinderella for the Duke" 5.0 out of 5 stars Reviewed in the United States on October 8, 2022

ALSO BY ABBY AYLES

The Keys to a Lockridge Heart
Melting a Duke's Winter Heart
A Loving Duke for the Shy Duchess
Freed by the Love of an Earl
The Earl's Wager for a Lady's Heart
The Lady in the Gilded Cage
A Reluctant Bride for the Baron
A Christmas Worth Remembering
A Guiding Light for the Lost Earl
The Earl Behind the Mask

Tales of Magnificent Ladies
The Odd Mystery of the Cursed Duke

A Second Chance for the Tormented Lady
Capturing the Viscount's Heart
The Lady's Patient
A Broken Heart's Redemption
The Lady The Duke And the Gentleman
Desire and Fear
A Tale of Two Sisters
What the Governess is Hiding

Betrayal and Redemption
Inconveniently Betrothed to an Earl
A Muse for the Lonely Marquess
Reforming the Rigid Duke
Stealing Away the Governess
A Healer for the Marquess's Heart
How to Train a Duke in the Ways of Love
Betrayal and Redemption
The Secret of a Lady's Heart
The Lady's Right Option

Forbidden Loves and Dashing Lords
The Lady of the Lighthouse
A Forbidden Gamble for the Duke's Heart

A Forbidden Bid for a Lady's Heart
A Forbidden Love for the Rebellious Baron
Saving His Lady from Scandal
A Lady's Forgiveness
Viscount's Hidden Truths
A Poisonous Flower for the Lady

Marriages by Mistake
The Lady's Gamble
Engaging Love
Caught in the Storm of a Duke's Heart
Marriage by Mistake
The Language of a Lady's Heart
The Governess and the Duke
Saving the Imprisoned Earl
Portrait of Love
From Denial to Desire
The Duke's Christmas Ball

The Dukes' Ladies
Entangled with the Duke
A Mysterious Governess for the Reluctant Earl
A Cinderella for the Duke

Falling for the Governess
Saving Lady Abigail
Secret Dreams of a Fearless Governess
A Daring Captain for Her Loyal Heart
Loving A Lady
Unlocking the Secrets of a Duke's Heart
The Duke's Rebellious Daughter
The Duke's Juliet

SCANDALS AND SEDUCTION IN REGENCY ENGLAND

Also in this series

Last Chance for the Charming Ladies
Redeeming Love for the Haunted Ladies
Broken Hearts and Doting Earls
The Keys to a Lockridge Heart
Regency Tales of Love and Mystery
Chronicles of Regency Love
Broken Dukes and Charming Ladies
The Ladies, The Dukes and Their Secrets
Regency Tales of Graceful Roses
The Secret to the Ladies' Hearts
The Return of the Courageous Ladies
Falling for the Hartfield Ladies
Extraordinary Tales of Regency Love
Dukes' Burning Hearts
Escaping a Scandal

Regency Loves of Secrecy and Redemption
Forbidden Loves and Dashing Lords
Fateful Romances in the Most Unexpected Places
The Mysteries of a Lady's Heart
Regency Widows Redemption
The Secrets of Their Heart
Lovely Dreams of Regency Ladies
Second Chances for Broken Hearts
Trapped Ladies
Light to the Marquesses' Hearts
Falling for the Mysterious Ladies
Tales of Secrecy and Enduring Love
Fateful Twists and Unexpected Loves
Regency Wallflowers
Regency Confessions
Ladies Laced with Grace
Journals of Regency Love
A Lady's Scarred Pride
How to Survive Love
Destined Hearts in Troubled Times
Ladies Loyal to their Hearts
The Mysteries of a Lady's Heart
Secrets and Scandals
A Lady's Secret Love
Falling for the Wrong Duke

GET ABBY'S EXCLUSIVE MATERIAL

*B*uilding a relationship with my readers is the very best thing about writing.

Join my newsletter for information on new books and deals plus a few free books!

You can get your books by clicking or visiting the link below

https://BookHip.com/JBWAHR

PS. Come join our Facebook Group if you want to interact with me and other authors from Starfall Publication on a daily basis, win FREE Giveaways and find out when new content is being released.

Join our Facebook Group

abbyayles.com/Facebook-Group

SECRET DREAMS OF A FEARLESS GOVERNESS

In his hour of need, an angel will bring light into his life. But angels are fragile things...

After the death of his parents, Edmund Hardwicke, the young Earl of Kelt, finds himself burdened with enormous responsibilities - none heavier than being in charge of his many younger siblings. When Joanna Warrick, the new governess, arrives at his home, she breathes life into everything. Like a wind of light and hope after the family's misfortunes, she even awakens Edmund's sleeping heart.

. . .

But a storm is brewing, and that storm has a name: Christopher Hardwicke. Edmund's younger brother will do everything in his power to see him suffer and ruined, and his unexpected arrival foretells nothing but trouble.

Now, Joanna will have to deftly navigate secrets, lies, and the battle of wills between two stubborn brothers who have both lost too much. But while her heart secretly dreams of a happy future and seeks to bring peace in a home divided, an old enemy reawakens, threatening them all...

1

Joanna Warrick looked up at the grand home in front of her. She barely had the courage to step out of the carriage, now that she was confronted with it. Her heart was heavy in her chest, and part of her wanted nothing more than to tell the driver to turn around and take her home.

But there was no home for her, not anymore. Or, to look at it another way, this house *was* her new home.

She sighed, and stepped down to the ground, taking the offered arm of the driver. He quickly turned away to fetch her luggage down, leaving her to her own devices.

She looked around, spinning slowly on the spot to take in the view around the house itself.

Acres of parkland stretched in every direction – the

carriage had travelled through it for some distance after entering the gates.

It was more impressive than her family's home had ever been, if for the grounds alone. But for the house, she could say with sincerity that it was not any more grand or well-kept than that of her father.

Yet here she was, ready to take up a position as little better than a servant inside it.

An older man, a butler by his appearance at the door, came down the steps to greet her.

"Miss Warrick, I presume?" he said.

"Yes," Joanna replied, nervously adjusting her bonnet.

"The children are waiting in the school room to meet you. Come, I will show you where you need to go."

Joanna glanced down at her bags, her only belongings in the world now, which the carriage driver had deposited on the floor at her feet.

"I'll ask one of the housemaids to take those to your room," the butler said. "My name is Jenkins. Please, do follow me."

Joanna nodded and hurried after him as he turned to walk briskly away. She did not quite trust her voice or her words at that moment. Of course, she had interacted with servants like Jenkins many a time.

The only problem was that she had done so as the daughter of the house, and as such, his superior. Now that things had changed and she had fallen so far, she barely knew how to act.

"I believe you have not met any of the Hardwicke family previously," Jenkins was saying.

"No," Joanna replied. "I... well, I lived far north of here. I've never even visited this part of England."

Jenkins looked back over his shoulder, fixing her with an inscrutable gaze for a moment. "I suppose your mother thought that would be for the best."

"Yes," Joanna said, hearing her own voice crack just a little. "She felt it would be less difficult if I became governess to a family we had not met in social circles."

The butler grunted slightly under his breath, which might have been taken for an agreement or for derision. Joanna did not feel tempted to ask which.

He led her through a grand open hall from the entrance, with corridors and doors snaking off in all directions. There was also a wide staircase leading upwards, though for the moment he took her to the right.

Down a corridor with wooden floorboards which rapped smartly under her shoes, and finally to another door right at the end, where he paused.

"Now, listen," Jenkins said, taking a breath and looking at her sternly. "They are children. That means you are in control. They must do as you say in terms of their education. You may not find that my lord, the Earl of Kelt, is open to conversation on this point. In other words, if they should misbehave, you will need to take them in hand – and quickly. If they see weakness in you, I assure you, you will be gone the way of the last governess."

"What happened to the last governess?" Joanna asked.

She wiped her hands, which for some reason hand suddenly become damp with perspiration, on the sides of her dress.

Jenkins' face softened, becoming almost avuncular. "Never mind about that, for now," he said. "They're waiting. Have you been informed of their names?"

Joanna nodded, looking up to the ceiling briefly as she recalled what had been sent to her in the letter confirming her appointment.

"They are Patience, who is sixteen; Samuel, who is nine; and the littlest Amy, who is five."

"Correct," Jenkins nodded. He cocked his head at the sound of a chiming from a grandfather clock somewhere back down the corridor. "I must go, and you are already late. Let's go in."

Without waiting for a confirmation from Joanna, who would really have liked to wait a few minutes more at least, he opened the door and stepped smartly inside.

The children had evidently been deep in conversation, for they all stopped talking at once and looked up at the doorway.

They were sitting on soft chairs inside the moderately-sized room, which held several bookcases, tables, and other learning instruments. Joanna saw a globe and a chalkboard before fixing her attention on the children.

"Are you the new governess?" the oldest girl asked. Patience's voice was short and terse, as if she had prepared already to dislike Joanna.

She had dark hair falling in ringlets down her back, tied with bright yellow ribbons, and a yellow gown to match. She was quite pretty, even despite the frown that settled on her features as she looked at them.

"Now, Miss Patience," Jenkins remonstrated gently, placing a hand on Joanna's shoulder. "This is Miss Warrick Warrick, your new governess. She has travelled far to be with you today."

"Warrick," Patience said thoughtfully, casting her eye across the room to a number of books that lay open on a table. "Aren't you a lady?"

Joanna cleared her throat uncomfortably. "I... My father was a baron," she said, quite unsure for a moment of what to say. Her cheeks burned, the shame of her situation coming to her fully.

"Why isn't he your father anymore?" Amy asked, piping up with a curious tilt of her head.

The youngest girl was darling, a picture of her older sister with the same ringlets, yet dressed in pink and with round, smiling cheeks.

"Don't be silly, Amy," Patience said, tossing her hair over her shoulder. "He's dead."

Joanna's heart almost stopped in her chest. It was cruel, to hear it told so simply. She was flustered, her hands fluttering together in front of her. She managed to calm them and clasp them together, letting them drop down in front of her body.

With a great effort, she could respond. "Miss Patience is correct," she said, clearing her throat to rid it of the obstruction before she continued. "My father passed away quite recently."

"What happened to him?" Samuel asked, although Jenkins was obviously squirming in discomfort at their line of questioning.

He was a small boy, pale and short for his age, and his clothes seemed too large. The dark hair on his head was cut short, though it was easy to see that he shared the curls of his sisters.

"I…" Joanna began, but looked to Jenkins for help, despairingly. How was she to talk about this with the young children who were to be her charges? How could she share with them her shame and grief, and they so young to understand it?

"I heard Edmund talking about it," Patience declared. "He was telling Christopher. The baron's heart failed him out of shame. They quite ran out of money, you see."

"My lady!" Jenkins burst out, fixing Patience with a furious glare. "That is quite enough for the moment. Your governess will take you through your lessons now."

He nodded to Joanna, then turned on his heel and left the room. Just like that, she was alone.

Joanna was reminded of a novel she had read perhaps a year before, in which one of the characters had been thrown to wolves to be eaten. This, she thought as the door closed behind him, was probably how it had felt.

She cleared her throat for the umpteenth time and tried to grasp some control.

"Children, I will need to take you through your paces first of all to see what lessons you are in need of. We'll commence with some tests."

All three children groaned, and Joanna gave them a small smile.

"It won't be too serious. You'll see. I just want to know what you know. There's nothing wrong with not knowing something yet, not for this test, at least."

She moved in front of the chalkboard and picked up the chalk, and tried not to think about her father. The collapse of the bank, into which he had invested all of the family's money, had been so hard on him.

She was not angry at him; he may not have had a good head for business, but he was her father, and he had always shown her love and affection.

It was that same lack of concern for money that had him gifting her silk ribbons and puppies and new bonnets every time he went to the city. And hadn't she enjoyed all of those gifts?

"Let's start with the basics," Joanna said, smiling down at little Amy. "We'll go through the three R's first. I want to see that you have a good foundation."

Patience sighed loudly. "Isn't this just for Amy's benefit?" she asked.

"Not at all," Joanna said, holding her smile without a pause this time. "I expect you and Mr. Samuel to know all of these basics already. You should pass easily, and if you don't, then I know what to work on first."

Though Patience made her displeasure known with a number of dramatic sighs and huffs, Joanna continued resolutely.

She found with some relief that the children were well-learned, and though Samuel was of an age where he should have gone away to school, he did not seem to have fallen too far behind what she had expected.

"Our last governess told me how to remember that," he said, proudly, after she had asked him to name some capitals from the globe.

"Oh?" Joanna asked, leaning closer for a moment.

Patience and Amy were distracted with their own exercises, and after checking with a glance that they were not listening, Joanna saw her chance.

"What exactly happened to your last governess?"

"Oh, Edmund didn't like her," Samuel explained. "He said she was too strict because she shouted at Patience."

Joanna glanced over at Patience again, but the older girl

was seemingly entranced by an examination of her own nails and fingers. "Was she your governess for a long time?"

"No," Samuel shrugged. "Just as long as the last one."

Joanna felt fingers of ice touching her spine. "How many governesses have you had, Samuel?"

The boy thought for a moment. "Well," he said, "since Mama and Papa died, I think... maybe ten."

"Ten!" Joanna felt her heart beating faster.

She had suspected that there had been one or two before her, but not ten. And all since their parents died? Perhaps it had been many years ago... but then, Amy was but five years old, wasn't she?

"When.... When did your parents die?"

"Well, I'm nine now, so, hmm..." Samuel said, counting on his fingers. "A year and three months."

Joanna stared at him, dumbfounded. To go through so many governesses, in just fifteen months? Some of them must have counted their stays in the days or weeks, rather than months!

"And why did they all leave?" She managed to ask after a moment's pause.

"Edmund didn't like them," Samuel said, turning his attention back to the globe.

Joanna stared at the short curls on his head as he peered at the names of places painted onto the wooden surface. How was she ever going to last in a place like this?

2

Edmund looked out of the window of the carriage, sighing. He could see that they were still a long way from home, and the day was not getting any earlier.

"Can't we go any faster?" He asked, leaning his head out to shout at the driver.

"No, my lord," the driver said. "I'm afraid the roads are very muddy today. All the rain overnight. It's pulling back our wheels and making the horses' hooves heavy."

Edmund sighed, and pulled his head back inside the carriage. What a mess. He was going to be late, and on the day that the children met their new governess.

It wasn't as though it could have been helped. There was so much to do up at the London office. His father had run a tight ship, but in the months following his death, things had become rather less restrained.

Now it was up to Edmund to put everything back in its place.

Although he felt he had been doing a good job, running things as his father had taught him, there were still a good many liberties that had been taken in his absence at the beginning.

He leafed through the papers he had brought along with him, so that he could continue working on the carriage journey home.

A note from Lord Kelverley made him pause, and shake his head in annoyance. The man had cornered him in the London office earlier that morning, trying to haggle him down on price.

"Your father was always a reasonable man, with a good head for business," Kelverley had said.

"Yes," Edmund had replied. "He had good enough sense not to offer you a lower price when you were dealing with him."

"But, my boy," Kelverley had entreated, although they were now equal in status. It was as if he had not noticed that his father's death made Edmund the new Earl. "Times have changed. People have less confidence in the company now."

Edmund had stood then, his chair scraping back across the wooden boards of the floor of his father's office.

"If you have less confidence in the company, you are more than welcome to take your business elsewhere. Since you do not, and since you come to me haggling like a fishwife, I can assume that you are attempting to test out whether I will give you some kind of discount out of inexperience.

"I can assure you, Lord Kelverley, that I am not going to fail. You will pay the same price you paid my father, or you will receive nothing at all."

That had stopped the old lord in his tracks, though it had done little good for the overall picture.

The truth was that many of their customers, the loyal base that Edmund's father had built up over the years, were not as eager to deal with his son.

They had, of course, expected Edmund to step up to run the business perhaps a decade or more from now.

Instead, he had been forced to take the position as head of the company at just twenty-three years old.

A year on, he knew they still thought him wet behind the ears, inexperienced, and liable to make mistakes.

Hadn't he proved himself yet? Over a year, and the company had not burned to the ground. Far from it: he was keeping it afloat successfully, and had even made inroads towards expansion.

The trouble now was maintaining their income enough in order to finance it.

Edmund rubbed a hand over his forehead, sweeping a few loose curls back off his brow.

"Oh, Father," he muttered, staring at Lord Kelverley's seal on the note. "What would you think of me now?"

Even as he said it, a foolish, prideful voice in the back of his head told him that his father would be pleased. That he had made the best of a bad situation, and that he hadn't floundered, despite being out of his depth.

All of that counted in his favour, and now that he knew what he was doing, he was sure he could allow the company to flourish.

The children were another matter. Edmund searched through the pile of papers for the advertisement he had seen, and read it over again.

Young lady from good family seeks a position as governess. Well-educated in French, pianoforte, deportment, drawing, history, use of the globes, and other areas.

It did not say much, but it had been enough to prompt him to contact the address held by the newspaper.

The arrangements had been made with Miss Warrick's mother, who had been keen to reassure him that she was an accomplished and pleasant young lady – in spite of the fact that her family's scandal had cost her the status she should have been granted.

Edmund closed his eyes for a brief moment, to think of his own parents.

It was still a wound that lingered in his chest. The family had fallen victim to a wasting illness that had grasped hold of both their parents and Samuel almost overnight.

Edmund, his second brother Christopher, Patience, and Amy had somehow been spared. Even one of their servants, a housemaid who had been with the family for many years, succumbed to it and died a few days after her master and mistress.

Edmund could only praise God that Samuel had survived. Though he was much weakened, and behind other boys of his age, he was at least alive.

The problem now, of course, was that Edmund had essentially become the head of the family in the space of only a few days, and now he was responsible for three children – and one adult in the form of Christopher, who needed perhaps the most supervision of all of them.

At last, the carriage entered through the gates of the Hardwicke grounds, and Edmund breathed a sigh of relief. It felt good to be home again, though he knew he had not completed all of the work he should have done during the ride.

He was simply too tired, and too worried about the children, to focus any longer.

He jumped down from the carriage without help, striding towards the door of his home with the sheaf of papers under his arm.

"Get the carriage cleaned up, Tom," he called up to his

driver. "I want those wheels clean for the morning. I've a feeling it will be drier, and we'll need to press on."

"Yes, my lord," Tom replied, jumping down from his seat and moving to unhitch the horses.

"Jenkins, good," Edmund continued, seeing his butler open the door as he approached. "Has the governess arrived?"

"Miss Warrick has been with the children since the afternoon, my lord. She was a little late to arrive."

Edmund nodded thoughtfully. It was something to note, though not perhaps something to judge this new woman on too quickly.

"The roads were awful today. I'm sure she ran into the same problems as I did."

"Very generous of you, sir," Jenkins said.

Edmund gave him a direct look, and the man had the good grace to seem abashed.

"Send her to dine with me. I'll take my meal shortly. I'll simply change from my travel clothes and be down."

"Yes, sir," Jenkins replied, scurrying away down the corridor towards the kitchens as fast as his old frame could.

3

"You're to meet him downstairs for your supper," Mary said.

Mary was a plain, mousey young housemaid, who had helped Joanna settle her things into her new, cramped quarters in the servants' wing.

Her things, such as they were: only a few dresses, one or two of them nice enough to wear to a social occasion, a bonnet, and two pairs of shoes.

The rest were a few small trinkets from home, and some material that she had been sewing to keep her occupied for the journey south.

Such was the total and sum of her worldly possessions. It did not feel like much, from a childhood spent with everything she could have asked for.

"Tonight?" Joanna asked, feeling stupid.

"Right now," Mary said, her eyes lighting up with near-panic. "You're to get dressed and go down right away."

Joanna considered that carefully, looking down at herself. Truth be told, she didn't have many options.

The dress she wore now was fine for her day to day duties, and while she would normally wish to dress herself up for dinner, this was a rather different affair.

She had no desire to outshine her employer, and it might be construed as vanity or pompousness if she were to dress above her station now.

After all, wasn't she just a servant? She might have been a lady once, but those days were done.

"Thank you, Mary," Joanna said. "I'll just fix my hair, and be down shortly."

Mary nodded and rushed out, apparently to go and ensure the dining room was clean and neat for her master's meal. Jenkins was already down there, laying out silverware and ordering the cooks about.

Joanna sighed, and examined herself in the small glass that stood propped on the windowsill of her room.

Her hair had been curled artfully overnight and placed into a neat chignon under her travelling hat.

Now, though, after a long day, the curls in front of her ears were straightening back out, and the chignon had come loose and messy.

She did her best to pin everything back into place, and

twirled the front parts of her hair around her fingers repeatedly to try to make them curl.

Finally, they only looked a little worse for wear, and she had to accept that it was the best she would be able to achieve.

Joanna's stomach leaped inside her as she stepped outside of her room. The path back towards the main body of the house, and the waiting dinner, seemed horribly short.

This was the first time that she was to meet her new employer – this seeming ogre of a man who had already dismissed ten governesses before her.

For a fleeting moment, she wondered whether unpacking had been unnecessary. Perhaps he would put her back in a carriage to her mother the next morning.

She approached the door, and saw Mary almost running down the corridor with a bundle of firewood in her arms.

"Mary!" Joanna called out in a half-whisper, causing the maid to pause and look her way. "Is he… of a pleasant mood?"

Mary shrugged, almost dropping her load. "He's been out working and travelling all day," she whispered back. "He was quite sour about my not having the fireplace ready. I must rush on!"

"Oh," Joanna replied, standing still now in the corridor and watching Mary go into the room.

From this spot, she could not be seen by anyone inside sitting at the table, and for a long moment she debated the possibility of simply standing here forever and never having to face him.

But she knew it was inevitable, and besides, perhaps Mary's work at the fire would distract Lord Kelt for long enough that her entrance need not be so much of a spectacle.

Joanna stepped through the open doorway, holding her breath, and almost immediately saw her new employer sitting at the head of his table.

She dipped into an ungainly, uncertain curtsey, almost tripping over her own feet.

"Miss Warrick, I presume?" Lord Kelt said.

Joanna could barely breathe. "Yes, Lord Kelt," she said.

"Sit," Lord Kelt said, his voice flat and sharp. "We have delayed dining for long enough already."

Joanna fumbled for the chair, drawing it out and falling down gratefully onto its cushioned seat. She was glad of the support just then.

"Chestnut soup, sir," Jenkins intoned, laying out a large bowl into the centre of the table. He began to ladle it out into individual portions for Joanna and Lord Kelt.

"You have met the children already," Lord Kelt said. It did not sound like a question, though Joanna supposed that she was still expected to answer it.

"Yes, Your Lordship," Joanna said. "I took some time to

acquaint myself with their current learning. Tomorrow I shall be able to form a plan for their continued lessons."

Lord Kelt grunted. "I trust you found them to be satisfactory."

Joanna smiled shyly. "They are quite accomplished. Even Miss Amy is quite ahead of where I expected to find her."

"Their education has not suffered since our parents left them in my care," he said. There was a frown drawing down over his eyes that felt almost like an accusation.

Had she insulted him perhaps, by suggesting that they might not have been developed? Oh, but she had not meant that at all!

"Indeed, that is evident," Joanna said quickly. "I only mean that they are intelligent children."

Lord Kelt said nothing, but began to eat his soup. Joanna followed suit, glad at least of the break.

But the longer they went without saying a word, the more uncomfortable the atmosphere became.

Soon she was wishing he would say something, anything at all. It was almost unbearable to sit like this, sipping soup in silence.

The metallic clanging of their spoons seemed almost to bounce off the walls, and Joanna hardly dared to swallow for how loud it sounded in her ears.

The crackling of the fire was barely any consolation at all, and she even began to fancy that the room was too hot.

The second course, a roasted meat pie with carrots and parsnips, filled the space with a momentary flurry of activity.

Lord Kelt spoke briefly with Jenkins, and Joanna seized this as her chance to at least make some small conversation.

If she was not the first to break the silence, then it was not as difficult – though she still felt out of place to speak to him without his first addressing her. Still, it was better than that interminable nothing.

"Are you often at work in the city, Lord Kelt?" she asked.

"Quite often," he replied. "Several days out of the week. It is necessary in order to ensure that the business stays running. My father kept a townhouse, but I do not care for the practice.

"I would rather travel daily. It means I can watch over the children's education and the upkeep of the house at the same time."

Joanna swallowed a piece of pie, harder than she had intended to. For an awful moment she believed she would choke.

The idea of him watching so closely over her work, when she knew already how exacting he could be, was not a comforting one.

"You care for them greatly," she said, as soon as she had recovered.

"Of course I do. They are my siblings. Nothing is more

important than family. Do you not believe that to be the case?"

Joanna looked up to find Lord Kelt staring directly at her, his gaze piercing through her.

She found she could not remember how to breathe for a moment. His dark eyes seemed to contain a world of meaning, and though she could not fathom what it might be, the pain that had marred him at his parents' death was plain to see.

"I do," she replied, simply and quietly. It was difficult to hold back her tears at that moment, and she blinked quickly, though she did not look away.

Something changed in his face, softening it and making it more pleasant. "Forgive me. I had quite forgotten that you, too, recently lost your father."

Joanna looked down at her plate and forced herself to resume eating her pie. "Thank you. It is a difficult time, for all of us."

"I have no doubt," he replied, recommencing his own meal.

Joanna took a few opportunities to sneak glances in his direction as they ate. Now that she had met his eyes, she was not quite as afraid to look at him.

He had a noble nose and the same dark hair as his siblings, which curled effortlessly along his temples without appearing disorderly. His colouring suggested time spent outdoors, though not so much as to be rough or unsightly.

In short, he was quite a handsome man. He could be even more so if it were not for the frown that seemed almost permanently etched on his features, and the dark circles under his eyes that indicated a lack of sleep.

"It must keep you very busy," Joanna said. "Your company, I mean."

"Yes," Lord Kelt said, looking even more tired for a moment, as if pointing it out only made him feel it the more.

"It has been a long day, today in particular. I wanted to be home earlier in order to ensure you were settling well with the children."

"We were quite comfortable," Joanna said. She felt a pity for him. It was obvious that the man needed rest, though he was not likely to get it with so much laying on his shoulders. She did not envy him.

With almost a start, though, she realised that her own position could be much the same: she had to work for her keep now, and could not spend her days in idle leisure or pleasurable pastimes as she had before.

"I hope you have enjoyed your dinner," Lord Kelt said, laying down his knife and leaning back in his chair. He was quite evidently finished with eating.

"Yes, thank you, your Lordship," Joanna said, dipping her head.

"It won't be a regular affair. I wanted to meet you on your arrival in our home, but from henceforth you will take your meals with the servants," he told her, wiping his mouth with a cloth napkin.

"Of course," Joanna said, more out of reflex than any real sense – for the commandment stung.

All her life she had been the young lady of the house, and she had had servants to do her own bidding. Now to be relegated amongst them was hard to bear.

But she tried to remain humble. It was, after all, her place now.

She trained her eyes carefully on the table and offered no complaint. It was better this way than getting nothing to eat at an empty table in an empty house.

"From tomorrow, I expect the children to be kept to a strict schedule. They are to learn as much as you can possibly teach them. Samuel, in particular," Lord Kelt said, getting up from his seat.

"You are to develop them, Miss Warrick, into the finest young people in the county. Are you able to accomplish that?"

Joanna thought of her three new charges as she stood: the kind Amy, weak but eager Samuel, and boisterous Patience.

Though she had little confidence in herself, it was true what she had said. The children were well-learned already, and if she had any skill at all in teaching them, they would develop further.

"Yes, Lord Kelt, I think I am."

"Don't think, Miss Warrick," he said over his shoulder as he left the room. "Believe. For if you are to remain in this household, accomplish it you must."

4

*E*dmund shuffled the papers on his desk again, trying hard to concentrate.

It was no good. He rang a small bell by his side, and waited to hear the familiar footsteps outside his door.

"Yes, my lord?"

"Jenkins, where are the children?"

Jenkins glanced behind him, as if he were expecting to find them there. "They are with their new governess, sir."

"And where is that?" Edmund asked, barely able to maintain his patience.

"Oh – they are in the schoolroom, sir," Jenkins said. "Miss Warrick did express some thought of a trip outside, but said it would wait until warmer weather, sir."

Edmund nodded. He pushed his papers into some

semblance of order on his desk and handed Jenkins two sealed envelopes.

"See that these are delivered, will you?" he asked, standing up.

Jenkins took them with a bow and was soon gone from sight.

Edmund stretched his arms above his head, feeling a relief at the movement. He had been sitting before his desk for too many hours already. A few more, and it would be time to dine with the children.

There were pressing matters that needed to be dealt with amongst his papers, but nothing was more urgent to him than his siblings. It was past time to ensure the progress of their education.

Edmund moved through his home fluently, knowing the corridors like the back of his hand. Better, perhaps, having lived there since the day he was born in an upstairs room.

Much of the estate was tied in painful memories of his mother and father, but all the same, this was where he would stay. It was his birth right, and his heritage.

This home had belonged to the Hardwickes since they took the seat of the Earl of Kelt some centuries before. He was not going to be the first to abandon it.

He slowed his pace as he approached the schoolroom, favouring silence and caution above speed. He waited until he could see into the room, through a small gap where the door had been left ajar, and paused there.

He had to know whether his brother and sisters were receiving the education they required. And if this new Miss Warrick were to raise her voice at them or mark the back of their hands with a ruler, well, she would hear from him about it.

"That's beautiful work, Miss Patience," he heard Miss Warrick saying.

Edmund leaned forward a little, and he could see Patience bending her head over some needlework. She was resting the hoop on her knees, and he could not see the design. Miss Warrick stood behind her, looking over her shoulder.

"Perhaps you could try a more complex stitch for the roses. Some French knots, perhaps, with couched threads to form the lines," Miss Warrick continued.

Patience twisted her face. "I dislike French knots. They always twist on the needle and get too tight, and I get a knot in my thread that pulls right through the fabric."

"Show me now," Miss Warrick said, tolerantly.

Edmund and she both watched as Patience drew the thread against her finger, spun it around the needle three times, and then attempted to push it back through the fabric.

"Ah, there," Miss Warrick said, reaching out to guide her fingers. "Keep some pressure on the thread, so it will stay in place. You see? Now draw it through.... Yes, like that... Very well done."

Edmund smiled at the self-satisfied look on his sister's face, but then swallowed it. So, the woman had managed to teach her a single stitch; it was hardly a grand accomplishment.

Whether the lesson would hold was another thing entirely again. He watched still, shifting his weight until he could just make out Amy's small form through the slightest space between the wall and the door.

"How are you doing with your writing, Miss Amy? Let me see," Miss Warrick said, leaning over the second girl now.

"Oh! That's very pretty indeed. But perhaps you might draw me some flowers during our art classes, little one. You must focus on your writing today."

"I'm sorry, Miss Warrick," Amy said, and she sounded so plaintive that it made Edmund's blood rush for a moment.

Surely, she was not afraid of the woman! Had she shouted at her, or punished her in some way?

"That's alright," Miss Warrick said. Her voice was kind and soft, and Edmund caught a glimpse of her smoothing down Amy's hair affectionately. "Now, do you remember what to write?"

Edmund puzzled over it. She sounded gentle now, and did not remonstrate with the child.

Perhaps she had changed her demeanour – perhaps even heard a sound of someone stepping outside.

Had he not been careful enough? But no, there was no indication that Miss Warrick had heard him at all.

"Is Edmund home today?" Samuel piped up. Edmund shifted his position, but from where he stood in the hall, he could not see his little brother, try as he might.

"Why, yes, I believe Lord Kelt is working in his office here today," Miss Warrick said.

"Can I go watch him?"

Edmund smiled to himself. Samuel was turning into a nuisance. He always wanted to watch his big brother work. For a short while, when they were between governesses, he had even allowed it.

But it was no good; the boy asked thousands of questions, so much so that Edmund had not been able to get anything done at all.

"No, no," Miss Warrick laughed. "You'll have to keep at your lessons. Your brother won't be too pleased if I let you escape me."

"I'll take my books," Samuel tried.

"I'm afraid the answer is no," Miss Warrick said. "You will see him at dinner. The harder you study, the quicker the time will pass. I should bury my nose in that book if I were you."

"I like it here better anyway," Amy said, her voice still so child-like compared to that of her older siblings. "Miss Warrick's so nice and pretty."

Miss Warrick laughed again, heartily this time. "Oh, Miss Amy, aren't you the sweetest thing," she said. "But you can't get around me that way. Come, let me see your script... oh, that is well-written."

"How do you think I should sew this part?" Patience asked. She sounded strangely shy, not at all like the strident young lady she normally was.

It took Edmund a long moment to realise that she was probably quite unused to asking for help. He had never heard her say such a thing, not to all the governesses whom he had employed.

"Let me see now... Ah, yes. Why don't you take this part, like so..."

Edmund shifted his feet and watched Miss Warrick sew deftly, having taken the embroidery hoop from Patience's hands. Her eyes were narrowed in concentration, and she quickly handed the hoop back, pointing out some technical details for Patience's benefit.

Edmund waited in the corridor, a frown settling deeper on his face as time wore on. There was nothing he had heard that lay any fault at Miss Warrick's door.

No, she was all but the perfect governess: kind, patient, measured, and graceful. She used the same light deftness to correct a mistake as to deflect the children's attempts to leave their books behind and play, or seek Edmund out in his office.

In fact, there was nothing he could reproach in her at all.

It was quite dissatisfying.

The grandfather clock in the main hall chimed, and Edmund quickly straightened up. He had quite lost track of time, listening to the children at their lessons.

Normally it would take him only a short while to form an assessment of a new governess, but he had been lulled into a relaxed state by Miss Warrick's calm and gentle voice.

She had attentively moved between the three children, despite the differences in their lessons and their development.

Now, to his alarm, he realised he had quite overstayed his intentions. The chime was a signal of the end of lessons, which meant –

The door to the schoolroom burst fully open, and Samuel nearly ran head-on into him.

"Edmund!" he exclaimed. "Why are you standing outside?"

"I'm... not standing," Edmund said, keeping his eyes on Samuel so that he would not have to look up at Miss Warrick.

"I was walking over to fetch you for dinner. I didn't know if your new governess had been told about the significance of the chime."

"We stopped for dinner yesterday," Samuel pointed out.

"Ah, yes," Edmund said. "Right. Well, come along, Amy and Patience. I'm sure Jenkins is ready to serve."

He looked up and noticed Miss Warrick lingering by the doorframe, watching them.

"They were well-behaved, I trust?" Edmund asked, though he knew the answer for himself.

"Little angels," Miss Warrick replied, smiling and tidying away a rogue strand of curls on Amy's head.

"Wonderful," Edmund said, hesitating. The way she stood there – did she think he would invite her to dine with them? He had made things clear the evening before.

She made no move to follow them, however, and after a moment he supposed that he was perhaps putting a meaning onto her actions that was not really there.

He took Amy's hand, nodded to Miss Warrick, and led Samuel away towards the main hall. Patience followed, brushing her long hair back over her shoulder with a careless grace.

After changing quickly to clothing more suitable for dining, Edmund sat at his table, watching his siblings attack their evening meal.

"So, are you enjoying your lessons?" he asked, trying not to sound too concerned.

"I love Miss Warrick," Amy said, grinning and popping a pea into her mouth with her hands. "She's really nice. And she drew me a horsey."

"It's called a horse, Amy," Patience said, sounding bored.

"Leave her be," Edmund chided. "And what of you, Patience? Do you like your new governess?"

"She's satisfactory," Patience said.

Edmund was taken aback. That was high praise, indeed. "Sammy?"

"I think she's really clever," Samuel said, furrowing his brow seriously. "She knows things."

"A good trait for a governess, I have to admit," Edmund said, amused. "So, you'd like to keep her."

"Yes, please!" Amy shouted, making Samuel jump in his chair and Edmund laugh.

"Don't shout!" Patience scolded her.

"Alright, everyone, that's enough," Edmund chuckled. "We'll keep her. For now, at least. Now, you be sure to tell me if you feel that something changes."

"Edmund, when is Christopher coming home?" Patience asked, changing the subject abruptly.

Edmund sighed, and put down his fork. He did not relish the idea of talking about Christopher. His closest brother in age, but perhaps the least in maturity.

Even Samuel had his moments of wisdom and insight, between his childish play. Christopher was in his own world, and wherever it was, it was not where he was meant to be.

"I'm not sure," Edmund admitted. "I have heard from

our friend, the Captain, that he did indeed enlist as he was supposed to. This time. They have him in training to be an officer. I expect he will be allowed to return home once he has completed his training."

"Is it dangerous?" Amy asked, her little round face transforming into a worried pout.

"I'm sure he is in no danger," Edmund told her. Privately he added to himself, not from the army at least. It was what Christopher got up to in his spare time that worried him the most.

The lad had always seemed right on the verge of causing a scandal. Edmund had supposed it might be better when he was enlisted securely, but with him away from home and no way to keep track of his actions, it somehow seemed even worse.

"Will he bring some friends back with him when he comes?" Patience asked.

Edmund threw her a sharp glance. What interest of hers was it if Christopher should bring home some soldiers? That did not sit well with him at all.

"I should hope not," he said. "Though, as you know, Christopher does as Christopher wishes. It's possible that he shall bring some fellow officers on leave.

"But if he does, I will stress this: you are absolutely not, under any circumstances, to fraternise with them. You will keep to your studies."

Patience looked upset, but she said nothing. She was becoming shrewd, that girl.

Edmund knew he was going to have to watch her closely. A failure to argue with him today likely meant a disobedience tomorrow.

"Off to bed, all of you," Edmund said, waving his hand since it was clear that they had all finished eating. "You have lessons in the morning, and I'm to London. We all need our rest."

He retired to his own chambers, pausing as he passed the short walk to the servants' quarters.

This new governess might be suitable, after all. He was just going to have to watch her closely to make sure of it.

5

Joanna began to adjust to her new life. It was not so difficult as she had feared, largely because of the fact that the children made her feel welcome.

Even if Patience would rather be anywhere else, and often made that known, Joanna felt that she was warming to her.

The idea that she might guide them through life had slowly begun to excite her. It gave her a purpose, a reason to strive every day.

And if the adjustment from lady to servant was harsh, it was softened many times over by the intervening months since the collapse of her family's fortunes, which had seen her sleeping in homes that were far less comfortable.

"Now, let's practice again, starting from the beginning," Joanna said, stretching out her arms to Patience.

She was teaching her a new dance, so that perhaps she would be able to enjoy dancing with a young gentleman at a ball in the near future.

At least, if Edmund should allow her to attend one.

"Have you ever danced with a man?" Patience asked, her eyes dreamy as she repeated the steps she had been taught.

Joanna knew that look well. She had seen it in her sister's eyes when she, too, was preparing for her first ball.

"Yes," Joanna admitted.

They both had: and it had been magical. Esther, her older sister by one year, had fallen head over heels for the son of a baron at that very first ball. Fortunate for her, as it turned out.

They had already married by the time Lord Warrick had lost the family fortune, and so she was protected by her husband from the worst of it.

"What was it like?" Patience asked.

"Oh," Joanna gave her a half-smile. "It was nice. Not so magical as I was led to believe. But then, I have never danced with a young man that I was falling in love with. I hear that is something quite else."

"From who?" Patience asked, spinning in place. "And where did you dance with them?"

"At a ball, of course," Joanna said.

She wished there was some way to change the subject away from her happier times. It was inevitable, really.

The girl was dreaming of life beyond the gates of the Hardwicke estate. Such things were natural.

"And my sister told me all about it. She's already married."

"Married!" Patience exclaimed. "How wonderful that must be."

"I'm certain she is very happy," Joanna said.

"But why were you at a ball?" Samuel asked, frowning from his seat in the corner.

"She used to be rich," Patience said, gracefully slipping behind Joanna and around her to complete the final steps of the dance. "Don't you ever remember anything?"

"Pay attention to your books, please, Samuel," Joanna said. She was grateful to at least have some way to divert the subject.

"So, you didn't fall in love with anyone?" Patience asked, standing and waiting now that she was done.

Joanna sighed. So much for a new topic. "No," she admitted. "But I am glad."

"Why?" asked Amy. She was supposed to be practicing her alphabet.

"Because if she had fallen in love, she would not be able to marry him now," Patience said slyly. "Not now her family is ruined."

"Enough dancing for today," Joanna said, feeling

harried. "Miss Patience, fetch your French book. I want to hear a translation of chapter five when the clock chimes three."

Patience groaned, but went to sit with her book.

Joanna went to the blackboard and began cleaning off the morning's lessons as an excuse to keep her back to the children while she composed herself.

It was hard, truly. She would need to strengthen herself against these kinds of conversations.

The truth of it was that all that was gone, forever gone, and the sooner she accepted it, the better it would be.

She would have to train first Patience and then, if Edmund allowed her to stay long enough, Amy in the rules of deportment.

She would help them find their own suitors, and then husbands, and perhaps even serve as a governess to their children one day if she was fortunate.

Marriage, and children of her own, were out of her reach now.

Joanna breathed deeply, wiping the chalk dust from her hands onto the front of her gown, and looked up at the ceiling for a moment to gather herself. Then she turned back and walked over to Samuel's seat to see his progress.

"How are you doing with your world map?" Joanna asked.

Samuel sighed. "I'm almost done."

"What's the matter?" Joanna asked, crouching down in front of his table.

The boy had a miserable expression, and he was resting his head on his hand, idly moving a pencil as if by automation.

Samuel cast an eye towards the window of the schoolroom, which looked out onto a vast grassy area to the side of the house. "I want to go outside."

"What for? It's cold out there today."

"I know," Samuel said, and sighed again, so deeply that you could have thought him an old man rather than a boy. "I just want to play sports again, like the other boys."

Joanna bit her lip. It was heart-breaking, the look on his face and the emotion in his words. She reached out and touched his free hand. "Do you miss being with your friends?"

"Yes," Samuel said. "I only got to spend a term with them. It was the winter break when I…"

"When you become unwell," Joanna filled in gently, squeezing his hand.

"And now Edmund won't let me go back."

Samuel's distress was obvious. He was imagining the other boys having all sorts of fun without him, no doubt, not to mention developing their education and playing sports.

But he was pale and thin, and Joanna had noted that he liked to sit down more often than stand. He would drop into a chair if he was unchecked for even a minute. There was no chance that he was strong enough yet to return to school.

"He's made the right choice, darling one. You aren't back to your full strength yet. But you will be, one day soon."

Samuel looked up at her, with a kind of rampant hope and excitement in his eyes. "Do you think so?"

"Of course. We'll work hard together, all four of us. When the weather is warmer, we'll have you running rings around us while we study. We'll get you hale and hearty again. How does that sound?" Joanna asked.

"It sounds magnificent," Samuel said, his eyes shining.

He went back to his map work with a renewed vigour, and Joanna stood, smiling.

She watched him for a moment, hoping that she had not lied to him. The illness had been a serious one, but he was alive.

While that was the case, she had hope that he could become just like any other boy of his age, with time.

Joanna moved over to the desk where Amy sat, completing another round of her young pupils.

The little girl was carefully drawing out her alphabet in long, slow strokes, joining up all of her letters. While her hand was not quite steady enough to make perfect loops, her practice was certainly going well.

"Why don't you try writing your letters a little faster?"

Joanna asked. "Like that – yes, there you go. Can you do the whole alphabet like that?"

Amy completed her task all the way to 'Z', and Joanna praised her roundly.

The letters were a little varied in size and shape, but the foundation was there. Before long, Amy would be writing fluently, needing only to learn her spelling and formal structures.

"Will you show me how to write 'Mama'?" Amy asked, the question coming as a complete surprise to Joanna.

"Of course I can. But why?"

"I want to write a message to Mama. I want to say how much I miss her," Amy explained, staring down at her page and the 'L' she was practicing, over and over.

"Of course," Joanna said, a twinge of sadness hitting her.

It did not seem right, that such a young child could only think to write a letter to her mother, instead of being with her. It was the way of the world, Joanna knew, and hardly an unusual case.

All the same, the thought of growing up without her own mother was almost unbearable.

Along with that came a fresh wave of grief at the loss of her father – a figure whom, of course, Amy had also lost. To see double the mourning at once, that was simply cruel.

"Do you miss your Papa?" Amy asked, turning her wide

brown eyes Joanna's way. Joanna felt how astute the girl was, despite her young years.

Children, she had noted previously, sometimes had a way of pinpointing emotions that adults had learned to ignore.

"Yes, I do," Joanna said, honestly. She smiled through the water that had gathered in her eyes as she stroked Amy's hair. "I miss him very much."

"I miss my Papa too. But I want to write a letter to Mama first."

"We'll work on it together," Joanna promised. "We'll start tomorrow, and practice all the words you need. Then you'll be able to write it on your own."

Quite unexpectedly, Amy turned in her seat and threw her arms around Joanna's neck, hugging her tightly. "Thank you, Miss Warrick," she said.

Joanna felt a lump in her throat, too large to formulate a reply around it. She simply patted Amy's back, and allowed her to cling on until she was done.

Then, when the little girl turned back to her alphabet practice, Joanna quickly wiped a tear away from her face and stood.

Glancing around the room, she saw Patience quickly looking away and back at her book. There was a small flush high in the girl's cheeks as if she had been caught watching.

Then, as if unable to control her eyes, she looked up again. A small, shy smile graced her mouth for a moment, before she tucked her hair behind her ears and concentrated on her books again.

Joanna walked to the window, and allowed herself a real smile out to the gardens below. Things had changed, yes, and that was hard.

But perhaps they were not going to be so awful.

6

Weeks had passed since his last questions, and Edmund thought it wise to bring the subject up at dinner once again.

"So, Amy, what did you learn today?" he asked, sipping at a small glass of wine in hopes of making his intentions seem more casual.

"We're writing a letter," she said, quite happily.

"Oh, really? A letter to whom?" Edmund asked.

"I learned a new type of dance," Patience said loudly, cutting across her younger sister's reply.

Edmund looked at her in surprise, and found her glaring across the table. Then she caught her brother's eye, and smiled sweetly. "Would you like to see it?"

"Not at dinner," Edmund replied, taken aback by her

interruption. "Perhaps later, when we have some space in the drawing room."

Samuel sighed. "Why do girls love dancing so much?" he asked.

Edmund gave him a smile and a conspiratorial wink. "You may find that you enjoy it yourself, when you are a grown man."

"Why?" Samuel asked, making a face.

"Well, for one thing, it allows you to converse and spend a pleasant while with fine young ladies."

Samuel shook his head, and put a bite of carrot in his mouth with a dismissive air that made Edmund laugh.

"Since we are talking of dancing," Patience said, with an air that instantly made Edmund suspicious. "I know we received a letter from the Haverhams. They have a ball taking place in three weeks. Everyone is talking about it. Could it be that it was an invitation they sent?"

Edmund sighed. He had hoped he could keep this a secret from Patience, but she had clearly been waiting for news of it.

"Yes, they did invite us to the ball."

"Oh, Edmund!" Patience cried out, smiling happily. "I'm so excited! Will you allow me to go into town for a new gown?"

Edmund frowned, and shook his head. "I don't see why you might need a new gown," he said, deliberately playing dense.

"Well, I can hardly go to a ball in an old dress. It must be something for the new season," Patience said, sounding as offended as if he had criticised her hair.

"But Patience, you aren't going to the ball," Edmund said. "No one is going to the ball. Not from this household."

"Should we run away?" Amy asked in a loud whisper to Samuel.

"There's no need for hysterics," Edmund cautioned, laying down his knife and fork to make his point seriously. "You're not ready to go to a ball yet, Patience. You shall have to live up to your name for a while longer."

"But I've waited so long!" Patience moaned. "Eliza Haverham is a month younger than me. She'll be there. In fact, the ball is in her honour."

"I refuse to judge you by the standards that others feel compelled to sink to," Edmund said, shaking his head again.

"If the Haverhams wish to introduce Lady Eliza into society before it is quite fit to do so, that is their choice. I shall not be making the same mistake."

"But... but..." Patience gasped, clutching her hands in front of her chest.

"There will be so many opportunities there. It's such a big gathering, there are bound to be many businessmen there. And wealthy men, brother. They might be interested in working with you. You should meet them."

Edmund thought this over for a second, taking another drink of his wine. The girl was right, of course.

It was a good opportunity – too good to pass up. This was the kind of gathering his father would have attended with relish, seeing it as a way to increase his fortune near enough overnight.

"Yes," he said, after a long moment. "Yes, I fancy you're correct. I should go to the ball."

"Oh, how wonderful!" Patience exclaimed. "I know we'll have so much fun, brother, I just know we will!"

"No, I said I should go. Not you," Edmund said. He pretended not to enjoy the way Patience's face dropped immediately into a sulky look of disappointment.

"This isn't fair," Patience said, her face reddening.

"You're not going, and that's final," Edmund said.

Patience gave a frustrated noise and stood up abruptly, the legs of her chair scraping back against the floor.

She turned with a harrumph and marched out of the room, not before fixing her brother with a wild glare.

Edmund sighed to himself. He wondered how many such glares, and how much silent treatment, he was going to have to endure over the coming three weeks.

No matter. His decision was final.

"Miss Warrick wouldn't let Patience be moody like that," Amy piped up.

"You're fond of her, aren't you, Amy?" Edmund asked.

He was glad of the opportunity to steer the conversation back in the direction he had originally intended.

Samuel scoffed. "Amy's in love with her," he said.

"Be kind, Samuel," Edmund said. "Your sister is allowed to have affections. Especially if they are deserved."

"She's deversed," Amy said, trying to imitate his word and failing. Her older siblings chuckled.

"Well, I'll take you at your word," Edmund said, smiling at his youngest charge.

"She is," Amy insisted stubbornly. "She's my favourite governess that we ever had. Even Patience likes her."

"Is that so?" Edmund asked, looking at Patience's empty chair. He thought about that piece of information, turning it over in his mind.

Maybe there was some room here for an advantage. Perhaps Miss Warrick would be able to help bring Patience in hand a little more.

After dinner, Edmund retired to his office room, sitting at his desk to work. There was much to be done, and it wouldn't wait until the morning.

Orders needed to be signed, and letters needed his response. There were complaints to deal with, and negotiations to be made.

He had almost made his way through a stack of documents brought with him in a case from London when he heard a knock at the door.

"Come in," he said, turning in his chair to face the door.

It was likely Jenkins, he thought, come to see if he would be needed any further for the night.

The head that appeared in the doorframe, however, was much younger and fairer. So much so, in fact, that he was quite taken aback to see it.

It was Miss Warwick, standing in the entrance with her hands clasped tightly in front of her and a determined expression.

"Lord Kelt, may I discuss something with you?" she asked. Her voice trembled slightly, but she looked up to meet his eyes all the same.

"Certainly," Edmund said, intrigued now. He laid down his quill and gave her his full attention. "Is it something about the children?"

"Yes," she said, turning to close the door behind her. There was a nervous energy in her actions, but she seemed reluctant to speak.

She paused before saying anything more, even though she opened her mouth as if she wanted to begin.

Was she coming to quit, already?

What would he do if that were the case? How would they cope?

No – what a ridiculous thought. Of course she wasn't coming to quit her position. That wouldn't make any sense. She had no reason to quit.

The children weren't misbehaving, not that he had heard of. And he had treated her well, hadn't he?

No, of course not. She wouldn't quit, not now.

Why was he getting so worked up about the idea of her leaving, anyway? It made no matter to him. There were other governesses out there, weren't there?

He brushed it aside in annoyance.

Better to simply find out what she wanted than to make assumptions.

"Is something wrong?" he asked, hoping it would prompt her to speak freely.

"Sir, I'm afraid it's about Miss Patience," Joanna said. "I don't want to overstep my bounds, but I thought it would be remiss of me not to come to you. She's been very upset tonight, and I found her almost inconsolable."

"About the dance," Edmund said, and sighed. He rubbed the bridge of his nose, shaking his head. "I've already told her that she is not to attend. It's simply not suitable."

"I understand that, my lord," Joanna said, dipping her head. "It's just that, as once a young lady myself, I also understand how she feels.

"It's a very difficult time for her. The thing is, sir, I think it might be beneficial for her to attend."

Edmund scoffed. Patience had the poor woman twisted around her little finger already.

He could already imagine what kind of a performance

she must have out on. "How so? I'm not going to bend to her will simply because she has thrown a tantrum."

"It's not that, sir," Joanna said, quickly. "Actually, I'm speaking as a governess, concerning her education.

"You see, I have been helping Miss Patience to practice her dances over the past weeks, and she is becoming quite accomplished. However, the practice in the school room is never quite adequate to replicate the feeling of being at a ball. I believe she needs to experience it for herself."

Edmund shook his head again. "No. I've to attend this ball in order to talk with some business associates of mine. I won't have the time to chaperone Patience and watch over her dancing. It's out of the question."

"You wouldn't need to, sir," Joanna said, and hesitated almost shyly. "I... well, I thought that I could chaperone her on your behalf. I will be able to make sure that everything flows smoothly.

"It will also afford me the chance to observe her in some social interactions, and assess whether there are any topics we ought to add to her deportment lessons."

Edmund wanted to tell her no again, but he found he was running out of excuses. Miss Warrick, it seemed, had thought of everything.

He was beginning to feel that whatever he might give her as a reason to leave Patience at home, Miss Warrick would already have a response prepared.

Not only that, but her request itself was enough to

make him hesitate. She was determined to argue on her charge's behalf, and Edmund sensed a deep care in her.

She had risked his displeasure by interrupting him in his office, and then again by arguing her case.

She must care a lot for Patience in order to take that risk, he realised. It was enough to make him consider it for a moment longer.

The more he thought about it, the more he liked it. There were many benefits here, and not all of them that Miss Warrick could have foreseen.

All in all, hers was a fine plan. He could watch Miss Warrick for signs of scandal, and at the same time, she might be able to help him out with finding some information about the other attendants of the ball.

Between them, they could create some interesting business deals. It would help him to ensure that she really was a suitable governess for the children, not just a charming young woman who made them smile.

All that whilst keeping Patience happy at the same time, and avoiding any further squabbles at the dinner table.

That was something he was keen to ensure, if only to preserve his sanity for the next few weeks.

And, he told himself, if he and Miss Warrick had to converse privately or even share a dance as part of this subterfuge, then that would just have to be the case.

Not that he would seek it out, of course. No, he would be there to engage in business instead.

Strangely, he even began to feel a slow stirring of excitement – even pleasure - at the prospect of accompanying his younger sister and her governess to the ball.

Fine, then. It all seemed to make sense.

"Alright," he said, breaking a silence that had fallen after Joanna's last words.

"It's settled. We will attend the ball, all three. You will be held responsible for Patience's behaviour, mark my words."

"Of course, my lord," Joanna said, breaking out into a brilliant smile that quite transformed her face into something lovely.

It was as if a candle had been lit in the room. Edmund found himself smiling back, though he quickly quelled the movement.

He tried to ignore, too, the strange feeling that welled up inside him at the sparkle in her eyes.

"I intend to hold you at your word, Miss Warrick," he said. "You'll watch over her."

"Thank you, sir," Joanna said, leaving the room with a graceful lightness in her step.

Edmund turned back to his desk and shuffled through his papers to find the invitation.

He took a fresh sheet and began to write out his response, accepting the invitation. He listed their three names, ensuring that the Haverhams would know who to expect.

As he wrote the words, a strange idea came over him.

It was that he had enjoyed seeing Miss Warrick give a genuine smile of happiness, and that he wouldn't at all mind making it happen more often.

What an odd thing that was to contemplate.

7

With Miss Patience excited about the prospect of finally getting to attend a ball, it became far easier to entreat her to practice her lessons.

She would talk of nothing else, and before long, Amy and Samuel took to sighing loudly every time she spoke.

They were bored of a topic that had no concern for them.

Amy was far too young to dream of dancing with young men, and the thought of mingling with elegant ladies was far from Samuel's mind as well. He was still impatient to return to the company of boys his own age.

Patience, though, was quite another matter.

She mastered another two dances in the space of a week. She was learning so quickly now that she had a reason to, that Joanna suspected she had in fact been holding back for a long time.

Even despite the added excitement, the days had begun to adopt an aura of normalcy. Joanna knew what to expect now, and things were simpler.

She would rise in the morning, prepare herself, and eat a snatched breakfast in the kitchens. Then she would go to the schoolroom and meet her charges for their early lessons.

Their programme varied, and Joanna tried to ensure that each child's education was balanced and strong.

While Amy laboured at learning her reading and writing, Samuel had more topics to tackle, including reading the globe and making his own maps.

Patience, meanwhile, had more yet to focus on, with her dancing and sewing.

The day seemed to pass quickly, and then Joanna would dine with the other servants.

Aside from Jenkins and Mary, there was also a cook, a groom, and Lord Kelt's driver. Some nights, the driver would not dine with them, having not returned yet from London.

Then the evening would come, and after her simple meal, Joanna would return to the schoolroom. This, she felt, was often easier than retiring to the sitting room.

While she was permitted to do so, there was always a

heavy silence, and she did not want to disturb the hard-working Lord Kelt.

So, her evenings were often spent alone. That was the time she found the most difficult.

Joanna's heart was still heavy with thoughts of her family. She missed them dearly.

Her mother was frail since her father's death, and she wished she could be with her. She wished to see her sister, Esther, too, and to talk animatedly with her as they had done for all her girlhood. They had been close as children, and never grew apart until Esther was married.

Hardest of all was missing her father. Joanna knew that, whatever the fates might allow, she would never see him again. Not in this life.

At least there was hope that she might meet the others of her family at some later stage. But her father was gone.

The thought brought her to tears. She held a faded ribbon, a once-red fabric that her father had bought her when she was a child, and cried into her hands.

Though she tried to be silent, her weeps turned into sobs at the deep loneliness that thoughts of her family brought with them.

"Miss Warrick?" A small, shy voice came from her side.

Joanna sat up abruptly, bringing her hands away from her face. She had not meant to be caught like this.

"... Miss Amy?" she said, almost dumbly. She was not

prepared to see the little girl at that moment and could not have been more surprised. She must have snuck in quietly.

"Are you sad?" Amy asked, cocking her head to one side.

"Oh," Joanna said, trying to find the words to answer the question.

She did not have to. Within a few moments, Amy had made a decision to take action. She stepped forward and wrapped her small arms firmly around Joanna's waist, hugging as tightly as she could.

After the initial surprise, Joanna wrapped her own arms around Amy, holding her close.

She managed to squeeze her eyes closed enough that the last tears fell from them, and then she took strength from the grip of the little girl.

They stayed this way for a while, until Amy clearly felt that her work was done.

"Do you miss your Papa?" she asked.

Joanna smiled, though the question almost made her eyes spill over again.

"Yes, I do. And my Mama and sister too. I have never gone so long without my family before."

"Don't be sad," she said, matter-of-factly. "We can play together."

Joanna laughed, and patted Amy on the head.

"Not at the moment, dear one. You ought to be in bed. What would Lord Kelt say if he saw you wandering around the halls at this hour?"

"He'd say, 'what a lovely girl you are'," Amy grinned proudly, doing an impression of her brother that managed to be both a million miles off and very close to the original.

Joanna laughed again and wiped off the tracks of tears from under her eyes. It was difficult to argue with that.

She reached for Amy's hand. "Come, now. Let's get you back to bed," she said, leading her out of the room.

The next morning was a Sunday, and so there were no lessons to be held. It was the only day when Joanna was not required, though truth be told, she had not much idea what to do with herself.

She went to the schoolroom just the same, to tidy up and to prepare her lessons for the week, after their morning at the church in the nearest village.

"Miss Warrick?"

The shy little voice always made her smile. Joanna turned from placing books back onto the shelves, to see Amy standing in the doorway with the cook.

As she watched, the cook bent and whispered something in Amy's ear, and gave her a nudge forward.

"I made you a present," Amy said, holding up a rag doll in front of her.

Joanna clasped a hand over her mouth. The doll was darling, if a little messy.

Amy had done her best, and from the neatness of some

of the stitches, Joanna suspected that she must have had some help from Patience as well as the cook.

"Oh, thank you, Miss Amy!" she said, taking the doll from her hands.

She recognised some of the cloth that cook used in the kitchen and smiled. She must have donated some of her old rags.

"What a kind and thoughtful gift."

"I made it so you won't be alone anymore," Amy said, her childish voice rounding out her words and imparting them with a sweet naivety.

Joanna leaned down and kissed her on the forehead.

"I will treasure it," she said. "You have made me very happy. Thank you."

Amy beamed, obviously pleased to have done a good job. She giggled and scampered out of the room.

Just as she left, she called back over her shoulder. "She's called Miss Prudence!"

Joanna laughed, examining Miss Prudence closely again and holding the doll under her chin.

"She was determined to make you a gift," the cook said, walking closer so that they would not be overheard. "Worked hard on it, too. Most all of it her own work."

"Not this neat stitching," Joanna said, pointing to a few examples with a smile. "And not done so quickly, in the matter of only a few hours."

The cook gave her a knowing look. "On that part I am sworn to secrecy," she said.

She leaned in even further, then, to whisper.

"We're mighty pleased to have you here, I must say, Miss Warrick. We're hoping this will keep the children settled. If they can finally have a governess who will stay, it will be so good for them."

Joanna's smile faltered a little, though only for a moment.

"On that point I am afraid you would be better off counselling Lord Kelt," she said. "I fear he is the one who must be convinced. I would not leave the children, unless it was him who bade me to go."

"Oh, don't you worry there," the cook said, smiling conspiratorially. "He's just as taken as they are. We all seen it. You're not to be chased off from this house any time soon."

The cook made her exit, but Joanna stood, holding the rag doll against her and thinking.

"Unless I make a mistake," she said, out loud now that there was no one to hear it.

Turning back to the shelves, she glanced from the window, and her eye was caught.

Walking to look out, she saw a magnificent chestnut horse trotting by, out in the grounds.

Lord Kelt was riding it, a greatcoat spread out across its

hindquarters. He had a stern look on his face, from what she could see at this distance.

She observed silently as he rode from left to right across her view.

Just as he was almost gone, he turned his head sharply. It seemed that he was looking right at her!

Joanna gasped, and threw herself to the side, away from the window.

What a silly reaction, she scolded herself, closing her eyes and breathing deeply. There was nothing wrong with looking out of a window.

Lord Kelt had been gone often lately, and Joanna wished that he would be around the home more.

Not that it should benefit her, of course. It was not as though it was her God-given place to sit with him in the sitting room at night.

Though, when he was home and she could sit by the fire to quietly sew, there was something about his silent presence that she found far less awkward than she had expected.

It was only the feeling that she might be holding him back from his work, or making him uncomfortable, that she disliked. And perhaps there was a way around that.

Maybe she could find some way, in time, to make herself useful to him.

Joanna wandered out of the schoolroom and down the hall, intending to put Miss Prudence away in her room.

As she passed by a large window in the hall, she noticed Samuel sitting on a bench before it with his feet on the seat and his knees up, his chin resting on his hand.

"Are you well, Mr. Samuel?" she asked, gathering close by him.

She saw that he was observing the same view that she had seen, and must have watched his brother ride by.

"Yes," Samuel replied, none too convincingly.

There was room on the bench by his feet. "What are you watching, there?" she asked.

"Nothing," Samuel sniffed.

Joanna decided not to push him on that point. She waited, looking out of the window alongside him.

"Did you see Edmund?" he asked, when she had been sitting silently for what must have been ten minutes or more.

"He rode past a while ago," Joanna said.

"Yes," Samuel confirmed. He reverted to silence for a while, resting his head on his hand and sniffling quietly.

"Do you miss your brother, Samuel?" Joanna asked, feeling that he needed a bit of help to confess what was wrong.

Samuel looked down at his own hands, picking at something on one of his fingers.

"Yes," he said, eventually. "I miss both of them."

"Your other brother doesn't live with you," Joanna said. She wasn't quite sure about the situation, though

Jenkins had mentioned something. The best way, she decided, was to tread delicately.

"Christopher joined the army," Samuel said. "He comes home sometimes. Edmund made him."

Joanna supressed a smile at the way he said it. "He made him join the army?"

"He said Christopher needed discipline," Samuel shrugged. "I guess he does. But I wanted him to stay home with us."

"Do you like spending time with Christopher?"

"Yes. But he fights with Edmund. I don't like when that happens. I wish they could both be home again like when Mama and Papa were here."

Joanna reached out and touched Samuel's hand, squeezing it for a moment.

"I know you miss them. I miss my family, too. We just have to keep each other company."

Samuel looked up at her then and smiled. His eyes were shiny with tears, but at least he was brave enough to smile. "We can do that," he agreed.

"Good," Joanna told him. "I'd like that very much. And we can look after your sisters, too."

"They need a lot of looking after," Samuel said, with heavy emphasis.

Joanna laughed and ruffled his hair. Samuel chuckled along with her, then got to his feet.

"I'm going to read a book. Thank you, Miss Warrick," he

said, calling the last words over his shoulder as he made his way down the corridor.

Joanna watched him go, and then looked out of the window for a while longer.

She, too, wished that Edmund could spend more time at home. It was better for the children, and that was better for her.

There was something good about him being there, too, something she couldn't quite explain. But for the children, she told herself, it was more important than anything else.

8

Edmund was just starting to feel accustomed to the new routine in the house, with Joanna as a part of their lives, when his middle brother arrived to throw everything off kilter again.

"Hello, brother," Christopher Hardwicke said, leaning against the doorframe of his office room at the home.

Edmund looked up in surprise. "You didn't send word that you were coming for a visit," he said, narrowing his eyes.

"Yes, brother, I'm very well, thank you for your concern," Christopher said, continuing the conversation on his own as if Edmund had not spoken. "The journey was fine. So kind of you to ask."

Edmund scowled. "Don't play games with me. What are you doing back?"

Christopher stood up straight, lifting his arms out to either side. "Aren't you pleased to see me? And looking so obedient, too?"

He had a point about the obedience. Edmund, and his father before him, had been trying to encourage Christopher for years to join the military. He had few options available to him as a second son, since there was no room for more than one hand on the tiller of the business.

Even if there had been, Christopher's hands were unsuited in the most obvious way.

The boy was irresponsible, and cared only for pleasure. With their father gone, it had fallen to Edmund to try to steer him in the right direction.

In the end he had had to resort to threats. Either Christopher enlisted in the army, or he would be cut out of his allowance and any inheritance that might be granted him.

"You're an officer, then?" Edmund grunted, eyeing his brother's sharp red uniform. It looked so new that he doubted it had been worn before today.

"Newly minted," Christopher said, pretending to polish one of the gold buttons on the front of his coat. "Aren't you proud of me, brother?"

"Not particularly," Edmund said, shuffling the papers on his desk. "I had to pay for that honour."

Christopher gave a mock sigh. Edmund knew he didn't care a thing about money, so long as he had some.

For all he paid attention, they could have been paupers or the richest family in the world. He would have spent it all with the same abandon no matter what.

"Why are you home? Are you looking for more money?" Edmund asked, fixing him with an even look.

He knew his brother well, and he wasn't about to imagine that Christopher was along for some family time.

"You wound me, brother," Christopher said. "Though now that you mention it, a little coin wouldn't go amiss."

"What did you spend the last bit I gave you on? Wine and women, I suppose?"

Christopher shrugged gracefully. "There was a little matter of a duel. Had to be avoided, you see. We settled it like real gentlemen, with a purse. Lady Chatsworth wanted to see which of us could provide her the finest gift for her birthday."

Edmund scoffed. Typical Christopher.

"So you purchased a trinket for a lady whose mother will never allow her to take a second son for a husband anyway. A good investment, as always with you."

"When have I ever failed to make a good investment?" Christopher said, picking up on the sarcasm in Edmund's tone.

"I may spend my coin on gifts, yes. But I find that it always pays to be generous, for what you will receive back."

"Such as impressive scars?" Edmund said, glancing pointedly at a small mark high on Christopher's cheek.

He had got it in a fencing duel over a woman, two years ago. Even though he probably would not marry for years yet, he was certainly getting in all kinds of courtship practice.

"It's unfair, really. Those poor ladies are waiting for a husband, and they even fancy that you might be it. You deceive them."

"Enough of all that," Christopher said, waving a hand in the air dismissively. Edmund noted, however, that he did not deny it.

"I'm done with my training at last, and I wanted to see my siblings. Is that so hard to believe? I'm also just in time for the ball, I believe."

"What ball?" Edmund asked sharply, seeing finally the real reason behind Christopher's appearance.

He had sniffed out a rumour of a social occasion. It was just like him to never pass up any opportunity to create a scandal.

"At the Haverhams'. I hear the invitations went out last week. I'm sure we received one, did we not?"

"We did," Edmund said, furrowing his brow and turning away. "But you're not just in time at all. I have already replied and confirmed my own attendance. Yours was not mentioned."

There were no circumstances under which Edmund would like to see Christopher attend the ball with him. He was a bad influence on Patience, for the first thing.

He also had no desire at all for Christopher to meet – or try to enchant – Miss Warrick. Why he felt that way, he couldn't exactly say; only that it was a thing he knew before he even had to think about it.

"That's no matter," Christopher said. "I shall come along with you all the same."

"No, you won't," Edmund said, resting his pen on the table again and facing Christopher.

"You cannot simply show up at the ball and expect that all will be well. You have not informed the Haverhams that you will be attending. There are rules to adhere to."

"Oh, rules," Christopher said, dismissively. "Who cares for them? You may be the only last man in England who does."

"You may be the only young man in England who thinks he is special," Edmund said, his tone dry.

"Ah, no, my mistake: that would be you and all of your peers. You cannot break the rules, Christopher. They exist. Your flippant nature does not mean they suddenly disappear."

"That's where you are wrong, brother. In the barracks -"

"No good sense will ever come from a sentence that starts 'in the barracks'," Edmund said. "You have to start taking things seriously. Society is not as forgiving as you seem to think it is."

"Perhaps I don't care for being forgiven," Christopher said.

That was too far. For a man like Christopher Hardwicke – or a boy, for all of his twenty years of life – to talk in such a way was obscene. A scandal of any kind would hit their family hard, and their business.

Edmund could not afford for that, not while he was still trying to establish himself as the head of the company.

There were rules – no matter what Christopher said. And the penalty for breaking them could be severe. He might even be ostracised, and his family tarred with the same brush.

Where would Patience, Samuel, and Amy be then? How would they be received when they wanted to enter society?

"That attitude is exactly why you will not be attending the ball," Edmund said.

He stood from his chair, emphasising his words as he faced up to his younger brother.

There was no chance that he would back down on this, not with the way Christopher was proving himself now.

"According to whose law?" Christopher retorted. "You aren't in a position to stop me, Edmund. Or have you forgotten that I'm an officer now? You ought to address me as Lieutenant."

"*Second* Lieutenant," Edmund said, gesturing towards the single emblem on Christopher's shoulder. "You don't even command any men of your own yet."

"But I will," Christopher said, drawing himself up to his

full height. "Which is more than you can say. I've enough training to put you on your back."

"Is that a threat, boy?" Edmund asked, his voice thundering with anger. "You would show me that level of disrespect?"

"Boy!" Christopher laughed. The sound was false and high – born of tension and mockery, not mirth. "I'm barely even your junior. Don't talk down to me as if you were Father."

"If I were Father, you'd be afraid to raise your voice. You may be only a few years younger than me in age, Christopher, but in maturity and responsibility, you are far further behind than that. Don't forget who controls your fortunes now."

"I don't need your fortune," Christopher sneered. "I have my appointment now. The army will pay me."

"And let's see how long you keep that rank if I withdraw my support. How far would you last if you had to become a Private, Christopher? Do you think you would even make it out of training if you weren't given special allowances?"

Christopher visibly bristled.

"Besides which, you're being ridiculous," Edmund continued. "You couldn't even afford to live on the small money you will take from the army. You aren't accustomed to it. You wouldn't even be able to keep up your social habits as they are now."

"Of course I would," Christopher said, his face red. "I could raise more money any time I wanted. I'd just have to entice this Lord or that Baron's son into a game of cards. Then I'd be well off enough."

"Gambling, too," Edmund said, shaking his head. "My, Christopher, you do bring such honour to the Hardwicke name."

"Fie on your name!" Christopher shouted. "As if you were such an established gentleman. I've heard the rumours, you know. They say that half our customers have abandoned us. No one trusts you. They call you Kelt's son, still."

"They will trust me," Edmund said, weary of having to defend this point. "And when they do, the business will thrive. I already have such provisions in place as might one day make us the richest family in England. And when I do, you will be crawling back on your knees to me to beg for an allowance."

"Or I shall marry rich," Christopher said, proudly. "I have enough duchesses and ladies to dangle on my hand."

"You shall not marry well at all if you continue in this way," Edmund scowled.

"What's more, I don't see why anyone should wish to marry a pauper. Which is what you will be, if I withdraw my money – for it is *my* money now, Christopher. I will leave you without a penny."

Christopher hesitated, his face changing colour and paling.

"You wouldn't leave me with nothing," he said, though his voice was less certain.

"I would happily do so, if it meant protecting our other brother and sisters from harm," Edmund said.

He met Christopher's gaze head on, eyeing him with a steely look that told of the truth behind his words. He meant everything he had said, and Christopher could see it.

"You are a beast of a brother," he said, though the fire was mostly gone from his words now. He was subdued – beaten.

"Call me what you will. Just know that I have your best interests in my mind, as well as those of the rest of us," Edmund said.

He could not afford to be gentle with Christopher, but at least he could emphasise the fact that he did not want to be cruel. "I will not see you ruined unless you drive me to it."

Christopher hesitated in the doorway. "You want me to defy my own spirit and become another man," he said, almost sounding miserable.

Edmund had heard enough. He pushed his chair back in under his desk with a heavy movement and strode towards Christopher.

"You are a child," he said. "Becoming a man at all would be some kind of improvement."

Edmund pushed past Christopher roughly, and out into the corridor, determined not to allow this conversation to continue any further.

When his eyes met those of his startled governess, his anger was too hard to allow anything but cold surprise.

9

Joanna had not intended to linger in the corridor and listen to the brothers arguing.

She had heard their voices raised as she came towards the door and had intended to turn away. But as she hesitated, she had seen Christopher step forward into the room, and heard their harsh words.

That had drawn her to stay, and to listen.

So, Christopher was here at last: it did not take her long to learn the identity of the strange and unfamiliar man in his red uniform. But all was not well with the two brothers, it seemed.

She had been on her way to speak to Edmund, wanting to raise concerns about how lonely Samuel seemed to be. She had thought that perhaps there could be a solution –

some time spent together, or even Samuel going into London on occasion.

But it was plain to see now that Edmund was not going to be in the mood for discussion.

It was the words they exchanged about Christopher attending the ball that made her pause. After all, that matter concerned her: she would be attending along with them.

And though she knew she should not have listened to their private conversation, their voices were so loud that she could hear it all.

She was not prepared for Edmund to leave the room. As soon as she knew that he was coming she could not help but let out a gasp.

Her face flooded with heat in embarrassment at being caught, and she knew that she must have appeared red as a robin's breast.

She expected her employer to shout at her, to chastise her for not knowing her place. Instead, he stared at her coldly and then swept by, down the corridor.

She turned to look after him, but only his coat swirling around the corner after him remained. He was gone, and she could not help but feel that she had made a grave error.

"Who are you?"

Joanna turned again, to see Christopher eyeing her with an interested look.

He had emerged from the office, too, and was leaning

casually against the doorframe with his arms folded over his chest. He did not at all look like a man who had just engaged in such a quarrel.

"Begging your pardon, sir," Joanna said, turning her eyes to the floor. "I'm the new governess. Miss Joanna Warrick."

"Well, well, Miss Warrick," Christopher said, his voice full of sly smiles that she could picture even if she dared not look up. "What is a pretty thing like you doing working as a governess?"

Joanna's face flared up again, and she stammered, unsure of how to respond.

"I – I'm not – I..." she took a breath and tried to compose herself. "My family were unable to support me."

"Is that so?" Christopher said. His feet shifted, leaning him a little closer towards her.

For a moment, Joanna was relieved that he did not sound put off or disgusted by her admission that she was in dire need of financial means. Then she hated herself for the feeling.

Of course she needed support: she was a governess. It was not a position that one generally took for the fun of it.

"Yes, sir," Joanna said, trying to turn away. "If you'll excuse me, sir, I should be getting back to my duties."

"Don't let me stop you, Miss Warrick."

Joanna hurried away from him, following after

Edmund. Although she was afraid to run into him again, she liked the idea of staying with Christopher even less.

There was something about his behaviour, his calm and unruffled tone after such a loud and wild quarrel, that unsettled her. How could he be so unmoved when Edmund had appeared so cold and angry?

She did not stop rushing until she had reached her own quarters and could close the door behind her for the privacy of solitude. Then she could at last sit down on her bed and consider what she had seen and heard.

Christopher was handsome, though in a more dashing way than his older brother. He had that scar on his cheek, which was immediately noticeable. His hair, too, was worn longer, and tied back behind his head. The red of his jacket was bright and the gold buttons shone.

Even so, she found herself comparing him to Edmund unfavourably.

In truth, she could say with a sincere feeling that she knew which of the two brothers she trusted most. It was an instinct in her, and not, she believed, drawn from her more experience of spending time with the older.

There was something about Christopher that was not pleasant, though she could not say precisely what it was.

Joanna decided to set her thoughts aside. In her room there was a treat waiting, something she had been looking forward to reading.

A letter from her older sister, the recently-married Esther Castleford.

It was still strange to her to hear a different surname appended to Esther, but that was how the letter was signed.

Joanna opened the letter up and began to read it, savouring every word from her treasured sister.

My dearest Joanna,

I do so miss you terribly. Allow me to start with that! A heart that has been separated from its sister must yearn much.

I hope it cannot be long before we are able to be reunited, even for a short time. You must let me know if your employer will permit you some time to see me. Perhaps he will go abroad and take the children with him? That should leave you some free time!

Oh Joanna, you must write me back and tell me everything. Are the children terribly darling? I suppose they must be. And is the house grand and inviting? Do they hold balls there and host esteemed guests? I want to know all about it.

Are they treating you well? I can hardly bear to think of you reduced to such a position. It is unfair, Joanna, terribly unfair. That I should be married just in time and you left so!

But let me tell you about the latest news with us.

My wonderful Lord Castleford is such a dear to me. He has purchased for me a new puppy, who is full of life and always eager to please. We have named him Spot. He is rather fun, though I confess I cannot quite keep up with his romps around the grounds. Lord Castleford says we shall have to train him to obey us so that he does not get ideas beyond his station.

We attended a ball last week with the Mifords. What fun it was!

Oh, you would have enjoyed it so, Joanna. We all had a good laugh at the antics of you-know-who. She still cannot learn even the simplest steps to any dance. The poor unsuspecting gentleman who requested her hand was quite sore by the end of the night for all the trampling over him.

I had some new gowns for the season, in yellow and lilac. Lord Castleford complains that my dresses are pretty enough but you know how it must be. A Baron's son ought to show that he can outfit his lady wife admirably!

The housekeeper here is quite fierce. I have tried to entreat her to change things to my liking and she is a stubborn old mare. I don't know if I should complain to Lord Castleford about her. What do you think?

Perhaps I should try to take charge on my own.

It's quite new still, being the lady of the house! I forget sometimes that I can order her about as I please. When she barks at me like a fearsome dog, I give in just like that.

Tell me, Joanna, how can I be stronger about this?

Well, I shall depart now and hope this letter reaches you safe and well.

Do write me, Joanna, I am anxious to hear from you.

Your ever-loving sister,

Lady Esther Castleford

Joanna read the words over and over again, a smile lingering on her face.

It was so wonderful to hear from her sister, and to know that Esther had not changed despite the distance between them.

Perhaps Joanna would never attend a ball as a lady again, or have to tend to her own household as a wife. But at least she could hear about it from Esther. That was enough, at least for the moment, to cheer her up.

Still, it wasn't as though she would never go to any ball – since she already had one coming up.

Being a chaperone was likely to be a very different experience from being the young lady who needed one, but she would be able to watch others dancing in their beautiful gowns and see young romances forming.

Joanna's pulse quickened at the thought of it. The music, the dancing, the conversation – all of it was going to be so much fun. Even to just be near it rather than really part of it was something.

And there was something else, too: she realised that she was looking forward to the prospect of spending more time in Edmund's presence.

Granted, she would not be there as his equal. But he had given her his trust in allowing her to chaperone Patience, and that was a real honour.

Joanna settled down at the small table in her room and picked up a quill. She had bought some paper in order that she might write to Esther, having already expected to receive a missive from her soon.

After a moment's thought, she began to write.

My dearest sister Esther,

I am so glad to hear from you. I miss you terribly also, and Mama and Papa.

It is quite different to be a member of a household, rather than a family. I wish often that I could see you all again, especially to spend more time with Papa.

The children are such lovely creatures, and even bring me gifts to lend me some cheer.

All the same, I do so hope to see my sister's face again soon.

Though please do not think that I am mistreated! Indeed, I am made to feel very welcome here. The children are wonderful.

There is Miss Patience, who is sixteen years old and quite beautiful already. She is impatient to attend her first ball. More on that anon!

Mr. Samuel is a delight, though he should be old enough to go off to school. The poor mite was struck with the same sickness that took his parents and has been left quite weak.

I have hope, however, that his condition will improve. After all, he is a robust boy, and still struggles even daily to regain his strength. His character, I believe, will see him through it.

My youngest charge is Miss Amy. She is such a darling, believe me, Esther. When I was feeling a little lonely, I was quite chagrined that she found me crying in the schoolroom. Me, supposed to be her strong governess!

Well, she is such a pleasant child that she soon made me a doll from rags that I am to keep as my companion against loneliness.

They are so well-learned already, I fear my job is perhaps the easiest it could possibly be.

The Earl of Kelt is gone often on business, and when he does return home it is often late in the evening. I have taken to spending most of my evenings in the schoolroom. I do not wish to disturb him as he has such important work to undertake.

But I shall be spending more time with him soon. I mentioned a ball earlier! Oh, Esther, I am to attend as the chaperone of Miss Patience. Lord Kelt wishes me to watch over her. He will be quite busy with his conversations and so I am required.

I can hardly wait to be in the midst of society again, even if I know it will not be quite as before.

Regarding your housekeeper, I think you should stand your ground with her. After all, Esther, you are the lady of the house – and don't forget it!

You ought to put her in her place. If she will not listen, why then you may as well go behind her and ask your other servants to follow your instructions only.

I do wish I could see your puppy. He sounds like quite a charm. Yours sounds so much like a happy house that I am relieved for you, dear sister. I only have to think of your happiness and mine is quite assured.

I may see about some time to visit you, though I fear Lord Kelt has no such plans to take a trip.

Your loving and happy sister,

Miss Joanna Warrick

After checking over her letter, Joanna smiled to herself and sealed it into an envelope.

How dull life would be if you could not converse by letter!

She wrote her sister's address on the front, thinking all the while of how long it would take for the message to arrive, and how long she might have to wait to read a response.

10

The night of the ball seemed to approach interminably fast.

Edmund could have wished for nothing more than to put it off forever, but no man could hold back time. Before he had time to gather himself, it was upon him.

At least Christopher had given up on his insistence of attending. That was one thing less to concern himself about. The threat of the removal of his allowance was enough, it seemed, despite all of his bluster.

The carriage stood ready to take them away to the Haverhams' estate, and Edmund stood waiting in the cold air with his pocket watch.

The time appeared to show correctly what he thought it did, but still he was missing two ladies who were supposed to be inside.

"If they are any much later, I shall have you drive us away without them," Edmund muttered to his driver, pacing back and forth in front of the carriage.

He turned to walk back across his own path again and saw them at last coming out of the house.

Patience was being hurried along by Joanna, though she kept trying to turn back and fuss with something.

"Please, Miss Patience, your hair is perfect," Joanna was insisting as they came closer. "You don't want to miss the first dance, now, do you?"

At that suggestion, Patience gave a squeal and began to move faster.

They reached the carriage and scrambled inside with the driver's help, Patience almost falling back with a yelp as one of her shoes caught on the step.

"Onwards, then, man," Edmund told the driver, helping himself up after them and closing the door in a rush. "I thought I was going to have to leave without you."

"Oh, you wouldn't!" Patience exclaimed.

She was still attempting to fuss with a strand of her hair. Joanna pulled her hands away from her neighbouring place on the seat and tucked it back in neatly.

"There," she said. "Now, stop touching it, or it will fall out again."

"You'll fix it for me, won't you?" Patience whined.

"Of course," Joanna smiled. "But try not to touch it all the same."

"I would have," Edmund said. "I was getting impatient."

"Getting?" Patience said. She was talking too loudly, jumping in too quickly. The excitement was obviously overwhelming her. "You're always impatient."

"Then you should know not to keep me waiting," Edmund pointed out. "I'm surprised that Miss Warrick could not get you ready quicker."

"I do apologise, my lord," Joanna said, bowing her head. "I tried, but there was a lot of preparation to be done."

Edmund made a noise and looked out of the window, leaving the women to chatter between themselves.

Patience could not stop fiddling with this ribbon or that hem, and Joanna had a great deal of trouble stopping her from fussing with everything.

He snuck his gaze back to observe them, watching as Joanna patiently took care of his younger sister.

She was dressed, he was surprised to note, in a gown that was of fair quality. It suited her well, and was not so old that it appeared unfashionable. Even if he was not an expert on gowns, he could see that.

In fact, with her hair done up and a light flush of excitement on her cheeks, she looked rather pretty.

Edmund found himself staring at her, and when her gaze met his, he quickly looked back out of the window again. Instead of the scenery flashing by, however, he was looking at Miss Warrick's reflection.

The journey was too short, and again Edmund found himself wishing he could put the ball off forever.

Watching Patience descend from the carriage as he held out his arm to help her, he observed her beauty and wondered if it was too late to take her back home.

Perhaps the driver could escort her there. Anything, surely, would be better than having to parade her around inside.

It was difficult to admit to himself, but Edmund really rather wished he could protect Patience indefinitely. If she were kept safely at home, she would never have to run into some bounder or cad who might break her heart – someone, he added to himself, not unlike Christopher.

He led Patience into the house on his arm as Joanna followed behind, emerging into a well-lit entrance hall and from there into a bustling ballroom.

The walls were painted a jaunty pastel yellow, and a string quartet were playing soft tunes as guests arrived.

"Miss Patience Hardwicke," the Master of Ceremonies announced, taking a number to pin to Patience's gown.

Edmund watched him, feeling quite out of sorts. Of course, there was no reason why this should be different to any of the other balls he had attended in his life. Somehow, though, seeing his sister announced like this made it a different matter altogether.

"Oh, this is so exciting!" Patience exclaimed, as they walked in to stand amongst the other guests. All were standing around and conversing, waiting for the dancing to begin. "When do you think we will start?"

"Very soon, I'm sure," Joanna said, when Edmund did not make any answer. "We have to wait for the hostess, first. Lady Haverham will call the first dance."

"Ah, Lord Kelt!" A voice came from behind them. "I thought I might meet you here. My wife, Lady Kelverley."

"Lord Kelverley," Edmund acknowledged, turning with a sinking feeling. It was just his luck that this odious man would be in attendance.

"Lady Kelverley. My sister, Miss Patience Hardwicke, and her governess, Miss Warrick."

"Charmed," Lady Kelverley put in.

She was approaching elderly, with her hair done up in a more old-fashioned style. She wore a dark gown, quite different to the light colours of the young ladies around her.

"Yes, what a lovely party you make," Lord Kelverley said. "Say, Edmund, I wondered if you had any news on the China ship."

Edmund gritted his teeth. Well, he had wanted to come here to talk business. So be it.

"Indeed, we're still waiting for news from the journey. The Captain had assured me that we would hear next week, and not before."

"Ah yes, a long journey I suppose," Kelverley blustered.

"What predictions have you on the stock? Any thoughts yet?"

Edmund resisted the urge to sigh. It might be a long night. "As I say, we'll likely know more next week."

The hostess, Lady Haverham, was calling the room to attention. Edmund saw Patience and Joanna turn to listen out of the corner of his eye, but Kelverley was not done.

"Now, what about the African matter? Lord Winsor heard rumours of something amiss. Tell me, is it dealt with? I should like to know if things are not going well."

"Believe me, the matter is in hand," Edmund said.

Why were these old men always doubting him? He had the experience and the knowledge – and he worked hard. Of course everything was under control.

"I don't know where Lord Winsor gets his information, but it is incorrect. Perhaps you should advise him not to listen to the gossip of charlatans."

As he turned, Edmund felt great alarm to see Patience being led away by a young man with the red hair of a Haverham.

He was about to start forward in protest, but Joanna stepped to his side.

"Lord Edward Haverham," she said quietly. "Third son. He asked to accompany Patience on her first dance, very politely too. I shall keep a watch on them. I have heard that Lord Edward's reputation is good. We should not be too concerned about him having wicked intentions."

Edmund looked down to see that Joanna was only partially mocking him. She wore a gentle smile, and with another glance at Patience, Edmund knew he had no reason to object.

He sighed, nodded, and watched her go into position.

"Not ready to let go of her just yet, Lord Kelt, eh?" Kelverley said, laughing. "She will have a grand old time. Young ladies like that think of nothing but dancing."

Edmund nodded, trying not to take offense with Kelverley's tone or the way he had read him so clearly.

He told himself that Joanna was watching, but still he could not help but glance over at Patience every few moments to be sure that there were no signs of improper conduct. All the while as Kelverley prattled on about Africa this and India that, Edmund was only half-listening.

He was thankful that Kelverley only required half an ear. The old man was complaining his same old complaints, and worrying in his usual way over the outcome of trade deals and shipments that would not be known until weeks or months in the future.

Even so, Edmund was forced to acknowledge that he might not have been the best conversational partner when he found he was expected to answer a question without having heard what it was.

"Hmm," he said, enigmatically, hoping that would suffice.

Thankfully it seemed to, as Kelverley launched on into a diatribe about the reliability of Welsh sailors.

Edmund realised that he was clenching and unclenching his fists and tried hard to relax. Each time that he looked over at Patience, he was almost angered to see her smiling.

Who was this boy, to pay her compliments and tell her witty jokes that made her laugh so?

At least half a dozen times, he wanted to go over and interrupt them, and pull Patience away.

At last, the long minuet was over, along with the torture that went with it. Edmund felt he could breathe again at last as Patience returned to his side, a little out of breath and flushed with happiness.

He was able to disentangle himself from Kelverley before the next dance began. Edmund turned, thinking that he would quiz Patience on her dance partner and his propriety, but the girl was already gone again.

He saw her being led away by a slim lad with dark hair, who must have been only eighteen or nineteen himself.

"Eldest son of Lord Winsom," Joanna supplied, predicting his need for information once more. "They will take just one dance together. I believe the boy is being pressured into dancing with as many ladies as possible by his mother, who looks rather formidable."

"Winsom," Edmund repeated, looking around the rest of the guests. "Pray, where's the boy's father?"

"Over by the carriage clock, there on the table," Joanna said, discreetly inclining her head towards the other side of the room.

"I need to speak with this man," Edmund said, but then hesitated, looking over at Patience.

"Go," Joanna told him. "I'll watch over Miss Patience, my lord. I won't take my eyes off her."

Edmund nodded sharply, and strode around the side of the dancers until he reached Lord Winsom.

There, he was forced to wait for the man to finish his conversation with a portly gentleman who had lost all hair but the heavy grey whiskers and sideburns on his head.

"Lord Kelt, isn't it?" Winsom said, turning at last as if recognising and greeting an old friend from years ago. "Fine ball, don't you think?"

"Quite," Edmund said, looking up and watching the dancers again. "It seems your boy is dancing with my sister."

"Ah, yes," Winsom said, watching them for a moment himself before turning his back on the scene. "They cut a fine figure."

Edmund watched them, then glanced over towards Joanna.

This was no good. Now he had both of them to keep an eye on. "Lord Kelverley tells me you have been listening to rumours about the African matter," he said, trying to keep himself on track.

"Oh, well, just a few things I heard here and there," Winsom said, flustered. His face turned a pale red, but he waved a hand in the air dismissively.

"I would hope that you might come to me with these rumours before talking to others," Edmund said, knowing that the threat in his voice was implied enough to not have to say it explicitly. "It would be the polite and gentlemanly thing to do."

"Well, now that you mention it, yes, of course, I'll be sure to..." Winsom started, his voice trailing off. "Are you quite alright, Lord Kelt? You seem a little... distracted."

Edmund looked back at him, and realised his head had been swinging back and forth as he checked on both Joanna and Patience.

"Yes, quite alright," he said. "Now, tell me where you heard about Africa. And from whom, if you will."

The man struggled his way through a vague answer about sailors and markets, as Edmund tried to force himself to pay attention.

Eventually, satisfied that Winsom had at least been put in his place, he took his leave and walked some distance away.

He did not quite return to Miss Warrick's side – not yet. He had noticed something peculiar while Winsom was speaking, and he wanted to see it with his full attention.

It had not escaped his notice that Miss Warrick was beautiful enough to catch eyes from all around the room, even if she might not have had quite as fancy or new a dress as the other ladies.

As he watched, however, Edmund never saw her return a single glance. Her eyes remained trained on Patience, and when they did flicker around the room, they landed only on the young men who were also watching her charge.

One scoundrel in a green velvet coat was watching Miss Warrick quite openly from a few groups of people away. Edmund saw him with a scowl, and how he even made some remark about her to his friends.

Whatever it was, a blond young man laughed. That made Edmund's fist clench tight again. Who was this young upstart?

Miss Warrick seemed not to notice him, until at last her eyes swung in his direction.

When she met his gaze, he gave her a sly smile, the type that no doubt had been found awfully successful with enchanting young ladies at many a ball.

Edmund felt his heart sink, thinking that now Miss Warrick would be distracted from her duties.

But she looked away from the young dandy without so much as a change in her expression and resumed her observations of Patience.

Edmund felt a pride in his chest then, that he had chosen a governess who was serious about her position and the lives of her pupils. She clearly had no thought towards social interactions, despite the heady environment of the ball.

He could only hope that the rest of the ball would continue to be so successful, but could it really be the case?

11

He returned to her side, giving the dandy a stern glare for good measure.

"Everything has been well, I take it?" he said.

Miss Warrick glanced up at him without surprise. She must have observed his approach.

"Quite well. Miss Patience is dancing finely. I am quite pleased with her progress."

Edmund smiled. "I'm sure she applies herself to her dancing lessons more than to any other."

Miss Warrick hid a laugh behind her hand. "I would not have put it in so many words, Lord Kelt," she said, though her tone revealed that he was correct.

Edmund began to look around the room, searching for another of the old men he no doubt needed to listen to for an interminably long time in order to secure their business.

With Miss Warrick watching over things, he would perhaps be able to relax a little more than he had thought. He had been unable to find any fault with her – and, indeed, it surprised him to realise that he was beginning to entertain the notion of trusting her.

What a strange thing that was. It had never happened with any of the previous governesses that he had hired – and subsequently dismissed.

Each one of them had, somehow or other, proven themselves to be unworthy of the position. And now here was this Miss Warrick, seemingly the perfect fit for the job, just like that...

Edmund excused himself and wandered over to engage a passing gentleman with large red whiskers, who he recognised by sight as a baron of some good standing.

"Who is that young woman?" the Baron asked, leaning in with a gruff voice as their conversation regarding trade began to come to a close.

"My sister?" Edmund asked, following his gaze to where Patience and Miss Warrick stood together. Yet another young man was approaching them, no doubt to lead Patience out for the next dance.

"No, no, I recognise Miss Patience. She looks like your mother, you know. I meant the young lady accompanying her."

"That is our governess, Miss Warrick. She is acting as a chaperone for Miss Patience tonight," Edmund said.

"Oh," the Baron said, an expression of surprise appearing above his bushy whiskers. "She is quite a fine-looking woman. I had thought she must be a visitor of yours, a cousin perhaps."

"She was a lady, before," Edmund said, though he felt an irritation at having to explain it.

Miss Warrick was a woman in her own right, and her status or lack of it was hardly relevant to her position.

"I believe there was some trouble with her father's fortune before his death. At any rate, her mother advertised her services as a governess, and I happened upon her details. She has been good with the children, thus far."

The Baron gave him what was no doubt intended to be a well-meaning elbow in the ribs.

"I couldn't have her as a governess in our house. The Baroness would get jealous, eh? Pretty thing like that. You ought to dance with her."

Edmund gave him a startled look. "Dance with her? Whatever for?"

The Baron scoffed, tapping his wife on her shoulder and getting her attention.

"My dear Baroness, don't you think Lord Kelt ought to dance with his young governess over there?"

The Baroness' gaze darted over to Miss Warrick and lingered, apparently assessing her. "She is of family?"

"Trouble with the family fortune," the Baron said. "Lord Kelt was just telling me."

"The best kind of governess," the Baroness nodded, proclaiming her opinion as if all had been settled. "The Earl should dance with her. Just once, as a courtesy. It would be polite."

"I really don't think I'm the best dance partner," Edmund said, shaking his head.

"Elizabeth," the Baroness called out, tugging the sleeve of a woman standing nearby. "Don't you think it's right that Lord Kelt ought to spare a dance for his governess? She's come to chaperone the sister."

Elizabeth, whoever she might have been, turned and gave her own assessment of the situation.

"It would be polite," she said. "After all, no one else will dance with the poor woman tonight."

Edmund gritted his teeth, trying very hard not to give them an answer he would regret. "I see you are determined to force my hand, Baron," he said, with an air of resignation.

"Quite so, Lord Kelt!" the Baron laughed heartily. "It's about time you had some fun, my dear lord. Your father was a shrewd businessman, but even he would spare some time for socialising at a ball."

Edmund sighed, and looked back at Miss Warrick.

Now that he thought about it, perhaps it would provide him with an excuse not to dance with any other ladies for the rest of the night if he had turned around the floor at least once.

It seemed, too, that his group were not going to let things drop. Of course, he could argue, but it might create a scene; and the Baron had seemed interested in the idea of placing an order or two in the coming week.

He walked up to her, thankful that Patience was already being led away – by the red-headed third Haverham son, no less. At least that meant she would not be left standing alone while he indulged in this ridiculous dance.

"Miss Warrick," he said, glancing over at the group that were now watching his progress closely, "I have been told in no uncertain terms that it is quite rude of me to leave you without a dancing partner."

Miss Warrick looked up at him in some confusion. "But I'm here as a chaperone," she said. "I did not think there would be any call for me to dance. And, who…?"

Edmund gave her a level look, until she began to blush furiously.

"Oh. I see," she said, looking down at his feet. "Are you asking me to dance, Lord Kelt?"

"Just one," Edmund said, extending his hand towards her. "We have an audience. We'd better get it out of the way as soon as possible."

Miss Warrick placed her hand on his without another word, and he carefully led her to join the other couples in the centre of the room.

He was all too aware of the fact that he was still under close scrutiny from the Baron and Baroness. It did not help that the red flush on Miss Warrick's cheeks had yet to die down.

In fact, as the first strains of music began and they moved towards one another, he even thought that it might have been getting more pronounced.

It was only as they passed around one another in the steps of the dance, and he looked down the line to see Patience dancing with her young admirer, that he realised Miss Warrick perhaps did not want to dance with him at all.

She did not have much choice when it came to refusing him – after all, he was her employer.

Perhaps that was why her cheeks still shone red, even while she executed the steps of the dance with perfect precision. Because the other young ladies dancing up and down the line had been asked by attractive young men who might one day ask for their hand in marriage – and she had had to wait for the pity of her employer to be paraded in front of all of them.

Such insensitivity he had shown! She must think him so cruel!

He tried to think of a way that he could improve the situation, but one did not easily come to mind. After all, to abandon the dance partway through would only give her more shame and draw more attention her way.

He settled on at least trying to say something nice. But a direct compliment might be seen as inappropriate.

He stuttered out the only thing he could think to say.

"Patience's dancing has improved much under your supervision," he said, as their heads passed by one another in the circular patterns of the dance.

"Thank you, my lord," Miss Warrick said. "She has obviously benefited greatly from having someone who cares enough about her to insist on the continuance of her education, in the absence of your parents."

Edmund felt a certain pride well up at her statement. "Our house has greatly benefitted from your skilled presence, more so than with our previous governesses. I am very glad to have found you," he said.

Then, feeling that he had gone too far, he quickly added: "For the children's sake, of course."

Miss Warrick inclined her head gracefully. "I have enjoyed my time with you greatly. With the children, I mean."

"And we, you," Edmund replied. "I have been impressed with your conduct as a chaperone. I know Patience is safe under your eye."

"You flatter me greatly," Miss Warrick said, flushing even deeper.

By now, Edmund began to wonder whether there could be any blood left in the rest of her body.

"You have earned it," he said.

He wanted to tell her that she looked quite beautiful as

they spun around one another, and that she was not so far from the ladies in attendance as he had expected.

He suspected, however, that this might come across as a thinly veiled insult, and so said nothing.

"I am quite happy that I have found my home with you," Miss Warrick said. "I feel more comfortable than I had thought possible."

"I hope you do not think me forward in saying that the home would not be the same, were you now to leave," Edmund replied, caught up in her sudden praise. "Your presence has improved us greatly."

"I do not know about that," Miss Warrick said, smiling shyly as she stepped away and then towards him again. "I was charmed on the first day of my arrival, and I remain so."

"You continue to surprise and delight me, Miss Warrick," Edmund said, just as the music came to an end.

They stood looking at each other, a little out of breath and lost in the awkwardness of their positions now that the dance was over.

At a loss for what to say, he added: "I talk of your work with the children, of course."

"Of course," Miss Warrick nodded. "The children. I was speaking of them, too."

She dipped a quick curtsey by way of concluding their dance, and after a short pause, rushed over to Patience to resume her chaperone duties.

Damn him. Why had he had to add that last comment?

The rest of the ball spun on around him, and he reluctantly returned to his conversations.

The Baron and Baroness complimented him on his footwork and his grace at dancing with an employee, and Edmund could not remove himself from their vicinity quickly enough.

He buried himself in negotiations and discussions with the patriarchs scattered around the sides of the room, and only occasionally found himself glancing to check on Miss Warrick and Patience.

As all good things are wont to do, the ball came to an end.

"I don't want to go yet," Patience whined, and Edmund found himself having to put a firm hand on her shoulder.

"The ball is over, sister," he said. "What do you expect to gain from staying? You will be here on your own."

Patience pouted but climbed into the carriage anyway. As Miss Warrick followed her, Edmund caught a smile of amusement on her face.

It echoed onto his own before he could stop it, and he realised that it was a genuine one.

Despite all of his misgivings, it had been a good evening. There had been no incident whatsoever involving either Patience or Miss Warrick – aside, perhaps, from their misjudged attempt at dancing together.

Deals had been made, and many of the men he had

seen this night would no doubt be appearing in his office over the following weeks, ready to sign contracts.

All in all, they had achieved their goals, and Patience was still giddy with the excitement of it all.

Miss Warrick helped her take down her hair inside the carriage, removing some pins that had become uncomfortable through the course of the night, and Edmund watched them with a feeling of satisfaction.

He could not remember the last time he felt strangely happy like this. Perhaps it had been a long time ago, in his boyhood.

But he had been a serious child; perhaps, he thought to himself, it was the first time he had ever really felt this way.

12

The ball was such an enjoyable night, but it was over so quickly.

Just to be back in that environment, revelling in the atmosphere and in the reflected fun that Patience exuded, was more than Joanna could have wished for.

Of course, it was not without a certain personal enjoyment. Being in the thick of it again, even if only temporarily while she danced with Edmund, had been like a return to her former life.

He had been such a skilled dancer – quite unexpectedly – and so kind in his words.

Though there was some bittersweet mixture of her feelings on that part.

He had been kind, yes, though only about her skill at her position of governess. Was it too much to wish that her days of being praised for a pretty hairstyle or a charming laugh were not behind her?

Though such flattery was not the most important thing in life, still, she felt a strange longing that he might have said something about her person while they danced.

Particularly from Edmund, though she could not explain why, she longed to hear such praise.

Still, when it was over, the next day dawned much the same as any other.

Their little spark of excitement was now in the past, and it seemed sad to think that it might be a long time again before they could participate in something similar.

Perhaps fortunately, and perhaps not, it was not long before Joanna had more excitement to deal with.

This excitement, however, was of an altogether different character, and one that she would have preferred to avoid if given the chance.

Despite having argued with Edmund so viciously on his last visit, Christopher Hardwicke did not stay away for long. Soon, they would all wish that he had – and perhaps for a much longer period than any of them had ever wished before.

Joanna was sitting in the schoolroom with a book, reading quietly to pass the time before she would retire to sleep, when she heard the sounds of a carriage rolling into the grounds.

She supposed it may have been a visitor for Lord Kelt

which he had neglected to tell her about – which was perfectly alright, considering that she was only there for the children.

She ignored the noise, and was thinking about going to her bedchamber after finishing the chapter she was reading.

A clattering from the hall, however, drew her attention once more.

When it was followed by a loud whoop, she could not contain her curiosity. Something did not feel right, and she swiftly moved out into the corridor to assess what was happening.

Back in the main hall, she soon found the source of the noise.

Christopher was there in his red uniform, laughing helplessly with an arm slung around the shoulders of another young man in the same colours.

They appeared to be attempting to support one another in standing up, but even as she watched, the other man dropped to the floor and clattered against a large vase once again.

"Second Lieutenant Hardwicke!" Joanna gasped out loud.

That was enough to draw the attention of both men. They paused for a moment, and then Christopher dropped his friend's arm to address her.

"Ahhh, the lovely Miss Warrick!" he proclaimed loudly.

"So delightful to see you again. Allow me to present my dear friend and fellow officer, Second Lieutenant Jasper Rivers."

Rivers began laughing again from his position on the floor, as if the whole matter was one irresistible joke.

"Shh!" Joanna hushed them urgently, casting a glance up the staircase.

This was not good. Edmund would be furious if he was woken up by his brother in such a state.

The two men had clearly been at their spirits for some time, and the empty bottle still clasped in Rivers' hand was a testament to the way their carriage journey must have gone.

"I'm sorry, Miss Warrick," the coach driver whispered.

Joanna started; she had not even seen him lingering in the shadows near the open doors.

"They insisted on coming in, and I couldn't persuade them to retire."

"The night is still young!" Rivers exclaimed, rolling himself into a sitting position. "Surely you don't expect us to retire when there is so much more fun to be had?"

Joanna stared at them in dismay. All she could picture was the look of fury on Edmund's face when he came down the stairs and found them. If they were not quietened down, it would only be a matter of time before he woke.

She made a quick decision, looking to the coach driver for help.

"Perhaps you could continue your fun in the sitting room, officers?" she said, hoping that her tone made it clear that it was a demand, not a suggestion.

It took both herself and the coachman to corral the drunken soldiers into the sitting room, and further persuasion to convince them to at least sit down. Both of them claimed that the floor was rising to attack them at least once, leading to a suggestion that they might go to war against it; it was only the coach driver's strong arm that prevented Christopher from drawing his sword and slashing away at it.

"No, but you'll stay with us, won't you, Miss Warrick?" Christopher asked, reaching out and grasping hold of her arm as she walked by him.

"I've to pay your driver," Joanna said sharply, attempting to pull her hand away. "He must return to the town for his next fare. You had forgotten to give him anything."

"Oh, that," Christopher said, waving a hand in the air dismissively. "Jasper, pay the man, won't you?"

Jasper mumbled something incomprehensible and thrust a hand into the air, containing a small leather pouch that jingled as it moved.

Joanna took it from his hand and extracted the driver's fare, slipping him an extra coin for the trouble he had taken.

She had only finished seeing him off at the door when

she heard a crashing noise coming from the sitting room, and had to rush back to see what had befallen them now.

"Oh, Miss Warrick, excellent timing," Christopher said, prompting a fresh round of laughter from Rivers. "We seem to be in need of your assistance."

A small side table loaded with a tea set, no doubt left behind by Edmund after the maid had already retired for the evening, had crashed over onto the ground, spilling everything.

A teacup and saucer were both completely smashed, and the teapot was leaking its last dregs onto a fine rug.

Joanna gasped and rushed forward to pick everything up quickly, as Christopher tried and failed to set the table back the right way up.

"Please sit down, Second Lieutenant Hardwicke," she said. "Please. Let me clear this up."

He fell down rather than sat down, next to his friend Rivers on the couch.

"Don't you think we should get more wine, Jasper?" Christopher moaned. "I do so feel that we should get more wine."

"What's going on?"

Joanna whirled around with her heart hammering in her chest, to see Patience standing in the doorway. She had drawn a thin robe on over her nightgown, though her hair was still twisted and tied up with rags.

"Miss Patience," Joanna said, hurrying over to her with

the remains of the teacup in her hands. "You should go back to bed. Lord Kelt is not going to be pleased if he finds us all here."

"Christopher?" Patience exclaimed, clearly not listening at all. "You're home!"

"Yes, my little chicken, I'm home," Christopher said, beaming and throwing his arms out towards her theatrically. "Come, give your big brother an embrace, a real welcome home."

Patience laughed and bounded over to squeeze him tightly, tucking her head under his chin as he patted her back.

"And an embrace for your big brother's best friend, too?" Rivers said, clearly eyeing Patience with a look that was not at all to Joanna's liking.

"*Miss Patience*," she snapped, throwing all the might she could muster into the words. "Come away and sit down by the fireplace before you catch a cold."

Patience sighed and rolled her eyes, but she came.

Just what she needed, Joanna thought, looking around the room in despair.

She had wanted to send Patience back up the stairs, but it seemed a compromise was necessary even to ensure that she would partake in proper behaviour.

Joanna lifted the table back into its proper position and deposited her handful of shards onto it, hurrying to pick up the teapot and the rest of the pieces of saucer before someone stepped on them.

"We were just discussing the need for more wine, dear sister. Wouldn't you like some?" Christopher said.

"Miss Patience does not drink wine," Joanna said, firmly, not even bothering to turn back to address them.

"Is Miss Patience allowed to speak except through the medium of her governess?" Rivers asked, causing Christopher to fall about laughing again.

"I think you officers may wish to be more concerned about how the pair of you will speak, if you wake Lord Kelt," Joanna said. "You may find that you have more explaining to do than you are capable of, sirs."

"She has a tongue, this one," Christopher said, with what almost sounded like admiration. "Does she address you this way in class, sister?"

"I'm a good student," Patience said, a little too primly. Rivers and Christopher guffawed together again.

"Miss Patience, I really think you may be better placed in your bed," Joanna said quietly, directing her comment to her charge alone.

"But everyone's having fun," Patience pouted. "And Christopher won't be home for long."

"You are correct, dear sister," Christopher said. "In fact, you may be shocked to learn that this visit was not planned in itself. We simply found ourselves a short distance from here with no more wine left to drink. So, we came. Now, where is that wine?"

Christopher lurched to his feet again and began to stagger around the room, unsteadily reaching for cabinet doors and making a generally poor job of searching the room.

"We should have music with our wine," Rivers said, waving his hands in the air as if to conduct an invisible orchestra.

"Should I play something for you?" Patience asked eagerly.

Joanna finished dusting her hands off above the table, everything now righted again, to catch a look on Patience's face that was not at all good news.

Following her gaze, she reassessed the Rivers fellow. His dark hair was long and tied at the nape of his neck, with a few strands working their way loose to hang about his face. He had a strong nose and full lips, and his eyes, now that Joanna looked closer, might well have been green.

Of all the soldiers Christopher brought back to parade in front of his impressionable young sister, it had to be one that looked like *that*.

"This is no time of night for music," Joanna said, hastily. "It is an hour for sleeping. You will wake not only Lord Kelt, but your other siblings too. The young ones need their rest."

"Perhaps they might appreciate the chance to come

and dance along with us," Rivers said slyly. "I see there is a pianoforte in the corner. Are you able to play it, my lady?"

"Of course I can," Patience said happily.

Both of them had ignored Joanna's words entirely.

"Wine!" Christopher exclaimed, finally brandishing aloft a bottle which he had found tucked inside a cabinet.

"That is port, actually," Joanna said, seeing the label.

"And can you sing, too, beautiful one?" Rivers asked.

"No, she cannot," Joanna said automatically, precisely at the same time at which Patience said: "Yes, I can!"

Christopher found his way back to the couch and settled himself again, working on dragging the cork out of the bottle of port.

"Are you going to entertain us, dear sister? I should think you don't know any of our army songs."

"You can teach me," Patience beamed, already making her way to sit on the pianoforte stool. "I'm a fast learner."

"Absolutely not," Joanna said.

She had heard an army song once when visiting London with her father, as they passed a group of drunken soldiers spilling out of a public house. It had been a bawdy affair, and she was not at all willing to allow Patience to learn one on her watch.

"Play something sweet, from my sweet sister," Christopher suggested, finally getting the cork out and taking a swig directly from the bottle before passing it to Rivers.

"Yes, I'm sure there is an angelic voice to match the angelic outside," Rivers suggested, taking his own swig.

Joanna wrung her hands. "Don't touch those keys," she said, running out of options. She could see no way to stop them if Patience did not listen.

Patience gave her a wide, innocent smile, and then pressed her fingers down and began to play.

Joanna felt quite light-headed.

Lord Kelt was going to wake up, and there was not a single chance in the world that he was going to be happy about any of this.

13

It was the distant sound of a pianoforte that first broke through his dreams.

For a brief confusing moment, he was somewhere between sleep and wakefulness, fancying himself still at the ball and about to dance with Miss Warrick again.

Then his eyes snapped open in the dark, and he knew that the sound was coming from within his own home.

He saw that the sky was still dark outside of his window, but the pianoforte was playing all the same. The notes rang through the house, completely impossible to ignore.

What could possibly be going on? Had someone gone mad?

Edmund struggled out of bed and into a housecoat that

hung over the back of a nearby chair, before wrenching his door open.

In the corridor he came across Samuel, peering down over the bannister into the main hall. Behind him, Amy was wandering out of her room, rubbing her eyes and clutching a rag doll sleepily.

"What's happening?" Samuel asked.

"Go back to bed," Edmund said, reaching over to mess his hair as he passed. "Both of you. Don't worry. The noise will stop soon."

"But…"

"No buts, Samuel. Go to sleep," Edmund threw over his shoulder as he jogged down the stairs.

The sound was clearly coming from the sitting room; he could have guessed it already, since it was the only room in the house equipped with a pianoforte.

It was supposed to be there only for Patience's occasional lessons and for the entertainment of guests, which they did not have at this –

Edmund pushed open the door, and saw the whole group of them in there, laughing and having fun.

The noise of the pianoforte faltered and stopped as Patience looked up and caught his eyes. "Brother," she began, quietly, but it soon lapsed into silence.

She must have known there was nothing she could say that would make him less angry.

"*What* is going on?" Edmund asked, into the sudden quiet of the previously-lively room.

"We're having a party, brother," Christopher said, managing to rouse himself up from the sofa. He was holding an open bottle of port in one hand. "Would you like something to drink? Come and join us."

"You are drunk, Christopher," Edmund said. "How disgraceful. What is your intention, in coming here and waking the whole household with this madness?"

"I told you he was a miserable sort," Christopher muttered to another soldier sitting beside him, who snickered in reply.

"They came in a coach, my lord," Miss Warrick said quietly. "I asked them to be quiet and retire to the guest rooms, but they would not."

"Miss Warrick," Edmund said, shaking his head.

He felt a cold rage towards her, a burning disappointment. "I expected better from you. Take Patience to her bed immediately."

"No!" Patience protested. "I'm having fun!"

But Miss Warrick bowed her head meekly and said, "Yes, my lord."

She walked over to Patience and took her by the arm, and despite her protests, the girl did not resist.

Edmund watched them leave the room, both of them with their faces cast down to the floor.

This was a black mark that he had not expected on

their governess' character. She should have known better than to allow her charge to fraternise with an unknown gentleman, and in her nightclothes no less.

To say nothing of this so-called 'entertainment', waking her younger siblings and scaring them in the deep of the night.

There was a pang of hurt, too, at this disappointment. He would have to send Miss Warrick away now and find a replacement, just when he had been warming to her character.

But a black mark like this was a stain. He could not trust her as a chaperone again if this was how she acted when his back was turned.

It would be painful to see her go, and full of regret. But she had forced his hand.

When the door closed behind them, Edmund turned back to his brother and the new interloper.

"What on God's earth do you think you are doing, Christopher?" he hissed furiously.

"We're just having fun, brother. Maybe you should relax. If you had any of it yourself, you might not be so angry all of the time."

"Angry?" Edmund repeated, hardly believing his ears. "I am angry at you, Christopher, because once again you play the fool and take nothing seriously. You woke Amy and Samuel. They were scared. Did you think nothing of them?"

"You should have let them come down and dance to the music," Christopher said, with a dreamy look in his eyes.

Edmund seethed. "And who, pray tell, is this?"

"Second Lieutenant Jasper Rivers at your service, sir," Rivers said, saluting clumsily and nearly falling off the couch in the process.

"You serve together, is that it?"

"Trained together also," Christopher pointed out.

"And who is he? Outside of the army, have you a rank, Rivers?"

"I'm a... a gent'man, m'lord," Rivers slurred.

"So, he is nothing but a lowly scoundrel," Edmund scoffed. "No title. And you bring him into our home to ogle your poor sister in her nightclothes?"

"She came down wearing that," Christopher said. "I didn't make her."

"You disgust me," Edmund said, pacing up and down in front of them. "I can barely believe the level you have fallen to. You think it is acceptable to engage in such drunken behaviour?"

"Slo... slow down," Christopher said, watching him and swaying back and forth as he passed by. "You're making me feel sick."

Rivers began snoring loudly from his place on the couch, and Christopher tittered.

Edmund had had enough.

"Get up," he said, seizing Christopher by the collar.

He hauled him out into the main hall and deposited him on the floor by the main entrance doors.

"Sit there and wait for the coach. You're going back to your base, and tonight."

It took their driver's help to move Rivers into the coach, though Christopher was still able to get in under his own steam – with a few false starts and falls.

"I apologise for asking you to take them at this hour," Edmund said to his driver, his breath forming clouds in the cold night air.

"But they simply cannot stay. Please, see them to the barracks. There you will have help to remove them, and return post-haste. I shall expect you in the late morning to take me onwards to London."

In the morning, Edmund woke at the normal hour.

He had barely slept at all since the interruption, which had not been long after he extinguished his candle, but there was no excuse for sitting around. There was work to be done, no matter what circumstances might be plaguing his home life.

In the hour or so before the coach driver would take him to the city, he still had much to do.

The first thing involved sitting at the desk in his study, going back over the advertisement he had placed in the paper last time he required a governess at short notice.

The text was more or less the same, given that it had been only a short while ago that he had used it.

This one had lasted longer than all of the others, he had to admit, and there was still a stab of remorse that almost stayed his hand as he wrote it out again. But he had to remain firm.

This was about what was best for the children, not his own personal feelings.

"You're still at home," Amy said, from the doorway of the study.

She was still rubbing her eyes, just as he had seen her last night, though now she was dressed and her hair had been brushed. "Are you going to stay with us today?"

Edmund put down his quill and turned to her. "No, Amy, my sweet. I'm just going to work late, that's all."

"Why?"

Edmund held out his arms to her, twisting around in his chair. Amy needed no further encouragement to bound over and climb up to sit on his knee.

"I have to go to work, Amy. I have to keep up the business now that Father – now that it's my responsibility."

"But you can stay at home for one day," Amy said, with an air of decisiveness.

Edmund laughed and planted a kiss on her forehead. "Not today. I'll be with you all weekend, I promise."

Amy sighed. "Okay then. I want a pony though."

"Nice try, little one," Edmund laughed again. "You'll just have to make do without either me or a pony. At least until you're old enough to ride by yourself."

"I bet Miss Warrick can teach me," Amy said, resting her little head against Edmund's shoulder and wriggling into a more comfortable position. "She knows everything."

"Not quite everything, sweet," Edmund said, feeling the heaviness settle on him again.

One thing she did not know, clearly, was how to stand up to Christopher.

"I love Miss Warrick. I hope she's here forever and ever," Amy said, wriggling again and then jumping down to the floor.

She wandered away, leaving Edmund staring after her, quite speechless.

It was true that the children had quite taken to her. Samuel, too. Even Patience seemed less determined to hate her than she had with every other governess.

Could he really risk exchanging her for another woman who might not be so quick to earn their love?

And when he thought about it, wasn't Christopher really the one who should be taken to task for all of this? He was unsure that any of the servants would really have been able to stop him from doing whatever he wanted, old Jenkins included.

Perhaps he was being too hard on Miss Warrick,

judging her in anger. The person who really deserved his ire was the one who had stumbled in drunk and unannounced.

"What are you doing, Edmund?" he asked himself, out loud.

Before he could think about it for too much longer, he took the scrap of paper from his desk and balled it up, throwing it to the floor. The original advertisement followed swiftly after it.

He put away his quill pen and ink, and cleared the desk entirely so that all temptation was gone.

There. The governess would stay – it was decided.

And if a small part of him was relieved not to lose her company, then that part need not be acknowledged.

Far be it from him to admit that he might perhaps like having her around for his own benefit, too.

14

Joanna had been sure that she would be dismissed after the anger she had seen on Edmund's face.

He had every right; she had been unable to stop all of it, and had failed in her most serious duty of protecting Patience.

But despite the guilt that she felt, Edmund did not so much as mention it again.

The first time she met him in the corridor after that night, he simply grunted from deep in his chest, gave her a level stare, and moved on.

She took the message of his stare, as she interpreted it, to heart.

Don't make another mistake like that again.

Joanna was determined not to let him down. The way he had trusted her at the ball, and the way he had praised her, had made her feel so alive and happy.

She would do anything, now, to return to that position again. She would make him respect and trust her once more, even if it took until the children were all grown up to do it.

The children, for their part, were another source of concern after the night that Jasper Rivers and Christopher crashed into the home.

While Samuel and Amy were still as good as gold, Patience was more than surly about the telling-off she had received from Edmund for her part in it.

He had more or less told her that she would not be attending any more balls for the summer so that she could reform her attitude towards the right way to act in polite society.

The two of them had screamed at one another for so long at dinner that night that Samuel and Amy had snuck away to find Joanna in the schoolroom and hide with her. Patience had thrown every fussy tantrum trick she could think of, but Edmund was unmoved.

Now, aside from the awkward silences at the dinner table that no doubt endured, Joanna was the one who was having to deal with Patience's temper.

She had lost all interest in her lessons, preferring

instead to bemoan her current situation and act as though she were the first young woman ever to feel slighted.

"Study a few pages from your French book," Joanna said, only a few days after the incident, as she prepared to set up Samuel and Amy with their lessons. By the time they were settled, she would be ready to come back and test Patience on what she had read.

"Shan't," said Patience, yawning loudly and going over to sit on the wide ledge of the schoolroom windowsill.

Joanna blinked, watching her. "Excuse me, Miss Patience?" she said, quite sure that she must have heard her wrong.

"Excuse yourself," Patience said, rudely. "I shan't take any more lessons. I have decided I am no longer going to do any of it."

Joanna continued to stare at her, open-mouthed.

She had never heard a girl say such insolent things! What should she do?

The thought of going to Edmund for help only made her shudder. She would be dismissed for certain if he thought that she was not able to control his sister.

Joanna cleared her throat quietly, trying to regain her composure. She turned back to the other two children, who were also staring open-mouthed, clearly wondering what would happen next.

"Mr. Samuel," Joanna said. "I'd like you to work on your

world map. Can you finish shading all of the African countries for me this morning?"

Samuel nodded wordlessly, reaching into his desk to take out the half-finished work without taking his eyes off Patience.

"Now, Miss Amy, we'll do some more reading for a little while this morning. Will you read out the next chapter of your book to me?" Joanna said, sitting down next to Amy as if nothing had happened.

Amy started slowly and cautiously, glancing over at Patience often.

The older girl did not move or turn around, simply looking out of the window.

Joanna racked her brains for what she should do.

What kind of action should she take? She was wholly unprepared for this kind of behaviour. Her sister had never acted out in this way, nor had her brother, and she had no model of what a governess was to do when discipline was so severely required.

She was quite at a loss.

When Amy finished her reading, Joanna realised she had barely heard any of it. She had been able to pay little enough attention to correct Amy's mistakes, and nothing more.

"Well done, Miss Amy," she said, feeling a slight shake in her hands as she took the book from her. She barely knew what to do next.

It was Samuel and Amy who saved her. They had been used to their sister's temperament for rather longer, and they evidently knew how to deal with it.

"Miss Warrick," Samuel called loudly. "Will you help me with my map? And can Amy join in?"

Joanna looked between the two of them for a moment, and noted how their little faces were set with a new kind of determination and enthusiasm.

She nodded, not quite yet understanding the meaning of their intentions. "Yes, alright. Let's work together, then."

The three of them moved their chairs so that they could sit around Samuel's desk, all looking down at the map.

"What kind of animals are here, Miss Warrick?" Samuel asked, pointing at a random spot. "I want to draw some on there."

"Tigers roam wild," Joanna said, peering down at the map. "Have you ever seen an illustration of a tiger?"

"Yes!" Samuel exclaimed. "They have stripes all down their backs and ferocious teeth."

Amy bared her teeth like an animal and let out a mighty roar, clawing the air with her fingers. "I'm a tiger," she explained.

Joanna laughed in spite of the tension she felt. "Very good, Miss Amy!"

"And what about here?" asked Samuel. He had a pencil in his hand and was already drawing a small, rather wobbly example of a tiger.

"Over here we can find zebras and lions," Joanna said.

"What's a zebie?" Amy asked.

"It's like a horse," Samuel said. "But that's all stripy too."

"Quite right," Joanna nodded. "They are striped black and white."

"Could you ride them?" Amy asked, her eyes shining with delight.

"I confess, I am not sure," Joanna laughed. "They are shaped like horses, so I do not see why not."

"I'm going to ask Edmund for a zebie," Amy declared.

"I will get a lion then," Samuel said, roaring in much the same way Amy's tiger had.

"What's the difference between a lion and a tiger, children?" Joanna asked.

"One's stripy," Amy put in.

"Um... maybe lions have lots of hair," Samuel added. "Oh, and they live in different places."

"Well done again," Joanna smiled. "But you should be very careful where you put your lion. Do you know why?"

"Because he eats zebras," Samuel said with a wicked grin.

"No!" Amy gasped, putting both hands to her cheeks. "He can't eat my zebie!"

Samuel and Joanna both laughed. "Don't worry, little one. All you need is a strong cage to keep the lion in so he doesn't get out."

Joanna stole a glance at Patience. The older girl kept

moving her head as if she was listening and wanted to turn around, but she said nothing.

Perhaps this was working – showing her how much fun they were all having without her.

"Where do monkeys live?" Amy asked, clearly moving on from the dilemma about her 'zebie'.

"Oh, well, they don't just live in one place," Joanna said. "In fact, you can find monkeys in a lot of places around the world. Like here, here, and here."

"Monkeys are funny," Samuel said, grinning. "We saw one once. One of Father's friends had a pet he brought back from the New World. He was like a little old man."

"What did he sound like?" Amy asked, wide-eyed.

"Don't you remember, Amy?" Samuel asked. "He made a noise like ooh-ooh-ooh. And he walked like this."

Samuel got out of his chair and crouched down, swinging his arms around loosely. Amy and Joanna were both in fits of laughter watching him.

"That's not quite right," Patience said from the window. She got up, carefully avoiding Joanna's eyes. "He wasn't crouching like that. He was walking on short legs. You just look silly."

"Show me," Amy insisted.

Patience shook her head. "It's not exactly ladylike. Samuel, just straighten your legs a bit – there, like that."

Patience walked over while Samuel continued

perfecting his impression, and took a nearby chair so that she could sit closer to them.

Joanna said nothing. The last thing she wanted to do now was to act smugly, or do something else that might trigger Patience to change her mind and flounce away again.

They sat around the desk for the rest of the morning, talking about different animals from around the world. It hadn't been part of Joanna's plan for the week's lessons, but she didn't mind.

So long as they were learning something, and enjoying themselves, she could let them continue.

By the end of the day, little Amy had quite worn herself out. With only an hour to go until dinner, Joanna decided that the little girl was in need of a nap. She could wake up for her meal and then return to bed, but she would not be able to stay awake for much longer without that nap.

Joanna lifted her into her arms, cradling Amy's sleepy head against her neck, and carried her out of the schoolroom. She was almost asleep by the time they reached her bed.

"Here you are," Joanna said, laying her down and drawing the covers over her.

"Night-night, Mama," Amy murmured.

Joanna could not help but draw in a soft gasp of air. She was hit by the surprise, and the unexpected pain of it.

The poor child. After losing her mother, she no longer had anyone to fill that role – Joanna was the closest thing she had.

Amy's eyes opened again at the sound of Joanna's gasp, and her cheeks flushed red. "Sorry, Miss Warrick," she whispered.

Joanna smiled, not wanting to discourage her. "Go to sleep, little one. It's alright."

She stroked Amy's hair back from her face and waited until her breathing evened out before standing up and leaving the room.

The poor mite. Joanna's heart was warmed by the idea that Amy would mistake her for her mother, even in such a sleepy state. The comparison was beyond flattering – it had to be.

But still, there was an ache in her chest for the fact that Amy had to miss her mother at all – and for the longing to see her own mother again someday.

That night after dining, Joanna retired to her room and thought of Esther. She had missed her sister dreadfully and had received a new message just a few days ago. She realised that she had not yet had the time to read it.

There were so many things that she needed to ask for advice about, but then again it wasn't as though Esther had any real experience with children either.

How should she deal with Patience? Well, that was one

question she might at least have partially answered for herself now.

What should she feel about the ball, and Edmund's insistence on dancing with her? That she had not dared to quite put out on the page, though she had laid out the event and hoped that Esther might comment.

She had decided to simply write everything she could think of and see what her sister had to say about it. Now, at last, she could find out.

She was not disappointed by her sister's attempt to answer her questions, though as she had suspected, her expertise was slim in these matters.

My dearest sister Joanna,

It sounds to me as though you are having your first troubles with your position, for which you should count yourself very lucky indeed.

It seems as though you have had a charmed relationship with your employer so far, for which you should be very grateful. I do not mean to scold, only to try uplifting your spirits.

I think it is fairly endearing that the children have taken to you quite so quickly. It almost sounds as though they regard you to be one of the family already.

What fortune you have had to find yourself among such people who are willing to accept you just as you are! And the children do seem darling.

To the help that you require with discipline, you are correct in surmising that I would not have enough experience to give you the advice you require.

I am so sorry that I cannot be of more help, but my advice to you would be to try and imagine yourself in Miss Patience's place. Perhaps you will be able to instruct her more keenly if you understand the motivations behind her behaviour.

It sounds that you are well on the way towards doing so, and I have no doubt, dear sister, that you will be able to solve this in your own way.

But I wish you would tell me more about the ball! How was Edmund's dancing? Was it really so terribly embarrassing to dance with your employer? From your words I should rather think that you found it enjoyable, no?

I believe from what I have read that he treats you with great respect. Do tell me if I am wrong.

How dashing, to have a man who sees that you are alone and puts it right! I find it all terribly romantic.

Now, I must tell you some of my own news. I hope that you will be of as good cheer as we are here. Indeed, it is the most wonderful news I have had the pleasure to share since the day that my dear lord asked for my hand in marriage.

For, as it is my great joy to tell you, I am at last with child!

I understand that things are not so simple for you as they were before, but I do hope that you will be able to come and be by my side in time for the birth. It will be of such great help to me, and I shall not fear for anything if you are with me.

Oh, my dearest, sweetest Joanna, how much better I shall feel if you are by my side to hold my hand!

Please do give me your response as soon as you are able – if your employer is willing to allow you some time with us, it will be the happiest boon and gift we receive all year.

Waiting urgently for your response, your happy sister,

Lady Esther Castleford.

15

It should have been a day like any other.

Edmund was simply riding to a nearby estate and back, visiting a neighbouring Earl who was interested in doing business and had to be buttered up with socialisation.

As it turned out, the old man was more interested in having Edmund spend dinner with his daughters than anything else, and he felt quite angry at the waste of his time.

Perhaps it was not the old man's fault: that was how things were done, out here in the countryside. But Edmund had many things to take care of, and such a delay as spending a whole day out of the city was unacceptable to him.

Rather than taking advantage of their hospitality, he decided to ride home that night.

It was a dark one, with little in the way of light from the moon, and clouds covered what stars there were. But still, he insisted.

It was less than an hour's ride on his horse, a fine steed who knew his way even in the dark, and then he could at least rest in his own bed.

His regret, however, stemmed from the bats that flew screeching from the trees as he rode across the distance between their two homes.

His stallion spooked and reared before charging away, leaving Edmund fallen to the ground behind him.

The pain was immediate, and excruciating. The horse returned when called, looking suitably sheepish at his own behaviour, and Edmund managed to pull himself up into the saddle using just one arm – for the other hung useless at his side, crushed as he fell and now radiating agony.

"Jenkins," he gasped, as he slid from the horse's back at the entrance to his home. "Jenkins, send the driver out for a doctor."

The old butler was almost out of his wits, startled to see his master in such a state – muddied, breathless, and hunched over, protecting his arm from any kind of movement.

"My lord! Immediately, I shall see to it... Oh, my lord, come, let me help you sit..."

"No, send for him now," Edmund gasped out. "I'll see myself inside. Just send for him."

Edmund's memory from then was spotted with periods of darkness.

He barely remembered the rest of the ride home, and he did not recall choosing a certain chair in the hallway to rest upon.

Some time later, he found himself with Miss Warrick crouched at his feet, and he had no idea when she must have arrived.

"Lord Kelt," she was saying, her expression very serious. "We must get you upstairs. Please. You can rest in your own chambers and wait for the doctor there. You must allow Jenkins to help you out of your muddy clothes and into something warm."

Edmund nodded, lurching to his feet.

His balance was thrown off by not being able to use one of his limbs, and every now and then he would try to make some unconscious movement and the pain would surge forth again.

"Come, my lord, come," Jenkins said, emotion quivering heavily in his voice. He was quite affected by it all, and Edmund tried to throw him a confident smile.

"No need for all that, Jenkins," he said, hoping that he sounded cheerful. "I'll be alright once the doctor comes. Broken the arm, I think."

Then there was more of a gap in his memory, time that was lost in a haze of pain.

Perhaps it had been so bad that his mind refused to collect it; perhaps he had been too focused on the pain to be able to understand what was occurring around him. Either way, he could not say.

"Ah, the patient is back with us," said a doctor, leaning over him when he finally knew that he was back in his own room again.

"Doctor? How long have you been here?" Edmund asked, momentarily struggling to sit upright and then giving up.

"Long enough to put a splint on that broken arm of yours," the doctor said, moving away towards the other side of the room where a heavy black bag sat open on a chair.

"You are quite lucky not to have done any further damage. It is a bad break, but I think it will heal just fine."

Edmund shot upright this time, ignoring the pain in his arm and pushing himself up with the one that was still healthy. "How long will it take to heal?"

"Weeks, I should think," the doctor said, tucking a roll of bandages away into his bag.

"Six of them, if not a couple more. You must rest the arm during that time, do you hear me? If you don't, you'll end up with an uneven heal. That's not good for gaining back your strength."

"Six weeks…" Edmund repeated. "Can it not be done any sooner than that?"

The doctor laughed. "I'm sorry, Lord Kelt, but it does take a little longer for a bone to heal than a simple cut. It is nature which dictates the time, not you or I."

Edmund watched him go, packing up his things and murmuring something to Jenkins in the doorway as he left.

Then it was only the old butler left in the room, and he began fussing with the covers on the bed and Edmund's pillows.

"How ever did you injure yourself in this way, my lord?" He asked, almost whining. "We were quite alarmed to see you returning home at such an hour, and in so much pain."

"I am fine now, Jenkins," Edmund said. "Do stop fussing, will you? It must be the middle of the night now."

"Indeed, my lord," Jenkins confirmed. "I sent the governess to her quarters to get some rest. The rest of the staff, too, are sleeping, and we did not think it right to wake the children. They would only be worried."

"You made the right choice, Jenkins," Edmund said. "Go now, and get some rest yourself. I will try to sleep for the rest of the night. In the morning, we must make provisions for how I can cover the work needed while I wait for this to heal."

Jenkins gave him a worried look, but said no more.

He took the only candle in the room to the doorway with him, leaving Edmund in darkness once he was gone.

It was a long night. Though Edmund had said he would rest, he found himself unable to sleep.

The pain was strong, and all he could think about besides that was the fact that he would need to find some alternative way to carry on leaving the business while he rested. The doctor had been clear.

But how could he keep up with his paperwork and letters if he was not able to use one of his arms?

It was just his damnable luck that it had to be his right arm, the one that he wrote with.

He managed to get some fitful sleep just before dawn, and then the light woke him once more.

He had made up his mind during the hours of night.

There was no opportunity for him to leave the work behind. Someone had to take responsibility. That someone had to be him, because Christopher was nowhere near ready enough to take on any kind of work for the business.

By the time Jenkins came in to serve him breakfast, Edmund had already struggled out of bed and attempted to dress himself. It was not as simple as it seemed without a working arm, and he had been having some difficulty getting his shirt on properly.

"Ah, Jenkins," he said. "Excellent timing, as always. Help me with this, will you?"

"Sir, I wonder if you should be dressing?" Jenkins

asked, though he came forward obediently. "The doctor did specify rest."

"Nonsense. I'm going to the city, as planned," Edmund said. "I've decided I'm not to be held back by this silly injury. What can I do, sitting around at home for six weeks? I have to work."

"Yes, sir," Jenkins said, though it was written plainly on his face that he did not agree with his employer's decision.

Edmund's arm kept plaguing him with each movement sending a fresh wave of pain. But he pressed on.

There was no time to be lost – he had to get going. He was already running late for his normal schedule.

To his credit, he made it all the way down the stairs, and into the courtyard. He was able to make it into his carriage, where Jenkins insisted upon accompanying him.

"You'll need my help, sir," he said. "I can make things easier for you when you reach the office. Please, my lord, allow me to assist you."

"Fine, fine," Edmund agreed, just wanting to get going as soon as possible. "You'll come with me. Look sharpish, then. We need to depart."

Once Jenkins was settled in the carriage alongside him, they set off moving.

The gravel driveway down to the house was uncomfortable, but at least they managed to make it.

It was when they emerged onto the road, which was

pitted with many holes, that Edmund's problems truly began.

He cried out in pain, then, the jolting of the carriage proved too much for his newly broken arm.

Jenkins had the good sense to call out to the driver to stop the carriage, and the horses came to a halt, panting in the morning air.

"Sir, will you now allow us to turn back?" Jenkins asked.

His old face was gentle, though he had a look that Edmund had seen many times in the past. It was the look of a servant who knew far better than his employer, and have finally been proven right.

"Alright," Edmund conceded, and the whole carriage was turned around post-haste to return to the house.

This brought with it new problems, however. If he could not go into work – as he now admitted that he could not – then work would have to come to him.

By the time the household was engaged in the hourly break the lunchtime, Edmund was installed once more in his chambers.

He had managed to convince Jenkins that he would be better off sitting in his office, in a comfortable chair, than languishing in bed all day long. That was as much as he could persuade him to allow, for the old man had become quite fierce in his attempts to protect Edmund from further harm.

A quiet knock at the door surprised him, for Edmund had already been served his luncheon by Mary, the household's maid.

"Enter," he called out, wondering who it could be.

"Lord Kelt, I wanted to bring you some presents from the children," Miss Warrick said, standing in the doorway.

She had a folded piece of paper in her hand, as well as an apple and a ragdoll. "They know about your broken arm, and they wanted to wish you to get better soon. I told them it was better if they applied themselves to their lessons and waited to see you in the evening. I thought that might be best."

"You thought correctly," Edmund told her. "I should not wish to interrupt their scheduled lessons with something as silly as this. What have you brought for me?"

"A card full of well wishes," Joanna smiled.

She walked forward towards his desk, placing the items down in easy reach.

"Miss Amy also wished you to have one of her dolls for comfort, and Mr. Samuel insisted on providing you with an apple. He has heard that it is a healthy fruit, and believes it will help you to recover faster."

Edmund chuckled. "They are good children, are they not? Even if they may be a little way off the mark with the idea of presents."

Joanna laughed along with him. "They mean well," she said.

"Their thoughts are truly with you, even if they are supposed to be studying. They have not stopped asking about your well-being all morning. I told them that you shall live, but I am not sure that they are fully convinced of this truth."

Edmund nodded. "For myself, I am hardly convinced of it either. I know I shall survive this wound, quite easily so, but I fear for the business. Jenkins has me practically under house arrest here. I don't know how I will be able to keep up with correspondence, particularly since it is my right arm which is broken."

"You are not able to write?" Miss Warrick asked, her forehead creasing with concern. "How are you to send your letters? Will Jenkins write them for you?"

Edmund guffawed. "No, that old bird is far too slow with a pen for my requirements.

"It is worse than that, anyway. I cannot even make it to the office in London to claim my correspondence. It will be building up on my desk as we speak."

"But you do not think of going out there? Jenkins told us all, the staff, that the doctor recommended rest for a full six weeks. You must recover the use of your arm, you cannot risk that it should heal badly."

Edmund sighed. He perhaps should not allow her to speak so plainly, given that she was his employee and nothing more, but he appreciated the concern with which she spoke.

It was touching to know that his full staff cared about his recovery, though that did not make it any easier for him to complete his work.

"I have already tried to attend my workplace, but it was not possible. The rattling of the carriage was too much for me to bear. I fear I am to be contained here for the full period of my rest, no matter what I may wish otherwise."

Miss Warrick lingered still in the room, though she had done what she came for. She seemed to be thinking, turning something over in her head while staring down at the desk.

"Perhaps I might be of some assistance?" she asked. "You know that I am lettered, and I can take dictation quite easily. I have done it for my own father at a time or two. If we were to give the children some hours off in the afternoon while you recover, which I believe would benefit them greatly by giving them some time to play, then I might become your secretary for a short while until your arm is healed again."

Edmund cocked his head, looking at her in a new light.

Of course, it was true that he trusted she could read and write, perhaps even better than himself. She was a teacher, after all. If he trusted her with the future of his brother and sisters and their education, then the least he could do was to trust her with writing a few letters each day.

"Your plan has some merit," he said. "But how shall I

know what to write? There is still the matter of bringing the paperwork here."

"If you have a man you can trust working in London, perhaps he can bring the letters to the house on a regular basis – or to the nearby town, where I could fetch them. Once a day, or once a week, whatever you may feel is suitable. Then you can see everything in a timely fashion and I can write the responses that you compose."

"You would volunteer your time for this?" he asked. "I will not pay you more because of this. It will be on your own head. Since it is a temporary engagement and not a new position for you, you will be paid as a governess still."

"I shall be a governess still," Miss Warrick smiled. "Wild dogs could not convince me to abandon the children. They must continue to learn. But a period of shorter lessons will not harm them. Why, I knew a family who would summer abroad without their governess every year, and those children turned out very well."

"Don't convince me too hard, Miss Warrick," Edmund smiled. "I might begin to think that your employment as a governess is unnecessary for several months of the year, and dismiss you forthwith."

Miss Warrick shook her head with a smile. "I think you jest with me," she said.

"That I do," Edmund laughed.

He, too, was thinking hard. The only other person who might be suited to run the company in his absence was the one person he could never allow to take control: Christopher.

The boy – still a boy, not at all a man in his behaviour – would run the place to the ground in the space of three weeks, let alone six. There was no possibility that Edmund would ever send him in his place.

And yet, who else was there?

"Fine," he said, decisively. "It is settled. Miss Warrick, you shall play the role of secretary while I need you. Your first order of business will be to write me up some instructions for those at the office. We had better do it now, so that it can be run up to London post-haste, and then we shall begin in earnest on the morrow. Are you up to the task?"

"Certainly, my lord," Miss Warrick said, sitting daintily in the chair at his desk.

She took out the quill pen and ink, and a leaf of fresh paper, and paused, looking at him expectantly.

Edmund dictated the letter, feeling quite unused to speaking his own words out loud like this. It was strange to see them appearing like magic on the paper, and he wondered if perhaps there was some idea to be had in the thought of getting a secretary for the longer term.

Maybe, after all this was over, he would look into the idea.

Miss Warrick took down the whole letter quite expertly, and when she showed it to him for a check, he found not a single error. He had to admit that he was impressed.

That was the moment he truly decided – she really would be his secretary for a short while. It had been a secret test of his, something for her to complete so that he might try the measure of her abilities.

In this, as in almost every other thing, he did not find her wanting.

16

*L*ife had been comfortable again since Joanna had volunteered to work as Edmund's secretary.

The awkward and uncomfortable atmosphere that had lingered after Christopher's last visit had at last been dissipated.

It was, however, inevitable that he would visit the house again sooner rather than later.

Perhaps it was only the children that looked forward to seeing him again, but Christopher came, all the same.

He had reason to celebrate with his family, for he had finally been given a promotion from his grade of Second Lieutenant.

He was now serving as a full Lieutenant, though Edmund expressed his doubts as to whether such a position could have been fully owned by his wayward brother.

Joanna knew that, as merely an employee of the house, she should not have heard such a sentiment; though it seemed as though Edmund could not hold back his frustration when Christopher arrived at the home again.

The main bone of contention, it seemed, was the fact that Christopher had insisted upon bringing his friend Jasper Rivers along with him once more.

"Little sister, have you missed me?" Christopher asked loudly as he swaggered into the main hall, leaving Jenkins and the coach driver to transport several bags of his belongings into the house. "I stand before you a ranked officer."

Patience squealed with glee, making the others present in the hall wince as she ran to embrace her brother. "Christopher! You're back!"

"Yes, and I have a few days to spare for once," Christopher said, looking up as Edmund entered the hall, no doubt alerted by the noise. "I hope you don't mind Jasper coming along with me, brother."

Edmund gave him a dark look, but nodded his assent.

It was hardly possible for him to turn the man away now, with him standing in the hall and evidently having been promised hospitality.

Joanna watched from the side of the hall, keeping an eye on Patience. She shared Edmund's misgivings, though her focus was on this new man, Rivers.

Her worry was that Patience, still young and naive in

her approach to the world, would be swept away by the glamour of this soldier's arrival.

How many times have they heard a similar story whispered in scandal, shared among the residents of the local town or passed like wildfire around a ball?

Joanna was also unhappy to see Christopher again, decked out in his newly badged uniform. He had clearly come only to show off his new rank, as well his friend, who he seemed to be rather impressed by.

Such braggart behaviour did not sit well with her.

"I thought that we might engage in a few days of fun," Christopher said, and immediately began a reason for Joanna to dislike him.

He clearly had no regard for the children's lessons, and thought that he could take them away from their study whenever he felt like entertaining himself.

She was not the only person who felt this way, as she could see from Edmund's expression immediately.

"The children are already engaged in their lessons," Edmund said. "Do you mean to interrupt their education so freely?"

"You take everything so seriously," Christopher said, laughing. "It will not harm them to have just a few days of fun. This house has become so dour. Allow them to smile and laugh like children for once, will you?"

Edmund bristled, and Joanna noted that his hands were clenching into fists and unclenching again. But his eyes darted towards Rivers, and he swallowed whatever angry words he had been about to say.

"I suppose you leave me no choice," he said. "The children are already excited by your offer. I will have to allow it."

The children, who had all gathered around to witness their brother's arrival, simultaneously cheered. Joanna did not hold that against them.

After all, when offered the chance to play, a child will always take it.

"First, let's get us settled in our rooms," Christopher said. "Jasper and I have had a long journey."

He gestured towards the bags that Jenkins had brought in, as if to say that they should now be put into their proper places.

Edmund snorted. "We have only one room prepared, since you did not see fit to inform us that your friend would be accompanying you. You will have to wait for Mary to set it up. In the meantime, perhaps you would like to rest in the sitting room."

Christopher stretched his arms above his head.

"No, we have been sitting for a long journey. I'd rather go down to the lake and perhaps indulge in some sports. What say you, Samuel?"

Samuel nodded vigorously, his face lighting up at the idea.

"Fine," Edmund said, curtly. "Miss Warrick, you will go

with them. You are excused from your other duties today."

Joanna looked at him with some surprise, but when she caught his expression, she understood.

He wanted her to watch over the children, and ensure that Christopher was not too reckless in his suggestions. She would not put it past him to allow them to drown in the lake while he admired his own reflection, and Edmund clearly felt the same.

"First we must change," Joanna said. "Miss Patience, Miss Amy, you will require sun dresses and bonnets. Come with me now and we shall prepare."

Christopher attempted to protest, but Joanna lifted little Amy onto her hip and took Patience by the hand so that there could be no argument.

She led them up the stairs, turning both her back and a blind ear to whatever Christopher had to say next.

Joanna changed her own clothes quickly, then rushed to help the children.

She was despairing at Christopher's decision to bring his handsome friend along. Where once she might have thought it good fortune to be in the presence of a dashing young officer, now, with little hope for her own future prospects, she was concerned only for protecting those of Patience.

With her family name, she ought to make a much finer match than Lieutenant Jasper Rivers – and quite easily so, given that he had no money besides his army wage.

Patience insisted on finishing fixing her hair and bonnet by herself while Joanna helped Amy, and the two of them arrived downstairs well before she had finished fussing.

Joanna took the opportunity to rearrange a vase of flowers in the hall, conveniently close to where Edmund was standing.

"My lord, I am anxious to keep Miss Patience apart from our guests as much as we can manage," she said, keeping her voice low so that only Edmund would hear.

He gave her a look of surprise, but soon regathered his composure and pretended they were discussing something no more serious than the weather. "You think she will be poorly influenced?"

"I cannot help but remember the pianoforte," Joanna said, casting her eyes over to the sitting room.

She hated to bring up the occasion which had left Edmund so disappointed in her, but the point had to be made.

"I think she will become rather giddy with this officer if she is allowed to spend time in his presence."

Edmund grunted. "But he is from no kind of family. I gather he worked his way into training from Private. Patience will not be swayed by the kind of man who has no fortune to offer her."

Joanna bit her lip. "My lord, forgive me, but she is just a

girl. She may be swayed by much. I think I would have been, when I was her age."

Edmund gave her another look, this time lingering for longer. She did not dare meet his eyes to see what kind of expression he was regarding her with.

"At any rate, we cannot be inhospitable to our guest," he said, at length. "We must allow Christopher his folly. I know he has done this only to irk me, but I refuse to bend to his level and throw our family name into disrepute by turning someone away. You will have to keep a close watch on Patience."

Joanna nodded, though a terrible anxiety was taking hold of her.

She knew well the way a young girl's heart could run. It would not be easy for her to keep them apart, nor to stop any affections from growing.

Down by the side of the lake, buried a long walk away from the house, they settled down with blankets and parasols. Amy, Patience, and Joanna rested on the shore while Rivers, Christopher, and Samuel began throwing around a cricket ball.

"Do you think we have fwogs in the lake?" Amy asked, her eyes trained keenly on the water.

"I should think it likely," Joanna told her. "There may be fish, too. If we were quiet and still, I have no doubt we would also meet a great many birds."

"Do the birds eat the fishies?" Amy asked, moving over

to peer more closely at the lake's surface.

Joanna quickly followed her, resisting the urge to take hold of the back of her dress just in case. Her hands hovered nearby, unwilling to risk her falling in.

"Yes, many of them do. But it depends on the size of the fishes. A small bird cannot eat a big fish," Joanna explained. "Do you see, over there on the far shore? There are some small birds playing near the reeds."

Amy exclaimed with delight, and watch the birds frolicking and picking at the ground for worms.

Joanna smiled to herself. The child was easily amused, but she hoped that natural curiosity would not fade as she grew older.

"Watch out!"

Joanna looked around in alarm, to see the cricket ball sailing perilously close to her face.

She ducked instinctively, and heard it hit the water with a loud splash.

"Oh, Samuel, why did you do that?" Christopher complained. "We'll have to fish it out now. We only brought the one ball with us."

"Sorry, Christopher," Samuel said, clutching his hands together. "I didn't mean to."

Joanna took one look at Samuel's piteous face and felt a righteous fury spread through her.

How dare Christopher tell him off like that? He should have known that Samuel's athletic gifts were much affected by his illness – besides which, he was only a child.

"Don't worry, Mr. Samuel," she called out. "It was only an accident. Perhaps you ought to take your game further from the lake. It was only a matter of time before the ball would go into the water, no matter who threw it."

Samuel looked a little cheered at her words, which helped ease the anger she felt.

Still, she gave Christopher a hard look as he passed by to try and find the ball. She did not care at that moment if he would start a fuss, or try to have her dismissed for insolence.

She would not have him talk to Samuel in that way.

Rivers walked by to join Christopher on the shore.

Both of them had spotted the ball, resting at the bottom of the lake in an area where the water was a little shallower. Now, their discussion seemed to centre around who would go in to get it.

"It's not too deep," Christopher said. "You can probably just wade in."

"I think you might even be able to reach it from here," Rivers argued. "If you lean, say."

"It's impossible to reach it that way without getting wet," Christopher argued. "You would be up to the shoulder."

"I don't mind," Rivers countered.

He shrugged off his vibrant red jacket quickly, placing it

with some reverence a clear distance from the muddier shore. In his shirtsleeves, he began rolling up the bottom of his breeches and taking off his shoes.

"Miss Patience, perhaps we should get some gentle exercise," Joanna suggested quickly. "A walk around the lake would do."

"I'm tired," Patience said, not taking her eyes off Rivers as he continued to prepare for his wade.

"Nonsense," Joanna said, getting up and standing over her with her hands on her hips.

"Come along, young lady. A good walk will do much for your health. If you are tired, it is because we have not walked enough in the past. Come now."

Patience got up reluctantly, and trailed along behind Joanna as she led Amy by the hand.

Joanna watched her closely, but could not find any way to dissuade her from staring at the men, even as they rounded the opposite side of the lake.

Rivers stood bare-footed with his breeches pulled up to his knees, and even rolled up the sleeves of his shirt, before wading into the water.

He gave a shout at the low temperature of the lake, causing Christopher to laugh until Rivers kicked a spray of water back towards him.

"Look at these birds over here," Joanna said, pointing to a clutch of them sitting closely to the shoreline. "See how they do not move when we approach? I would bet they are protecting something, likely a nest. If they had nothing to stay for, they would scatter as soon as they heard us coming."

"Where's the nest?" Amy asked eagerly, looking amongst the reeds for some sign of it.

Patience, however, still had not looked away from Rivers, and Joanna found herself running out of tactics to distract her.

He waded further out into the lake, until the bottom of his breeches was wet even despite the rolling. Then he reached down, plunging his arm in up to the shoulder and emerging with the ball clasped in his hand.

"He found it," Patience said, excitedly.

On the other shore, Samuel and Christopher both whooped and cheered while River waded back, carrying the ball aloft as if it were a great trophy.

"Perhaps we should rest here awhile, and take a look at these trees," Joanna said, taking Patience by the arm. "We may be able to gather some wildflowers that would look darling in a vase in the main hall."

Patience was clearly disappointed, but allowed herself to be pulled away. "We will miss the boys' games," she said.

"I am sure Mr. Samuel will be fine with Lieutenant Christopher," Joanna said, deliberately misunderstanding her meaning.

She took one last glance over her shoulder as Patience and Amy walked ahead into a small grove. Rivers was back on the shore and dressing again, rolling down his breeches to their proper place.

Joanna noted how the water, dripping from his arm, caused his white shirt to cling closely to his body, and shook her head.

She had the feeling that she had pulled her charge away just in time.

When they returned, Samuel was tired out, sitting on the blankets to watch Christopher and Rivers throwing and catching the ball. Rivers had never picked up his jacket, playing in his shirtsleeves instead.

"I think the children ought to return to the house," Joanna called out, catching their attention. "We have been gone some hours. It is time for them to eat."

"Fine. I'm hungry anyway," Christopher said, slipping the ball into his pocket. "Jasper and I will head back too."

Joanna turned around to gather the blankets back into the basket she had carried over, and felt a chill seize her heart.

Patience had fetched the red jacket from where it lay on the grass and was carrying it over, holding it in front of her with an almost reverential expression.

"Here's your jacket, Lieutenant," she said, passing it over to Rivers.

"I thank you, my beautiful lady," Rivers said, effecting a bow as he took it from her. He shrugged it on, giving her a dazzling smile in the process.

Joanna marched forward quickly with the basket tucked under one of her arms, and hooked the other around Patience's elbow.

"Come, Miss Patience," she said. "We are all prepared. Let's return to the house. Take your sister's hand, there."

Amy eagerly grabbed hold of Patience's hand to skip alongside them.

Though Patience looked mightily displeased, she could not protest. Samuel, Rivers, and Christopher ended up walking ahead of them, though Samuel eventually dropped back, unable to keep up with their pace.

The three days of the officers' visit were perhaps the longest of Joanna's life. She felt exhausted, having to watch closely over Patience at every moment.

On the second night, she even caught her trying to sneak down to the sitting room after she was supposed to have retired from the night.

From then, Joanna took to stalking the corridors until she was confident that Patience had at last fallen asleep.

Rivers was a scoundrel, a rogue, and a cad – of that she had no doubt, even if she had no actual proof. She was quite certain that he was deliberately making a pose of himself around Patience, and that it was all a carefully designed ploy to get himself married into a wealthy family.

Joanna said nothing of her suspicions, knowing that she could not prove them.

But when the two men left, finally, on the fourth day,

and Patience stood waving at their carriage with a tear in her eye, Joanna knew she had been right.

And she knew that it was the biggest relief of her year to watch that carriage disappear down the driveway, out of sight of her young charge.

17

It soon became part of their normal routine for Miss Warrick to appear in his office chamber after luncheon was concluded.

The children would retire to their own pursuits – often they could hear them, calling and whooping out on the grounds of the house, enjoying their own fun. Though he would not say to them, for fear of provoking mutiny against lessons in the future, it was pleasant to hear them having a good time again.

There had been far too little laughter in the house since the illness had come and gone.

It was Miss Warrick who continued to surprise him the most, as she had done since the first day she set foot in their home.

She was more than capable of acting as his secretary,

and he even began to wonder why she had wasted herself as a governess. He did not say this out loud, since it might encourage her to seek employment elsewhere.

"What did you think, Miss Warrick?" he asked one evening, as they finished putting together the paperwork for a particularly difficult trade agreement.

"Am I a fool to offer them such a good rate? I do believe they will bring us plenty of business in the future, and it could equate to quite a fortune. Though I could ask for more in this deal, and earn more profit without risk."

"No, sir," Miss Warrick said quickly, shaking her head. "I see it as you are in the right. My father would often say that the best way to a secure future was to nurture the finest relationships. Although, I do not know if his advice is the best to take."

Miss Warrick looked so low as she recalled her father's fall from success that Edmund felt a painful pity for her.

"I believe it to be sound advice," he said. "My own father told me much the same. There is always room for error, even when following the best possible course. The advice is not at fault."

Miss Warrick nodded sadly.

"And what of this matter with the workers?" Edmund asked, wanting to distract her so that she might smile again. "Do you think it right to raise their wages? Their protests have been strong."

"Certainly, sir," Miss Warrick nodded.

"The work they have done for you and your father is good. The price of living increases from time to time, and the value of our currency may change. I think it would only be right to ensure they all have enough to support their families by."

"You have it right," Edmund nodded. "I thought as much myself. The older members of the company have argued that we should loss profits if we pay them more, but I think we must be fair to all men rather than greedy. The company will remain strong even with the extra expenses."

Miss Warrick smiled and finished tidying up the papers on his desk. "Do you need me for anything else tonight?"

Edmund wanted to have an excuse to ask her to stay, but he had none left.

"No, Miss Warrick. Thank you for your work today. You may retire."

Miss Warrick left the room, Edmund watching her go with a strange feeling in his chest.

They had such similar views on so many things that he thought it a marvel she had happened upon his home. How could he have ever chosen a more perfect governess to live with them? The more work they did together, the more in tune he felt they were.

It was a funny thing, he thought, that as he returned to his bedchamber for the night, she was the last thing on his mind in the darkness.

In the afternoon, Edmund was going through his correspondence, reading a few personal letters that had come directly from the mail coach. Miss Warrick waited by his side, ready to put pen to paper should he wish to write a response to any of his letters.

He thought to himself that he had become quite used to having her ready in such a position, and wondered, when his arm was healed, if he might struggle to remember how to do it all by himself.

One letter caught the attention more than the rest. It was sealed with a golden stamp, quite ostentatiously, and a fine script had been used to carefully detail his name and address on the envelope.

It was, in short, quite impressive.

"What an interesting envelope," Miss Warrick remarked, watching as he pried open the seal. "They must have gone to great effort to present it so nicely."

"Hmm," Edmund agreed, finally getting it open.

Inside was a thick piece of card, lettered in the same script.

"It seems another of our neighbours is holding a ball. The Winsoms, this time. I suppose they felt duty-bound to invite us all, since we have started doing business together. Even Christopher and Patience are noted by name on the card."

"When is it?" Miss Warrick asked, sitting up a little straighter in her chair.

Edmund studied the details, but then tossed it aside onto the pile of papers that he no longer needed.

"It matters not. We won't be going, of course."

He had briefly considered going, as he opened the envelope. But even as he did so, he had seen a vision swimming before his eyes:

The last ball they had attended at the Haverham's house. He remembered how fine it was to dance with Miss Warrick, such an expert partner who never put a foot wrong. He remembered the pressure he had faced to dance with her, even when it had not been his intention.

But more than anything, he had remembered the look on her face – the bright red colour that stained her cheeks for the entirety of the experience.

As soon as he remembered that, all he could imagine in his mind's eye was a repeat occurrence of the very same. He pictured Miss Warrick, once again drawn to dance with him against her will, and utterly embarrassed to be seen with her employer in such a way.

She would have to be there, if they were to attend, because Patience needed a chaperone. And if he was to go, then Patience would have to come. Otherwise, he would never hear the end of it.

No, the only solution was not to attend at all – none of them. That had to be the end of it.

"Oh," Miss Warrick said, seemingly taken aback. "But… I know that Miss Patience will be most eager to attend."

"She is still under punishment for her part in the whole pianoforte affair," Edmund said gruffly. "Besides which, she has had her public practice now. You cannot convince me that she needs more chances to try out the dances that you learn in the schoolroom. She appears to be doing just fine."

"Of course," Miss Warrick nodded meekly. "And do you not wish to attend yourself, in order to take care of business matters?"

"I am injured still," Edmund said, lifting his arm to show the splint, as if she could have forgotten. It was still tied in a silk sling around his neck.

"I would not be able to dance sufficiently, and if I am too injured to go to the city, then I am too injured to go to a ball. I hardly think the doctor would call it resting."

"No, quite right," Miss Warrick agreed, bending her eyes upon the table.

She had no further objections, it seemed. Well, that solidified things. It proved that she had no desire to go to any ball with him, perhaps for fear that she might be forced to dance again. Edmund knew then that he had made the right choice.

"I've a letter to send to Lord Winsom as it happens anyway," Edmund said. "Take this down on a new sheet, will you?"

Miss Warrick obediently took out a new sheet of paper, and began readying her quill.

"Start with the usual honorifics," Edmund said.

He stood from his chair and began to wander over to the window. He had taken to walking around the place while dictating to Miss Warrick, as it was more comfortable than sitting and staring at her for hours on end. At least, it felt a little less awkward.

He had to admit that one of the things he was going to miss, once his arm was healed, was this sense of freedom. Imagine, walking around a room whilst simultaneously writing a letter!

He found that he was able to think better, while his body was otherwise occupied in wandering about or looking down out of the window into the garden.

Edmund waited for the sound of Miss Warrick's quill to stop scratching on the paper, indicating that she had begun the letter as instructed.

"I am writing to you regarding the latest development in the African colonies," he began. "I should have thought you would be eager to learn that your investment has been flourishing, and that we now await news from the ship of its swift arrival."

As he spoke, Edmonds looked down into the garden, following his now usual habit.

Down there, he was happy to spy Samuel wandering around on his own. He had noticed that his younger brother was becoming more adventurous of late, striking out by himself and no longer waiting for others to take the lead.

"Say, I do believe that Samuel is doing a lot better these days," Edmund said, distracted from his letter.

Behind him, he heard a sigh. Miss Warrick laid her quill down on the table with a heavy clatter, and there was a rustling of paper. "Give me a minute, sir," she said. "I thought you were still dictating."

Edmund laughed. "I do apologise, Miss Warrick," he said. "I was quite distracted. Samuel is down there, playing in the garden. He is running about like a madman, but I confess I am quite pleased to see it. He appears to be getting back into fine shape."

"I have noticed that he is getting stronger," Miss Warrick agreed. "I have tried to encourage him to get back into playing sports, though it is difficult considering that he has no boys of his own age to play with."

Edmonds turned to look at her with some surprise. "Do you believe that he is well enough already to return to school with his peers?"

He had not suspected that this would be the case so soon, and had even plans for the eventuality of keeping Samuel at home for another year or more.

"Perhaps when the new school year begins," Miss Warrick agreed. "In the meantime, I wonder if there is anyone who might be able to keep him a little more active. I would like him to build upon this new fitness and even increase it before he returns to a school environment."

Edmund considered this. "I suppose it should normally

fall to me," he said. "Sadly, I am not much use in playing cricket or tennis with my arm in a sling. Christopher I am not expecting to see again for some time. Jenkins is too elderly. Maybe I can ask around, and see if there is anyone on the staff who has a young relative."

"I think that would be good for him," Miss Warrick said, smiling. "At any rate, it does him some good to run around, even if it is on his own. I am glad the weather has stayed pleasant. It had allowed him to put these afternoons to good use, while I am employed as your secretary."

Edmund looked down out of the window again, watching Samuel pretend to fight with a broken stick as a sword.

"I'm quite grateful to you, Miss Warrick," he said, staring down so that he would not have to turn and meet her eye.

"I have been meaning to say this for some time. It warms my heart to see Samuel brought so back to life. I had begun to lose hope that he would ever return to his former self, and yet here he is; not so far away as he once was."

"It is my purpose to raise all of them, in all areas," Miss Warrick said. "I would not be doing my job correctly if I did not instruct him in fitness as well as in more studious subjects. He is a capable boy, and very eager. He only needed a little push."

Edmund watched him a little longer, thinking all the while about how lucky they were.

Despite her modest words, he knew exactly who he had to thank for Samuel's turnaround.

If he had not employed Miss Warrick those months ago, then the poor boy would still be sickly and pale. Already there was more meat on his bones, and he no longer needed to sit every quarter of the hour.

That was Miss Warrick's work, and hers alone.

18

A school morning rose, and Joanna always found that she was more eager than ever to wake up in the morning and hurry down to her duties.

She had never believed that she would find such a purpose in life as she did now, knowing that the children depended on her for their education.

Indeed, it was such a pleasure to complete her duties each day that there was no longer any reason for her to hide away.

After finishing Edmund's letters and paperwork for the day, and dining with the other servants, she would then retire to the sitting room.

She had taken up sewing a few little things for herself now that she had her wages saved up, and was completely happy to sit in the quiet room in Edmund's company, simply sewing until her fingers were sore and she decided to retire for the night.

He had raised no objection to her being there, and their silence was no longer the awkward quiet between employer and employee.

It was the comfortable silence of two people who had already conversed readily throughout the day, and now had no need to say any more while they relaxed.

There were no longer any problems with Patience. Samuel was getting healthier each week, and Amy was as eager and sweet as ever.

Joanna found herself wondering if things could ever be more perfect than they were.

And when a traitorous voice in the back of her head whispered that it would be more joyous if the children were *her* children, and she the lady of the house, she chose to ignore it.

"Miss Warrick," Amy said, quietly, while her siblings were engaged in reading their own books. "What will you do when we're all growed up?"

"Grown up," Joanna corrected her, half-absent-mindedly. "I shall perhaps have to find new employment. Though by the time you are grown, sweet little one, your sister may already have her first children, or Lord Kelt may be married with children of his own. In that case, I would hope that I may be allowed to remain and continue as governess here."

"I hope that happens," Amy said, dangling her legs in the space under her chair and swinging them backwards and forwards. She could not quite yet reach the ground. "Will you stay here forever?"

Joanna was taken aback, as always with this darling child. She always said the most loving and genuine things, that struck right home in Joanna's heart.

But what followed after was a barb of sadness, because she knew that she could not say yes. "It is not up to me, Miss Amy," she said softly. "It will be your brother's decision, for the most part. If I am no longer wanted, then I will have to go."

"I will always want you," Amy declared in her matter-of-fact way. "So, you can stay."

Joanna chuckled lightly. "Thank you, Miss," she said. "I'll keep that in mind."

Talking of babies had reminded her that there was something else she needed to do.

She had still not spoken to Edmund about her sister's pregnancy, and the idea of going to be by her side when the baby was due.

She had been half-afraid to ask it, since he had been so kind to her, particularly in not dismissing her when Rivers had first come to the house. She was grateful to him, and felt perhaps a self-flattering notion that he needed her, now.

If she went away, maybe she would prove that to be

a lie.

Still, the question had to be asked; the turning of the skies would not wait, and if she did not ask soon, the baby would be arriving into the world without her presence.

As soon as she left the children for her luncheon and hurried from there to Edmund's office, she made up her mind that she must ask – and today.

She paused outside his office door, remembering the nerves that had hammered her heart when she first waited outside of a door to meet him. Strangely, she felt much the same today.

What a difference the time had made – and yet no difference at all.

Joanna took a deep breath and opened the door before she could change her mind.

"Lord Kelt," she said. "I've a request to make."

"Hmm?" Edmund opened his eyes and looked at her.

For a second, they both just stared. Joanna felt her cheeks beginning to burn.

Edmund was nestled cosily in his padded armchair, and had evidently fallen asleep after eating luncheon. His hair was somewhat mussed with sleep, and his eyes barely opened. She had woken him.

"I'm sorry, my lord, I'll come back later," she said, hurriedly reaching for the door handle again.

"No," Edmund said, stirring himself.

He rubbed his eyes, and she was reminded of how

young he was. Even though he was a serious man, with many responsibilities heaped on his shoulders, he was only a few years her senior. She often forgot that that was the case.

"Wait. I'm awake. Come in. We should work."

"I didn't mean to…" Joanna began, fidgeting awkwardly in the doorway.

"Neither did I. You have done me a favour. I can't sleep the afternoon away," Edmund said, gesturing to the desk. "Come, really. Sit."

Joanna took her customary place at the desk, her mind now only just catching up to what she had seen.

She thought of how restful Edmund had looked when she came in the door, almost angelic even, and was regretful that she had interrupted his sleep.

But he was insistent, and she could not refuse the request of her employer.

"I had something that I wanted to ask of you," she said, hesitantly, not wanting to give up the intentions that had brought her to the room in the first place.

"Go ahead, Miss Warrick," Edmund said nodding his head permissively.

"It's about my sister, Lady Esther Castleford," Joanna said. "I have received word from her of the most joyous news – she is with child."

"Then congratulations are in order to her," said

Edmund. "I take it there is some purpose to your sharing this news with me, beyond wishing to spread good cheer?"

"Yes, sir," Joanna said. "She has requested that, as her sister, I join by her side to help her through the childbirth. She is most anxious that I'd be there for her in what will be both a difficult and a wondrous time."

Edmund inclined his head slowly. "So, you are requesting some leave of absence in order to visit her?"

"If you require my services and cannot allow me to go, then I shall stay," said Joanna.

She wanted to make it clear that she understood her position here. She was an employee, and if he refused her request, that would be that.

But she fervently wished that he would give her the chance to support her sister. She waited, her heart pounding, to hear his verdict.

"How long until the baby is due?" Edmund asked.

"Only a couple of months," said Joanna. "I feel I should have raised the matter sooner, but things have been so hectic here. I was not sure whether you would be in a position to let me go."

Edmund thought the matter over for a moment, placing two of his long fingers across his lips. Then he gestured expansively with them, a small shrug.

"I see no reason why you cannot go," he said. "You have done well in your work here, and if you feel that the children need supervision during the time you are away, I will bring in someone on a temporary basis.

"However, if we plan to put Samuel back in school in the autumn, then perhaps a short break first from studies will do him well."

Joanna felt a rush of gratitude through her very cool. "Thank you, Lord Kelt," she said.

She had not realised exactly how much she wanted to go until he granted her permission, and the words were spoken from the heart. Her gratitude was more genuine than perhaps it had ever been before.

"Nonsense," said Edmund. "I would not hold you back from your family. Of anyone in our beautiful green countryside, perhaps our family is the one that understands the most exactly how valuable it is to spend time with those you love while they are with you."

Joanna inclined her head sadly, giving a moment's thought to both her own father and the parents of the Hardwicke household.

This sadness was a touchstone for both of them, it seemed, and barely a week would pass before one or the other of them referenced it in some way.

But this, she felt, was just one more matter in which she had a connection to her employer that made them well-suited to spending time with one another.

Anyone who had not suffered a loss such as theirs, she

felt, might be less sympathetic to the sadness that ran like veins through the very flesh of their lives.

So, that was done – and the agreement was made. Joanna wrote Esther immediately, letting her know that she would be with her sooner rather than later. Edmund had granted her a full month away, if she needed to use it.

He did, however, express a heartfelt wish that there would be no complications with the childbirth, thus allowing Joanna to return sooner – and not, he hastened to assure her, because he was begrudging of the time.

Letters were greatly on Joanna's mind that week, and perhaps that is why she was more attuned to notice when Patience was writing during class.

Normally, she might have assumed that the girl was just doing her work as instructed, and let her be. But, as she worked diligently with a studious Samuel on his advanced arithmetic, a small suspicion arose in her mind that Patience was writing something that looked suspiciously letter-like.

"What is that?" she asked, getting up from her place by Samuel and rounding the desk quickly.

Patience tried to quickly put the paper away inside one of her books, but Joanna was there quicker.

She pulled the piece of paper quickly from the younger girl's hand, despite her protests.

"That's private," Patience said.

Joanna completely ignored her, quickly scanning the words she had been writing.

It was clearly a letter, and more than that – a letter for a recipient that she should not have been corresponding with.

Dear Lieutenant Rivers,

I have been thinking of you since you were here with my brother. We had such fun together over those few days, and I wish they could be here again.

You were so dashing in your red uniform, I have been able to think of nothing else.

Please do tell me when you are next on leave, for I should very much like to see you again. Do you think you will come back to...

Joanna was shocked. "This letter is meant for Jasper Rivers," she said, quite forgetting his title in the moment. She was beyond shocked – into anger already. "Have you been corresponding with him?"

"No," Patience said.

Her face was flaming red, and she had a sulky look about her – as if she might alternately begin to cry or throw something across the room.

"I just wanted to write him something. I wasn't really going to send it."

"Then why did you write it?" Joanna demanded.

She stood over Patience, not allowing her to worm away. She ignored Samuel and Amy, who were both watching them with wide eyes.

"I just wanted to pretend. It was silliness, nothing more. I don't even know where I should send it in order to reach him," Patience said.

She tossed her hair defiantly back over her shoulders.

Joanna sat down in a chair close to her, putting the letter down on the table between them.

"This is extremely important, Miss Patience. Tell me the truth now. Are you corresponding with Lieutenant Rivers?"

"No, I told you," Patience insisted. She looked away, her eyes sliding to the floor. "I was just... playing."

Joanna hesitated, biting her lip.

She read the letter over again. There was nothing incriminating there – nothing that would point to an ongoing correspondence, or a real desire to meet.

"Do you promise me that was all this was?" Joanna asked. "Do you swear it?"

"Yes, I swear it," Patience said, still not meeting her eyes. Her cheeks were flaming yet brighter, and she looked on the verge of tears now. "Don't tell Edmund."

Joanna weighed that in her mind.

She had a duty to tell Edmund, really, not only as Patience's governess but as her appointed chaperone. She had warned him that something like this could happen, so he could hardly be surprised.

But Patience had been settling back into her lessons

lately, and Joanna wanted no repeat of the incident in which she had refused to take her lessons.

Nor did she want her causing trouble, the kind of trouble that had led to countless governesses before her being dismissed.

In short, it was important for Patience to like her – both for her place in the household, and for her continuing enjoyment of her position.

It was a fine edge to walk along, between keeping Patience's trust and keeping Edmund's. Perhaps this truly was nothing, like the girl said.

Looking at the embarrassment on her face, Joanna wanted to believe it.

No, she did believe it. How many girlish fantasies had her and the sister gone through while they were the same age? If her mother and father knew of half the daydreams they had entertained, they would no doubt be shocked beyond measure.

And, indeed, Patience had no sister of her own age to speak to about these things. She had only little Amy, who was far too young to understand the same feelings and emotions that were growing for the first time in Patience's breast.

She could go easy on her this time, couldn't she? If it meant regaining her trust a little more, supporting her through a confusing time in her life?

Joanna looked at Patience carefully, and said, "I will

keep this to myself. But you must promise me absolutely that you will not attempt to write to Lieutenant Rivers on your own. You must not engage with him, is that clear?"

Patience nodded, having the good grace to look thoroughly abashed.

Joanna decided that that would be enough. They need not take it any further, so long as nothing more happened.

She had no way of knowing that this would be a source of regret, before the month was out.

19

When Christopher returned home for another short stay the next week, he had the good sense not to bring any friends with him this time.

He had no doubt got wind of the fact that his brother was more than annoyed with his behaviour, and saw the need to toe the line, at least for a short while.

Christopher never behaved well for long, but a short threat or a burst of anger was all that was needed to put him back in his place once more.

Edmund was suspicious about his reasons for even coming home this time.

What kind of entertainment did he expect to have? There was no ball to attend, no friends to spend his time with, and he certainly did not choose to engage in any kind of activities with Edmund.

Still, with no kind of evidence of anything untoward, Edmund had nothing to do but sit upon his suspicions and wait for Christopher to reveal himself.

He was walking through the house one morning, trying to find an item of his father's that he must have misplaced, when he came upon Christopher standing at the window.

At first, Edmund did not approach him, wondering instead what he might have been looking at. Edmund stole into a neighbouring room, and looked down upon the same view.

Below the windows, a sunny day was unfolding upon the lawns of the family home. There were some stone benches arranged artfully on this outlook, where one might sit and look back at the house or towards the surrounding countryside, as one pleased.

Here, Joanna had gathered the children to take their morning lessons, giving them a taste of fresh air at the same time as their education.

Edmund watched them for a moment, wondering what Christopher might find interesting in this scene. A strange, gnawing suspicion was growing up on him now. It was one that he almost dared not act on, for fear that it might be true.

Could his brother have some kind of interest in their young governess?

The thought was instantly odious to him. Of course, Christopher have been known to chase after all kinds of women – duchesses, ladies, and even another servant that had once been with the family. His intentions were never good, and that was what worried Edmund.

Could it possibly be that he had some kind of affections towards Miss Warrick?

That couldn't be. He couldn't allow it to be.

Miss Warrick was the best governess they had ever had, without a doubt, and he could not have her corrupted by Christopher's poor behaviour. It might end up thoroughly disturbing the children's education, or even subjecting them to a scandal first-hand.

This, he told himself, was unacceptable. Something had to be done.

Edmund rounded the corridor, rushing into the room where he had seen Christopher and finding him in the same place at the window.

"What are you looking at?" he asked brusquely, although he already knew the answer.

"This fine, sunny day," Christopher answered glibly. He turned a wide smile towards his brother.

"Do you not have any kind of industry with which to engage your time?" Edmund asked. "Something more useful than gazing at the sun?"

"I am on leave, dear brother," Christopher said, spreading his arms expansively. "I am a man of leisure."

Edmund snorted. "Perhaps you ought to take your

leisure elsewhere, to some place where it cannot cause any damage."

"Whatever can you mean by that?" Christopher asked, his eyes turning wide with innocence.

"You know very well what I mean," Edmund said, gesturing towards the window. "Let's not mince words. Christopher, I absolutely forbid it. Do you understand?"

"I fear I do not," Christopher said, laying a hand delicately on his chest as if in shock.

The tone of merriment in his voice, however, suggested otherwise.

"You are only amusing yourself," Edmund said darkly, joining him at the window and looking out at the group below them.

"I mean to say that she is out of bounds. I won't have another governess corrupted by you. Not this time."

"What is it about this one that is so special?" Christopher asked. "Does my brother have affections of his own to give?"

Edmund glowered at him. "Our siblings are quite enamoured of her, and it would break their heart if she had to go away."

"Ah, and that is the only reason," Christopher said, nodding sagely.

"Listen, boy," Edmund said, drawing himself up to his full height. He had had quite enough.

"If you so much as touch a hair on Miss Warrick's head

I will string you up for it. Do you not think that the well-being of our brother and sisters is more important than your stupid need to show off? You're supposed to be courting a Duchess's third daughter or something along those lines, anyway, from what I have heard."

"They speak of me in the City?" Christopher asked, leaning forward with more interest. "Fascinating. What do they tell you?"

"Only things that make me blush with shame at being your relation," Edmund said.

"Well, they tell you nothing, then," Christopher said, and sighed. "As it happens, the third daughter of a duchess no longer has any interest in me."

"So it is true? All of it?" Edmund snapped.

He had indeed heard tales which made him worried indeed, though he always waved them off as mere rumour and speculation when others asked.

"Not all of it, I'm sure," Christopher said. He hooked his knee up onto the window seat, looking down into the garden again. "In fact, it was not as scandalous as you may wish to believe."

"Then tell me," Edmund said, exasperated. "How am I supposed to trust what you say if you tell me nothing?"

"Lady Juliana Reffern and I met last summer," Christopher said. "At a ball, naturally. I started courting her soon after. You remember – I spent some weeks in the countryside."

"We live in the countryside, Christopher," Edmund snorted. "You mean you went further south."

"Yes, well. We spent some agreeable time there. Her father was most accommodating, and there was quite a crowd of us. At any rate, Lady Juliana and I got along quite famously."

"All in the eye of chaperones?" Edmund probed.

"Yes, of course," Christopher said, as if offended. "Although, alas, there was an incident with a fountain which was quite regrettable."

"The fountain story was true!" Edmund exploded, taking a step towards his brother in anger.

"Be calm, brother, and let me tell my tale," Christopher tutted.

"Lady Juliana is quite a beauty, you see, so she had many admirers. Still does, I am sure. That is why I resorted to purchasing small items of jewellery in order to demonstrate my affections."

"Hm," Edmund tossed his head. "I recall those fripperies."

"And then Lady Juliana appeared at a ball in London, where I was invited along with half of the officers in my barracks, and she was on the arm of some third-rate Lord with an estate out in Devon. That was how I learned that she had been betrothed," Christopher said, punctuating his final words by plucking a loose thread from his breeches and breaking it with a bitter expression.

Edmund felt a stirring of pity. So, Christopher was suffering from a broken heart – was that it?

"If you're in need of some advice," Edmund began, thinking that he should at least step in the way that a big brother ought to.

"I would ask Father," Christopher snapped. "And I mean that literally, because he will still be more help than you even in the grave."

Edmund regarded him for a moment. Perhaps Christopher was feeling vulnerable after spilling his heart like that, but it was no reason for him to evoke such harsh thoughts.

"If you're going to be a spoiled brat, you will continue to receive less help from me than you think," Edmund said. "I will withdraw my support entirely if you aren't careful."

"Oh, tosh," Christopher snapped, before turning him an eerily cheerful grin that was clearly false. "You wouldn't do that to your beloved brother."

"I mean it, Christopher. This time I'm really serious. Keep your trouble-making away from our door."

Christopher gave him an amiable smile. "Of course, dear brother," he said. "I agree to your terms. Might my head remain on my shoulders now?"

Edmund sighed. "For the moment, at least," he said, and left the room.

It was a shame that Christopher would not accept help, or even allow himself to admit to having feelings of the sort that clearly troubled him. Edmund could not do a thing to aid him if he would not even admit it.

After that last exchange, Edmund could not help but feel a creeping sensation that he may have only served to stoke the fire of his brother's mischief.

If that was the case, then he knew he would come to regret ever attempting to interfere – for he could not risk losing the governess.

And with his capricious moods, who knew if Christopher might see such a simple conversation as this as a reason to disrupt the stability of the household in any way that he could.

20

The summer brought with it a haze of joyful days spent teaching the children under a bright blue sky.

The weather was so delightful that every day seemed tailor-made for playing outside, and she even took them down to the lake on more than one occasion to explore certain lessons there.

It was Christopher, however, who proved to be the most interesting new visitor – not the sun.

His presence, as always, provoked a testiness within Patience which would not permit her to pay as close attention to her lessons as Joanna would have liked.

More than that, his attention, too, was focused on Joanna herself – something that she found mildly unsettling at best.

"Miss Warrick," he announced, finding her outside the kitchen after she had dined with the other servants. It could hardly have been a coincidence that he was there, since there was no other reason for him to be in this part of the house so late in the evening.

"Lieutenant Hardwicke," Joanna said, bowing her head slightly.

She wished he would let her past; she had thought of retiring to her room with a book and reading a few chapters before sleeping.

"I was out in town this morning," he said.

This was no news to her; she had heard all about it from Patience, who wanted desperately to go with him and had been ordered to stay at home.

"I found something that was completely out of place. It should have been here, all this time."

Joanna frowned, puzzled by his words, as he held out a closed fist. He turned it over and opened it to reveal two slim blue ribbons, made of shining satin.

"How pretty," Joanna murmured, not quite sure yet what the significance of his gesture was.

"I am glad you think so," Christopher said. "I knew they would match that day dress of yours completely. They will make a jaunty look if you twist them through your hair."

It took a moment longer still for Joanna to realise that he was making her a gift.

"Oh! My lord... these are for me?"

"Yes, indeed," Christopher said, flashing her a brilliant and amused smile. "Are you so unused to receiving gifts? I fear you have been badly treated here."

"Forgive my manners," Joanna said hurriedly, blushing at being caught out. "What I mean to say is thank you, my lord. It is a very thoughtful gift."

"Take them, please," Christopher urged, chuckling at her.

Joanna reached out and took the two ribbons from his open palm.

As she touched them and was about to draw them away, his hand closed lightly all of a sudden, his fingers dancing over hers.

Joanna gasped out loud, almost dropping the ribbons in surprise.

Christopher laughed louder then, and released her, stepping away. "I look forward to seeing what colour they bring to your eyes, Miss Warrick," he said, with a twinkle in his eyes.

He drew away down the corridor then, leaving her standing, feeling quite stupid, as she watched his retreating back.

She stood there a moment longer, looking down at the ribbons in her hand. They were warm with the heat of his body, and she could not quite shake the feel of his fingers from her skin.

How lucky it was that no one else had been walking by to see it. They might think her quite improper.

She had no interest at all of a romantic nature for Christopher, and she was quite startled that he should think to bring her a gift like this.

What was his meaning behind it? Could he be quite serious? Or was it some trick to humiliate her further on down the line?

At any rate, she did not wish to risk the displeasure of her employer. She would wear them in her hair on the morrow, she decided as she went up the stairs towards her chamber.

Of course, she mused as she placed the ribbons on her bedside table and began to undress, there was one good thing about Christopher Hardwicke: his last name.

Becoming the wife of Christopher was not an idea that appealed to her, for he was boorish and headstrong, and altogether too brash. But to become Lady Joanna Hardwicke – well, that was another thing again.

She lay back in bed, feeling the thin covers under her hands as she dreamed about it.

Yes – to be a wife. Not solely for the sake of becoming a lady again, though that would have suited her fine. No; it was the children she thought of.

For if she were his wife, she would not be a governess who might be dismissed or grown out of. She would be a part of their lives forever – a surrogate mother of sorts, even.

That would have enough sweetness to endure the sour heart of even a man like Christopher.

But she reminded herself, it was all a fantasy only. Whatever Christopher's intentions were, they certainly could not be honourable.

Most likely, she decided to herself, it was all a plot to anger Edmund – and that was something she could not be part of.

Christopher stayed for the rest of the week, even if his presence was a clear annoyance to Edmund. When Joanna sat by his side to help him with his letters, every day he seemed surlier and worse-tempered. He even scolded her several times, with an air of impatience which warned her not to test him.

She had regretted immediately wearing the blue ribbons in her hair the next day, when Edmund had praised them and how they matched her dress. He had even asked her about where she got them from; she had given a vague answer about the market in town, knowing that it was not a full lie if that was indeed where Christopher had purchased them.

But it was the night of the proposed ball that was to

push things to their fullest limit, leaving Joanna with no choice but to intervene as best as she could.

Joanna had been tidying up the schoolroom and found a loose pink ribbon – exactly the kind that she knew Patience had been wearing in her hair that day.

It was a fact that was made all the more obvious to her by the unavoidable truth that it was exactly the same kind of ribbon that Christopher had bought for her – simply a different colour.

Patience was rather particular about her belongings, especially those that related to fashion or beauty. Joanna decided with a sigh that she would return it to her immediately.

The rest of the household had retired already – Joanna had only been staying up late to tidy because she was unable to sleep, for thinking about Esther and her baby.

No matter. Even if Patience was already sleeping, Joanna reasoned that she would be able to slip into the room and leave it on her dresser without waking her. That should be a simple enough task, and it would prevent panic in the morning when Patience thought her ribbon was lost.

She hurried up the stairs, then slowed down to creep as quietly as she could to Patience's door.

With a measured care, Joanna reached out for the door handle and turned it slowly, pushing through as smoothly as possible so as not to make a noise.

She moved over to the dresser in the dark room, navigating by memory rather than sight in the gloom. She had left her candle out in the corridor in case the light might wake Patience.

She placed the ribbon down gently and was just turning to go when she realised that the curtains were hanging open about the window.

She ought to close them; the sun might wake Patience too early when it rose.

As Joanna started to approach them, the moon moved out from behind a cloud in the sky, shining a soft light right into the room.

It was as good a demonstration as any that the curtains were needed, for the whole chamber was now bathed in enough light to see by. Joanna turned to glance at Patience, hoping that she was not waking already, but was soon stopped in her tracks and forced to look again.

The bed was empty.

Patience was simply not there.

Joanna felt her heart pounding, but tried to push away the encroaching sense of panic.

Patience could not get far at all on her own, so it made sense that she would at least be somewhere in the house. The question was, where would she be hiding at this hour?

Joanna swept up her candle, being careful to close the door behind her so as not to raise alarm for anyone else that might be wandering the corridors.

She headed first downstairs, to the sitting room where

the pianoforte sat silent and no guests lounged on the sofas or comfortable chairs near the fire.

The other reception rooms downstairs were likewise empty and cold, the fireplaces all having been extinguished for the warm summer's days. That left only the upstairs rooms, where the family stayed, and the servants' quarters.

It was not likely that Patience would be fraternising with the servants. She had no interest in them, and barely even spoke to Mary or Jenkins unless she was asking for something.

With that in mind, Joanna reasoned that she might be in another room.

Perhaps she was with Amy or Samuel? If either of them had already woken earlier in the evening with a nightmare, perhaps, they might have gone to their sister, looking for help.

It was not totally implausible, and so Joanna crept up the stairs once more, repeating her routine in an attempt to keep from waking anyone.

With her candle shielded by one hand to shed only the barest light that she could manage, Joanna peered first into Amy's chamber and then Samuel's, and found them both soundly sleeping – and alone.

There was no sign that they had been disturbed at all since being put to bed, and another check of Patience's room confirmed that she had not yet returned.

But where else could she be?

Joanna did not want to look in on the two men of the household – after all, it would be improper. But this was becoming something of an emergency, and she was increasingly worried for Patience's safety.

The girl would not wander off alone into the night, would she? There had been no indication yet that she walked in her sleep as some were wont to do.

Yet if she had strayed out there in just a nightgown, she would be in great danger for her health. The night was clear, and it was the height of summer, but that did not mean she would not catch a cold if she were out there. That thought drove Joanna on to be sure.

She hesitated outside Edmund's door, then turned away.

Perhaps she could leave him until last. After all, she would need to wake him to join in the search if she was not able to find Patience.

The thought of creeping into his room at night while he slept was almost unconscionable, too. She would not do it unless it was forced.

So, that left just Christopher.

Joanna hesitated outside of his door again, trying to steel her nerves. It would not be particularly within the bounds of decent propriety, to be discovered alone in the room of this young Lieutenant in the night. Even more so, given his reputation. But Patience's safety was at stake, and that was enough to push Joanna onwards.

She cautiously opened the door, as quietly and slowly as she had ever done before, stopping and catching her breath to listen for a single noise in the darkened room. She heard nothing – not even the sound of breathing.

A suspicion came over her, and she lifted her candle.

Joanna saw that this bed, too, was empty – and still made neatly, as if it had not been touched at all since the morning before.

Christopher was gone.

Now things were beginning to fall together in front of her eyes. Joanna sunk into a waiting chair, surveying the empty room and thinking about what she knew.

Patience was gone. Christopher was gone. And it was the night of the ball that Edmund had decided none of them would visit.

Now it all made sense.

Christopher must have taken Patience to the ball, against Edmund's wishes and without his knowledge.

What should she do?

Joanna sat with her mind racing, trying to see the best way forward.

If she woke Edmund and told him what had happened, he would be furious. There would be another big row with Christopher for certain, and both of them would be punished in some way.

Patience, she knew, would not see that Joanna was only doing her duty. No; the girl was headstrong and proud, and she always wanted her own way. That meant that if she found out Joanna had raised the alarm, she would never forgive her. She would be surly again and refuse to listen or take part in lessons.

Taking the scenario to its logical conclusion, Joanna could see only one outcome.

Edmund would dismiss her if she was not able to perform her duties as governess correctly. He only allowed her to stay because the children liked her so much, and he had already made it clear that another failure would not be tolerated.

But what if he found out that Patience was missing, and that Joanna had known? Would she not then be in even more trouble? She imagined that he would dismiss her on the spot, and she would be forced to pack her bags and be on the next coach. Perhaps he would not even allow her to say goodbye.

The situation was impossible! No matter where she turned, it seemed that the only outcome would be that she lost her position and was cast out into the world again. She would have nowhere to go, and she desperately did not want to lose her place here. She was so fond of the household, and she wanted nothing more than to stay with them.

There was but one option that left her with her position intact. That was if Patience and Christopher returned without raising the alarm, and Edmund never found out that they had gone.

Of course, it risked much. It required the missing siblings to return under cover of darkness and absolute silence, so as not to wake Edmund or any of the other servants. It required them to keep the secret, without throwing it Edmund's face one day when they rowed again.

And there was also another face to it that was particularly pertinent to Joanna.

That was that she was remiss in her duties if she did not look after Patience. Having the girl off in society without her true guardian, or the chaperone that said guardian had appointed, risked her coming in for some scandal.

And there was yet the possibility that the news would reach Edmund some other way – through the mouths of those who had also attended the ball and seen Patience there.

Joanna sat, toying with the blue ribbons that she had pulled down out of her hair, twisting them between her fingers. She felt completely a-flutter, with both her mind and her stomach tied in knots.

What should she do? There seemed no possible outcome that was good on all counts.

It was very late, and past time that she should have raised the alarm already. By now, Edmund might indeed wonder if she had waited on purpose to give Patience some time to enjoy herself.

Oh, it was all coming unravelled! How she wished that she had a crystal ball or some other instrument of magic, that she might be able to look into the air and see that Patience was well!

Joanna waited, heavy with indecisiveness. She could not sit any longer, and began pacing across the floor. She was well aware that she should not be in Christopher's room, had no right or reason to be there, but now she also feared slipping out into the corridor and having someone else see her there.

The sound of hoofbeats and the grating of wheels on the driveway led her to the window. There, under the light of the moon, she saw a carriage approaching. It was pulled by two horses, a smaller affair with less space than the family carriage.

She knew it on sight: it was the vehicle that Christopher had been using to make his visits.

Joanna gathered her skirts and rushed down the stairs as quickly as she could without raising any noise.

She had just arrived at the front door and flung it wide open when the carriage pulled up outside, the horses blowing and snorting.

Christopher stepped out of the carriage first when the coachman, who gave Joanna an apologetic look, went to open the door on the side of the vehicle. He turned then and offered a hand to Patience, helping her step down daintily.

"Where have you been?" Joanna hissed quietly, stepping over to them, even though she full well knew the answer.

"Ah, Miss Warrick," Christopher said, smiling gaily. "Don't be alarmed. We've had quite the fabulous evening."

"We went dancing," Patience laughed. "I'm not surprised you are jealous to not have been invited."

"Shh!" Joanna cautioned them, glancing back towards the house. "Speak quietly, or you will wake Lord Kelt. Lieutenant, I have been beside myself with worry. How could you take Miss Patience out to the ball in secret, against our Lord's wishes?"

Christopher laughed, though quietly. "Do not fret, little Miss Warrick," he said, smiling and linking his arm through hers as if he were escorting her on a country walk. "It was a masquerade ball. Miss Patience and I both wore masks. No one even knows we were there."

Joanna's anger faltered. Could it really be true? If this was a saving grace, a way that she would not have to lose her position, then she would grasp it with both hands – as a dying man, an anchor.

"You are sure that no one saw you?"

"Quite sure, Miss," Christopher said. "And, see: I even persuaded a friend to lend Patience a gown so that she would not be recognised by the fabric. I will hide it in my carriage again tomorrow and return it post haste. I was at her side all night and chaperoned her to your own high standards, I assure you."

Joanna allowed herself to relax a smidgeon. "Lord Kelt will never find out?" she asked, needing still that last little piece of reassurance.

"Never," Christopher said, turning to face her earnestly. "Especially not, my dear Miss, if you take Patience up to her room now and have her tucked safely into bed. Will you do that for me?"

Joanna nodded dumbly, taking Patience by the arm to hurry her inside the house.

She did not like the idea of deceiving Edmund one bit, but if it was the only thing that would allow her to stay, then so be it. She would keep her silence.

21

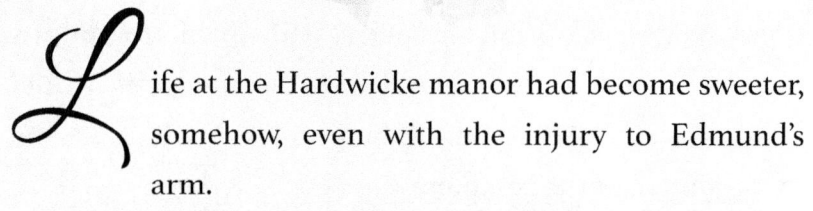

*L*ife at the Hardwicke manor had become sweeter, somehow, even with the injury to Edmund's arm.

Spending more time at home was doing him good, and he was happy to see more of his family. Miss Warrick's help, too, had become an invaluable resource.

He had found himself restrained on more than one occasion from the harsh words he would normally have reserved for the mistakes she made from time to time. He had to remind himself that Miss Warrick was not a trained secretary, nor a hired one.

Edmund tried to be a fair man and a level-headed employer, though he did not always succeed. At times, when his arm caused him pain and the work was urgent, he could snap at her more harshly than he had intended.

"Forgive me, my lord," she would say immediately each time, ducking her head and fetching a new sheet of paper to correct her mistakes. "I will endeavour not to let this happen again."

Then he would soften inevitably and feel a heaviness in his heart for having scolded her. "Your work otherwise is good, Miss Warrick," he would tell her. "I thank you for your efforts. Let us begin this letter again."

As the evening came, they found themselves working later and later. Finally, even though it was time to break for dinner, they reached a point where all the work was not done. Being away from the office, and unable to address matters in person that should have required but a brief conversation, was leaving Edmund far behind on the management of the company.

"Miss Warrick," he suggested, hearing bells ring downstairs to summon him to his dinner, "I wonder if we might return here after we both have dined. I do not wish to keep you awake late into the night, but these duties do seem to increase each week. Will you return and write a few letters more?"

"Of course, my lord," Joanna nodded, giving him a brief smile as they left the room behind.

He was never entirely convinced of whether she was very eager to do her work, or whether she was simply good at pretending that she enjoyed following the orders he gave. For, after all, she had not much choice but to follow them.

It was around this time that a change came over them, a new circumstance which had not before been the norm.

One late night after dinner, Edmund found himself sleepier than he had supposed. He had been hardly able to rest the night before, having spent so much time thinking about the letters that still needed to be addressed and wondering about the fate of the company's ship from Africa. It had not docked as expected, and was now over a week late. There was always some worry like this with his trade, that a ship and its cargo would be lost at great expense.

So, as their arrangement of continuing to work after dinner was new, and as Edmund had much fatigue, he forgot to think about Miss Warrick waiting for him in his small office. After dinner, he simply retired to bed, putting himself under the covers and letting his eyes fall closed.

It was only a light slumber that he managed, however, for he woke up quite suddenly a short while later when the door to his chamber swung open.

It was not clear what it was that induced Edmund to keep his eyes closed and feign sleep even when he was wide awake. It was a small suspicion, perhaps, on the part of his subconscious mind that Christopher might sneak in whilst searching for money.

There was a small "Oh," and then he knew that it was Miss Warrick that had entered the room.

Since he was already awake, and the situation was now quite an awkward one, he could think of no way to feign his awakening that would not be awful for them both. Thus, he kept his eyes closed, and tried to regulate his breathing to an even and calm pattern.

He had expected that Miss Warrick would close the door and leave quite shortly, as she would no doubt be flustered to have come upon him in this way.

He knew well what the mishap had been: on waiting for him in his office, she perhaps imagined that he was reading or collecting his thoughts in his chamber instead. Perhaps she even intuited that he had quite forgotten. Expecting him to be awake, she had quite naturally come in, never imagining that he would be sleeping.

But there was a long time, an interminably long time it seemed, in which he heard nothing.

Then at last her light footsteps tapped their way towards the door and closed it.

It was sheer fortune that he did not commence the embarrassment again right away, for his instinct had been to shift his position and even open his eyes. But he did not do so immediately, and this gave him the chance to hear what came next before he reacted.

For Miss Warrick was still in the room, as he knew from

the gentle steps that padded over somewhere close to his bureau.

There was a small, quiet creak from the chair that rested in front of it, and then nothing for a long while again.

She was sitting there, he knew, at his bureau, and watching him. Even without his eyes open, Edmund could feel her gaze lying heavy on him.

It was not quite so unwelcome as he would have supposed, however. Rather it was like the weight of a warm blanket, placed over you with care.

Why did Edmund not at least feign waking, or attempt to stir so that she would be alerted and leave the room? Why did he not chase her away? It was not quite proper for her to stay, and yet there was something that kept him still and quiet.

It was, after all, a warm feeling to have someone watching over you. He had not experienced this since his days as a boy, when his mother would do the same.

But could it truly just be a gratitude at the idea of having someone mind his dreams for him that kept him quiet?

Could it truly be only that which made him fail to mention it the next morning, when he woke to find the room empty and Miss Warrick retired?

Was it truly only that which made him feign sleep

again the next night when she crept in after their work was done? Or the next? Or the next?

Whatever his inner reasons, Edmund kept up the pretence. And from that night, Miss Warrick was by his side as he slept, with all the calming presence of a guardian angel.

22

"Miss Warrick," Jenkins said, holding out an envelope with a frown wrinkling his elderly face. "There is some correspondence for you. It was marked urgent."

Joanna took the letter from him, concern washing over her like a flood.

It was not unusual for her to receive messages from her sister, of course, but urgent mailings were a new thing entirely. She had never in her life recalled an occasion when a letter for her would have been marked as urgent.

She tore open the envelope there in the corridor, not wanting to stand on ceremony or retire to privacy when such worry filled her mind. Surely, she thought, it could only be bad news!

Miss Joanna Warrick,

I am writing you on your sister's behalf. There has been some difficulty and her child appears to be coming now. I know you had arranged to visit us in some two months, when we believed it would come into the world, but we beg you for Esther's sake to come as soon as you can.

Yours,

Lord Castleford

Joanna read the letter over three times, trying to find the trick or the joke that would reveal itself to her.

Surely, this letter was not to be taken in all seriousness? Surely, Esther could not be giving birth to her child two months early?

Joanna sank into a chair in the hall, fearing that her legs would no longer hold her up.

"Are you quite well, Miss Warrick?" Jenkins asked.

Joanna found that she could not quite gather the strength to reply.

Mary was passing by them with a broom, fresh from sweeping some area of the house. "What's going on? Miss Warrick, you look mighty pale," she said.

"Not now, Mary," Jenkins said, shooing her away. "I fear she has received some bad news. Return to your duties, now, there's no time for idle gossip."

Joanna was grateful for his interference, but the shock was beginning to wear off. "It's about my sister," she said.

"Ah," Jenkins replied, moving to sit beside her. "Lady Castleford was with child, was she not?"

Joanna nodded dimly. She stared at the paper again, as if there was a chance that it might have a different message this time.

"They say that she has gone into labour. It is two months early."

Jenkins nodded seriously. "You plan to request leave from Lord Kelt?" he asked.

"I must go," Joanna said. "I will likely miss the birth, but I must go all the same. The family will need me. Either as an aid to Esther while she becomes accustomed to life as a mother, or..."

"Or to attend the funeral," Jenkins replied, with an apologetic look. "This is much to lay on your shoulders, Miss Warrick. Allow me to petition Lord Kelt on your behalf. I have little doubt that he will allow you to go, even if it is earlier than planned. You should go to your chamber and prepare yourself for the journey. I shall have the carriage readied for you."

Joanna stood, unsteady on her feet but imbued with a sense of purpose now that he had directed her what to do.

"Thank you, Jenkins," she hurried out as she made her way up the stairs.

When she was done packing the small belongings she had into a case, and had changed into a dress more suitable for travelling, Joanna returned to the main hall.

There, she found not just Jenkins but also Edmund waiting for her, to her surprise.

"Miss Warrick," Edmund said. "Jenkins has given me the details of your situation. I give you leave to go. I understand how important it is that you be with your sister at this time."

"Thank you, my lord," Joanna said, dipping her head.

It was partially an act of deference, and partly an attempt to hide the tears that were swimming in her eyes.

"Will you be able to complete your work? I am dreadfully sorry that I cannot continue to take down your correspondence for you while I am away."

"I will manage just fine," Edmund assured her warmly. "Give our thoughts to your sister. I sincerely wish that you will find both her and the baby in good health when you arrive."

"Thank you," Joanna said again, gathering herself and rushing to the carriage as the driver took her case.

The journey was a long one, but it passed by under heavy thoughts, so that Joanna could barely tell how long it had been.

She saw the night beginning to fall outside the windows of the carriage with some surprise, and realised that they must be close to Esther's home.

All through the day she had struggled with her hopes and her fears. She prayed for a healthy baby boy, but closed her eyes in fear at the thought of her sister not surviving the birth.

It was not a good sign for a baby to come early, that much she knew.

The trees, fields, and villages had passed by in such a blur that it was not until they nearly reached their destination that Joanna thought to wonder at Edmund's kindness.

He had sent his own personal carriage for her, rather than forcing her to wait for the mail coach. The horses would be tired, and would have to rest the night before returning home. To be without his carriage for two days on her behalf was kindness indeed!

She thought of Amy, Samuel, and Patience then. There had been no time to bid them farewell, nor to explain to them why she would not be arriving for the lesson that they were awaiting that morning.

She hoped they would not be upset, and that Edmund was not angry at their education being interrupted so.

Joanna had never visited her sister at her new home, and as the carriage pulled in to the estate, she could only raise her eyes in wonder. The building was much larger than she had thought, though it certainly paled in comparison to Edmund's manor. A small area of land was fenced off across the horizon, though within it there was much landscaping and trees grown in pretty rows.

The carriage rolled to a stop at last in front of the entrance, and Joanna hastened to disembark. A small party was there to meet her already, consisting of a butler and a stable boy who immediately began to lead away the horses.

"Miss Warrick?" the butler asked.

"Yes," Joanna said, rushing to him from the carriage and passing him towards the house. "Am I too late?"

"The baby is born," the butler informed her, hurrying to keep up. "If you will turn to your left and up the stairs, Miss. Lady Castleford has been asking after your arrival. She is most keen to see you."

Joanna's heart was in her throat as she took the stairs two at a time, lifting her skirt to avoid tripping.

"Are they both well?" she asked, feeling overjoyed already at the news that her sister was at least still in this world.

"The baby is small," the butler said, trailing behind her by now. "Though both appear to be in good health. Third door to your right, Miss Warrick!"

Joanna would not have needed his directions at any rate, because there was a veritable stream of people coming and going from the room.

The door was open, and several women were bustling around with sheets and towels and tubs of water.

Joanna came to the door and looked in, and her heart almost burst with relief and happiness. "Esther!" she exclaimed, rushing forward to her sister's side.

"Oh, Joanna!" Esther replied, holding out one of her arms in greeting from her bed.

The other was cradling a tiny face, all that could be

seen of the new-born infant who was tightly swaddled in layers of cloth.

"I am so happy to see you," Joanna told her, leaning in to her sister's embrace and then settling on an empty chair beside her. "I am sorry not to have come sooner."

"There was no chance you could have made it," another voice said, and Joanna looked up to see Lord Castleford sitting opposite her. "We did not even know if the message would reach you in time, let alone bring you here. It was a reasonably short birth, so I am told."

"There was no trouble?" Joanna asked.

"Only the panic this little one caused us by coming early," Esther said.

She looked tired, and her hair was stuck down against her head with drying sweat, but still she had a happier glow than Joanna had ever seen on her.

"I was quite sick with worry when the contractions began. The midwife tells me it is not so unusual to have him arrive this quick."

"Him," Joanna repeated, breathing the word, realising what it fully meant. "You have your first son."

"We are naming him Charles," Lord Castleford put in. "After my grandfather."

"Lord Charles Castleford," Joanna sighed happily, reaching out a hand to stroke the baby's peaceful face.

He was sleeping calmly, quite some contrast from how the scene must have looked on his arrival.

"She was lucky, this one," the midwife said, clucking her tongue. "It could have been a difficult one. I have lost many a young mother to an early birth."

Joanna turned to look at her with some alarm. "Is that so?" she asked.

"You should direct your prayers to thankfulness tonight," the midwife nodded. "The Lord God intervened on my lady's behalf. It must have been so, to have such a charmed birth two months ahead of date."

Joanna whispered a fervent prayer under her breath that very instant, just in case she might be thought ungrateful.

To have arrived with Esther lost would have been too much to bear indeed.

The demands placed on a new mother were plenty. Esther was to learn very quickly how to swaddle and clothe, how to change the child, how to wash him, how to hold him so that his head was kept upright. She had to feed him also, and many other things that were completely new to her experience.

"Oh, Esther," Joanna sighed, at least once every day. "He is so perfect, this son of yours."

"The most perfect and handsome," Esther would reply, giving her son a fond and dreamy smile.

Little Charles would only make the smallest sounds in reply, a kind of gurgling or gasping depending on the level of his emotion.

At last, however, a day rose when Joanna knew she was beginning to outstay her welcome.

Though she knew Esther would have welcomed her with open arms for the rest of her life, there was the small matter of paying her own upkeep – not to mention that the young family deserved some time to themselves.

"I have been away for more than a week already," Joanna sighed, allowing little Charles to grasp hold of one of her fingers in his whole fist.

"I have so enjoyed your company, sister," Esther said. "Are you sure you do not wish to stay longer?"

"There is the matter of my employment to attend to," Joanna said, giving her a small smile of admonishment. "That area is unknown to you, I know well, but it brings certain responsibilities."

"Do not chide me for being married," Esther tutted. "It should have been your lot, too, if father had held things together just a little longer."

"It was not his fault," Joanna said, looking down at the floor. "I did not mean anything by it. I suppose I am a little jealous. I had always dreamed of beginning a family of my own."

"You do not think you will have one, someday?" Esther

asked. She left off rattling a toy in front of Charles' face to look at her sister closely.

"What chance have I now?" Joanna said hopelessly. "I am just a servant. I have no fortune attached to me, no dowry. I have not even a father to argue on my behalf. No, I think I will live out my days as a governess."

"Perhaps one day you can come home to us," Esther suggested. "Charles will be in need of a governess before he goes away to school. We may have another child yet, who would follow him."

"Is it not too early to be thinking of that?" Joanna teased, nudging her sister. "You have only just managed this one."

"Still," Esther said, giving her a hopeful gaze.

Joanna smiled, though in her heart she was conflicted. "Perhaps it may be so. Though I think you will need me sooner than the Hardwickes are done with my services. So long as I remain the governess they desire me to be."

"Oh, I have no doubts on that count," Esther said, returning her attention to baby Charles. "From what you tell me, I believe the Earl is quite taken with you. Perhaps we might even hear wedding bells there."

"Esther!" Joanna exclaimed, standing up. She was scandalised, and she felt her face growing hot. "Do not jest about such things. How can you bring my reputation into question so?"

"I meant nothing by it," Esther said, taken aback. "Are

you really so nettled? I only observed that he seems to trust in your work. There was the matter of the ball, too."

"The Earl was kind enough to dance with me at the ball because I was a pitiful, lonely figure," Joanna said, tears pricking at her eyelids. "That was all. It is cruel of you to make such a remark. I will not be accused of bringing that house into disrepute."

"I meant nothing by it," Esther repeated, quietly.

There was silence between them for a moment, but Joanna felt her temper cooling rapidly.

She had no desire to nurture ill will against her sister, and besides, it had been a tiring week. Some leeway was certainly required.

"Are you going to be well, without my help?" Joanna asked.

"Oh, sweet sister, I am quite myself again," Esther smiled. "Though I am still weary, I think myself capable. I shall miss you much. Are you sure you cannot stay longer?"

"The trip was unplanned," Joanna said sadly. "It would be unfair to leave them without me for too long. Lord Kelt has a broken arm, and I was acting as his secretary while he was bound to stay at home. I am neglecting two duties, now. Alas that I cannot be both there and here at once. My heart is torn, believe me, but I feel it is the right thing to do."

"Could you not write to the Earl?" Esther pressed. "Ask

him for an extension of your time? Do you think he would refuse it?"

"He would grant it if I asked," Joanna told her, shaking her head gently. "And that is why I cannot. A good nature is not to be abused."

"Then come here, sister," Esther said, holding out her arms once more. She clasped Joanna close, kissing her warmly. "I wish you a good journey. Your help has been so appreciated here. You will write to me as soon as you return?"

"As soon as I return," Joanna promised, planting a small kiss on baby Charles' head before stepping back.

23

It was with some surprise that Edmund saw Miss Warrick alighting from a coach in front of his home when he glanced out of an upstairs window.

There had been no advance notice of her arrival, and he would have sent the family carriage to pick her up if he had known.

Still, it was not without a rush of happiness that he saw her stepping down from the coach and handing her bag to Jenkins.

Her presence had been much missed, and not just for the children. Amy and Samuel had been nigh-on dejected that she had been unable to bid them a farewell, and Edmund himself had been wishing for her help daily with his correspondence.

As it turned out, Jenkins had been fairly well capable of

dealing with urgent letters when they came up. A man from the office had also come out one day last week to spend a full day going over important contracts and other new documents that could not wait.

But still, Edmund had deferred as much as possible, leaving the letters untouched on his desk.

In the end, he had even had to send Jenkins away. The man had been getting altogether too competent, and Edmund had even worried that all of the letters would be dealt with and done. He invented some pressing need to see all of the family silverware polished and laid out in order to distract the man.

If he was being truly honest with himself, he might have admitted that he wanted Miss Warrick to deal with the letters personally.

If he had been even more honest, he might even had been able to admit that the letters were no more than a pretext, and that in fact it was her company that he desired.

Still, it was a matter of stubborn pride for Edmund that, on this occasion at least, he was not at all prepared to be honest with himself.

"Miss Warrick," he said, greeting her as he came down the stairs into the main hall.

She had just arrived and was in the process of taking off her bonnet. She looked a little weary from the road, though not at all unwell. In fact, her cheeks had something of a flush of health about them.

"Lord Kelt," Miss Warrick smiled. "I am returned."

There was a squeeze in his chest at that smile. He had not dared to examine closely how much he had missed it in the days since her departure. "All is well?" he asked.

"Both mother and child," Miss Warrick nodded. "They had a healthy baby boy. Small, but they say he is a fighter. My sister is very happy."

"I am glad to hear it," Edmund said, somewhat surprised to find that he did indeed mean it.

Normally in these situations he would make small talk only, but it brought him pleasure to know that Miss Warrick's family were safe. What strange new things he was always finding out about himself since he had hired this governess.

Miss Warrick tucked her bonnet under her arm and looked up at the clock in the hall. It was the late afternoon already, and she chewed her lip for a moment as if thinking.

"I can be ready to assist you in perhaps twenty minutes if you require some letters writing today, my lord," she said.

Edmund was a little startled, but pleased that she was so eager to return to work.

"If you are weary from your travels, there is no need," he said. "Though I would be grateful of the help."

Miss Warrick nodded, smiling again. "Then I shall be in your office anon."

Edmund watched her go up the stairs with a kind of

amazement. How was it that she could return from such a momentous trip and yet make herself useful again almost instantly?

He admired her work ethic greatly, being a man who saw no sense in resting himself.

He waited for her in the office, sitting in the chair away from the desk as was their habit.

There had been a momentary lapse in which he made to sit at the desk himself, as he had done in her absence, before he remembered to keep up the pretence. He had deliberately stacked up a large pile of letters which required answers, to give her the immediate impression that there was much work to be done.

"Goodness," she said, as she came to sit before the desk, fully changed out of her travelling clothes. "It appears there is not a moment to lose. I am quite sorry to have left you with so much to work through."

"Not at all," Edmund said, waving his good hand dismissively. He admired how fresh she appeared, with something so simple as a change of clothes.

"It was not your fault. I was simply unable to achieve much without the use of your hand in place of mine. We must just press on as the circumstances dictate."

"And speaking of dictating," Miss Warrick said with a smile, "I have here at the top of my pile a missive from Sir Gregory. Would you like me to take down a response?"

Edmund nodded and began to dictate his answers to

her, and they settled quickly back into working as they had become used to.

Within just the space of a few letters it was as if they had never been apart. Everything felt comfortable again, and wholesome, just the way that it was intended to be.

"Now, tell me about your sister," Edmund said, standing and stretching his legs as Miss Warrick finished stamping the day's letters with his seal. They were not done with the pile, but the dinner bell was ringing, and he had announced their work finished for the day.

"She is the Lady Castleford, is that not correct?"

"Yes, my lord," Miss Warrick told him. "Her husband, Lord Castleford, is just as happy as she with the baby's arrival. He has his first heir. He is such a charming man. I believe he dotes on my sister completely."

"I see," Edmund nodded, feeling a pang of something deep within his chest.

What was that twinge he felt? Something like... jealousy? Surely it could not be.

"And are they settled in a fine home?"

"Oh, yes, very fine," Miss Warrick said. "Of course, it is nothing like your home here, my lord. It is quite considerably smaller, and the grounds are encompassed only in what the eye can see."

"Very good," Edmund nodded, feeling a little more satisfied.

There, see? The couple lived on a smaller estate and

could not possibly be one half as wealthy as the Hardwickes. They had no Earldom, either.

There was no possible reason for him to harbour any feelings of jealousy towards them, no matter their circumstances.

Besides, he was a young man yet. Marriage and children – those were things that naturally came later in life. He was not to be expected to have achieved such goals already.

"Will you need me to return after dinner, my lord?" Miss Warrick asked, looking expectantly at the large stack of letters still waiting for a response.

Edmund hesitated. He did wish to press on, but still, he could not overwork her. She must have been tired from her travels, despite the rosy colour in her cheeks.

"No, Miss Warrick, that will be all for today," he told her, trying not to feel disappointed at the thought. "You should get some rest after your journey."

"Thank you, my lord," Miss Warrick smiled, her skirt swaying behind her as she departed the room.

Edmund felt another disappointment, then, as he realised she would have no pretext to return to his room that night.

Indeed, he had been missing that knowledge that she was watching over him, and it was even difficult to sleep for the first few nights she had been gone. Now, he supposed, they had broken the tradition; she would not return.

So it was that he felt an immense sense of relief when, later that night after the whole household was asleep, he heard the quiet creak of his door opening. Shortly after there was the familiar squeak of the chair as her weight settled upon it, and then silence.

Edmund was almost off to sleep when he heard the next sound, something so totally unexpected that he almost opened his eyes.

It was only extreme self-control that kept him still and silent, and reminded him after a moment to breathe deeply as if in sleep.

"I have missed you," Miss Warrick had whispered into the dark room, so quietly that he could almost believe that he had not heard it at all.

Edmund listened hard, trying to quieten even the sound of his breathing so that he could strain for any more words that she might utter, but none came.

At last, she rose from her chair and tiptoed back to the door, which creaked in farewell as she left the room.

Then, at last, Edmund could open his eyes, staring into the darkness and wondering at what he had heard – and in what sense it was meant.

By the time he fell into dreams, he had himself convinced that she spoke not to him as a person – but to the household as a whole.

Quite naturally, he knew, she would miss the children, and perhaps even the other servants whom she had grown fond of. She was an industrious woman; thus, it was perhaps even the work itself she had spoken of missing.

And there was even the thought that crossed his mind, that he had heard nothing at all, or something else entirely.

Perhaps she had only let out a sigh, and at that moment, his ears conspired to hear something that was not at all there. Yes, perhaps that was it.

He did not allow himself to entertain the startling and wonderful possibility that she might have been missing him personally, and him alone.

24

Joanna settled back in to her daily routine with ease.

It seemed that she had been away for so long while she was at Esther's home, but the reality was that it was only a week. It could hardly have been expected that much would change in that time, though Samuel and Amy were a little grumpy with her on her return.

"Miss Warrick," Samuel said at last, solemn and frowning. "You have to promise to say goodbye when you go again."

"No," Amy cut in. "She must promise not to go away at all."

Joanna laughed then, out of love and because she was touched that they were so hurt by the fact that she had not bid them farewell.

"I have been told, and I have heard you," she said. "I shall not go away without saying goodbye again."

"Or go anywhere," Amy corrected, without a moment's pause.

"I might go somewhere," Joanna laughed again. "But I promise that you will know before I do."

She felt some surprise in her heart to know that she believed she could withhold this promise. For so many months, she had been living in fear of losing her position.

Recent weeks, however, had left her more comfortable and settled in the household. She felt as if she would at least be given time to pack her bags and make her farewells, and perhaps even serve out a period of notice, if Edmund did decide to dismiss her.

That was, at least, so long as he never found out about the ball.

Patience was almost unnervingly sweet and obedient now that she had seen Joanna keep her secret. It was as though she thought she was on to a special formula: that if she was a good girl for her governess, then she could be wicked when her brother came calling.

At any rate, Joanna was in no rush yet to correct her – not as long as she was behaving well.

There was one crucial part of her education that Joanna had not tackled yet, and since she was beginning to be presented in society already, she felt it was high time that Patience receive some instruction.

That was of the running of the household, and to run it correctly, Joanna had always felt that a woman should have a thorough knowledge of all of the tasks expected of her servants.

So it was that she rose with the early summer dawn towards the end of the week, knowing that Mary, Cook, and Jenkins would have risen to begin their daily chores at the same time. She dressed quickly and hurried to Patience's room, knocking loudly on the door before she entered.

"Good morning, Miss Patience, rise and shine," Joanna said, though her words caught in her throat when she looked at the empty bed.

This was becoming somewhat of a habit. Patience was, once again, nowhere to be seen.

Joanna closed the door behind her, thinking for a moment. Then she opened it again, wanting to confirm something that her eyes had registered.

There it was: Patience's bed was tidy and well-made, without any sign that it had been lain in. Last time, she had at least made the pretence of sleeping.

Something about this was different.

Christopher was home for his leave; he had arrived the day before. Joanna had gladly managed to avoid his presence for the evening, but he had spent some time with the family.

Had he convinced Patience to get herself into trouble again?

She could not explain how the sight of that bed sent a chill up her spine, but Joanna felt that something urgent had to be done.

She could not spend the time to search each room one by one as she had done the night of the ball. The household was already waking, besides, and she would surely attract the attention of the servants. Thus, what better course of action than to enlist their help?"

"Jenkins!" she called urgently, keeping her voice pitched low so that she would not raise any alarm, as she saw him crossing the main hall.

He looked up as she hurried down the stairs, her skirt nearly tangling around her feet in her haste.

"What is it, Miss Warrick? You are pale," Jenkins said, frowning at her. "Slow down before you tumble."

"It's Miss Patience," Joanna burst out, almost falling against him as she came to a stop. "She is not in her chamber. I do not believe the bed has been slept in."

It was Jenkins' turn to become pale, the blood draining from his face at her words. "You are sure?"

"Not sure," Joanna said. "Only that she is not there, and she should be sleeping still. We ought to search the house in case she woke early."

"Quite right," Jenkins said, his face taking on a business-like expression. "I shall rally Mary and send her to fetch the driver so that he can search the stables and other outhouses. You should go first to Cook. Check that she is not in the kitchen and then go to the schoolroom. Cook is to look through the servants' quarters. If you find her or no, we shall meet in the main hall."

Joanna nodded and rushed away, fairly running towards the kitchens.

She did not know why her heart was beating so fast, when there was not yet any evidence that the girl was gone. She tried to tell herself that Patience was probably in the library, or strolling down by the lake, or doing something else entirely inappropriate and yet utterly safe.

"Cook!" Joanna gasped, leaning against the kitchen door for support as she tried to catch her breath.

Cook was a large red-headed woman named Sarah, who wielded her ladle with such authority that everyone who knew her simply called her by her position. She was perhaps ten years older than Joanna, a maid still, and likely to become a spinster. Her rages were legendary, though they revolved solely around kitchen disasters; at all other times, she was sweet as honey.

"What is it, dear?" Cook asked, looking down at the bowl of porridge she was stirring. "I'm making breakfast."

"It's Miss Patience," Joanna said, wincing at the thought of interrupting her cooking – though needs must.

"She is not in her bed. We are searching the house – Jenkins requested that you check the servants' quarters, and then meet him in the hall."

"Oh," Cook said, and then a darker look swept over her face. "Oh," she said again, this time in a far different tone.

"What is it?" Joanna asked, stepping forward.

A cold grip of fear had taken over her heart at the sound of that tone.

"It might not be anything," Cook said, setting down her ladle with a guilty look.

"Tell me, Cook, please," Joanna said. She was trying hard not to snap, but the woman was scaring her.

"It's, ah, the little miss," Cook said, wiping her hands on her apron and avoiding Joanna's eyes.

"Well, she seemed so lovestruck, you see, and far be it from me to stop matters of the heart. I thought it was only harmless, nothing would come of it. So I told her I would help."

"Help what?" Joanna asked, almost close to screaming now. Could this dumpling of a woman not get the story out any faster?

"Well, she only wanted to exchange letters with the young man," Cook said, wringing her hands against the cloth of her apron now.

"All I had to do was send them to her, and pass his on when they arrived addressed to me."

Joanna stared at her for a few moments, letting her words sink in. Could it really be?

Could it really be what she was thinking?

"She was writing to Jasper Rivers," Joanna said, with the certainty of a statement.

"Yes," Cook admitted, covering her face with her hands. "You don't think...?"

"I do think," Joanna said, turning on her heel. "I have to go get help. She has run away to be with him."

The urgency of the situation had increased tenfold.

Was Patience out there with Jasper already? Had she been out all night?

Joanna lifted her skirts now and ran at full speed through the corridor, across the main hall, up the stairs, and right to Christopher's door.

There was no longer a moment to lose.

She banged hurriedly on the wood, hearing a shuffling noise instantly on the other side of the door. He was home, then.

Christopher pulled to door open and Joanna nearly fell into the room. She had not realised she had been leaning on it, trying to get her breath back.

"Where is Miss Patience?" she burst out, as soon as she saw him.

Christopher rubbed his eyes.

"What?" he asked, his throat scratchy with sleep.

He had come to the door in only his breeches and at any other time Joanna would have been scandalised. But there was no time even for propriety if Patience's future was at stake.

"Your sister. Where is she?" Joanna asked again. "Think. Did you take her anywhere? Or did she tell you she was going?"

"No," Christopher said. He yawned, and the scent of alcohol wafted on the air towards Joanna. "Why?"

"Is Jasper Rivers on leave at the same time as you?" Joanna pressed.

"Lieutenant Rivers," Christopher corrected, leaning against the doorframe.

"Is he on leave?"

"Yes, of course," Christopher said. He shifted on his feet and swayed a little. "What's the problem, little governess?"

"Miss Patience is missing," Joanna said, close to tears. "I know she was infatuated with your friend. They have been writing letters to one another. Please, tell me that you know where she is."

Christopher looked at her for a moment, and then laughed. "Jasper and my sister?" he asked. "I didn't know he was the letter-writing type."

"Please, my lord," Joanna begged. "This is important. I fear that she has gone to him."

"That sly old dog," Christopher said, laughing again.

He almost over-balanced, taking half a step backwards to avoid falling over.

"You're drunk," Joanna said, realising with despair that the alcohol she had smelt on his breath was not just the product of the night prior. It was still in his system.

"You're mean," Christopher countered.

Joanna stared at him for a moment longer and then gave up.

It was a lost cause. He was too drunk even to understand the gravity of the situation.

She spun on her heel, leaving him where he stood, and rushed further along the corridor.

"Jenkins," she called over the bannister, no longer caring about keeping her voice down. "Has she been found?"

"No, Miss Warrick," Jenkins said, turning from his conversation with the coach driver.

He looked the picture of paternal concern, his face drawn and pale. Mary stood by, anxiously clutching the hem of her apron.

"Then I am waking Lord Kelt," Joanna said. "I believe she has fled the house. Please, talk to Cook. She may have the key to all of this."

She turned without waiting for a reply, and flew back towards Edmund's door.

She took a brief moment after lifting her hand to hammer at it, feeling her heart pounding so loudly in her chest that surely it alone would be enough to wake him.

Then she knocked, and shouted his name at the same time, knowing that the time to hesitate was over.

There was a long pause as she stood there, trembling, waiting for a response. She heard noises inside the room and did not knock again, wishing that Edmund would appear faster.

At last, he opened the door. He had dressed in a full shirt and suit, although in haste, and his hair was mussed still from sleep.

He looked at her, and the picture of terror she must have made, and his brows drew over his face in concern.

"What is it, Miss Warrick?" he asked, glancing into the corridor behind her as if expecting to see the problem made clear.

"It's Miss Patience," Joanna said, the tears fighting more than ever to break from her eyes as her voice cracked. "I think she has run away to be with Jasper Rivers."

25

He stared down at the governess, his brain failing to make comprehension of the words she had said for a long moment.

"Patience," he repeated finally, turning the words through his own head. "Is run away? To be with Jasper Rivers?"

"I am sorry," Miss Warrick said, shaking her head.

Fresh tears were beginning to roll down her cheeks. Strangely, the sight, which he had thought would injure him greatly, was only something to observe from a state of profound numbness.

Edmund paused, somehow unable to move for a moment. Thoughts were not crashing through his mind, but rather sailing around loosely, as if in a great void.

How Father would berate him now, he thought, for losing his sister's honour as if it were nothing more than a handkerchief to be misplaced.

"Please, my lord," Miss Warrick begged him, clearly distressed at his failure to move or speak.

What she wished for him to do was unclear, but it was enough to stir him into action at once.

It was as though night turned to day. "We must discover where she has gone," Edmund said. "Did she leave a note?"

"No, my lord," Miss Warrick said, turning to walk alongside him as he began to stride down the corridor. "We only found that she was gone this morning, with no explanation. But she has been exchanging letters with Rivers – I believe, letters of love."

Edmund stopped walking abruptly, turning to face her. "You knew of this?"

"Only today," Miss Warrick stammered, her voice faltering. "I – I knew she was enamoured – only thought it was a – a passing fancy…"

"You never thought it prudent to tell me?" Edmund demanded, towering over her.

There was a feeling inside of him that he was entirely unfamiliar with: a rage towards Miss Warrick, who had only ever disappointed him once thus far.

"I'm sorry," Miss Warrick said miserably, seeming to diminish in stature. "I wanted Miss Patience to trust me.

She swore to me it was nothing, only a daydream. She told me they had not been in contact."

"Your job here is not to be liked and trusted, Miss Warrick," Edmund thundered, using his full height above her. "Your position is to protect and educate the children who have been placed in your care. This foolish pride of yours has cost my sister her virtue!"

Miss Warrick covered her face with her hands, weeping. "I have failed her, I know. And... and there was more."

"More?" Edmund shouted.

He was not full of pride to see Miss Warrick flinch at his voice, but he had more urgency to know the truth than to comfort her.

"The ball... you told her she was not to attend. I... I discovered her room empty that night as well. Lieutenant Hardwicke had taken her. They bade me not to tell you a word, my lord. He... he promised nothing untoward..."

Miss Warrick broke off into sobs, her shoulders heaving.

Edmund's heart was thawed much by the sight of her distress, and another picture was forming in his mind of the truth.

It was Christopher's friend who had captured Patience, the friend he himself had brought to the house.

It was Christopher who took her to a ball without permission, and no doubt beetled poor Miss Warrick into covering it all up.

It was Christopher, Edmund saw, who was to blame.

"There is an answer to this somewhere," Edmund said. "Miss Warrick, find your composure. We must discover those letters. Please, begin a search of her room. I will speak to Christopher."

"He is quite useless at this moment, my lord," Miss Warrick said, gasping for breath as she sought to restrain her tears. "He is drunk. I asked for his assistance and he was... I do not want to say too much, but I fear he was amused."

"I see," Edmund replied. A muscle in his jaw clenched so tightly that it was painful. "Then there is but one thing I need to discuss with him. Begin your search. I will join you shortly."

Miss Warrick hurried to Patience's room, where the door already stood ajar, wiping her face with her hands as she went.

Edmund waited for her to disappear, then turned and kicked Christopher's door hard enough for it to rattle in its frame.

Three times he kicked before he heard a groan and a rustling noise from inside the room.

"Edmund," Christopher said, rubbing his face. "My head is a fresh hell this morning. Please, do not wake me again."

"This will be my left hand, Christopher, since my right

is incapacitated. Thus, I am sure it will not provide the full force with which it is intended," Edmund said, regarding his brother coolly.

"What?" Christopher asked, scrunching up his eyes against the sun.

He was still holding that face when Edmund's fist flew towards him, which was lucky indeed, since it landed precisely on the radius of his left eye.

When Edmund entered Patience's room, Miss Warrick was already shifting through a pile of letters scattered across the bed. An upended keepsake box was left by them, clearly emptied of its contents.

"The most recent," she said, brandishing it aloft as she saw him.

She seemed quite recovered, enough to have remembered her drive and responsibility, though her face was still pale. "It mentions something of an inn with a sign of a white horse."

"I know it," Edmund nodded, darting back into the corridor. "Come. We must waste no time!"

He took the stairs two at a time, shouting orders at Jenkins and the driver on the way down. In the end it was Jenkins, Miss Warrick, and he that piled into the carriage, leaving instructions with Mary to distract the children sufficiently when they awoke.

"It is a three-hour drive from here to the inn," Edmund

explained as they set off, the carriage rattling down the long driveway at a swift pace. "I believe our man can do it in two, if he pushes the horses fast enough. I do not know how far we are behind her."

"There was certainly no coach or carriage noted last night, my lord," Jenkins informed him. "The driver told me he retired late, and there had been nothing. There may be perhaps only a four-hour window in which Miss Patience left her room."

"I do not believe they would have brought any coach to the house," Miss Warrick put in. "They would have tried the utmost secrecy. The letter speaks of a walk. Perhaps she met the coach in the town."

"So, our window is smaller still," Edmund noted. "It would have taken her perhaps an hour to walk there."

"With those odds, we are but a short distance behind," Miss Warrick said. "We can catch them yet."

Edmund thought on these reassuring words, but his heart could not absorb them.

s

He hit out, knocking his fist hard against the side of the carriage. "Damn it all!" he exclaimed.

Jenkins and Miss Warrick were silent. They kept their own thoughts.

Edmund lowered his head into one hand, uttering a swift prayer in his mind that his sister was not ruined yet.

The journey was uncomfortable and far too long. Every

uneven piece of road made the carriage jolt up and down at high speed, making Edmund's bones ache and sending pains through his arm.

The physical discomfort, however, was nothing compared to the turmoil inside his mind.

He stared out of the window and watched the countryside roll by.

Jenkins and Miss Warrick, for the most part, did the same. Occasionally Jenkins would mutter something or point out a landmark as they passed, no doubt with the intension of providing reassurance that they were racing on towards their goal.

Edmund could only find the fortitude to nod silently at these interjections, wishing all the while that they could be further on in their chase.

Two hours passed this way, and at last Edmund felt the motion of the carriage begin to slow. He thrust his head out of the window to converse with the driver, looking at the landscape around them.

"Why do you slow?" he asked.

"Right ahead, my lord," the driver said, gesturing with the whip in his hand. "The coach. We are not far from the inn, and should see ahead of us as soon as we crest this hill. But the coach, I believe it is a private vehicle."

Edmund leaned out further, looking past his own horses to examine the coach which was just reaching the summit of the hill itself.

It was a plain black affair, with a bend to one of the back wheels that creaked precariously with each rotation. Even from this distance, it was audible. It was moving slowly.

"Catch it," Edmund said, decisively.

The driver cracked the whip, and Edmund pulled himself back into the interior of the carriage just as it lurched forward at high speed again.

"Brace yourself, Jenkins," he said, loudly, over the new rattling of their vehicle. "We are in pursuit!"

It took only a matter of a few minutes to catch up with the coach and then draw alongside. Edmund peered closely towards it, but there were curtains drawn tightly over the windows.

Even so, just beyond one sliver of a gap at the edge, he made out a slice of hair and a portion of a woman's face.

A face he knew very well indeed.

He hammered quickly on the roof of the carriage, a signal meant for the driver. They pulled ahead in front of the coach, and then slowed once more, forcing the other driver to gradually bring his steeds to a halt.

At the last minute, Edmund's driver turned his horses at an angle, blocking the road almost completely with their length and that of the carriage.

Trapped, the coach stopped only a short distance away, with the driver swearing at the interruption.

Edmund wasted no time in disembarking from the

carriage, allowing Jenkins to help Miss Warrick down behind him. He marched to the coach and flung the door open, finding with a grim satisfaction his sister's pale and shocked face staring back at him.

"What is the meaning of this?" Jasper Rivers asked from the opposite seat.

As Edmund leaned inside the coach and made himself known, Rivers, too, paled.

"You, sir, had best hold your tongue for the entire length of my presence here," Edmund warned him, with the quiet certainty of a man who does not made an idle threat. "If you do not, I shall not be held responsible for what happens to it."

Rivers opened his mouth, looked at Edmund's face, and then closed it again with a gulp.

"Patience, were you seen by anyone?" Edmund asked, turning his attention back to the other side of the coach.

"Leave us alone," Patience said shrilly. "I'm not coming back."

"I'll be the judge of that. Did you meet anyone on the road? Or were the curtains kept closed for the journey?"

"We're in love," Patience declared, though there was a tremulous edge to her voice.

"No one saw us," River said, quietly.

Edmund turned and lifted a finger, holding it up as a warning. He had told the idiot boy not to speak, but since it was useful information, he moved on with only a dark look in his direction.

"Then you are coming home, and you are doing so immediately," Edmund said, grasping hold of Patience's arm.

"No!" she squeaked, pulling her hand back out of his grip. "Jasper, tell him! I'm not leaving."

Jasper made no noise at all, even though Patience looked at him beseechingly.

Edmund offered his hand again, but she jerked away from him, turning her nose in the air and shuffling across to the far door so that he could not reach her without stepping inside the coach.

Edmund sighed in exasperation. He wanted to hit something again, so he climbed down from the step and took a deep breath of the morning air instead. The fields around them were deserted, and there was not so much as a bird on the road in either direction. The inn was just visible ahead, though it seemed quiet at this early hour.

"May I?" Miss Warrick asked quietly.

Edmund looked up, at Jenkins and Miss Warrick standing patiently by.

They both wore the same solemn expression, with their hands clasped formally in front of them. Edmund almost wanted to laugh. Jenkins had been with the family since before Patience was born, and yet here was Miss Warrick, showing the same level of concern after less than a year.

"You may," he said, curtly.

He was willing to attempt anything to take her home; if she would not be persuaded, he had no qualms about picking Patience up over his shoulder and carrying her kicking and screaming to the carriage.

Miss Warrick stepped up into the interior of the coach, sitting down next to Patience.

Edmund listened from outside, feeling impatient. He certainly did not want anyone else to come along and witness their predicament.

"Miss Patience, this must stop now," Miss Warrick said, gently. "You must come home with us."

"I shan't," Patience said. "You can't control me anymore. I am to be Lieutenant Rivers' wife."

"He will not marry you," Miss Warrick said.

There was a certainty in her voice that Edmund admired, especially given how close she sat to the very man who could refute her statement if he wished.

"He will not risk your brother's ire. He is not going to stop you going home."

"Don't be absurd," Patience laughed haughtily. "Jasper loves me. Don't you, Jasper? We're going on to start a new life."

"Will you do so without a fortune?" Miss Warrick asked. "Lord Kelt will not allow you anything if you are ruined woman, nor if you marry against his blessing."

"Don't you, Jasper?" Patience interrupted, clearly impatient to hear the reply she was waiting for.

There was only uncomfortable silence within the coach.

"Men like him are not interested in marriage, Miss Patience, and certainly not for love," Miss Warrick said.

"Perhaps he thought that your brother would take pity and allow you some pounds per year that you could both live on. But since he is poor himself, without such an agreement he will ruin you and abandon you."

"That isn't true," Patience said, her voice becoming higher pitched still. "Jasper, tell her."

There was a longer silence still, and then Jasper cleared his throat. "Perhaps it would be best if you returned to your family," the man said.

Edmund could have cheered out loud. He knew, of course, that to do so would not be prudent. She still needed to be swayed.

"Come with me now, then," Miss Warrick said. "Please. I will take you home."

Edmund held his breath when he saw Miss Warrick begin to descend from the coach, accepting Jenkins' hand.

When Patience followed her down to the road, he breathed again at last, full of relief.

Jenkins fetched a bag containing Patience's luggage from the top of the coach, while Edmund returned to the interior.

"Rivers," he said, his voice low. "I know you are aware that I am a man of considerable means and influence. Should you breathe a word of this misadventure to a single soul, your life shall become one of abject misery and poverty. I shall have you stripped of your rank and cast out of the army, and you shall be in the poor house within the year."

"You couldn't do that," Rivers attempted to protest. "You haven't a rank yourself. The army wouldn't listen."

Edmund leaned close to him. "If I have no influence with the army, then how do you suppose my lazy, drunkard brother managed to get himself a rank despite being disciplined so many times he ought to have been court-martialled?"

Rivers swallowed. It was clear from his eyes that he had understood the point.

Edmund stepped down then and, seeing that the others were now safely waiting inside his carriage, signalled for the horses to be turned around.

For his final act, he turned to the driver of the coach.

"How much for your silence?" he asked, getting right to the point.

The coach driver named an outrageously high price. Edmund reached into his jacket and pulled out the notes, handing them over without a moment of hesitation.

"Not one word, my lord," the coach driver said, his eyes lighting up with joy as he held the paper.

"Do one extra task for me," Edmund said.

"Of course, my lord, you name it," the driver said.

"Leave your passenger on the road here and let him find his own way back to civilisation," Edmund told him, before returning to sit opposite his sister for the long drive home.

26

Christopher departed the day after the incident, sporting an impressively purple eye which, Joanna felt, was more than deserved.

Though Amy and Samuel were curious about what had happened, the topic was banned in the household after Edmund locked himself in the sitting room with Patience for a long, drawn-out shouting match that had everyone avoiding one another's eyes.

Mary and Cook had been told that Patience was alone in the carriage when they found her. Only Jenkins and the driver knew the truth, and Jenkins would rather pluck out his own eyes than harm the reputation of what he saw as 'his' family. The driver's silence was also assured, and so it seemed that a tragedy had been avoided.

Joanna tried to bring a sense of normalcy back for the

children, resuming their lessons immediately as if nothing had happened.

It was clear to all of them that something had changed, however; Patience was quiet now, and no longer outspoken or headstrong in class. She would simply do what she was told, silently and with no complaints.

Though it made things easier for Joanna, she found herself wishing that Patience was back to her normal self.

She took the children outside for a day of reading by the lake. She had picked out important texts for all of them to read: a simple story book designed to help Amy begin her French, an account of exploration and discovery of new lands for Samuel, and a tome on running the household for Patience.

Joanna even chose a novel for herself, a gothic tale set in an old manor, and settled in to read alongside them.

She ended up watching Patience and thinking things over more than she read.

She had come to care for the young woman just as much as she would a close relative, and though she was only her responsibility for a little while longer, that did not mean that she had any desire for her potential to go to waste.

Patience was not truly a troubled girl, though she had her own issues. All of them, though, should be resolved if Joanna was to consider her role as governess complete.

After all, was she not supposed to prepare her for life as

a married woman? And would she not be remiss if she did not stop her from tumbling headfirst into ruin?

Ruin may well have been averted in the case of Jasper Rivers, but that did not mean that Patience was entirely saved. After all, she might fly towards whichever young gentleman came courting next.

It was not a problem of disobedience, Joanna could see. It was not merely a wish to displease her brother or cause some scandal. On the contrary, Patience seemed contrite at the trouble she had caused.

But if that were the case, it meant that there was something deeper beneath Patience's plan to run off and marry her soldier.

And, that being so, the risk of it happening again with another gentleman was not entirely averted. Something more had to be done to prevent that from happening.

By the time she returned to the house for luncheon, and to change to her duties as secretary for Edmund, she had begun to formulate a plan that might help her young charge.

"Lord Kelt, I wanted to talk to you about Miss Patience," she said, more than a little hesitantly, instead of picking up her quill to begin writing letters.

He had not wanted to discuss the subject since they returned, and she was anxious not to stir his anger again.

"Go on," Edmund said, though his tone was dark and warning.

"She is sixteen," Joanna began, taking a deep breath. "Nearly seventeen, indeed. I do not wish to overstep my bounds, but I fear that if she is not allowed to act her age, then disaster may follow."

"Whatever do you mean?" Edmund asked, frowning.

Joanna felt that this was not going as well as she had hoped – but nevertheless, she persisted with her argument.

"At her age, she ought to be attending balls and showing her face in society. We ought to have guests in the household, young men from appropriate families sent here to court her. To hold a ball here in the house, even. It is what will be expected for her. Already, the other young ladies of her age are seeking a husband that they may marry in a few years' time."

"And you think this pertinent how?" Edmund snapped. "She has already strayed once. We cannot afford another."

"That is precisely my point, my lord," Joanna said, refusing to back down even though Edmund's tone worried her.

"She is restless. Her female heart is yearning for romance and fantasy. Let her play out that role in public, where all can see that her conduct is becoming. Let her find a match who will be suitable. She is bored, and she has only met one man who ever attempted to woo her. Of course it was natural that she should fall for his charms."

Edmund hesitated. A troubled look passed over his face. "She is not so old as all that," he protested.

"I am afraid she is, my lord," Joanna said, ducking her head.

"I confess, when I was her age, I was quite enamoured of at least three gentleman who had offered me a dance, all at the same time. All of them were passing fancies, in the end. But Miss Patience has not had the chance to know the difference."

Edmund reddened slightly and cleared his throat.

"Forgive me, Miss Warrick," he said awkwardly. "I sometimes fall to recall that you have been a young lady in the same position yourself."

"I hope I am not quite as elderly a spinster as that yet," Joanna laughed.

Edmund reddened further, and shook his head.

"I do not mean that at all. You are quite charming. No, I just meant that you are far more responsible than Patience is."

"I have had reason to learn," Joanna said. "But Miss Patience has much growing to do in a short space of time.

"You will see how she begins to change once she is out in society. She will learn how things go, and will mature at the same rate as her suitors' chances. She will be ready to marry respectably before you know it."

Edmund sighed, looking away to the far side of the room.

"Perhaps that is what I am afraid of," he admitted. "I suppose I would like her to stay a little girl forever."

Joanna's heart was warmed by his reaction. He looked so forlorn at the mere thought of his siblings growing up.

"Rest easy, my lord. Amy is some years behind her still. You will have a little girl in your care for a long while to come."

Edmund shot her a gentle smile, though it was tinged with regret.

"I just wish that our parents were here to stand by her side, the way that they should have been," he said. "It is my father who should be leading her to balls, not I. My mother who should be arranging suitors and visits."

"I understand that it is difficult," Joanna said, bowing her head.

She could not, in fact, imagine how hard it must have been to face the continuation of life alone. Of course, that was part of the point.

"But you are not alone. Jenkins served your parents for decades, and he knew of their wishes. He can guide you. I, too, have experienced it all first-hand. And there are friendly families in this district who would each be happy to take Miss Patience under their wing, with her best interests at heart."

"You may be right," Edmund sighed, rubbing his forehead. He paused, then made a gesture of defeat. "Then read to me the invitations we have received lately. I know you have been keeping them secretly."

Joanna smiled, and opened a small drawer to the side of the desk.

There, wrapped with ribbons and impressive seals, were a pile of invitations that had been coming in all summer. She had been saving them, just in case Edmund would change his mind.

"Shall we begin with the most recent, or those invitations for balls which are soon to be upon us?" she asked, unfolding the neat cards and laying them out on the desk.

"Whichever you feel is best, Miss Warrick," Edmund said, with an air of resignation that made her chuckle to herself.

By the end of the afternoon, they had sent off letters of acceptance to five invitations, which was a considerably small number of those they had received.

It seemed that everyone in the area knew the Hardwickes had a girl who was ready to be courted, and more than that – that the Earl was himself a single man.

Joanna tried to push away the twinge of jealousy that came at that thought. After all, her days of being courted were long over.

She did not count Christopher, who clearly had some kind of ulterior motive hidden away up his sleeve.

And even if she had been in a position to accept a proposal of marriage, it was hardly likely to come from Lord Kelt.

Still, the very thought of him taking a wife sent a cold

darkness up her spine, that nested in her head and would not depart.

Such a woman entering the household would cause utter disruption, and would leave her future there in doubt. Supposing the new wife did not approve of Edmund's choice of governess? She would be likely to be dismissed forthwith.

She might wish to change things, or send Samuel away to school before he was ready. She would have the final say over the children's education, not Joanna, and so she would be forced to bend to any orders that were placed upon her.

The thought filled her with horror, so much so that she almost wished to rip up the responses she had painstakingly written out and throw them in the fire.

Edmund was expecting them to be delivered, however, and there was no way around it now that he had agreed to attend.

With resignation, Joanna handed the finished letters to Jenkins, allowing him to take them for the morning's post. She told herself that she was only being unkind.

Who would wish for Edmund to be alone the rest of his life, without a wife by his side?

No, there would be a marriage one day, and she would simply have to accept it. That was her lot, as governess.

27

It was with mixed feelings that Edmund watched the doctor cut away the bandages from his arm and remove the splint.

"How does it feel?" he asked, encouraging him to flex his long-dormant muscles.

Edmund turned his arm over, twisting the elbow, and moved all of his fingers.

It all seemed to work just as it had before. He reached out for an apple on the table, picked it up, and took a bite out of its flesh.

"I believe it is all in good working order," he said, lifting his apple as proof.

"Excellently done," the doctor proclaimed, as if he had achieved some great task in simply healing at a normal speed. "You are fine to return to life as normal, Lord Kelt. I shan't think you will be hearing from me anytime soon, barring another one of your accidents."

"Please do not be offended, Doctor, but I sincerely hope not to see you for some time," Edmund said, moving his arm about freely in some wonder at how strange it felt to be able to do so again.

The doctor chuckled. "I understand perfectly," he said. "Well, it was a pleasure."

He held out a hand to shake, and Edmund took it, glad to be able to do so once more.

Edmund wandered out of his room, watching the doctor go, and trailed after him to the main hall just as the man was leaving. Jenkins, Mary, the driver, Miss Warrick, and the three children had gathered to hear his news.

"All well again," he said, lifting his arm as proof. "Well, children, this means you have your governess all to yourself again. I will be able to travel to the London office again from now on, and write my own letters, too."

"Oh," Samuel said sadly.

"I am flattered, Mr. Samuel," Miss Warrick said dryly.

"Oh, no," Samuel said quickly. "Not that. I just meant, I liked having Edmund at home with us."

"Me too," Amy declared.

Edmund smiled, and ruffled her hair. "Well, perhaps I can arrange it so that I am not at the office for so many hours a day. Would you like that?"

A chorus of agreement followed, making him chuckle.

"There is only one problem," he said. "If I am to return early each day, I will still require Miss Warrick to attend some correspondence in the evenings on a regular basis. Can that be managed, Miss Warrick?"

Miss Warrick smiled and dipped her head in a nod. "Yes, my lord," she said. "I am at your disposal."

Edmund smiled back briefly, though he quickly extinguished the expression for fear that an altogether too familiar warmth was held within it.

Bidding farewell to his time with Miss Warrick had been a source of unhappiness for him, and he was pleased with himself for coming up with a reason to continue it on the spot.

He had to bless Samuel and Amy for providing him with the excuse.

Now that he was able to travel to the city again or ride about in the carriage as he pleased, Edmund returned to work with a vengeance. He spent his hours at the office, and was pleased to find that the entire business had not disintegrated in his prolonged absence.

There was, however, a certain slack attitude to paperwork that appeared to have built up, and he was quick to correct this in his employees.

The long days were necessary after so much time away. Customers and merchants both demanded his time for meetings face to face, and it was necessary also to appear at certain events in order to make it clear that he was back at his post.

People could not be allowed to whisper that he was neglecting his duties, or held away by some mystery illness that would take his life.

Indeed, there had been plenty of whispering by the time that he returned. He knew it was not a good omen, given his father's untimely death, that he should be detained away from the office by health reasons.

Still, he did not appreciate the churlish nature of what had been his father's best clients, that they would gossip about him in corners like fishwives.

Many of these rumours and whisperings made their way back to his ears, by design rather than luck. He had cultivated quite a network of trust with the employees of his company, and of messenger boys and couriers besides.

At the docks, there were scruffy street urchins who knew that a piece of information might net them a shiny coin with which to take their supper.

This was valuable stuff, and he was able to use it to his advantage. It was quite simple to slip in the particular words a man might have used behind his back when meeting him for the first time, and to allow him to realise with a slow dawning horror that his conversation had been reported.

For the most part, they would fawn and put on airs

then, and he had managed to negotiate a few contracts at a better price as a result.

All of this made him terribly busy, but it was not to be avoided. Despite his promise to the children, there were some days when he could not but return late at night, missing dinner and arriving only in time to retire.

It was on the first of these nights that he arrived at his home, surprised to see a candle burning in the window of the schoolroom where all the rest of the house was growing dark and quiet.

"Miss Warrick?" he said, pausing at the door of the schoolroom.

"Oh!" Miss Warrick exclaimed, hastily putting down the book that she had been engrossed in. "Lord Kelt, you are returned."

"I am surprised that you are still awake," Edmund said. "That must be a very interesting book."

"No," Miss Warrick said, then shook her head with a sheepish look. "I mean, yes, it's a good book. I just wanted to wait in case you needed me to do anything."

"Oh, heavens," Edmund said, shaking his head in return. "No, no, you have no need to stay up late on my account. I wouldn't ask you to work at this hour. You must be fresh for the children in the morning."

"It's no trouble," Miss Warrick said, flushing a little. "I don't mind waiting."

"All the same, I don't wish to take advantage," Edmund

said, wondering why on earth he was pressing the matter when he found it quite pleasing that she had done so.

"All the same," Miss Warrick said agreeably, smiling.

Edmund had the feeling that he had lost, although it was hardly any kind of argument.

His feelings were confirmed on the next occasion when he was kept late at the office, for he saw the candle burning in the schoolroom window once again.

It made him feel a bit of a cad to demand that she stay awake simply to match his schedule, though the sting was taken out of it by the fact that she insisted.

Over the weeks, it became a special treat of his to come down the driveway and peer out of his carriage window to find that light burning in the schoolroom.

Edmund was touched to know that there was someone watching out for him, even if everyone else in the household had gone to sleep.

It was a warming feeling to see that flame, steadfast and true, every time he came home.

And every night, no matter if he arrived late or early, he would lay awake in the darkness until he heard the sound of Miss Warrick stealing into the room and sitting down in his chair.

Such was this comfortable arrangement that Edmund could not wish for any alteration in it, even to make his work easier or to bring a wife to run the household. No, he was quite satisfied beyond measure.

All that was set to change, as it always did, when Christopher returned home for his next period of leave; and after several months of peace, it was all fated to be broken again by his arrival like a cat amongst the pigeons of their simple life.

28

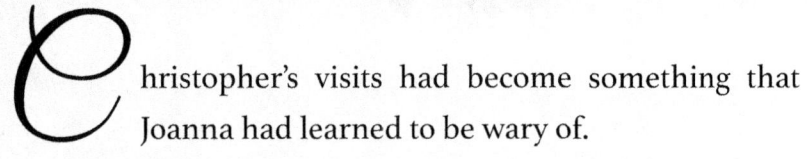

Christopher's visits had become something that Joanna had learned to be wary of.

It seemed that every time he arrived, he brought only trouble with him. Thus it was with some apprehension that she learned he was going to return on leave once more as the seasons began to change.

She had made up her mind to avoid him, but it was not to be possible; on the first day of his arrival, he swaggered by to the schoolroom, still dressed in his red uniform.

"Christopher!" Samuel exclaimed, drawing the attention of the others.

For once, it was not Patience who sprung up to greet her favourite brother. The whole sorry affair with Jasper had done damage to their relationship as well, it seemed.

"Good day, brother," Christopher said jovially. "Sisters. Miss Warrick."

"Can we go and play with Christopher?" Amy asked, in a plaintive tone that she clearly thought was more likely to get her own way. She even clasped her hands together in front of her as if she were praying. "Pleeeease?"

Joanna glanced at the clock. It was almost the end of their lesson time, and there was no chance that the children would concentrate now that they knew Christopher was home.

She sighed, knowing the battle was lost before she even entered it.

"Go on," she agreed, finally.

Christopher chuckled. "Meet me outside in a few minutes. Samuel, fetch the cricket bat and ball. We'll have ourselves a game."

Amy and Samuel ran out of the door shouting in excitement, and Patience followed them, if more slowly. She even cast an eye back towards Joanna, who gave her a subtle nod of encouragement.

The faster the girl could get back to normal, the quicker her heart would mend. It was not right for her to lose her liveliness over a silly mistake.

Joanna began to pick up and tidy away the books they had been studying, not wanting to turn and face Christopher.

There was something about his presence that seemed

foreboding, today – an augur of things to come. It crackled in the air between them like a living force, even though she could not yet give it a name.

"Miss Warrick," he said, stepping into the room and blocking her path between the tables. "I wonder if I might have a moment of your time."

Joanna did not want to give him any of her time at all, but it was necessary to at least be polite. "Of course, Lieutenant," she agreed, waiting for him to reveal what it was that he wanted.

"Miss Warrick," Christopher began, with the air of a man launching into a prepared speech.

"You have proven yourself a very capable woman, and endeared yourself completely to my family. I think it impossible now to imagine you as anything less than a part of it. More than that, I have had the opportunity to see firsthand that you are a handsome woman of good breeding and good sense. What I intend to ask of you, Miss Warrick, is no less than your hand in marriage."

Joanna stared at him for a moment, completely taken by surprise.

Was this the culmination of his gifts and his lingering looks? She not even dreamed for a moment that he could be heading in this direction. Her heart was beating quickly in response, alarmed and surprised and, yes, flattered.

She turned away from him for a moment, trying to process her thoughts without his eyes on her face.

"Miss Warrick?" Christopher prompted.

"Allow me but one moment," she said.

It was almost cruel, this proposal of his. Joanna had learned to give up hope of the idea of ever being married.

If she did find a spouse, she had also learned to assume that he might be low-born, a servant or someone like herself who had fallen from fortune. It would be a marriage of love, not of convenience, for how could it ever be convenient for someone to marry her now?

To marry so exceptionally well, into a great family, was something that had already passed beyond her – even if it was only to the second son. There had been no possibility of something like this in her mind, and certainly no design.

An opportunity like this, she felt, would never pass her way again. She would never again be petitioned by a gentleman such as this, standing in his family manor in his smart red uniform.

This was the last time she would be allowed the possibility of changing her station and returning to something like the life that she had known.

And even so, she knew in her heart what the answer must be.

She could not marry Christopher. It was not just that he was immature and a scoundrel, though those things he certainly was. It was not just that she barely knew him, or that what she did know troubled her greatly. It was not even just the fact that it would feel as though she were abandoning her real duty to the children.

All of those were excellent reasons, and there were more, such as the fact that she had to wonder if his offer was even intended to be truly genuine. If he was anything like his friend Rivers, then he would abandon her long before they reached the altar.

But all of those excellent reasons paled in comparison to the one reason she had now to admit to herself, that she had concealed from her own mind for so long.

The one thing she had not wanted to look in the eye, knowing that it would cause her more harm than anything she had felt before and that it might linger for the rest of her life.

It was the fact that she was truly, deeply, without any hope of it being requited, absolutely in love with Edmund Hardwicke.

Joanna turned back to Christopher, and watched his hopeful expression crumble under her serious gaze.

"I am flattered beyond measure, Lieutenant," she said. "Still, I am afraid that I am compelled to refuse your offer. I hope that you will not be too greatly injured."

Christopher clasped a hand over his heart dramatically, as if he had been shot there; but he smiled and nodded his head.

"I suppose I even expected as much," he said. "You are far too sensible to be linked with a man like myself."

Joanna was surprised that he understood her thinking, and almost denied it out of politeness. Then she decided against it.

If there was ever a time when a man and woman should be honest with one another, it was at the time of a marriage proposal.

"Now that your proposal is refused, perhaps you will tell me something honestly," Joanna said. "You have no hope of changing my mind, but I should like to know the truth."

Christopher scratched the back of his neck awkwardly. He never had come across as the kind of man who was comfortable giving out the truth. Even the suggestion of it apparently made him uneasy.

"What is it?" he asked.

"Did you make this proposal just now with the intention of causing hurt to your brother?" Joanna asked.

There was a moment's pause, and then Christopher burst into forced laughter. "Samuel is just a child. Why should I wish to hurt him?"

"Please do not take me for a fool, Lieutenant," Joanna said. "You know to whom I was referring."

The smile died away from Christopher's face. He dropped his pretence, then, clearly knowing that he was rumbled.

"Yes," he said, at length. "He hit me, you know. Right in the eye."

"I have more than enough reason to believe you deserved it," Joanna said levelly.

She did not want to waste this opportunity. After they left this room, they were servant and master again. She would speak her mind, now, while she had at least the small allowance of the fact that she might have been his betrothed.

Christopher opened and then closed his mouth again. "I do not believe that to be the case from my own perspective," he said, finally. "Still. It matters not. You did not fall into my trap. I shall have to find some other way to injure Edmund."

"Perhaps, instead, your energy would be better poured into the pursuit of your career," Joanna said, feeling more like a teacher chiding a student than she ever had.

"Lord Kelt does not deserve your animosity. He is father to this whole household, now, without so much as a wife of his own. He carries all on his shoulders. You must see how much that weighs on him."

Christopher made a face. "He does not see how things weigh upon my own shoulders," he said, slumping down onto the side of one of the desks as a seat.

"Whatever can you mean?" Joanna asked. She remained standing before him. "Your life is ruled by the army. You have no cares such as running a business or taking responsibility for children."

"Not that he ever questioned whether I would want

such a thing, damn him!" Christopher said, slapping the palm of his hand onto the desk with a crack.

Joanna had never seen such a side of Christopher, nor imagined that he might harbour such feelings.

She moved forward and sat primly on the edge of the desk opposite him.

"You have desires for a family of your own?" she asked.

"I have desires such as any man may have," Christopher replied. "You say my life is ruled by the army, but it is not true. It is ruled by a heart – just like any life."

"There is someone else you would wish to wed?" Joanna asked, with some surprise. "I know that you cannot mean me."

Christopher gave her a wry smile. "My apologies for that," he said. "In truth, it matters not who I marry. For I cannot have – her. I may as well be miserable with someone else."

"Who is she?" Joanna prompted.

Christopher sighed again, throwing his hands up in the air in a gesture of helplessness.

"Lady Juliana Reffern. Only the third daughter of a Duchess. If she were anyone else, I would barely have any competition at all. But, Miss Warrick, you must believe me when I tell you that she is the most beautiful woman in all of England."

Joanna bit her lip to hold back a smile. "Even I have heard tell of Lady Juliana Reffern," she said. "They say she was the delight and charm of the whole city last season."

"And she was all mine," Christopher said. "Until that scoundrel of a lord stole her away from me. They were betrothed in the winter."

"I am sure there is another lady waiting out there for you," Joanna said warmly. "You must turn your heart away from revenge, misery, and pain. You won't find her there. You will find her only by being open to love again."

"Easier said than done," Christopher sniffed.

"But soonest done, soonest mended," Joanna smiled.

"At any rate, the children are waiting for me," he said, getting up abruptly and turning on his heel. "I suppose there is no need for me to ask you to keep this conversation of ours private, away from Edmund's ears?"

"None whatsoever," Joanna replied.

She, after all, had no wish to be linked to a courtship with this man, even if by association alone. Besides, Christopher clearly thought that the idea of losing a governess that the children liked would be harmful to Edmund.

Since that was the case, there was no possibility that Joanna would be the one to hint at that news.

Above that, she considered it a solemn duty laid upon her to keep Christopher's secret heartbreak to herself.

He had confided in her, and it could not have been easy. Surely, if she were anyone else, he would not have dared to breathe it; it was only her sheer lack of importance that made her a target for confession.

She turned and continued to tidy the schoolroom, trying to ignore the shaking in her hands.

Two very important things had happened in the past while.

First, she had turned down what was likely to be the last good proposal she was ever likely to hear.

And second, she had finally embraced fully in her heart that her desire to serve her employer as usefully as possible came not from a sense of pride in her work, but from a love that she knew was never destined to be returned.

Outside, Joanna heard the children shouting and looked out to see Samuel trying to hit the cricket ball as Christopher threw it. Yes; it was just like Christopher, to be so unaffected despite the magnitude of what had passed between them. To him, she supposed, it was almost nothing.

Joanna sat at the window, looking out and trying to calm her racing heart.

"Oh, Joanna," she sighed out loud to herself. "What have you got yourself into this time? What a foolish fancy to have."

She pretended to watch the game a while longer, seeing neither the people nor the scenery. Instead, she was gazing out into her future, and she was forced once again to confront the fact that there was only a small amount of comfort in what she saw.

At that moment, all she wanted was her sister, to lean a head on her shoulder and have her share some sisterly wisdom.

But Esther was far away living out her own fairy tale, with her husband and her child. Sitting in the empty schoolroom, Joanna felt all of a sudden as if she were more alone than she had ever been.

29

"*E*dmund?"

The little voice at his door made him start and look up.

Edmund had planned to be home from the office today, since he knew that Christopher was coming off his leave and he did not want to leave him unsupervised. Even so, there was work to be done, and so he was sitting at his desk and going over the words of a particularly complex contract for the third time.

"What is it, Amy?" Edmund asked, beckoning his little sister forward.

As if released from a string, she bounded forward and climbed onto his knee.

She looked upset, and with an inward groaning,

Edmund concluded that it could only possibly have something to do with Christopher's return.

Amy hugged him tightly, and Edmund patted her head.

"Tell me what the matter is, sweetling," he said. "Why are you upset?"

"I'm not," Amy said, grumpily.

Edmund bent his head to see that she was pouting, obstinately staring at his coat rather than meeting his eyes.

She fiddled with a silver button attached to the front, twisting it around in such a fashion that he began to fear she would pull it off.

"Stop that for a moment, Amy," he said gently, trying to coax her to open up. "If you don't tell me what you're thinking about, I can't help you. It's my job as your big brother to help you, so you must let me."

Amy sighed dramatically and buried her head into his shoulder. "It's just not fair," she said, her voice muffled by the fabric.

"What isn't, dearest?" Edmund asked, cradling her weight.

He wanted to sigh and tell her to get on with it, but she was not an adult. Besides, if something had upset her enough to cause this display, he wanted to get to the bottom of it as thoroughly as possible.

"I don't want Miss Warrick to go," Amy whined, and sniffled against his collar.

That made Edmund's heart jump against his ribcage.

To go? Where was Miss Warrick going? And when, and with whom? No one had been to consult him about this. What could Amy possibly know that he did not?

"What do you mean?" he asked, trying not to demand an answer but to keep his gentle tone.

All the same, his pulse had quickened, and he was struck by an urge to put Amy down and go to find out what was happening for himself.

"She's our best governess," Amy said, twisting around on his knee. "I like her a lot."

"I know you do," Edmund said. "She's still your governess, though, isn't she?"

Amy sighed. "Maybe," she conceded.

"Why aren't you sure?" Edmund asked. He felt he was starting to chip away at things, bit by bit, even if Amy was not giving him much to go on.

"She'll be our sister now," Amy declared, then shifted again. She seemed to be thinking. "I suppose that will be nice. She will be a nice sister."

"Miss Warrick will be your sister?" Edmund repeated, not quite understanding what he was hearing or where Amy was getting her information from.

"I suppose I am happy for that," Amy said, sighing noisily. "I just already had a sister. Now I don't have a governess. And she will go away like Christopher does."

"Amy, darling," Edmund said, leaning away to look at

her face again. "Tell me why you think Miss Warrick will be your sister, instead of your governess."

"Christopher came home," Amy said, as if that explained everything.

"Yes, I thought I heard his carriage arrive," Edmund replied. "But what does Christopher have to do with it?"

"Well, because they are getting married," Amy explained matter-of-factly, swinging one of her feet backwards and forwards in the air.

Edmund stared at her without full comprehension for a long moment.

Miss Warrick and Christopher, getting married? This was the first he had heard of even a suggestion of the idea!

But he remembered Christopher watching her from the window, and a sense of dread began to creep over him.

"Can you tell me exactly what happened, Amy?" Edmund asked.

"Christopher came home," Amy said, in an exasperated tone as if she was annoyed at having to repeat herself. "Then he talked to Miss Warrick when we were getting the crickets."

Crickets…?

Edmund threw that aside for now, trying to focus on what mattered. "What did you hear them say?" he asked.

"Christopher said that Miss Warrick is a woman and has ears for the family. Then, um… she is apart from it and has good hands and good scent. And he in-ends to ask her hand for a marriage."

Edmund filtered Amy's report through his mind, trying to make sense of what she had heard and what must really have been said.

"I see," he replied. "And what did Miss Warrick say?"

"She said nothing," Amy replied. "Maybe she was crying and happy."

"Then what happened?"

"I came outside but I was sad. So I came to see you. They are all playing crickets."

Edmund turned this over again.

So, Miss Warrick had accepted the proposal and then gone out to join Christopher in a game of cricket?

He supposed they must both be very happy.

Amy was already wiggling free of his grasp and dropping to the floor, from where she strode purposefully for the door.

"Where are you going, Amy?" he asked.

"Crickets," Amy declared, vanishing into the corridor.

Left alone, Edmund sunk back against the support of his chair and mulled it all over.

The idea of Miss Warrick accepting a marriage proposal from Christopher somehow made him want to snatch up the inkwell from his desk and dash it against the wall.

He did not, for it would have been nigh on impossible to clean up, and besides, the inkwell had been his father's.

There was nothing quite else that would have allowed him to express precisely how he felt at that moment.

So, it seemed that his warning to Christopher had been taken as a personal challenge after all. Damn the boy! Had he even real feelings for Miss Warrick, or was it all part of his endless game?

And hadn't Edmund predicted this even when Miss Warrick first arrived? She was pretty and slight, and cultured despite her fallen status.

Of course she would have been attractive to Christopher. It was those same qualities that had attracted himself.

But Christopher was a cad, a scoundrel. Edmund doubted that he had ever even felt the true stirrings of love, but only played with hearts as in a game that he enjoyed thoroughly.

Could it be possible that he would toy with Miss Warrick so? Oh, but Edmund would skin him alive!

He rose and walked to his window, looking down into the grounds and finding Samuel and Christopher practicing their cricket technique while Patience and Amy looked on.

"Throw it faster!" Samuel shouted, wielding his bat with fierce determination.

Edmund had to close his eyes and back away. Was it all really coming undone like this?

He thought back to all of the help that Miss Warrick had been, all of the times she had stepped into the breach when he needed assistance.

She had been patient and kind to the children, useful and efficient as his secretary, and charming in every conversation. She was prettier in a plain dress than any woman he had ever seen in fripperies at a ball, and she watched over him with a grace that warmed his very soul.

For some time, he had known – even if he had never admitted it to himself – that his affections for her were growing. He had called it attachment when he thought of it at all, but perhaps a more accurate term would have been love.

He thought of losing all of that warmth from his home, from his very life, and it squeezed on his heart like a tight fist.

Edmund sat down at his desk and took out his quill, and a fresh piece of parchment.

With regret and pain lacing his features, he laboriously wrote out a notice of how much money he would afford Christopher and his new wife per year to ensure their comfort. It was the right thing to do, after all.

As soon as they came clean and announced their betrothal, he would share with them the news.

He placed the paper away in a drawer of his desk, no longer wishing to look at it.

How long did he have before they would come to him,

breathless with excitement, to tell him all? Perhaps no more than a few hours, at the longest. Only that amount of time in which he could still harbour denial.

Edmund reached for a bottle of whisky that was kept inside a secret drawer of the desk, and poured himself one small glass. A stiff drink would help him to keep his composure, he reasoned. He was going to need it in order to look Christopher in the eye and pretend to be pleased.

One thing was abundantly clear, and that was that things would have to change immediately.

He could not bear to let them continue as they were, not knowing it would all soon be over anyway. Miss Warrick would have to be governess only, and remove herself from his side.

Edmund sat in his study and waited, and though Christopher did not come to him at all that day, he thought he detected a hint of merriment in his eyes when they finally sat down to dine.

Christopher had a secret, and it seemed that he was going to have his fun with it before he revealed all.

Fine, then; let him have it his way. Edmund would wait, and not let on that he already knew. The boy could have his fun. What did it matter, anyway?

30

Joanna was relieved to be free of Christopher's gaze once he had gone to play with the children, and yet more relieved still when the family were called to dinner.

She could avoid him easily for the rest of the night, which would give her time to recover somewhat from her embarrassment.

She retired to her chamber earlier than usual, wanting no risk of a chance encounter in the corridors should she linger for longer. Despite the fact that they had left things in an amiable fashion, she was uneasy at the thought of it all.

It had been a queer proposal, and their conversation had been out of place. Returning to the role of servant and master required some time and distance.

Her great consolation and joy was the fact that a letter had arrived from Esther, and hearing from her sister was enough to put a smile back onto her face. All the more so, since she knew now that there was something she had to share in return.

Though she would not tell another soul about Christopher's offer, her sister was removed enough from the situation and a trusted confidante.

Still, first there was the matter of reading what her sister had to say.

Joanna tore open the envelope excitedly, reading her sister's familiar hand with a greed for news.

Dearest Joanna,

Oh, my dear, I know I should write to you in response to your last letter. There are many questions and things to discuss. But I hope you will afford me some leave to give you my reply to those matters another time, for I have an important item of news to impart!

I can barely contain my excitement, and I know that you will feel the same for me.

Joanna, it is the best, the most wonderful news. I am with child again!

Charles is still requiring my attention most of the time, but I hope that we shall be able to give him a younger sister.

I know from my own experience that a sister is the most precious thing in the world to have, so I hope that I can give that to him.

If I do – well – I should not hint – but I think I have already chosen a name!

My lord Castleford is so beside himself with happiness. We shall grow our brood most readily, as we both dote on Charles so that I think we should both like to have a great deal more.

We shall fill our hall here with laughing faces and tiny feet.

Oh, Joanna! Eight months more before I can bring into the world another babe to join our family. You were such a comfort to me before, so I hope you can join me again. This time I hope our little one will wait until the appointed time! The midwife tells me that it gets easier with each one.

I shall end here as I must write next to Mama – but I send you my love, Joanna, and ask you to pray for my child!

Ask God to bless us with a girl in due time!

All my love and affection,

Lady Esther Castleford

Joanna read the letter over again with a growing sense of dismay.

Yes, it was a wonderful piece of news that Esther should be able to grow her family, but Joanna feared for her health. The last birth had been so sudden and difficult, with much risk to both mother and baby.

Was there not equal risk that the same would take place again?

Joanna paced her room, wringing her hands. This was a dilemma indeed.

She wished that her sister would be safer, more careful.

It should not have been thought of to try for a child so soon again, with Charles still but a babe in arms and Esther only just recovered from the ordeal she endured with him.

But what was she to do? The deed was done. Esther was with child. Such a condition could not be reversed.

And beyond that, Esther was a wife now – a lady. It was her duty, expected of her, to bear her lord many children and raise them in health and happiness. There had to be an heir to their title and lands, and more to distinguish their family further and gain connections with others.

It was the way things were done, and that was that. Even if Joanna worried terribly for her, there was nothing to be done about it.

Esther was happy, and she supposed that, for that reason, she ought to be happy too.

That thought played on her mind, and it was not without some reluctance that she turned to address it.

Sitting down on her bed with the letter safely tucked away in her desk, Joanna took out the blue ribbons that Christopher had bought her and twisted and turned them in her hands.

The fabric was innocuous, a little nothing… Yet it held a deeper meaning, belied by its appearance.

It represented his feelings, or at least his supposed feelings. It was a measure of his intentions to propose, surely a signpost that he had intended to show that he was courting her.

Joanna had dismissed it out of hand at the time, but it must have been his plan all along. She thought of the tales she had overheard of Christopher buying jewellery and gems for other women, and smiled to herself self-deprecatingly. She supposed he thought she was beneath such gifts.

Trinkets, anyway, that she would have felt honour-bound to return even if he had offered them. It would not have been appropriate to keep them after having refused his proposal in such a way.

And was she mad, to have done so?

Joanna stood and paced again, unable to keep still. The thought of Esther growing her family by another head already, with Joanna still unwed and unlikely to be so, made her miserably jealous.

She wanted children of her own, too, and a husband to please. Perhaps for the first time, Joanna allowed herself to acknowledge this fact: she desperately wanted to be married, and yet it was not something likely to ever happen for her now.

Not especially after she had turned down the hand of an Earl's second son, all out of pride and misplaced affection for his brother.

Oh, what a fool she must be! Should she go and tell him that she had changed her mind?

No, but it was too late. They had spoken frankly, and Christopher had even admitted that he was not badly wounded by her refusal. To try and accept it now would only offer her shame, and perhaps his cruel laughter in her face.

Joanna sat down again on the bed, and even curled under the covers, trying to convince herself to sleep. How would it be if she were too tired to rise and do her duties in the morning?

The children needed her.

Yes, the children. That was a thought that gave her comfort. Even if she was not to have children of her own, she at least had these charges under her wing. They were beautiful children, a joy to teach, and that was more than many women could hope for.

While Patience was still a little standoffish, lost in her own world and halfway to being a woman already, it was different with Amy and Samuel. They were almost children of her own, lost without a mother and father as they were.

The door to Joanna's chamber creaked open then, and she sat bolt upright, out of shock and fear.

Who could it be at this late hour? Was it Christopher, that scoundrel, seeking to bring dishonour on her head by appearing in her room at such an inappropriate hour for the sole cause of irritating his brother?

But no. A small head peered around the door, and Joanna recognised Amy's soft curls. She let out a sigh of relief.

"Miss Amy?" she asked, keeping her voice quiet so as

not to cause any disturbance to others asleep down the corridor. "What is it?"

Amy studiously entered the room and closed the door behind her, affecting a silent care that let it click shut with a quiet noise only. Then she tiptoed across the wooden floorboards, raising her legs high into the air to avoid making a sound.

"Miss Warrick," Amy whispered loudly, as soon as she was close by the bed. "I couldn't sleep."

"And you shan't sleep wandering around the house like this," Joanna admonished her. "Why did you come to me?"

"I want to sleep with you," Amy said, indicating the patchwork quilt across the bed.

"What's wrong with sleeping in your own room?" Joanna asked, trying to be gentle even while persuading her to go back to bed.

Amy made a face. "It's cold," she whispered.

Joanna paused for a moment. She wanted to ensure that Amy would sleep, but it was unorthodox for her to sleep in the room of a servant. She ought to have been with her sister, if anything.

"What of Miss Patience?" Joanna whispered. "She might keep you warm."

"Patience snores," Amy said, so matter-of-factly that Joanna had to stifle a laugh.

At last, she had no recourse.

"Climb in, then," she said, shuffling backwards and patting the empty space on the mattress.

Amy used her knees to heft herself up onto the bed, and she had soon wriggled herself into a comfortable position that somehow took up most of the available space. Joanna bit her lip to keep herself from laughing again.

"Miss Warrick, will you stay with us?" Amy asked.

Joanna frowned. "Of course I will stay with you," she said. "What's brought this on?"

"I just wondered," Amy said, sighing and nestling down closer into the blankets. "It's too bright."

Joanna took the hint and leaned over to blow out the candle beside her bed.

She lay down again, and felt the little body of her young charge moving to snug against her for warmth.

"Night-night, Miss Warrick," Amy said sleepily, her words already muffled and obscured by the blanket.

"Night-night," Joanna whispered, listening for Amy's breathing shallowing out as she fell asleep.

She lay awake for some time longer, considering her situation and all the angles of it.

All things taken into account, she decided that she was a lucky woman. She had a home, a roof over her head – and a grand one, at that.

She had found a family who liked and respected her even on her first assignment as a governess, and she loved the children as if they were her own.

She was blessed, too, with the fact that Samuel had been held back from school. In any other circumstance she would not have had the pleasure of teaching him.

She had, too, a wonderful household, with Jenkins who was as avuncular as they came, the clumsy yet amenable Mary, and even Cook with her talent for pastries.

Add to that, too, her employer, who treated her kindly and even allowed her to take on more responsibilities.

All in all, she was happy, she concluded. Perhaps a family of her own might have been a happier goal, but there was nothing for it. Since this was to be her lot in life, she was abundantly satisfied to know that her circumstances could have been far worse.

That, she decided as she closed her eyes and fell asleep at last, would have to be her outlook and approach: to remember just how lucky she was and feel gratitude, not remorse or sorrow.

31

*E*dmund kept to the resolve he had made with himself. Things had to change, and they had to change immediately.

He had not quite brought himself to the task of addressing her directly, but he had left for the office early the next morning with Miss Warrick on his mind. She need not know that he was aware of her betrothal, but it was certainly inappropriate to let things carry on as they were.

He did not know what kind of game Christopher intended to play, and how long he would wait before giving the confession of his happiness. But since this timeframe was yet to be determined, the only thing Edmund could do was to take matters into his own hands as far as he was able.

So it was that he returned late from his office, having

stayed to get the work done with a secretary in London who could do the job more admirably.

After all, it was the man's position within the company to take on such work. How Edmund had ever countenanced giving such tasks to another was beyond him.

When he approached the house in his carriage, everyone was asleep. He had felt no worry at leaving Christopher alone in the house now that he knew the deal had been made. It was as if he no longer feared what mischief the boy could get up to; as if the taking of Miss Warrick's hand had been the thing to worry about all along.

So, what did it matter now if he were left unsupervised?

But Edmund saw, with not a little consternation and chagrin, that the light of the candle was burning for him in the schoolroom, as always.

This was to be it, then. Now was his moment in which he must make matters clear, and break the long tradition they had held between them.

It was not right for Christopher's intended wife to be waiting on the arrival of another man, servant or no servant.

He strode into the house and into his study, placing some papers on his desk and tidying them into piles. He knew he would not have long to wait, and so he busied himself, attempting to ignore the way his heart fluttered inside his chest with trepidation.

"My lord?" Miss Warrick asked, from the doorway, and he found all of a sudden that he could not turn to face her.

"Your services are not needed, Miss Warrick," Edmund said, stacking away a group of letters that he had already repositioned twice.

"Oh, I see," Miss Warrick said, with some surprise.

There was a moment of hesitation before she continued.

"I shall bid you goodnight then, my lord, and return to assist you tomorrow."

"No," Edmund said quickly, straightening up. "Not tomorrow, neither. What I intend to say, Miss Warrick, is that your services are not required at all. I have no need of a secretary. I have enlisted the time of the man at the office whose task it should have been all along. My papers will be done in London from now on."

Edmund waited, but he did not hear her steps retreating or the door closing behind her.

At last, he turned, facing her as he had not wished to do.

"Is there anything else, Miss Warrick?" he asked, employing a haughty tone designed to remind her that it was he who would decide when there was something more to add. It was not her place to linger after having been dismissed.

"N-no," Miss Warrick stuttered.

Her face was pale, and a picture of dismay.

"Forgive me, my lord. I... I just wish to know if I have displeased you in any way."

"I have explained to you already," Edmund said, on the verge of losing his patience.

Why couldn't she see that he needed her out of his sight, and immediately? He could hardly bear to look at her.

"The work was never yours to do. You ought to focus on your duties as governess, while they are yours to hold. It should never have been any other way. I am simply returning things to their rightful state."

Miss Warrick swallowed, hard, and looked down at the floor. Edmund saw water gathering in her eyes, and did his best not to allow the same thing to happen to his own.

"I am deeply sorry, my lord, if I have caused you any inconvenience," she managed, before dipping her head in an approximation of a curtsey and hurrying away.

The swishing of her skirts followed her down the corridor as her footsteps retreated, and Edmund found himself sagging against his desk for support.

It was a hard thing that he had done, and he had no wish to do it. Still, it had to be that way now that everything was to change.

He felt even a little surprised that Miss Warrick had reacted so strongly – after all, she must know that things would change if she were to become Christopher's wife.

Still, there again, she did not know that Edmund knew; and in circles he went, pushing it around in his head.

Edmund retired to his chamber almost immediately, having no wish to stay in that room any longer.

Once there, he did something that he had never in fact had cause to do in his whole life: he reached for an ancient, half-rusted key and locked his chamber door.

It was infinitely easier than locking his heart or his thoughts, but he had to start somewhere.

It had been not half an hour of lying awake in bed, staring up at the ceiling in the darkness, before he heard her stealthy footsteps creeping along the corridor.

She was quiet, but he had learned to listen for her, and there was a tell-tale creak on a floorboard just down the hall that always signalled her presence.

Edmund's heartbeat quickened, beating rapidly in his chest as she approached the door.

There was the lightest, smallest noise as she knocked. One would have to be wide awake as he was to detect it. Had he been asleep, it would have been lost in the quiet of the night, as was her intention.

Edmund waited. If she took gentle hold of the doorknob, he knew there would be a tiny squeak of complaint from the metal as she would turn it around. If she tried to open the door, it would stick with a clang, the lock hitting the inside of its cage on the doorframe.

He was uncertain what he wanted her to do. He could

not determine his own treacherous heart. But she did nothing.

Edmund lay staring at the door, even though all was dark and he could see nothing. Even the hallway was dark, without candle flame, and he could not make out so much as her shadow under the door. But he knew she was there.

Finally, though Edmund could barely hear it over the sound of his own heartbeat in his ears, the softest whisper permeated the door.

"I am sorry…"

It could have been the lament of a ghost, a whisper there and then gone, words scattered on the floorboards like ashes, a dream that, in the morning, Edmund would be unsure if it had been real.

Then she must have stepped away, and Edmund heard the creak of a floorboard down the hall, and knew that she was gone.

He did not sleep for many hours that night, and when he did, it was only to be tormented with dreams of his brother's wedding.

Miss Warrick avoided Edmund's presence, it seemed, for a long while.

Several weeks passed by and she did not appear in the sitting room, as she had sometimes been invited to do of an evening before they began writing letters together. Nor did she come by his study when he was home, even to talk about the children.

Indeed, whole days went by when he did not so much as see her in passing by accident.

Christopher lingered, choosing to spend his whole leave at home for once, but he still did not share his good news.

Edmund grew more enraged with each passing day. How dare he keep something so important a secret from his own brother? The man who, by rights, controlled any fortune he did not make for himself?

It was tantamount to failing to tell a father. For less than that, many a man had been disowned.

"My lord."

Edmund started at the interruption, turning to see Miss Warrick standing at his door. It was a Saturday, and he had spent the day at home, though there was still, as always, some correspondence to be done.

He had been whiling away the time watching Christopher play catch with Samuel outside the window, silently seething. His anger was almost at a boiling point by now, and he was barely keeping it under control.

It was with some small guilt, therefore, that he turned to face Miss Warrick at last – not to mention a healthy dash of discomfort.

"Miss Warrick," Edmund said, attempting to pretend as though he had been looking at nothing in particular.

He returned to stand by his desk and started shuffling through some papers. "Nothing is the matter with the children, I hope?"

"No, my lord," she said, hesitantly, in a voice so small and weak that he barely caught it at first.

Edmund leafed through a few more sheets, frowning at them as if they held information of the utmost importance.

Miss Warrick did not speak again, and he was forced to look up at her.

"Well?" he asked. "What is it that brings you to interrupt my work, Miss Warrick?"

"Forgive me, my lord," Miss Warrick said, her face dropping as she turned immediately to go. "I did not think to inconvenience you. I will leave you in peace."

Edmund felt his heart drop at the same rate as her departure, and felt a compulsion to call out.

He was being too cruel, perhaps. She had done nothing wrong – in her position, any woman would have been forced to accept Christopher's proposal. It was her only hope at a comfortable life, one not spent serving others.

"Wait," Edmund said, unsure of whether he stopped her from compassion or from longing for her company. "Turn back. What is troubling you, Miss Warrick?"

She faced him again, though the hesitation had not left her. She seemed unsure of what to do with her hands, tangling them around a length of blue ribbon over and over again.

"It is just," Miss Warrick began, and then her face crumpled in a manner which was most alarming.

Edmund laid his papers down on the desk immediately, though he was held back from rushing to her side. She was, after all, his brother's woman.

"Miss Warrick?" he prompted, fighting to keep his growing concern from his voice.

"It is just," she rallied with some effort. "That I feel I must have failed you in some way. I tried my hardest to serve you well as a secretary, my lord. Please, tell me my fault that I may correct it. I wish to be of use for as long as I may."

Edmund was almost choked, seeing the emotion writ upon her face.

So, for all this time she had imagined him angry at some supposed failure in her deeds as a secretary. How irksome it was to see that she had not the slightest inclination of how she had wounded him, how her secret had festered between them.

A rage boiled up in Edmund again, the rage he had so far reserved for Christopher. Now it was full to spilling over, and there was no preventing it.

"There was never any problem with your letter-writing skills, Miss Warrick," Edmund said icily, keeping his back straight and his gaze firm.

"Though you are but an uneducated woman, you have matched any clerk or secretary from my firm. No, it was not that which caused me to force you from my aid. It was your emotions towards my brother that sealed your fate. Surely you see that you cannot work for me any longer – in any capacity."

Edmund let his words hit their mark, seeing the look of shock upon her face, and he snatched up his riding cloak from where it lay over the back of his chair.

He pushed past her then, his boots ringing smartly on the floor as he stormed away, as far from her as he could manage.

At that moment he was no longer thinking logically, or trying to remain calm. Instead, all he thought of was the need to remove himself from the vicinity of his brother and the vixen who had ensnared him.

Ensnared both of them, as it happened.

Edmund strode to the stables before he really even knew that was where he was going, sweeping his cloak onto his shoulders as he went. He shouted an order to Jenkins to gather him some victuals as he passed by the old man, who was skulking about in the corridor as usual.

"Saddle my stallion," Edmund barked to the coach driver, who served also as stable hand when they were not in motion.

He was incensed by the delay, pulling on soft riding gloves and changing his boots with the impatience of a man who would prefer to have left hours ago. He almost leapt onto the horse before the driver was done, causing the man to cry out in alarm and check the girth one more time.

Jenkins hurried out of the house with a bundle in his arms, which he quickly transferred to the saddlebags of the prancing stallion.

The steed sensed his master's impatience to be off and would not suffer to be held in check.

With all things done, Edmund shouted a warning to his servants to stand clear, and gave the stallion his head.

They charged out of the yard and into the countryside, the wind streaming over them as they fled the house. Edmund did not even give a backward glance to his home, for he feared that if he did, he would see them looking back at him.

32

*J*oanna was in shock.

It had taken her a long moment even to digest Edmund's words, and then the first of them to hit home was the understanding that he was dismissing her from her post as governess.

This realisation had her sinking to her knees. Small mercy it was that he had already left the room, for she would have been most ashamed for him to witness how his words laid her low.

To be without the children! To leave this place, which had become such a comfortable and natural home, behind!

But most of all – to be without him – to be away from her Lord Edmund...

Joanna stayed there for a time, unmoving except for the

tears beginning to leak from her eyes, and it was only hoofbeats outside the window that made her start and rise.

She rushed to the casement, only to see Edmund riding away on his stallion at great speed. His riding cloak flared out behind him on the wind, and he rode on despite the dark, cloudy skies that gathered above him.

Joanna felt a moment of true despair to imagine him caught in a storm, alone, and all because of her own doing.

But, wait: what was it that he had meant? He had spoken of her emotions towards his brother – surely he intended her to understand he was speaking of Christopher, not of Samuel.

If he feared she had grown too close to the children, regarding them as her own, then he should have mentioned Amy at the least.

So, Christopher then – and what could he mean?

There was the proposal, of course. It was bound to appear straight in her mind, the most recent and most startling display of any kind of emotion between them.

True, also, that she had been avoiding Christopher since then. Could it be that Edmund thought she could no longer continue, having dishonoured Christopher by so flatly turning him down?

But, no; that was not the story that Christopher would tell, she was sure of it. There was no reason for him to admit his defeat. She had vowed never to reveal it, and it would only appear as shame for him. So, then, what?

"Miss Warrick?" a shy voice came from the corridor.

"Miss Amy," Joanna said, refusing to turn around so that the child would not see the tears on her face as she hurriedly tried to wipe them away.

"Why are you in Edmund's room?" Amy asked, with the sly curiosity that only the young possess.

"I was just talking with him," Joanna explained hastily, attempting to compose herself. "I shall be leaving momentarily."

"Why did he go out riding?" Amy wondered. "It's a storm."

"I don't know," Joanna said, a little more flatly than she had intended.

She turned then, trying to soften her words with a smile that could not quite reach any part of her face but her lips. "I don't think he wanted to see me anymore."

"Why not?" Amy asked, swinging her weight from the doorknob and making the door rock to and fro.

Joanna hesitated, trying to find some way to explain this. She had not expected to be confronted by one of the children so soon, but she felt she had to come clean.

They must know that she was leaving them. It would have been a betrayal to leave without saying goodbye.

"Is it 'cause of Christopher?" Amy asked, cutting off Joanna's need to explain in that easy way that came from total innocence.

"What do you know about the Lieutenant?" Joanna

asked carefully, thinking that perhaps Amy knew more than she was letting on.

"Me and Edmund are sad," Amy said, shrugging. "But I decided it's okay if you're to be my sister."

"Why should I become your sister?" Joanna asked, coming closer to Amy now and peering down into her face.

"When you marry Christopher," Amy said simply, and let go of the doorknob. "I'm going to find Mary and make her play."

"Alright, sweet," Joanna said distantly, watching her run off down the corridor.

So, this was the crux of it.

Somehow, from some corner, Edmund had received the idea that Joanna was to marry Christopher after all.

Had it been from the soldier himself? She wouldn't have put it past that scoundrel to cause mischief in such a way. Perhaps he even intended to punish her by shutting her out from the family she so loved.

Looking back, things began to fit into their rightful places.

It was after the proposal that Edmund had declared he no longer needed her services as secretary. Now this outburst – all stemming from the one fact: that he thought she had accepted.

Oh, what a mess it all was!

Joanna sunk down in her customary chair at Edmund's writing desk, seeing the familiar implements before her.

What was she to do? The record must be set straight, but he was gone from the estate, and who knew when he would be back. Perhaps he would never even listen to her, expecting as he did that she would be gone.

The deception would fall apart rapidly when no wedding was held, but that would be far too late.

She had been dismissed. It did not matter whether the reasons were untrue. He was her employer, and it was her duty now to leave.

But there was perhaps one recourse left – one thing that might save her. Here she was, at the very desk where she had written letter after letter for him, time and again.

Why not rely on the same to save her?

She picked out a quill pen and a fresh sheet of paper, even though a voice in the back of her head reminded her that to do so was technically stealing from her employer.

She pushed these doubts away and set to work, laboriously trying to find a way to express her meaning.

My lord Kelt,

Please accept my humble apologies that a misunderstanding has come to pass, but I fear the situation is not as you believe it.

I am not betrothed to Lieutenant Hardwicke, nor could I ever be. I am in love only with yo-

No, that would not do!

Joanna stopped writing with a groan of frustration and crumpled the paper up immediately. She tore it once or twice for good measure and threw the whole mess into the fireplace. It was not lit, but she would light it later and destroy the damning draft.

She could not admit such a thing so freely. It was inappropriate, and just as likely to lose her position all over again.

No, she had to restrain herself. She should correct the misunderstanding, and nothing more.

She took a fresh piece of paper and started again, breathing deeply this time and trying to keep her shaking hands under control.

My lord Kelt,

Please forgive me for being so forward in writing to you so, but I fear there has been a terrible misunderstanding.

From Miss Amy I am given to understand that it is your belief that I am betrothed to Lieutenant Hardwicke, soon to be his wife.

I do not know how such a misunderstanding came to pass, but it is not true. I remain as I ever was since coming to your family – a humble governess only.

There was a proposal, but I did not think it a fitting match for such an esteemed nobleman and soldier to be linked with one such as I. I do not wish to be marked as a vicious social climber, and there is no love between us that would have us forsake the rules of society.

My lord, I beseech you to allow me to remain a governess in your household. I know that it is most unbecoming of me to beg, but it is my only hope. I feel such dear love for the children as if they were my own, and to be parted from them now brings such unbearable pain.

It is true also that I have enjoyed greatly serving you as your secretary, in whatever capacity I could. Our time together has been amongst my happiest memories, and I harbour a most sincere wish that we might be friends again, inasmuch as a servant can be friends with her master.

Please, if there is any way I may stay in my position here, allow me to do whatever is necessary to keep it.

Yours in faithful service,

Miss Joanna Warrick.

Joanna looked over her own words again, and felt tears threatening to spill out from her eyes once more.

She hastily blotted the page and folded it nearly, writing Edmund's name on the front, so that she would not blur the words by crying upon them.

She pushed the letter to the middle of his desk, resting it where it would be easiest seen, and allowed the sobs to come over her then.

Oh, what a great despair it was, to have done everything in her power and now be forced to wait to learn what the outcome would be!

At any other time, she would have thought such a letter to be impertinent. Indeed, she should never have dared to express herself so. But this was a desperate time, and desperate measures had to be taken.

Since her position was lost anyway, what difference

could it make? Perhaps he would want her gone for her brazen self-expression, but at least she would have tried. And she had not gone so far as to confess her love. That would be enough.

Joanna rose from her chair at last, concerned that perhaps Edmund might return from his ride and find her still sitting there.

In a burnished glass above the mantlepiece, she caught sight of her own reflection. Her face was sullied by tears, red around the eyes and yet so wan and pale everywhere else.

She reached up to scrub away the marks and found her skin burning hot to the touch, so hot that she snatched her hands away in alarm.

No matter. It was no doubt a physical symptom of her emotional distress. She had still to light the fire, to scrub away the evidence of her first attempt at a letter – the one she should not have written.

Joanna turned to look for the fire lighting tools, and to find the irons with which to stoke and move the fire. They were there by the fireplace, but somehow also so far away that they seemed unreachable.

Swaying for balance, Joanna reached out and caught hold of the mantlepiece for support. The cool stone felt impossibly cold under her fingers, almost as if it would freeze her to death. And what was this feeling in her head, now, as if it were fit to burst?

Oh, she was being so silly. To get so worked up about such a thing! Governesses lost their positions all the time, she told herself. It was no reason to swoon like an embarrassed schoolgirl.

She had done all she could, and now she had to see to this one last duty.

Joanna made another effort, letting go of the mantlepiece and rubbing her forehead to try to remove some of the pain. It was so hot still, the skin seeming almost to give off waves of heat that she could feel from a distance away.

Almost without knowing that she was doing it, Joanna leaned forward and pressed her forehead against the stone of the mantlepiece, craving that coolness to seep into her skin.

It was like a jolt of lightning, the shock was so great. She cried out in spite of herself, feeling the cold meet the fierce heat of her head.

The headache evolved into something new, reacting to the temperature shift, and she began to see black circles before her eyes.

With a groan, Joanna pushed herself away from the stone once more and made to grab for the fire irons. Even though they seemed so close, her arms were not long enough, and they slipped further and further away.

She tried to push herself towards them but the room was moving in the wrong direction, and tilting up on itself besides.

The ceiling rose to greet her, and then Joanna felt a sharp crack across her shoulders, and then the black circles enveloped her gaze until she could see no more.

33

The sickness was come again upon the Hardwicke family.

When Joanna came to, she found herself in her own bed, tucked inside her chamber with the blankets wrapped tightly around her body.

She was dressed in only a shift, and yet the blazing fire in the room made it so warm that she could not bear to remain still.

She pushed her way out of the blankets, finding her arms surprisingly weak, and swung her body around to allow her feet to touch the floor. It was the coolest thing in the room, and she took pleasure from its touch, feeling beads of sweat move down her back.

"Oh, no, Miss, you've to stay tucked up!" Mary

exclaimed, dropping a bowl of water so rapidly onto Joanna's chair that it spilled over the sides.

"Mary?" Joanna managed, finding her throat dry and tight.

"Please, Miss, you're not well. Lay back down again, do. Please, Miss, or Jenkins will box my ear for it."

Joanna sighed. "Some water?" she asked.

Mary made for the large bowl, already with a rag halfway within it, and Joanna shook her head.

"No!" she called out, regretting the rough feeling in her throat. "To drink."

"Oh, of course," Mary said, tutting at herself and reaching for a jug on the dresser. "Here, Miss. Drink up."

Joanna accepted the cup of water gratefully and drank it down. "What happened?" she asked. Her throat felt better with the water inside it, but she was still groggy and sore.

"You came down with – with the sickness, Miss," Mary said quietly, as if it was news she did not want to share.

Joanna tried to meet her eyes, but the maid kept her head ducked down. "The sickness?"

"Yes, Miss," Mary said, tucking her hair behind her ears with a tremble of her lip. "Jenkins says your symptoms are the same as what took the Lord and Lady, before. Everyone is mighty frighted."

Joanna tried to stand, but found herself dizzy. "More water, please, Mary. Is everyone else alright?"

Mary poured her another cup, fidgeting on the spot. She couldn't seem to keep her feet still. "Jenkins said as I wasn't to tell you," she said.

"Tell me what?" Joanna demanded immediately, drinking the second cup of water and feeling her head clear just a little.

"Well," Mary said, twisting a strand of hair between her fingers awkwardly and glancing towards the door.

"Tell me this instant," Joanna said, drawing herself up with a strength that she did not feel.

"Yes, Miss. Um, it's Miss Patience and Miss Amy. They're sick too."

Joanna felt her stomach dropping out through her feet.

The two young girls, ill as well? Oh – and it was so cruel! To have them suffer the same illness that had killed their parents, and weakened their brother so much!

"Where are they?" Joanna asked.

She shuffled forwards to the end of her bed, casting about her. She found a day dress hanging on the back of her chair and reached for it, drawing it over to herself.

"They're in their own beds, Miss. Me and Jenkins and Cook is looking after them."

"Show me," Joanna said. She stepped into her skirt and began to draw it up over her body. "Help me put this on so that I can go to them."

Mary dithered a little more before giving in to the authoritative tone in Joanna's voice. She obviously felt that she was no match for her, and began fussing around her, helping her lace up the dress.

"Oh, Miss, you're burning so," she tutted, laying a hand on the back of Joanna's neck.

"It is nothing," Joanna said. "I must be through the worst of it by now. Take me to them at once, Mary, no more fussing now."

"Yes, Miss," Mary said meekly, leading her out of the room and only stopping to snatch up the bowl of water she had carried in in the first place.

They walked along the corridor, which was strangely quiet and subdued.

As they passed the top of the stairs down to the main hall, Joanna caught a glimpse of Samuel sitting glumly on a chair below.

He leapt to his feet when he saw them passing by. "Miss Warrick!" he exclaimed.

"I'm quite alright, Mr. Samuel," Joanna said, raising a hand to reassure him. "I go to tend your sisters."

"But Jenkins said…"

"I'm going to be fine, I promise you," Joanna insisted, forcing a smile.

She tried to keep her breathing controlled. Already she was fighting for air, after such a little exertion.

"Can I come with you?" Samuel asked, coming to the foot of the stairs.

"No, young master!" Mary exclaimed quickly. "Jenkins says he's to stay down there so as the sickness can't reach him again."

Joanna thought about it. "He's probably right," she said. "Mr. Samuel, don't come up. Please, listen to Jenkins. He wants to keep you safe."

"But I want to help!" Samuel whined.

"You are helping," Joanna told him, starting her walk along the corridor again so that he could not argue. "You're letting us worry about your sisters without having to tend you, too. Please. Wait for us to do our work."

He did not answer, but neither did he come up the stairs.

Joanna glimpsed him traipsing back to his chair as they passed further down the corridor and out of sight.

The wing in which the family kept their chambers was more inhabited. Jenkins and Cook were there, standing by Patience's door and conversing in low tones.

"Miss Warrick! You oughtn't be out of bed," Cook scolded, seeing them coming.

"I'm quite fine," Joanna said, approaching them. "Please, do not argue with me. I must help. How are the girls?"

"Deeply asleep," Jenkins reported, with a heavily furrowed brow. "We have not been able to wake them, and they burn. Are you really recovered?"

"I am here to serve, and serve I will," Joanna said sternly, giving him a level look which she hoped he would not argue with. "What needs to be done?"

Jenkins exchanged a look with both Cook and Mary, but at last sighed in surrender.

"We must keep the girls wrapped up tightly. I have been cooling their faces with water, and placing some drops on their lips so that they may at least drink. We keep the fires burning around the clock. It is the only way that they will survive."

Joanna nodded. "I will help. What of Lord Kelt? Or Lieutenant Hardwicke?"

"Gone," Jenkins said, twitching his mouth in displeasure. "My lord rode out yesterday and has not been seen since. The Lieutenant went out to search for him, hoping he has not taken ill as well."

Joanna's heart lurched. She had not thought, until that moment, that Edmund might be in danger. If he had ridden off because of her, only to fall from his horse, sick...! She could not forgive herself!

Joanna swayed a little, overcome by the sudden fear that he might not even be amongst the living.

"It has been a whole day already?"

"Miss Warrick, if you're not feeling well..." Jenkins began, but Joanna waved her hand.

"No, Jenkins, I'm fine. I'm just concerned. I hope the Lieutenant finds him soon."

Jenkins gave her a fatherly look which told her she was not the only one feeling concern, but she turned from him and went to check on the first of her charges.

The fever was raging so wildly in Patience's body that the whole room had a different smell when Joanna stepped inside.

She lay wrapped in blankets with her eyes closed, but she had not the peaceful expression of a sleeper. Rather, her forehead was creased with a frown, and she even moved fitfully every few moments.

Joanna knelt and touched her hand to Patience's brow, finding it hot to the touch.

She lifted a rag from the bowl beside the bed and started to sponge her face, soothing away the heat with the calming droplets of water.

Patience stirred slightly and even made a small groaning noise, but she did not open her eyes or attempt to make a more solid movement.

Joanna understood that she was still locked away deep within the fever, and whatever she saw or heard there, was the stuff of dreams.

Joanna stayed by her side for a long time, pausing in her ministrations only to occasionally apply the water to her own brow when she felt the heat getting too much for her.

She did not mind about the water dripping onto her

dress. She was already soaked through with sweat, a consequence of the fire being lit on a summer day.

Mary came as the evening began to draw in, bidding Joanna to take some rest and eat, but she instead moved to Amy's room where Jenkins was tending the young girl. She looked so frail and helpless that Joanna had to hold back a sob.

"Miss Warrick, have you eaten?" Jenkins asked, turning around to see her in the doorway.

Joanna shook her head wordlessly. She could not take her eyes from Amy's face.

Perhaps Jenkins understood that she would not have been persuaded to leave her by earth, wind, or fire. "Stay with Miss Amy a short while. I will bring you something."

Joanna stayed with Amy through the night, picking fitfully at the meat pie and pickled vegetables that Cook had served up.

It was a good pie – as always – but Joanna had no appetite. She watched nervously for every movement of Amy's small body, and each groan or whimper that issued from the child seemed to pierce right into her heart.

When the night had fully set in, the sound of hooves clattering across the stones outside the house made Joanna rise to her feet and peer down.

She could see nothing that would make out who was there – only the small glow of a lantern near the doorway, too far to reveal who dismounted from his horse.

Could it be Edmund? It had to be!

With one last check that Amy was unchanged, Joanna rushed out of the door. She clutched at the balustrade for support as she neared the stairs, watching the main hall to see who would enter.

"I'm afraid not," Christopher was saying, as he walked in, turning his head to Jenkins.

Next to Joanna, Mary rushed to her side. "Is it our lord?" she asked, breathlessly.

"I'm sorry to disappoint you," Christopher called up to them. For once, he seemed genuinely full of regret.

"I could not find him. I found no sign of his horse, either. Tomorrow I'll ride east. The driver will join the search on one of the spare horses, going north. If we do not find him then, it only leaves south."

Joanna found that she was gasping for breath, stricken by panic. She held a hand over her mouth to stop desperate cries from leaking out of it.

"They'll find him, Miss," Mary said, patting her shoulder. "They will. I know it. He won't stay from home too long."

"I only hope he is found – alive," Joanna said, retreating to Amy's side where she could cry without being seen by anyone awake.

The next day dawned the same.

Jenkins had forced Joanna to get some rest in the latter

part of the night, though she insisted in sleeping in Amy's room, setting up her own blankets on the floor.

When she woke, the stern butler demanded that she eat a full breakfast before she was allowed to return to her tasks.

"We cannot lose you as well, Miss Warrick," he said gruffly. "You know I will not force you to retire. Your help is appreciated. But you must look to your own self. If you are too unwell, you must allow us to tend you as well."

Joanna nodded in agreement, though privately she knew that she would do no such thing.

There were only four of them – Jenkins, Cook, Mary, and herself – to tend to the children as it was. If she should retire, then the others would be stretched so thin as not to be able to eat or sleep themselves. She could not leave them in this way.

Horse hooves woke Joanna late at night, as she dozed while Cook watched over Amy.

They were both on their feet in an instant, though Joanna found herself needing to hold onto the bedframe for support until the room stopped spinning.

They all gathered at the top of the stairs again, unwilling to go too far from the sick rooms but desperate to know what news came.

"Did you find him?" Samuel called from the doorway.

He stood shivering in the night air, still dressed as for day. He had been sleeping downstairs in the sitting room, and Joanna felt a pang at seeing him. He, too, must have been despairing for any kind of hope.

"No," Christopher said, his voice low and dull as he entered the house. "I'm sorry, Sam. Not today either."

"Why not?" Samuel demanded.

It was the kind of question only a boy would think to ask, but Christopher seemed to take it to heart. He closed his eyes for a moment.

"We looked as hard as we could. I pray that he has found shelter at some neighbour's home. We rode all day. I thrashed the horse so that we could go to the south as well, as far as we dared with the night coming in. We could not find any trace of him."

"You're giving up?" Samuel asked, dismayed.

Joanna felt her heart sink, too.

If they had searched in all directions and Edmund was not to be found, where was he? Could he have come to harm?

"I have to," Christopher said, sighing and rubbing a hand across his eyes.

"Listen, Sam. We'll hope and pray that Edmund went to visit someone. But for now I am needed here. I must help tend your sisters. We pray that Edmund will return tomorrow, unaware that anything has been happening."

"No," Samuel said, beginning to cry.

Christopher knelt down and embraced his younger

brother roughly, cradling Samuel's head against his shoulder.

As one, Joanna, Cook, and Jenkins moved away from the balustrade and back to the girls' rooms. They had no wish to impede upon a private moment.

The next day was different. Joanna woke a little past dawn to find not Cook, but Christopher sitting beside Amy's bed.

The bright flare of the sun through the window had her squinting her eyes, and she could barely make out his features for a long moment after awakening.

"Does she improve?" Joanna asked, raising her head hopefully.

"No," Christopher said, and sighed. "But she is no worse."

"That is mercy at least," Joanna said, joining him to reach out and touch Amy's forehead.

She was hot still, and showed no sign of cooling off despite the water they mopped her brow with day and night.

"The doctor refuses to visit us," Christopher said, sounding as if he were talking from a long distance away.

"He says we know how to treat the sickness, and it is too contagious to risk spreading it around the rest of the countryside. He bade us stay inside the house until it is passed, all of us. I did not tell him that we stayed out searching for Edmund."

"Was there really no sign?" Joanna asked. She harboured a small fear that perhaps Christopher had lied to save the others, when in truth Edmund's body had been discovered cold and lifeless in a ditch.

"None," Christopher shook his head. "I truly suspect he is with some friend. Though which friend, I wish I knew. I did not even know that Edmund had any."

"That is cruel," Joanna said, before she thought to stop herself. "He has much responsibility."

"You are right," Christopher said, glancing at her. He looked at Amy, then back at Joanna, more closely this time. "Are you feeling well, yourself?"

"I am fine," Joanna said, batting his concern away. "It's just a little too warm."

"You look as though you may be coming down with the sickness," Christopher said, reaching out to touch her forehead.

Joanna dodged backwards, out of his range. "I already have it," she said, quietly.

Christopher started. "What? You mean to say…"

"I think I may even have been the first," she said. "I fainted after Edmund left."

"Why do you not rest?" Christopher admonished. "You could be making yourself worse. You should get to bed!"

"I cannot," Joanna said. "The children."

"The children need a living governess," Christopher told her fiercely.

"There are so few of us to tend them," Joanna protested.

"I am not leaving their side," Christopher said. "I cannot lose both my parents and my sisters too. I will not allow it. Wherever Edmund is, damn him, he will need to stay there or return on his own steam. The coach driver aids us with carrying water and letting us sleep in shifts. We are enough, now."

"I am strong enough," Joanna said. "Please. Let me stay."

Christopher eyed her crossly. "You're a stubborn woman, Miss Warrick," he said. "I find myself rather glad not to have to battle you on a marital field."

"You have had a lucky escape, Lieutenant," Joanna said, giving him a weak smile.

"Then at least fetch us some breakfast. I will wait with Amy. Cook is preparing trays for us all."

"I will," Joanna said, rising to her feet.

She stepped towards the centre of the room, but the fireplace was so hot that she had to stagger back from it.

"Are you sure you are well?" Christopher asked, watching her. His words seemed to come to her as if from the other end of a tunnel. "Miss Warrick, you are dripping with sweat."

"It is nothing," Joanna said, moving onwards again

towards the door. She was determined to show him that he was wrong, that she could manage.

The thing of it was that the door was moving further away from her no matter how hard she tried to chase it, and before she knew it, there was no door before her at all – only a familiar blackness which, at last, allowed her the chance to feel a cool touch on her skin.

34

Edmund knew that he was possibly being childish.

It had been a few days since he rode away from the house, and he had left no word of his plans. Indeed, he had not known them himself when he set off.

It was pure chance that threw him in the direction of the Haverham estate. He had not even known he would go there until his horse snorted and blew at the sight of a herd of deer roaming within a fence, and then he was hailed by Lord Haverham himself.

It was growing dark already by the time he was drawn in for a brandy in the sitting room, and then they would not hear of him riding home through the night.

They insisted that he should stay with them and rest, rather than risk his stallion turning a hoof in the dark and ending up lame – or worse. Besides which, a storm had begun to blow, and the wind was hammering mightily at the windows.

Lord Haverham, in particular, was keen indeed to make Edmund's acquaintance more closely.

Edmund soon came to realise that the motive lay in his third son, Edward, the red-headed lad who had seen fit to dance with Patience at the ball. It seemed that he wanted more than dancing, and was seeking to court Patience in the next season.

At first the idea was strange to Edmund: he had been given to thinking, all the while that he was growing up, that Patience and Amy would marry well. Very well, in fact. Particularly Patience, who was to be the first daughter married off, and would thus no doubt get a large dowry.

But, of course, things had shifted and changed when his father died. Now he, Edmund, was the Earl, not his father; and subsequently, Patience was no longer the daughter of an Earl, but rather sister to one.

Put in that context, he soon came to see that the third son of a well-respected lord was not as badly matched as he had first thought.

Edmund had intended to ride away on the next morning, to return home – hoping that he would find Miss Warrick already abandoned her position, and perhaps even gone away to stay with relatives until she could be married to Christopher.

That was his intention, but it was not to be granted by Lady Haverham, who had designs on his time already.

She insisted that he join the family for a lengthy stroll around their grounds and a discussion of the neighbouring estate, which they also owned.

Since their second son was set to join the priesthood, Edmund took it to be their intimation that this might be Patience's future home if she were to marry their third.

He dined with them that night, having worked up a great appetite from their exertion, which had taken them right to the far-flung reaches of the Haverham estate.

The next day he felt at ease, revelling in the unexpected and unaccustomed feeling of having nothing at all to do. Still, by the time the afternoon came around, he was growing tired of it. He had been a busy man for too long already to be able to rest for long.

"Now, then, I thank you greatly for your hospitality, Lady Haverham," Edmund said. "However, I ought really to be returning home. They should be expecting me there."

"Oh, but my dear Lord Kelt!" Lady Haverham exclaimed, her delicately freckled features falling into a mask of dismay. "You were to be our guest of honour at tonight's dinner. Do say you will stay – I have asked our kitchen to prepare something special."

Edmund shot a glance towards the horizon, over which his home lay.

There was work to be done, surely, and he had no

doubt that there might be some gossip about where he had gone.

But he was due a day off, wasn't he? More than that. He had ever been the studious son, right up until the moment when he was forced to be the responsible man of the house.

They would survive without him one more day – all of them would. He hired men for this very purpose, to keep the office ticking over.

And he had a staff who were quite capable – not to mention that Christopher was at home, and it would do him good to assume some responsibility for once.

All things considered, there was nothing he could possibly stand to lose by having dinner with the Haverhams.

Besides, if they were truly serious about making a pitch for Patience's hand, he felt he ought to spend more time with this Edward, and find out what he was all about.

The next step after this would be inviting the young lad and perhaps a few of his siblings or friends to visit Hardwicke Hall. In that sense, it was perhaps essential that Edmund get the measure of him – and decide whether it was better that Christopher be home or away at the time the guests arrived.

"Do you suppose you will go abroad this summer, Lord Kelt?" Lady Haverham asked at the table, clearly trying to get a handle on his social calendar.

"No, Lady Haverham," Edmund replied, with some amusement. "Did you hear that I had injured my arm? Some short months ago, I had a fall from my horse."

"Nothing serious, I hope," Lord Haverham mumbled.

Edmund felt sure that he would have heard through their business connections, but he explained all the same.

"A break," he said. "I am only just out of the sling. Thus, any social plans we had made were quite put off for some time, and I was even kept away from the office. I must make up the time, so there will be no travel for us."

"Your youngest brother, Mr. Samuel – I hear he is not at school," the elder Haverham son piped up, earning a stern look from his mother.

"That is not your business, Henry," she warned.

"It is quite alright," Edmund said, shaking his head. "Samuel learns from our governess. He was laid quite low by the sickness that took our parents and is still yet to fully recover. He is most eager to rejoin his classmates, however."

"I heard rumour that the sickness is back in the county again," Edward said, sipping from his glass. "They were talking of it at the ball last week. A neighbour of ours has not been seen for weeks, and a messenger dispatched there found the house shut in quarantine."

Edmund started in his chair. Could it really be true?

"Which neighbour?" he asked quickly, setting down his own glass to focus on the young man.

"I'm not sure," Edward shrugged sheepishly. "I do apologise. I was not paying full attention. To the west, I think. Whoever is renting Mossford Park this year."

"How ghastly," Lady Haverham said with a shudder. "I do not know if this is an appropriate topic for the dinner table."

"Sorry, Mother," the boy said, pushing a half-cut carrot around his plate so as to avoid meeting her gaze.

"I think I should go back to my own hall," Edmund said, feeling a growing sense of uneasiness.

Perhaps the rumour was only a rumour, but it had reminded him of one thing very clearly: what was important to him.

And that was his family, above all else. He should be with them.

"In the morning, surely, dear Lord Kelt," Lady Haverham said. "You mustn't ride this late. It should be full dark before you were even out of our gates."

"My lady is quite right," Lord Haverham said, his voice low and rumbling. "We'll set you loose with some provisions tomorrow, so that you don't get hungry on the journey."

"I thank you for that," Edmund said, inclining his head.

The delay made his feet itch, but they were right. It was foolhardy to ride this late into the evening. There was enough distance between here and his home that it would be gone midnight when he arrived, and without the lanterns of the carriage to light the way, it would be treacherous going.

He had little appetite left, however. The reminder of his family's great tragedy had seen to that.

He made his excuses and left the room, retiring to the guest chamber the Haverhams had been kind enough to prepare for him.

He could not have imagined that the feeling of dread creeping across his scalp was real enough, or that it was inspired by a cause that should have had him flying through the night if he had known the truth of it.

"Ah! Lord Kelt," Lord Haverham exclaimed the next morning, as Edmund tried to make quick his escape.

"Lord Haverham," Edmund responded, turning on his heel ruefully to face his host. "What luck that we have stumbled on one another. I was just preparing myself to depart."

"Oh, come, sit with me a while," Lord Haverham said. "I wanted to go over a few things with you concerning the business."

"Really, I wanted to return soon. My family must be worried about my whereabouts," Edmund tried, giving the other man what he hoped was an apologetic smile.

"Nonsense, they can wait a few hours longer," Lord Haverham insisted. "I have a proposal that I think you will be very interested in. What with my lady wife's long walks, we have not had quite enough time yet to discuss deals which might benefit both of our families."

Edmund hesitated.

Of course, he wanted to return home - that was completely true. But the other man might offer him something lucrative, particularly since he seemed interested in forging a deeper bond between their two households.

It wouldn't make sense for him to argue a deal that might disadvantage his future daughter-in-law's fortune, after all.

Edmund nodded at last, regretful that he could not slip away, but knowing an opportunity when he saw one.

"Alright. Lead on, Lord Haverham."

What followed was a lengthy discussion on the merits of trade in the Indies, and of particular types of sailing vessel - and it bored Edmund thoroughly.

By the time that the man had finally got around to his point, the sun had risen almost to noon already.

"Now, then," Lord Haverham said, expectantly, leaning forward in his chair. "What say you, Lord Kelt?"

Edmund blinked at him for a moment. He had quite drifted away during the last few minutes of his speech.

"Go through it for me again," he said, trying to appear as though he was thinking the deal over rather than that he had missed it entirely.

Once repeated, the deal was incredibly fair – more than

fair, in fact. It would allow Edmund to make a healthy profit, and would benefit him for some seasons to come.

"I think it sounds agreeable, Lord Haverham," Edmund said, nodding his head. "I'll ask the office to draw up a contract, to be signed by both of us anon. Then we shall begin shipping."

"Then let us seal it with a handshake," Lord Haverham said, holding out his arm.

He clasped Edmund's elbow with his opposing hand when they shook, and gave him a sly wink. "And may this not be the last of the deals that links the Haverhams and the Hardwickes."

"Indeed," Edmund agreed, careful to say no more.

There was much to consider, and agreeing to a betrothal now – without Patience's consideration – would be more than foolhardy. He knew the rages that his sister could exhibit and had no wish to be on the receiving end of one, particularly not after absenting himself from the house for several days.

It was late afternoon by the time he was finally in sight of Hardwicke Hall, nestled on top of the hill on the horizon.

He urged his stallion on at the sight of it, not fully realising until then how heartsick he had been at staying away from home.

When he reached the grounds and headed for the stables, he was more than surprised not to be met by his driver. Nor was there any sign of Jenkins to be had, though all the other horses were quietly stabled.

Where was everyone?

Edmund put the stallion away himself, and headed for the house, ready to give his servants a piece of his mind towards their dereliction of duty.

35

"Hello?" Edmund called out, looking around the eerily quiet main hall of his home.

There was hardly a noise – it was as if the entire place had been deserted in his absence.

"Edmund?"

He turned to see Samuel standing at the far end of the corridor, looking anxiously towards him.

"Samuel, what is going on?" he asked.

He received no answer. Instead, Samuel charged right at him all of a sudden, running as fast as his thin legs could carry him.

He knocked Edmund's wind out as he tackled him, throwing his arms around his waist and holding on tightly.

"What ever is the matter?" Edmund asked, completely bemused.

His arms encircled Samuel's body by habit, and he was surprised to find that the boy was shaking.

"We thought you were dead," Samuel said, and Edmund realised that the shaking came from sobs that wracked his body.

"Now then," Edmund said gently, extracting himself from Samuel's arms so that he could lift the boy's chin and look him in the face. "I was only gone for a couple of days. What's all this fuss about?"

"We thought you might have fallen from your horse," Samuel said tearfully. "Christopher looked for you for two days. He couldn't find any trace of you."

"Christopher did?" Edmund said, raising his eyebrows. "But there was nothing to fear. I stayed with the Haverhams, that is all. They were most hospitable."

"But we thought you were sick, too," Samuel whimpered, drawing his sleeve across his face.

So, the rumours of the sickness had reached this far already?

Edmund wondered who could have brought the news. The driver, perhaps, or Christopher returning from a jaunt in town. "No one's sick, Sammy. It's just a rumour."

"They are!" Samuel cried, his voice rising in pitch. "Patience and Amy and Miss Warrick – they are!"

Edmund stared at him, straightening his back. "What?"

"They're sick, all of them. Like Mama and Papa all over again. They made me stay down here so I won't catch it this time," Samuel sniffed. His face was the picture of misery.

"Stay here, Samuel," Edmund said, tearing away from him and starting towards the stairs at a run.

"But, Edmund!" Samuel called after him.

"Stay there!" Edmund repeated, shouting it over his shoulder as he took the stairs two at a time.

He burst into Patience's room first, the first door he came to.

Cook was there with Jenkins, and both of them looked up wearily as he entered.

"My lord," Jenkins gasped. "We had all but given up hope. We prayed for your return."

Edmund took in their stricken faces, and then strode past them to sink to the floor at Patience's side.

Her face was red and slick with sweat and water, and she moved slightly in her sleep, twitching and frowning.

"How long has it been?" Edmund asked, finding his voice suddenly raw.

"We found them the afternoon you left, my lord. Miss Amy fainted while playing a game with the children, and Miss Patience not long after. It was not until we went to fetch Miss Warrick for her aid that we discovered she, too, had fainted. She was lying on the floor of your study."

Edmund covered his face for a moment, almost overcome.

It had been the very hour in which he left! He had

turned and fled the house in the hour of his family's need, and jollied along with the Haverhams while they lay here dying!

"There has been no change since then?" Edmund managed, reaching for Patience's hand where it lay on the covers.

"No, my lord, the girls remain the same," Jenkins said.

He sounded tired. The worry must have been driving him half out of his mind.

"Miss Warrick rallied admirably and helped us with their care. I fear she pushed herself too far, but she would not be dissuaded. It was not until this morning that she fell into a faint again."

Edmund turned on him. "You let her tend them while she was herself sick?" he asked.

"My lord, she could not be stopped," Cook said, gently.

She tucked her chin down into her neck when Edmund looked in her direction. She was not used to speaking directly with him, and he had no doubt that his gaze was a terrifying one at that moment.

"She cares deeply for the children. She would not hear of any suggestion that she should leave them."

"Where is she now?" Edmund asked.

"With Miss Amy," Jenkins said, gesturing towards Amy's chamber.

Edmund leaned over and kissed Patience's forehead

tenderly, stroking her hand before placing it back on the covers.

"Just as well," he said. "I will visit them next."

He stood and walked the short distance along the corridor, Jenkins trailing quietly at his heels.

In Amy's room was a sight of fresh despair: the tiny, frail body looking apt to drown in a sea of blankets, still in much the same state as her sister.

Christopher sat in a chair beside the bed, sponging a wet cloth across her brow.

He wore dark circles under his eyes, and his uniform looked to have seen better days. He even had a few days' growth of stubble on his chin, light as it was, and his hair was half pulled out of the low ponytail he kept it in customarily.

"Brother," he said, with an expression of clear relief.

"I am sorry," Edmund said immediately, quite overcome at the thought he had been absent for all of this trouble.

He could see that what Samuel had said was true: Christopher's clothes looked travelled in, and he was obviously worse for wear.

"You are alive," Christopher said, shaking his head as he got to his feet. "You don't know how much of a gift that is."

The two men embraced, without any of the awkwardness or bitterness that normally accompanied their exchanges.

Edmund felt the tight grip of a man who thought another family member lost, and experienced great shame.

How he had drunk and feasted and laughed with the Haverhams! How he had engaged in their trifling pastimes and pleasantries!

"I didn't know," he said, gruffly, and Christopher sat down again with a sad smile.

"It is forgotten," he said. "I am truly happy to see you whole. If it were not for the fact that our sisters remain in danger, I would toast you with a drink."

"I do not doubt that," Edmund said wryly.

He leaned over to touch Amy's forehead, feeling her hot to the touch.

He was already wracked with helplessness. He wanted so desperately to take some kind of decisive action that would keep his sisters safe, but he knew that there was none. It was only a matter of time, and waiting.

He turned, then, and allowed himself at last to observe Miss Warrick, laying on a cot by the door with more blankets piled around her.

The room was stiflingly hot, and there was a heavy, cloying smell over everything. She looked as though she could not possibly be in need of covers, but Edmund knew it was necessary to sweat out the fever.

"She fell, this morning," Christopher said. "I tried to convince her to take some rest, but she would not. She has not woken since."

Edmund knelt at her side on the wooden floor, and felt her temperature. "She's so hot. You have been wetting her forehead?"

"Yes, brother," Christopher sighed. "Both of them. It seems to make no difference. They still frown and struggle so."

"What of Mary? And the driver? Do they assist?"

"Yes, both of them. They are sleeping now. We take shifts. We will be glad of your joining us. Someone must relieve Cook or we won't eat."

Edmund had not taken his eyes off Miss Warrick.

Even flushed, and with her hair pressed tightly onto her head with sweat, she was a beauty. The fact she had cared so for the children only increased her charm.

"I must go for a moment," he said, getting up abruptly. He could not bear to look at her anymore. "I have something to do. When I return, I will relieve Cook. I trust I can leave them in your capable hands."

"And mine, my lord," Jenkins murmured, stepping out of his way with a reassuring nod as he headed for the door.

Edmund clutched at the bannister above the hall, gasping for breath.

How could this have taken place? The sickness, come to Hardwicke Hall again!

He closed his eyes to prevent the tears from squeezing through them.

To see Patience and Amy laid low was terrible, an agony

that he never thought he would have to endure. And to see Miss Warrick struck similarly, and be unable to reach out and hold her as he longed to...

It was beyond his grasp, however. Christopher was there, and he would look after his betrothed, as was his duty. Why he still did not admit to it and end the silly charade, Edmund could not say, but it was undoubtedly a time of suffering.

Perhaps he did not want to bring false happy news, given that the outcome was far from assured.

Edmund tried to get control of his emotions, fighting a mighty battle within himself to remain composed.

At last he struck the balustrade with an open hand and marched away to his study, thinking that he might find some quiet there away from the smell of sickness and the crackling of the fires.

The room was cold, and a fine layer of dust was illuminated on the sill by the window. He supposed that not a single person had stepped inside since Miss Warrick was discovered there.

Damn it all! Why had it not happened a day later? She might have been far from here, and safe, when the sickness struck!

What was this, on his desk?

Edmund saw his own name scrawled on a piece of folded parchment and reached for it, puzzled. How long had that lain there...?

He opened it, and saw his own name written again in Miss Warrick's hand like a bolt through the chest.

What message had she left for him, before swooning into what could possibly now be her deathbed?

Though he read it through five times, he could barely make sense of it. The words towards the bottom were scrawled in an increasingly untidy hand, as though Miss Warrick had been unable to control her pen, but he could read them clearly all the same.

It was their meaning that was alien to him.

He had got it all wrong. All of it.

Edmund rushed along the corridor then, and back into the room where Christopher still watched anxiously over Amy's laboured breathing.

"You are not betrothed?" Edmund demanded.

"What?"

Christopher looked as if he might have asked him whether he was a purple pig, or if the sky were made of bread.

"You!" Edmund said exasperatedly, pointing first at Christopher and then at Miss Warrick with exaggerated movements. "You are not betrothed?"

Christopher looked at him blankly for a moment before an understanding cleared his face. "I am not, brother," he said. "Please, allow me to explain."

"I thought you were betrothed," Edmund breathed.

"I see that. It must have been a misunderstanding. In

fact, I did make an ill-timed and ill-considered proposal to Miss Warrick. She had the far better sense to turn me down. It was a rather embarrassing incident, Edmund, and one I did not wish to share."

"I sent her away," Edmund said, dimly.

"Pardon?"

"I thought you were betrothed, so I sent her away," he said, feeling an utter misery at what a cad he had been. "I told her to leave us and then I rode away."

"Oh, Edmund," Christopher said, giving him a look of disapproval that he had never before had reason to wear. "You could have asked me. There was nothing between us. Not even for that moment. It was a silly mistake."

Edmund stared at him, and at the prone Miss Warrick again, and then left the room as sharply as he had entered it.

He returned to his study and placed the letter on his desk, pacing around it as if it were able to give him the resolution he required.

Damn it all, he had endangered the poor woman's life. She had clearly been distressed when she wrote the letter, and wanted so desperately to prove her value to the family that she had ignored her own health in favour of the children.

What kind of a monster was he, to make such an accusation without proving it first?

Edmund sunk into his chair, holding his head in his hands.

This was all a giant mess, and he was a giant fool. There was no other way of looking at it.

He realised he had been staring absently at the fireplace for some time when he at last noticed that it was not only wood waiting to be burned there. He had not used it for some time, since the summer had set in, and he could not remember throwing anything in himself.

Yet there, scattered amongst the logs, were a few scraps of parchment.

Edmund roused himself and leaned over to pick them up, finding them scattered in a number of places as if they had been dropped in carelessly.

They were torn as well as scrunched up, and as he began to straighten them back out, he caught Miss Warrick's hand.

How curious – it seemed to be an earlier draft of his letter. He laid them out on the desk, quickly fitting them together, and then –

Could it be?

I am not betrothed to Lieutenant Christopher, nor could I ever be, she had written. *I am in love only with yo-*

Could this truly be some form of confession?

Edmund stared at the words on the page, trying to find another way in which they fit together.

I am in love only with your family, perhaps, an expression of motherly affections rather than romantic ones.

Or, I am in love only with youth! An expression of vanity!

Tenuous, it seemed, and Edmund could not figure out what other meaning there could possibly be than an admission of affection for himself.

But he had jumped to conclusions about Miss Warrick's affections before, and that had gone just about as badly as was possible.

No, he wouldn't read anything into this. Not yet.

He carefully screwed up each piece of parchment again and placed them inside the fireplace, not truly sure of why he did it.

Even as he tried to hold it down, flames of a different kind were already taking over his heart – of hope, that perhaps his feelings might after all be reciprocated.

Edmund returned to Patience's room with a renewed vigour and determination.

Whatever the case may be, one thing was certain: all was not lost. Not yet. Patience, Amy, and Miss Warrick might all still be saved.

And if she was, then she had no reason to leave them, given that she was not at all betrothed.

He paused at the doorway. "Cook, I'm to relieve you," he said.

"Oh, my lord," Cook said, scrambling to her feet from

where she sat by the bed. "She improves. See how she improves. She is no longer so hot."

"Truly?" Edmund asked.

He rushed forward and laid a hand on Patience's forehead, feeling it considerably cooler than before. She did not groan or twitch at his touch, either.

"Do you think she is through the worst of it?" Edmund asked quickly.

"You are as good a judge as I, my lord. You remember the first time."

"It was much like this," Edmund said. His heart was hammering fast as he took the chair, grasping Patience's hand. "Samuel recovered slowly, but he cooled after a week or so. This has only been a few days, no? She may recover completely."

"Oh, I pray for it," Cook said excitedly, clasping her hands tightly in front of her. "Please, God, let it be true! I will pray for it!"

"We'll need provisions," Edmund instructed her. "For the rest of the household as well as the girls, if they should wait. Perhaps a simple broth that they can try when they awake."

"Yes, my lord, oh yes, I will make it at once," Cook said, fair running out of the room in her haste to serve.

36

She dreamed that she was on board a ship, in the sea.

When she turned to look at where they had come from, she realised it was only the lake at Hardwicke Hall.

Their ship was not a ship at all, but rather a small boat, and the sun was beating down mercilessly over everything.

"I am so hot," she murmured crossly, tugging at the sleeve of her winter dress and wishing she had not worn quite so many petticoats.

"Take them off then," Christopher said lazily, sunning himself on the deck.

Joanna tutted. "That would not be becoming of a lady," she said.

"Suit yourself," Christopher replied, and dived off the boat and into the lake in one smooth motion.

All at once, the sky darkened, and storm clouds began to gather above the lake.

A flash of lightning hit the surface of the water, and Joanna screamed.

The boat rocked from side to side in the onslaught of waves, pushing her around in the middle of the lake. She took up an oar and tried to row, but succeeded only in turning in a circle.

"I am lost!" she cried out, seeing the waves rising up to meet the boat. "Somebody, help me!"

"This way, Miss Warrick," Edmund said, calling to her from the shore. He held a rope in his hand, and slowly pulled her in towards the shore. "Gently does it. That's it."

Joanna wept as the boat sunk into the soft sand at the shore, and she took Edmund's hand as he helped her down. "I thought I was lost," she said.

"You're home now," Edmund told her, his grip firm on her hand. "Don't worry. We're all here to look after you."

Joanna looked up to a bright sky. The sunshine was bearing down on her again, and it was so hot, so hot.

"Drink some of this," Edmund said, holding up a handful of stagnant water from the lake. "It will cool you down."

"I can't drink that," Joanna balked, stepping backwards.

"But it's needed for the baby," Edmund insisted, pouring it down her throat and spilling it down her neck.

Joanna looked down to see her belly rising round and

swollen, and felt the kick from inside. "I must protect the baby," she said.

"He is coming early," Edmund told her, squeezing her hand again. "You must come home to us now."

"But how should I get there?" Joanna asked desperately, looking back at the house.

It was so far away, and all the distance between here and there was scorched and dry under the burning sun.

Something was wrong. There was such a delay in each answer that she sought. It was as though she were trapped in one space, and they in another. Though they touched her, she knew somehow that they must be far apart.

"Run!" Christopher shouted, coming up on her left side, and Edmund held her fast on her right, and they all ran together with as much speed as they could muster, until everything around was only a blur and in the distance there was only one tiny speck of light.

37

"That's it, dear girl," Edmund murmured quietly. "Drink up. We'll get you out of this room in a moment and downstairs. You could do with some fresh air."

"I can't bear to be here a moment longer," Patience said, her voice dry and brittle from her sickness. "Where is Samuel? Was he affected?"

"No, we bade him wait downstairs," Edmund said. "I couldn't risk him catching it again. He's been beside himself. He'll be very pleased to see you up and about again."

"Don't push yourself too far, Miss Patience," Cook clucked disapprovingly. "We don't want you falling ill again. Just take your time."

"She's right," Edmund smiled. He never thought that

Cook could be so forthright, but she was a fierce mother bear when it came to the welfare of the children.

"I'll be careful," Patience said. "I'd like to bathe, at least."

"We can arrange that," Cook said. "If Lord Kelt leaves us be for a while."

Edmund took the hint and stood up. "I'll check in on you later," he promised.

"Don't look for me here," Patience said. "I'll be down with Samuel."

"Edmund?" A breathless Christopher appeared in the doorway. "Come, quickly. I think Amy is starting to wake."

Edmund hurried after him.

In Amy's room, Jenkins was hovering anxiously over the bed, while Mary watched from Miss Warrick's side.

"Does she stir?" Edmund demanded, moving closer.

"Little by little," Jenkins said, not taking his eyes from Amy's face.

Christopher and Edmund joined him on either side of the bed, kneeling down and each taking one of her little hands in their own.

Amy made a face, and stirred a little. She made a dry, croaking noise in the back of her throat. She was no longer hot to the touch.

"Papa?" she said, her voice cracking and breaking off into a whine.

Edmund and Christopher exchanged a glance. "I'm here, sweetling," he said. "It's me, your brother Edmund."

"And Christopher, too," Christopher put in, not to be outdone.

Amy's eyes slowly fluttered open. "My throat hurts," she said.

Jenkins rushed her a cup of water, and quickly held it to her lips so that she could drink.

"Good girl, that's it," Edmund said, supporting the back of her neck so that she would not choke.

"Can you sit up?" Christopher asked.

Amy groaned a couple of times in the back of her throat, but she did it, shuffling herself back so that she could rest against the pillows.

"Well done, brave girl," Edmund breathed. "You're doing so well."

"It's too hot in here," Amy complained groggily, pushing the blankets away from her.

Edmund hesitated, and glanced at Miss Warrick. She was still insensible. In Patience's room they had extinguished the fire completely, but it was not possible while one still lingered in the grasp of the sickness.

"Would you like to go downstairs?" Edmund asked.

Amy nodded silently, pushing the back of her hands across her face to clear the sticky hair away where it had become plastered down over her forehead.

Christopher reached out his hands, and to Edmund's

surprise, Amy climbed into them without a moment's thought.

She allowed him to lead her from the room with her small hand clasped in his, and Edmund was left alone with Jenkins and Miss Warrick.

"Do you think she would be more comfortable in her own chamber, Jenkins?" Edmund asked. "Now that Amy is awake, we've no reason to keep her in here."

"Forgive me, my lord, but the servants' quarters are more... sparsely furnished," Jenkins said, dipping his head. "Not that we make any kind of complaint, of course. That is as it should be."

Edmund grimaced. "You're right. I suppose, though it may be her chamber, it is not really her home. She would be more comforted to wake up on her own estate, though I gather that is sold some time ago."

He sighed, taking hold of Miss Warrick's hand and squeezing it.

"It is most difficult, my lord," Jenkins agreed.

Edmund was hit with a flash of inspiration. "What if we moved her to my chamber?" he asked. "I can sleep elsewhere for now. She would be most comfortable there. After what she has done for the children, it is the least I can offer."

"As you see fit, my lord," Jenkins nodded, but Edmund could see from the gleam in his eyes that he approved.

"Mary, see to it that the room is prepared," Edmund

said. "I want the fire nice and hot before we move her. Then we can start cleaning up in here."

"Yes, my lord," Mary agreed, quickly scrambling out of the door.

Within a short matter of time, they were ready to move her. Christopher had taken to supervising Amy and Patience downstairs, and Cook was readying a dinner for them all, but Jenkins and the coach driver stood by, ready to assist as Edmund prepared to move Miss Warrick.

Suggestions had been made, but in the end, the only sensible way he could think of to move her was to carry her from the room himself.

It made sure that she would not be dropped, and also allowed the quickest possible move from one place to another. Edmund was concerned that even being away from the fire for a short time might set her back, but sleeping on a cot on the floor was no way to heal either.

Miss Warrick began to move, as if trying to escape, and to groan as soon as he touched her. Undeterred, he lifted her up into his arms, wrapped in layers of blankets still so that she would remain comfortable.

"This way, Miss Warrick," Edmund said, talking to her as if she were awake. "Gently does it. That's it."

She seemed to quiet a little, and at last he was able to lay her down in her new bed, and she seemed to calm completely.

Throughout it all her eyes remained closed, and

Edmund feared that she had suffered more deeply from the fever than Amy or Patience.

"You're home now," Edmund told her, taking up a firm grip on her hand once more. "Don't worry. We're all here to look after you."

He hoped that his words might reach her in some way, and give her some small kind of comfort. Even if that was all he could do – and heaven forbid that that were the case – it would be a small something.

She did not deserve to go from this world thinking him angry with her, and that her position had been lost.

He would have begged her, paid her double, and given her as much as she wanted on top of that if she would return to being a governess now.

If only she would wake and rise from the bed to return to her duties, he would give her the world.

Edmund dined beside her in a comfortable chair, watching her every move and adjusting her pillows or dabbing her face with cool water when it seemed necessary.

The room was sweltering, but he did not mind. He would have endured a hundred times worse.

"Should I make up another room for you, my lord?" Mary asked, coming to take his empty dishes away late in the evening.

"No. I'll stay here," Edmund said. "Mary, have someone come to join me in a few hours, will you? I don't want to risk falling asleep and leaving her alone. Anyone, so long as it isn't Jenkins. The old man needs some sleep, himself."

"Yes, my lord," Mary said, dipping a curtsey as she left.

Miss Warrick stirred a little and moaned again, and Edmund stood to press a cup of water to her lips.

"Drink some of this," Edmund said, still talking to her even if he did not know why.

She twisted her head away slowly, and he held the base of her neck to prop her up more easily. "It will cool you down."

She did not drink, exactly, but the water entered her mouth; and so, satisfied with this, Edmund returned to his chair, resuming his watchful duty.

When he woke in the morning of the third day since his return, the sun was streaming through the windows again.

Mary set aside some embroidery she had been working on clumsily through the night, by the light of the candle, and started to fuss around him, as had been the routine while he watched over Miss Warrick.

"Any change?" he asked, leaning over to touch Miss Warrick's forehead and finding it still hot.

His back complained at the motion, having been ensconced in the chair all night, but he ignored it.

"No change, my lord," Mary said regretfully. "She burns still."

Edmund sighed. "Thank you, Mary. You may take your rest now. I will watch over her."

"Yes, my lord. Cook says she'll serve breakfast anon and bring you up a tray."

Edmund nodded absently as she left. He was thinking about his parents, and Samuel, and their experiences with the sickness.

He knew that it did not take long for the damage done to become long-lasting. Samuel had burned longer than this, and lost all of his strength.

Patience and Amy seemed well enough now that they were through it, which must mean that they recovered early enough to avoid further troubles.

And that, in turn, meant that Miss Warrick may only have a short window in which she would need to wake up – or worse would come.

He took hold of her hand, stroking her soft skin, feeling the limp flesh and how it did not respond at all to his touch.

How he wished that she would move, even a little, even if just to fit her small fingers into his and hold his hand in return. He squeezed, but nothing happened.

"Miss Warrick, it's time to wake up," Edmund told her, squeezing her hand again. "You must come home to us now."

Miss Warrick groaned, and Edmund leaned closer, hoping that his words were having some effect.

"You pushed yourself too hard," he said. "But I am not angry. We all need you here, Miss Warrick. You are of great importance to us. Please, now. You must find some strength to return to us."

There was the sound of a throat cleared in the doorway, and Edmund looked over to see Cook standing there.

"Breakfast, my lord," she said, not meeting his eyes.

"Thank you, Cook," Edmund said gruffly, feeling his own cheeks burn a little. He had not thought that he would be overheard. "Set it down on the dresser, here."

Cook did as she was bidden, and then withdrew to the hall again. "I think she will recover, my lord," she said hesitantly, pausing and looking back.

"You are confident in that?" Edmund asked, raising his eyebrows.

"I feel it," Cook said. "She's a strong young woman. She won't abandon us."

"Thank you," Edmund said again, and meant it.

With Cook's departure, they were alone again.

Edmund thought of picking up a book to read or even stepping to look out of the window, but he might have missed something: a flicker of movement, a groan, an essential moment in which Miss Warrick's brow needed to be mopped.

He applied some cool water to her face again, noting how small twitches brought her closer to the source of the water when he did so. She was in there, somewhere. He knew it.

The food grew cold beside him, and Jenkins gave him a

disapproving look when he came to replace it with some cold luncheon meats.

"My lord, you must eat," he said. "I beseech you. We cannot have any more illness in this house."

Edmund took his point, though he wondered when the man had decided it was acceptable to offer orders to his master instead of the other way around.

"I will," he promised. "Are the rest of you well-rested? Your service has been much appreciated these few days. I know you have sacrificed your own sleep and time."

"We are, thank you, my lord," Jenkins nodded. "Slowly, we begin a return to normality."

"Almost," Edmund said, casting a sad gaze back to Miss Warrick.

He started from his chair, then, and grasped up a cup of water, for her eyes were fluttering and she was moving her head.

"Miss Warrick?" he said, slipping a hand behind her head to support her neck. "Are you with us?"

Miss Warrick groaned, and her eyes opened fully, though she did not yet speak. She seemed unable to handle even the light of the chamber, and squinted around like a kitten.

"Here, drink this," Edmund urged, putting the cup to her lips.

He knew from experience that the thirst was great upon

waking from the sickness, and that water was an essential need.

She drank slowly, and even managed to raise her head a little more under her own power before sinking back onto the pillow.

"How long?" she croaked out, focusing on Edmund at last.

"It has been three days since you swooned again," Edmund said. "I came home shortly after. Over a week since you fell ill."

Miss Warrick opened and closed her eyes slowly, seeming to adjust to her surroundings. "Where am I?" she asked.

Edmund smiled. "I thought you should be familiar with it," he said, teasing her gently. "It is my chamber."

Miss Warrick took this in, as well as his position in the chair. "You watched over me?"

"Yes, Miss Warrick. Quite some reversal of our positions. The children are recovered. All are healthy now save yourself."

"I am mighty glad to hear it," Miss Warrick said, settling further against her pillows with a tired sigh. "I worried for them."

"Too much," Edmund said. "You almost dug yourself an early grave."

Miss Warrick said nothing to that, and Edmund leaned

over to gently place the back of his fingers against her forehead.

"Your fever is broken," he told her. "You will be well now. But you may need further rest."

"I am so tired," Miss Warrick said, and even attempted a chuckle. "I have quite worn myself out with sleeping."

Edmund smiled at that. "This time I will leave you some privacy," he said. "Please, sleep. When you wake again, eat these luncheon meats. You will need sustenance."

He rose then, and left the room as her eyes closed once more. Pulling the door shut behind him, he met Jenkins' eyes with a happy smile.

"Will you stay here, Jenkins? You should be able to hear if she needs assistance."

"I will, my lord," Jenkins said with a grin. "I am most happy that she is recovered. Will you spread the joyous news?"

"I will," Edmund promised, stretching out his shoulders and feeling the ache of three nights' sleep in a chair.

38

For days, everything was a struggle.

Joanna felt as though she had undergone the most strenuous physical test of her life, and more. It took until the end of her first day awake before she could so much as lift herself into a sitting position in bed, and then she was most chagrined to realise that she could not return it to its rightful owner.

"I shall sleep in a guest room," Edmund told her with a smile. "I would not dream of disturbing you until you are more yourself again. What kind of gentleman would I be?"

Her shame grew when she could not but move her feet to the floor the next day, before she had to retire again and sleep.

But finally, with the help of Mary, she was able to stand

and remove herself from the bed, and half-stagger along the hall to her own chamber on the third day.

Removing her sweat-soaked day dress and undergarments was a blessing the likes of which she had never known. Her skin smelled like fever, and sluicing it off in a tin tub was a great joy – even if she needed Mary's help even to climb into it.

Feeling the last vestiges curl away from her hair in the water brought back some of her self again, and she felt much refreshed once dried and dressed in clean garments.

"Burn it, Mary," Joanna said when the maid held up her gown with a questioning look. "Even if it were to cost all my yearly wage to replace it, I don't think I could ever wear it again."

Mary giggled, but she took it away all the same and followed her wishes.

Joanna was beginning to feel stronger, even if only by small steps. She did not want to linger too long; there were duties that she had to get on with, after all.

"Miss Warrick," Christopher said, appearing in her doorway as if reading her thoughts. "How are you feeling? The children are asking after you, and I told them I would make a report."

"I should be down there myself," Joanna said. "Let me gather my strength, and I will come down to the schoolroom. The day is not yet wasted, and I can begin their instruction again."

Christopher shook his head. "You work too hard," he said. "The children are on enforced rest anyway. Patience and Amy are much recovered, but there is no need to push things too far. Though I am told that your presence is welcome in the drawing room, should you feel up to it."

Joanna nodded. "I think I can manage that," she said. "I shall just ask Mary to help me with my hair."

Christopher cocked his head. "Is it so terribly unfashionable to wear it down around your shoulders so?"

Joanna smiled. "I think it unprofessional, Lieutenant. I must be the very picture of presentation in order to instruct Amy and Patience."

"But today you are off-duty," Christopher reminded her. "Come. If you wish, I will give you my arm and you can come down with me. Poor Mary can't be asked to cart you around all day, like a workhorse."

Joanna blinked at his choice of words, only causing him to laugh uproariously.

"Well, Lieutenant, when you put it like that," she said, as his levity subsided. "I would be most honoured to accept your invitation."

Christopher nodded and moved to her side, holding his arm out with the elbow extended so that she could hook hers through it.

Once she had slowly pulled herself to her feet, he waited to be sure that she was stable before moving off, keeping to her gentle pace.

"Take as much time as you need on the stairs," Christopher said, as they approached the descent to the main hall.

"It is getting up them again later which concerns me," Joanna said, smiling ruefully. "Perhaps we might go down close to the side, so that I may hold onto the bannister as well as your arm."

Her legs were like jelly, shaking each time she lowered the weight of her body down another step.

It was only her firm grip on the bannister and Christopher's watchful strength which kept her from tumbling down all the way to the bottom.

At last, the ordeal was over and they stood in the main hall.

Joanna took a moment to breathe and collect herself, and Christopher waited patiently until she nodded that it was alright to go on.

She was not quite prepared for what awaited her when they pushed open the door to the drawing room.

The whole family were seated on various chairs and sofas, relaxing together and engaged in their own activities. Edmund sat reading the newspaper on one side of a well-cushioned French sofa, while Samuel was amusing himself with the pages he had already discarded on a nearby chair.

Patience and Amy sat close by one another on a chaise, each engaged in embroidery, Amy peering her small head over her sister's work to copy her actions. They were both draped with soft blankets over their knees, and Jenkins stood by at the back of the room, ready to serve in any way that he might be required.

Each of them turned to her with an expression of delight as she entered, and Samuel even sprang to his feet.

"Miss Warrick!" the children exclaimed.

"You're alright," Patience said joyfully.

"Quite so," Joanna said, flushing to be greeted with such warm affection. "The Lieutenant thought I ought to prove to you all that I was yet living."

"Admirably done," Edmund said, looking at Christopher with a spark in his eye. "Come, allow Miss Warrick to sit down by me. The cushions are most comfortable."

Joanna allowed herself to be led over and sank gratefully onto the soft sofa.

Before she had time to adjust to her new seat, a blanket appeared from nowhere and was thrown over her legs.

"Do let us know if you require anything, Miss Warrick," Edmund added. "Jenkins has been instructed that you are to receive all you need for rest and recuperation."

"That isn't necessary," Joanna said, flushing again. "You are all far too kind."

"Only as kind as you deserve, Miss Warrick," Christopher said gallantly, sitting down by the empty fireplace and stretching his legs out in front of him.

Joanna could only smile and blush further, looking around at the happy faces surrounding her.

They soon resumed their idle chatter and pastimes, and

she began to feel just as at home as if she had been sitting amongst her own family.

That thought almost brought her to tears, and she was forced to hang her head for a time, looking down at her blanket to blink the moisture away.

"Are you quite alright, Miss Warrick?" Edmund asked, with some concern.

"Oh, yes, my lord," Joanna said, finding no other words that could be sufficient to express her happiness at that moment.

To be accepted in this way, only if for a short time while she recovered from the sickness, was more of a gift than she had ever thought to receive again.

"You know, I wanted to ask your opinion," Edmund said, keeping his voice low and darting a look in Patience's direction. "Lord Edward Haverham. The third son – do you recall him?"

"He danced with Miss Patience, twice if I remember correctly," Joanna nodded. "The red-headed young man."

"Yes, exactly him," Edmund replied. He hesitated, and lowered his voice yet further. "Did you find the impression of a suitable young man in him?"

Joanna followed his gaze towards Patience, and caught his meaning. "You mean, as a beau, my lord?"

"I was with the Haverhams lately," Edmund confided. "Lord Haverham has expressed his interest in having his lad court our Patience. What did you think of him?"

"He was well-mannered enough," Joanna said, thinking back. "I think the Lady's impression of him was a good one. He certainly cuts a dashing figure, for a young lord."

"I had thought to perhaps allow some courtship," Edmund said thoughtfully, checking that Patience was not paying attention.

"They can linger a year or so. There is no need to rush them together, but the family wanted to visit us anon. Perhaps when we have recovered a little more, it can be arranged."

"I think it might be wise, my lord," Joanna agreed.

He seemed to take that as answer enough, and settled back to his newspaper, satisfied.

They passed away the hours of the afternoon in this fashion, and though Joanna had nothing with which to occupy herself, she was tired enough that to simply sit and observe was sufficient.

She admired the way that Patience took time with her sister, helping her complete difficult stitches, and how Edmund soon moved on to conversing about Latin conjugations with Samuel.

As the day wore on, they engaged in short but strenuous debates on a number of matters, and Christopher showed Samuel the correct way to carry out a military salute.

Amy scrambled onto Joanna's knee, where she had only

enough strength to allow her to sit and to listen to her childish stories about fairies and elves.

It had been a most magical day; the kind of day that Joanna felt she would one day wonder about.

Had it all been real, or simply an extension of her feverish dreams? Could she really be so fortunate as all this?

The fatigue hung heavy in her bones, however, and by that she knew it all to be true. She even dozed off at one quiet point as the hour grew late, and was only woken by the family rising to go to the dining room.

"Will you dine with us, Miss Warrick? I think your recovery warrants a special occasion," Edmund offered.

Joanna gave him a rueful smile. "I am sorry to miss it, my lord, but I fear I have not the strength nor the appetite. I shall be satisfied with a bit of Cook's broth and then shall retire to my chamber."

"As you wish," Edmund said, allowing the others to file out of the room as he remained seated beside her. "Is there anything more we can do for you?"

"No, for the moment. I have enjoyed a delightful day, my lord. I thank you greatly."

"Have you energy yet for a little more excitement?" Edmund asked. "Leave us, Jenkins, if you will."

The butler stepped out of the room with a knowing look, and Joanna turned her eyes back to Edmund in wonder.

"There is something I have been wanting to say to you, Miss Warrick," he said.

With a flash of inspiration, Joanna thought she understood his meaning. "I do not require any sort of apology, my lord," she said. "It was a misunderstanding only. I am only pleased beyond measure to be allowed to stay."

"It is not that," Edmund said with a self-conscious laugh. "Though you do, in fact, require and deserve an apology. My behaviour was beyond boorish."

"It was no such thing, my lord," Joanna said, shaking her head. "I forgive it entirely. It was only a misunderstanding."

"Well, but you see, there was a reason behind my actions," Edmund said.

He sighed, and stood, beginning to pace in front of her.

"I find myself quite unused to this kind of talk. You will forgive me, I hope, if I am not as eloquent as I would otherwise wish to be."

"Certainly," Joanna said.

There was a growing concern inside of her that had begun to gnaw at her belly. What could it be that he needed to discuss which was so difficult?

"You see, I had a realisation while you were lying a-bed, Miss Warrick. We were frightened, all of us, that you might not wake up. Your sacrifice and insistence in looking after the children made your sickness all the worse, and we began to think it had taken too great a toll."

Joanna opened her mouth to apologise for causing worry, but Edmund held up a hand.

"No, Miss Warrick, let me finish what I have to say, lest I lose the nerve to say it," he said. "Imagining that you would never wake again, I found it a reality that I could not bear. The thought of continuing life without your presence was simply outside of consideration. I could not fathom an existence without your person beside me.

"I have known for some time, Miss Warrick, that I harbour feelings not entirely appropriate for an employer and his governess. When I thought you betrothed to Christopher I, well, I pushed them away. I tried very hard to be happy for you both, but I could not. I knew then that I was jealous, foolishly and hopelessly jealous, and I could not bear to have you here a moment longer if I could not have you for myself.

"I rode away with those thoughts in my mind, and it is my great shame that I did so. Had I stayed and listened to reason, you need not have suffered so. Nor I, for I might have learned of my mistake earlier. For that, I am truly sorry."

Joanna's head was spinning. She could only stare at him in amazement.

Somewhere in his speech she had registered talk of feelings, though they seemed lost almost in his urgency to apologise. Had she truly heard him correctly?

"I forgive you for that," she said, quietly, staring at him with her eyes as wide as they could manage to go.

"But that is not quite the point I wanted to reach. I have become tangled up in myself," Edmund said, shaking his head.

He sat down again next to her, turning his whole body towards her to address her directly.

"Miss Warrick, my point is this. Having been faced twice with the prospect of losing you, I do not wish to face it a third time."

"What are you saying, my lord?" Joanna breathed, hardly daring to believe that she had understood him correctly.

"That I love you, Miss Warrick, I love you most dearly. Furthermore, that I would like nothing more than for you to become my wife," Edmund said, his eyes searching her face earnestly. "Please, Miss Warrick. Allow me to take your hand in marriage."

Joanna simply stared back at him for the longest moment, until she felt hot tears falling down her face.

"Have I offended you?" Edmund asked urgently, pulling back with an expression of chagrin.

"No, my lord," Joanna whispered. "Forgive me. I am just so desperately happy."

Edmund's countenance changed, and it seemed as though a light shone from within him to illuminate the smile upon his face. "Does this mean that you will accept?"

"Yes," she said. "Oh, yes, my lord, yes. A thousand times yes."

If she had had the energy, Joanna would have leapt from her seat and danced a jig. As it was, she was content only to sit while he clapped his hands in delight, and then drew closer, cupping the side of her face in one of his hands.

He met her lips in a tender, soft kiss, a kiss that lit her whole body to the core with the same illumination as his, and they both laughed with joy, until he rested his forehead against hers in happy harmony.

39

The summer was almost drawing to a close before the Haverhams made good on their promised visit.

The rooms of Hardwicke Hall swelled with eight extra bodies: the Lord and Lady, their three sons, a maid, a valet, and even their own cook, whom they had brought along much to Cook's displeasure.

"I think it is going well," Edmund confided, sitting down on the picnic blanket next to Joanna.

"She is quite taken with him already," Joanna agreed, smoothing her hands over the blanket on her lap.

She was still not recovered sufficiently for them to wed, though she could at least join them when there was somewhere to sit.

The whole party had decided to take advantage of the

late summer weather by enjoying a picnic out by the lake, and the Haverham boys were engaging Christopher and Samuel in a hearty game of cricket.

Patience, for her part, was beginning to find it difficult to remove her eyes from the third son's every move.

"Perhaps there is a chance that we have found a good match," Edmund suggested, thinking of how neat and easy it would all be if Patience were to set her heart on the first lad who came courting.

"I should give them a little more time first," Joanna said, with a smile that crinkled the corners of her eyes. "I remember how many courtships and imagined romances it took for my sister to settle on her lord."

"Have you heard from Lady Castleford of late?" Edmund asked.

"The pregnancy goes well," Joanna replied. "She is hopeful that I will be well enough to travel when the time comes."

Edmund reached over and took her gloved hand in his.

He had insisted that her day dress, ruined by the sickness, be replaced. Against her arguments and protestations, he had replaced everything with a wardrobe of new garments, amongst them hats and pretty lace gloves and gowns suitable for balls.

"By then we may go as man and wife," he said. "I shall look forward greatly to meeting your sister. If you are not much more recovered, I can at least accompany you and see that you are not overtired."

Joanna smiled again. "That would be a most wonderful arrangement," she agreed. "I'm sure Esther would be thrilled to meet you. She has heard so much of you, after all."

"I shall have to get her to dig out those old letters and read them to me," Edmund teased. "I trust that I won't find anything too uncomplimentary about myself."

"I shall instruct her to burn them forthwith," Joanna laughed.

"Are you playing, Edmund?" Christopher shouted from the vicinity of the game. "We require another batsman for our team."

"Oh, dear," Edmund said, shaking his head ruefully. "Will you think less of me if I prove to you now my utter lack of skill at our fair country's finest sport?"

"No less of you than I would if you refused to join their fun," Joanna said, tapping the covers of the books she had brought with her out to the lawns. "Go. I shall be kept company by Mr Shelley and Lord Byron."

Edmund made a face. "Who are these scoundrels? I shall chase them away from my betrothed," he told her.

"You shall do no such thing," Joanna replied. "Nor shall you use me any longer as an excuse not to play cricket."

Edmund groaned, and got to his feet, eliciting a cheer from the members of his team.

They would not, he thought, be cheering for long once they saw him bat.

He joined in with gusto, his heart made light by the fact that he could glance over whenever he wanted and observe his dear Miss Warrick sitting with her head in a book, propped up on soft cushions that they had carried out especially for her use.

His sisters were engaged in making daisy chains, and the whole party was made more fun and more boisterous by the inclusion of the Haverham boys.

Each of them was a fair testament to their father's good sense and their mother's loving care, and Edmund confessed to himself that he was enjoying their company.

If their families should end up joined in matrimony further down the line, it should be no great hardship.

And if this was to be no more than the first passing fancy which would see Patience have her head turned by some finer match, then so be it.

In the late afternoon they packed up their games and their picnic materials, and returned to Hardwicke Hall to dine.

"Tell me, Miss Warrick," Lady Haverham said, nestling next to her at the table. "Have you made plans for your wedding day as yet?"

Joanna looked up at Edmund with a plea for help in her eyes. "Not quite yet, Lady Haverham," she admitted.

"Why ever not?" Lady Haverham enquired, pushing further as the Lady was always wont to do.

Edmund saw the need to intervene.

He knew that Joanna was embarrassed: it was her weakness, as she still recovered from the sickness, that held them back from finalising their plans. She wanted at least to be able to walk for a longer time, and stand to greet their guests, before they were wed.

Anyone with eyes could have seen that she was tired, but Lady Haverham was not one to stay her questions on the basis of such evidence.

"I have been quite busy in London," Edmund said, cutting in so that Joanna did not have to make a reply. "The business, sadly, takes much of my time. Soon, though, I am hoping to hand the reigns to my brother for a short time so that we might enjoy our wedding."

Christopher fairly beamed with pride. "I'll be taking my leave from the army for a short time," he added. "I've been granted permission from my superiors. It will be an interesting opportunity to see how things are away from the military."

"How trusting," Lord Haverham joked, elbowing Edmund heartily. "I should have imagined that our Lord Kelt would never allow another man at the helm of his company."

"You may have been right," Edmund replied good-naturedly. "But Christopher has proven himself to me. I trust that he will do things in my stead with the correct sense."

"I will endeavour for nothing less," Christopher put in.

"And if not," Edmund added with a sly sideways glance and a wink at Joanna, "I can always return early and take over before we are totally ruined."

The table burst into guffaws of laughter at Christopher's injured expression.

"Say, Lieutenant," the eldest Haverham put in. "Weren't you lately connected to Lady Juliana Reffern?"

"There was never any formal arrangement," Christopher said, his mood changing abruptly. He looked down at his plate, pushing food around merely rather than eating it. "I believe she went and got betrothed to some other fellow."

"We were just talking about it," the red-headed boy went on. "Such an upset. Some say she intended to cause a scandal."

"What, by agreeing marriage with a mere lord?" Christopher asked, and snorted. "I hardly think it the scandal of the year."

"No, by what came next," Edward Haverham cut in with a twinkle in his eye. "You haven't heard?"

Christopher leaned forward in interest. "There had been a development? I have kept myself quite apart from that set since the happy news. I did not hear of any other occurrence."

"Well," the third Haverham son began, clearly delighting in the chance to share a titbit of gossip. "She broke it off with him, last month. There was quite a to-do about it.

"She went to a dance the next week and he turned up to try to convince her to change her mind. Such a scene it was! By the time it was done, her retinue were required to whisk her away to home to avoid any damage to her reputation. The poor lord got drunk and tried to fight with her cousin about it."

Lady Haverham gasped in disapproval, though Edmund would not be surprised if she had heard the story before.

"Such behaviour, and in public too. He ought to be censured for it. What is decided between families should not be paraded for all the world to see afterwards."

"He was quite heartbroken," the elder Haverham put in with a note of sympathy.

"I can imagine so," Christopher breathed.

He seemed to be fascinated by some spot on the distant wall, and talked to it rather than anyone at the table.

"She is a stunning beauty."

"Perhaps her family decided the match was not an appropriate one," Joanna said quietly.

"Quite so!" Lady Haverham agreed. "Well, it was ridiculous really. A girl of such breeding should not be paired off with a mere lord. There are plenty of dukes with second or third sons who would have been better. Mixing the ranks so unevenly is a recipe for unhappiness on both sides."

Joanna looked up and met Edmund's eyes. He shook his head at her, forbidding her to listen to such nonsense.

"The rank is not quite so much an arbiter of happiness when the couple have an equal class of heart," he said sternly.

Lady Haverham looked between Edmund and Joanna, and had at least the good grace to show a small flush on her cheeks.

"O-of course," she stuttered. "When love is concerned. Though I do not think there was truly love between them."

"I have heard that her heart belonged truly to another," the middle Haverham boy, who was hardly ever heard, spoke up.

Christopher looked at him then, piercingly, as if trying to determine whether his words had a ring of truth.

"Well," Edmund said, hoping to steer the conversation in another direction. "I am sure some other scandal will break to distract everyone from it before long. Lord Haverham, have you made any plans as yet for the winter?"

"We'll proceed as normal," Lord Haverham replied, draining his cup of wine. "We shall all gather for the winter celebration and enjoy some feasting, I should imagine. We have no particular plans."

The conversation moved on in that direction, and

Edmund was able to spare some moments to catch Joanna's eye.

He gave her a reassuring smile, hoping that she would take it as it was intended.

There was no opinion from Earth or heaven that would have him dissuaded from marrying her, and he wanted her to know that.

A trace of worry lingered on her face, but she smiled back at him all the same.

That was enough, for now. He could settle for that.

"Of course, you must come to join us in the winter," Lady Haverham was saying. "There is always more fun to be had with guests. We do so enjoy having our friends come to stay, don't we, my lord?"

Lord Haverham grunted in agreement. "Gives the boys something to entertain themselves, too. A bit of sports or a few excursions here or there. Though we shall have lost one of them to the clergy by then."

The middle son bowed his head bashfully. Edmund gathered that Lord Haverham was not quite approving of his choice, though it was tradition for a family with so many sons to donate at least one of them to the service of God.

"And what of young Edward?" he asked, nodding towards the younger boy. "Has he reached some decision regarding his future as of yet?"

"He is considering the navy," Lord Haverham replied,

with a significant amount more pride. "Of course, the army wants him. But we shall see what prospects they can each offer him. Either way, I expect he will be an officer, and a decorated one at that, before next year is out."

"That is an interesting prospect," Edmund said, turning this information over in his mind.

Patience did seem to like a soldier, after all. No doubt this would only raise the young Haverham in her esteem.

Still, he was to be away in battle for long stretches, and Edmund did not know if she would truly enjoy being a soldier or sailor's wife.

The conversation turned again, and soon they were all finished with their dining; with a sigh of regret, Edmund led his contingent of men away for a glass of whisky, wishing instead that he were able to join his beloved in her drawing room.

"My lady," Mary said, dipping a curtsey to Joanna as the women gathered to rise.

Edmund watched as Joanna shook her head, her usual disagreement.

"I am not your Lady yet, Mary," she said. "Nor do I intend to be. We have served together, do remember that."

"You have it the wrong way around, Miss Warrick," Mary said with a smile. "You always was a lady to me."

Edmund hid a smile of his own as he ducked out of the room to join the men, congratulating himself once again at the admirable job he had done of choosing a bride.

EPILOGUE

Edmund stood fidgeting in his new suit, waiting restlessly for the guests to finish filing in to their seats.

"Why ever does it take so long?" he complained to Christopher, who stood by his side.

"Hush, brother," Christopher said, with obvious amusement. "You will make a spectacle of yourself. Stand still."

"I cannot stand still," Edmund hissed.

"Look at how well Amy and Patience are waiting," Christopher said calmly, taking every opportunity to tease his brother. "Aren't they just darling in those bonnets?"

Edmund looked at his sisters, standing in their white dresses. They had been chosen as bridesmaids, of course, and though they had been very excited to prepare for the day, now they indeed stood calmly.

"They are children," Edmund sniffed. "They don't understand the gravity of the situation."

Christopher chuckled. "I see. It is the gravity which makes you move about as though you were trying to invent a new dance."

"What kind of devilment is it that leads you to mock your eldest brother on his wedding day?" Edmund complained.

"Only the same devilment that leads me to mock him any day of the week."

"You are a cruel man," Edmund said. "Is my watch chain still hanging right?"

"Just the same as it was when you asked me last, not five minutes ago."

"I cannot help it," Edmund said. "I wish this infernal ceremony would begin. What is it that we are waiting for?"

"Only for your guests to be seated and your delightful bride to prepare herself. Nothing of any importance," Christopher replied with a heavy dose of sarcasm.

"Well, they could sit down quicker, I think."

"Hush, now, brother," Christopher said, gripping his shoulder and squeezing. "Your bride approaches."

Joanna appeared and began to walk down the aisle, and Edmund felt his heart fluttering against his ribs like a caged bird. It must have swollen at least ten times in size.

Joanna was radiant; a silver gown with pale blue trimmings decked her entire form, and matching silver slippers peeked out from beneath the hem with each step that she walked.

She was exquisite, a being not of this Earth, an angel that Edmund had no business deserving.

He watched her come with a lump in his throat that would not be cleared away, and if it were possible, he felt his love grow even further when she ducked her head shyly under his adoring gaze.

The ceremony seemed to pass by in a daze. Out in the pews were friends and relatives – Lord and Lady Castleford, she bearing the heavy belly of later pregnancy; the Haverhams, taking up their own red-headed row entirely; employees and partners at the company; their entire staff, except for Cook, who had insisted on staying behind to prepare a feast; cousins and nieces and nephews and aunts and uncles.

Even Joanna's mother had made the trip, though they had had to send her the money for the coach.

Edmund realised with a start that the vicar was waiting patiently for him to say something, and snapped out of the reverie that had overcome him.

It was such a magical day that it seemed almost not to be happening.

"With this ring I thee wed, with my body I thee worship, and with all my worldly goods I thee endow: In the Name of the Father, and of the Son, and of the Holy Ghost. Amen," he recited, slipping a ring onto Joanna's finger.

Their eyes met with the kind of misty happiness that comes only from exquisite and delirious joy, and he knew that she felt as unreal as he did.

The gold band fitted perfectly onto her finger, and a cheer went up from the people in the church.

Edmund turned to exchange grins with Christopher and Samuel, visibly only as vague figures through the moisture that had gathered in his eyes.

"Come," Edmund said to his new wife, interlacing his fingers with hers. "Let us sign the registry, Lady Kelt."

Joanna gave a gasp of delight at the first mention of her new name, and followed him. Through their connected arms he felt a shaking in her that concerned him.

"Are you tired, my sweet? We can sit," he offered.

"I am just so happy," Joanna laughed. "I barely know how to exist."

He laughed in return, and bent to place a kiss on her temple. His wife's temple. The thought was a strange and yet completely right one.

The register having been signed, they retired from the village to Hardwicke Hall, where their esteemed guests had also been invited.

There, as promised, Cook had laid on a sumptuous breakfast of rolls, eggs, ham, bread, fish, tea, and other delectable foods. Crowning it all was a dense fruit cake that Cook had spent many hours slaving over, and which took pride of place in the centre of the table.

The congratulations were many, but Edmund soon brought a chair so that Joanna could sit; he could feel the weakness overcoming her again, and did not want her to tire out. Though she protested, he assured her that no one would think any the less.

Amy soon came to sit on Joanna's lap, which was her accustomed place, and Patience even drew up a chair alongside them, once she had grown thoroughly tired of teasing the third Haverham son.

Their guests lingered for a few hours, eating and talking merrily. Christopher finally approached the happy couple as the celebrations were winding down, congratulating them once again on their marriage.

"Edmund, I have news of my own," Christopher said, his eyes shining with happiness. "I ought to wait and let you have your day, but I fear it will burst out of me.

"I wrote a letter to Lady Juliana Reffern. It was a fool's hope that she would reply with one of her own, but she did! A very formal and proper answer, as you can well imagine, but she agreed to my request to visit her."

Edmund embraced his brother in congratulations. "I am most happy for you, Christopher. It is time that you settled down."

"Settle down? No one mentioned anything about a proposal, dear brother. The lady simply agreed to meet with me," Christopher said, but Edmund could tell settling down was not a prospect that truly bothered his brother anymore.

"Still," he insisted, "a simple meeting is where the path of our destiny sometimes begins."

"You talk like an old man," Christopher laughed. "And only wed a matter of hours yourself!"

Edmund laughed along with him. "Christopher, you are unaware of the wisdom that was imparted to me by God the moment our hands were joined. I am sure you will know it too, when you are a grown man."

Christopher gawped at his jibe. "Who is this man, and whither has my brother been taken?" he responded.

Edmund clapped him on the back. "Today, Christopher," he said. "I have been replaced with a happy man. I hope that he shall stay for a long time to come."

"That is my hope also," Christopher said, giving him a genuine warmth that had been missing so often from their past.

"Are you ready to depart, my lord?" the coach driver asked, approaching them with Jenkins at his side.

"Quite ready, I suppose," Edmund said, looking down at his wife for confirmation. "We have only to bid our guests farewell, and we can be on our way."

"I am so jealous," Patience complained. "You shall spend all your spring in Europe, and I am to be stuck here as always."

"You'll be here with me," Christopher opined. "That is compensation enough."

"I have already promised to take you abroad next year," Edmund cut in, to prevent Patience from making harsh reply. "You shall have to make do with that, all of you."

"But I shall die just thinking of Rome and Paris and the places you will go without me," Patience sighed dramatically.

"Come, my lady wife," Edmund said, ignoring Patience forthwith. "Shall we embark on our honeymoon?"

Joanna smiled up at him. "I gather that we shall," she said, rising up gracefully to take his arm and begin the rest of their lives.

THE END

Did you enjoy *Secret Dreams of a Fearless Governess*? Check out the story of *Juliana* and *Christopher* in *A Daring Captain for Her Loyal Heart* here.

If you want a Bonus Scene of this book visit the link below (or just click it): https://abbyayles.com/aa-020-exep/

A DARING CAPTAIN FOR HER LOYAL HEART

Preview

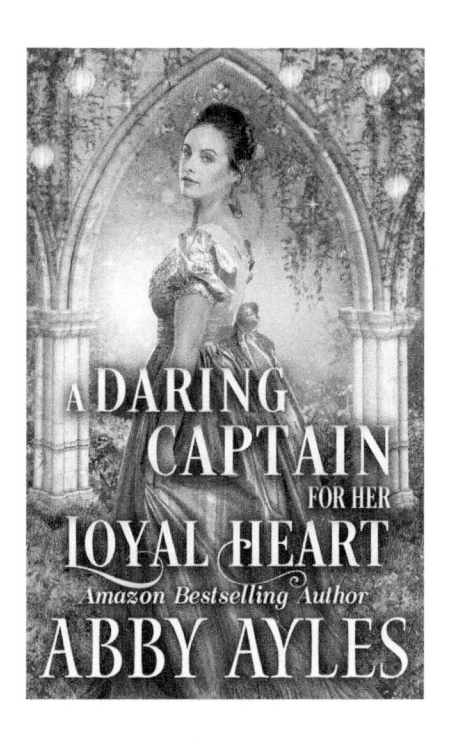

Read it now!
http://abbyayles.com/AmB024

The heart knows no boundaries when it comes to love... and he chose her.

No other man has been shrouded by rumors and mystery as much as Lieutenant Christopher Hardwicke. Reckless, mischievous, scoundrel. But the rumors are hardly ever true: his heart has always belonged to one girl, and one girl alone - a lady so far above his station that society dictates he should never dare hope for her. But Christopher is not prone to ever giving up. And this lady is worth going to war for.

No other woman has been accompanied by rumors and scandal as much as Lady Juliana Reffern. Arrogant, whimsical, the girl who dared break an engagement. But a scandal is hardly ever fair: her heart has always remained true, given to the dashing soldier she can't forget – a man who she patiently waits for, a rock that resists the oncoming tides of society's expectations.

. . .

But her family has had enough. And this time, Juliana may not succeed in thwarting another marriage.

Now, Christopher and Juliana will have to race against the clock, to earn the redemption that might be their last chance at a future. But this road is full of obstacles, and the most dangerous of them are those that are hidden just below the surface…

If you like engaging characters, heart-wrenching twists and turns, and lots of romance, then you'll love "A Daring Captain for her Loyal Heart!"

Buy "A Daring Captain for her Loyal Heart" and unlock the exciting story of Juliana today!

Also available with Kindle Unlimited!

Read it now!
http://abbyayles.com/AmB024

1

The two men faced off against one another, the tension between them palpable to any onlooker. The moments ticked by at an unbearably slow pace, as they looked each other up and down, waiting for an opening.

The tension burst as one rushed at the other, tackling him around the waist and forcing him back a few paces. The other was quick to react, hooking his arm around the first man's head and locking it into position so that he could not struggle loose.

They twisted and turned, each fighting for the upper hand. They exchanged no words, only grunted with the strain and the effort.

One finally found an opening, landing a blow to the

other's ribs – but it was a soft blow, and one that signaled only the end of the fight.

"Alright, I yield," Christopher Hardwicke laughed, letting go of his friend's neck and stepping backward. "You got me again, Rivers."

Jasper Rivers straightened up, flashing him a grin of victory. "As always," he said. "You're lucky I didn't really have a knife."

"I'm not sure why you would pull a knife on your best friend," Christopher laughed. "It would be terribly unsporting."

Jasper brushed himself off, laughing in return. "Not to mention that the Captain would be none too happy with us for thinning the ranks of our own army."

"You're right about that," Christopher smirked. "Though if you ask me, this army could do with fewer officers – at least, the ones above us. More room for us to move up."

"Well, give us some time," Jasper said, picking up his scabbard and reattaching it to his belt. "We've only just got here. Once we know the score a little more, we might find there's an opening somewhere."

Christopher shrugged. He had already made some inquiries since they were reassigned to their new barracks.

"All the officer positions are full here. Just about everywhere, it seems. I've put out a few queries, but I don't think there's a captain missing in the whole of the south of England."

"Hm. We'll have to do something about that," Jasper said.

Christopher raised an eyebrow. "I don't see that we can. Besides, we'll be busy enough with everything this season."

"You have some plans?" Jasper asked. "I hope you're not expecting to leave me behind."

Christopher laughed. "Never, old chum. You know we both have lodgings for our leave in Bath. But I do think perhaps you might want to stay at the barracks when I go back to visit home."

Jasper pulled a face. Nothing more needed to be said: they both knew what had happened last time Jasper had visited Hardwicke Hall.

It had been a terrible to-do; Jasper had succeeded in persuading Christopher's younger sister, Patience, to run away with him, and it was only at the last minute that they were stopped with Patience's honor still intact.

Jasper flopped down on his cot, making himself comfortable. "I suppose I should never show my face in front of Edmund again."

"My brother is not the forgiving kind," Christopher agreed.

In fact, Edmund, the Earl of Kelt, had been incensed to know that Christopher still fraternized with Jasper – but he was not in the military, and he did not know what it was like.

Bonds that were forged here were strong, and when two men still served together, it was not as though they could avoid one another.

Besides which, they were officers. That meant they treated one another with honor. And since no real harm had been done – except for Patience complaining and sulking for weeks straight – Christopher had let the matter go.

Perhaps if he really had run away with her, it would have been a different matter.

Edmund, on the other hand, had no bond with Jasper. He had given Christopher a black eye for bringing his friend to the family home, so there was no telling how far he would go if he ever saw Jasper again. Even the calming influence of his wife would likely not be enough to hold him back.

"Still, all is well with the family?" Jasper asked, even managing not to sound as if he couldn't care a fig.

"Oh, yes," Christopher said, trying to ignore the treacherous spike of jealousy when he thought of how happy they were. "Edmund is settled in very nicely with his new wife. They are expecting a child soon."

Jasper snorted. "I bet that will be the end of it for your siblings," he remarked, picking at something on the inside of one of his fingernails.

"What do you mean by that?"

"Well, once he has a child of his own, I doubt the Earl will want to mess around playing father to the others. He'll have his hands full. The girls will be married off as soon as possible and ignored otherwise."

"You can't think so!" Christopher exclaimed.

"Why not? It's a tale as old as time. The new lion takes over the pack, and he kills the cubs of the old king. People are always more dedicated to their own children. I was only packed off to the army because my mother remarried."

Christopher frowned. "You have him wrong," he said. "Since our parents died, Edmund has only ever taken his duties seriously. Besides, Samuel is away at school, and Patience should be married before long anyway. By the time the new child is walking around unaided, he'll only have Amy left with him. She's not exactly a burden."

"If you believe it to be so, I cannot argue. Granted, the only impression I have of him is that of an extremely angry man," Jasper commented.

"Well, you do have that effect on most people."

"Since my birth," Jasper admitted cheerily. "It's always been a particular skill of mine."

"And what of your family? They are well?" Christopher asked, mostly out of politeness.

Jasper waved a hand dismissively. "All well. Why shouldn't they be? Nothing new to report. But tell me, will Edmund hire a new governess? I do so enjoy a governess."

"You won't get your hands on her, even if he does," Christopher said, scowling at the shameful memory of his own attempt to woo Joanna – the former governess who was now his brother's bride. That was something he wished that he could forget.

"You'll have to make do with the ladies of Bath."

"You're still set on making the trip again this season, then?"

"Of course. I've already announced my leave to the Captain. I'm staying with another officer, and I've arranged a room for you in the same house. Lady Juliana will be in town at the same time."

Jasper gave him a sly look. "You old dog. Returning to old grounds, eh?"

Christopher turned away from him and tidied his trunk, aimlessly, afraid that he might be seen to blush.

"It's not exactly like that. Nothing happened between us last season. When I court her, it will be for the first time."

Jasper followed him to elbow him in the ribs. "I'm sure."

Christopher gave a yelp of protest, and quickly turned to tackle his friend. "Don't start this again," he said, as they began to play at fighting once more. The sting of red in his cheeks only served to make Christopher wrestle Jasper harder.

After confusing minutes of straining and matching strength against strength, Christopher managed at last to get a hand up to Jasper's throat, clenched around the handle of an imaginary knife.

"I yield! I yield!" Jasper cried with a grin, seemingly only more satisfied by his friend's embarrassment.

Satisfied, Christopher let him go.

His thoughts about Juliana were his own, and he didn't wish to share them with anybody – least of all Jasper, who wouldn't understand.

He wouldn't understand staying up at nights, envisioning only one woman's face, your ears ringing with only one woman's laughter. He wouldn't understand counting the days until he saw her again. Planning, hoping, dreaming, imagining.

Most of it, Christopher didn't understand either. But if there was one thing he did understand, it was this:

A tree had taken root inside his heart last year, and it was growing and growing whether he wanted it or not. A willow tree of smiles and glances, of warmth and starlight, lean and strong and persistent.

There was no point in trying to uproot it. It had reached the core of his heart and had become entangled with it.

If there was one thing that helped him rise every day, that helped him survive the bleak days of life in the army, was the dream he could be in her presence again. And he would.

He would see Juliana again. And this time, everything would be different.

Read it now!

http://abbyayles.com/AmB024

2

*L*ady Juliana Reffern lounged by her window, basking in the light of the sun as it flowed over her long, dark hair. Still, she refused to be cheerful. After all, she was in trouble – and it had been made more than clear to her.

Weeks had gone by, and still her stepfather had not relented in his unhappiness with her.

"It's all just so unfair," she sulked. "He won't let me do anything."

"Well, you did rather cause a scandal," said Lady Mary Westenholme.

The two girls were firm friends, with Lady Mary visiting Juliana for weeks at a time – though she was no longer allowed to return the favor.

"It doesn't mean I should be confined only to my

home," Juliana protested. "It's not as though I would be unsupervised were I to visit with you. Your mother and father have always been most scrupulous."

"Perhaps your mother and stepfather want to ensure that you do not meet any more young lords," Mary teased gently.

Juliana sighed. It was not as though Mary didn't have a point. Everyone had been rather taken with the idea of her marrying the Viscount of Drevon when they started courting over the winter.

Her mother had made some small comments about the match not being quite equal since Juliana was the daughter of the current Duchess of Prighton. Juliana's stepfather, however, had soon corrected his wife on that matter – Juliana was only the third daughter of the house, after all.

"He was just so boring," Juliana sighed.

Mary knew instinctively who her friend was speaking of – after all, there had been talk of little else in the last months.

"Just because a man is boring, does not mean that he would not make a fine husband," she said, primly.

Juliana rolled her eyes. "You sound just like the Duke," she said. "I do not know why they could not understand it at all. Lord Drevon and I were matched so quickly, after all. These things are sometimes done in mistake."

"Try telling that to his family," Mary said heavily. "I

hear they had already agreed to a lease on what was to be your future home."

Juliana made a face. "A horrid, poky little estate. I wouldn't have had it. No, it was entirely unsuitable."

Mary picked up the book she had been reading, and pretended to study it once more. "I do worry that, compared to Prighton Hall, you will find very few estates in the whole of the country that match up to your expectations."

"Just one that I have heard of," Juliana said dreamily, getting up to sit on the window seat.

"Oh, not Hardwicke Hall," Mary groaned. "Are you not done with that soldier yet?"

"He's not a common soldier," Juliana corrected her sternly. "He's a Lieutenant now. He was only in training when we first met last summer, but now he has his commission."

"Even so. He shan't earn much at all from the army, and you know he won't ever inherit Hardwicke Hall. You'd have to live somewhere else."

Juliana picked up an old rag doll from beside her bed and threw it at Mary. "Will you not be satisfied until I am deeply unhappy?"

Mary ignored the doll, allowing it to land ineffectually beside her. "You should not even be talking of him, Juliana. If the Duke hears you, who knows what punishment he will decide upon."

"He is already exceedingly angry with me," Juliana sighed, looking out across the gardens where the flowers were just beginning to stir from their winter sleep. "I do not truly believe he could go any further."

"I am quite sure that he could," Mary warned her. "At least, for the moment, he has allowed me to stay."

Juliana looked at her friend with some concern. Much plainer than herself, with her light hair that resembled straw even when she attempted to coerce it into a fashionable hairstyle, Mary was not considered a great beauty.

Those people were fools, and blind, according to Juliana, who couldn't see Mary as anything less than beautiful. She was also one of the few people upon whom Juliana could truly rely. Her two sisters were already grown and married, and lived on their own estates.

To think of life with Mary banished for good gave her enough pause to quiet her down. "I suppose I should not have spoken to Lieutenant Hardwicke as I did," she said.

"Lieutenant again now, is it?" Mary said, flashing her a smile as if to make her feel better again. "Only yesterday it was his Christian name you were insistent upon using."

"You have a point about our conversation being overheard," Juliana said, a little sourly.

"Well, you are right about that," Mary agreed, putting her book down again and abandoning the pretense. "You should not have given him to believe he had a chance at your hand."

"But he does," Juliana insisted, throwing her hands up in the air. "At least, if I have anything to say about it."

"According to the Duke, you do not," Mary cautioned her. "I know your mother has given you the freedom to believe you might marry your choice of man, but remember who has the final say.

"The Duke will want to ensure that you marry well, so that he does not have to worry so much about providing you an allowance. A military man will surely need that."

"The Earl of Hardwicke has riches enough," Juliana sulked. "He could provide for us. Anyway, it is all a moot point if we cannot get to Bath."

There was a pause, and Mary joined her on the window seat. "Do you really think the Duke will prevent you from going this season?"

"Yes," Juliana said, gripping her friend's hand. "And that means he will prevent you too, since we were supposed to stay with my aunt. If only we could change his mind."

"I do not think he will bend," Mary shook her head, squeezing her hand back.

"It is no matter to me, really, Juliana. Perhaps a spring in the countryside will be fun for us. The flowers will be all blooming, and I am sure it will be quite lovely to walk around the grounds when the weather is fair."

"That should provide us entertainment for a day. What of the other weeks?" Juliana huffed, leaning her chin on her hand as she stared out of the window.

"It will be so dreary here. To think of all the others, having fun and dancing and walking about town. They shall all have new gowns too, and we shall miss the latest styles. By the time we come to the summer balls, we shall end up a laughing-stock for our old-fashioned looks."

Mary giggled. "I think it will not be quite so bad as all that, Juliana," she said.

Juliana sighed. It was just like Mary to not be upset about missing the Season. She was always happier in quiet company, and she had hardly danced at all last year. Juliana had been waiting for her to blossom, but she seemed stubbornly intent on not doing so.

"Don't you wish we could at least go to meet some of the new gentlemen who might be on the scene?" Juliana asked.

"I will be happy to marry whomever my parents choose," Mary said, dutiful and diffident as ever. "Or if a gentleman should happen to choose me himself, it will be fine enough. I don't long for the drama and politics of courtship."

"You only say that because you have not yet fallen in love," Juliana protested. "You will change your mind once it happens. Then you will care very much about who you are permitted to marry."

"Well, at any rate, it will not happen this spring," Mary said. "If we are not at Bath, then we shall not meet anyone new."

"I just wish I knew of a way to change his mind," Juliana said. "Or at least to get us there. Even if we have to agree to other restrictions…"

"I see that your mind is at work," Mary said, quite seriously. "I fear that I should be quite worried."

Juliana responded only by giving her friend a wicked grin, causing them both to fall in laughter together.

Her mind was indeed at work. And it would not rest until it came up with a way for her to see Christopher again.

Read it now!
http://abbyayles.com/AmB024

3

"What else do I need with me?" Christopher wondered out loud, staring at his trunk as if the answer would magically come to him.

"Whatever else you haven't yet got," Jasper said lazily, not getting up from where he lay on his bed.

He was thumbing through a little printed magazine, the kind that told dashing tales of heroes on the battlefield and women who swooned at their rescue.

"I don't know what I would do without your help," Christopher said with a heavy dose of sarcasm.

"Any time you need me," Jasper replied, flicking onto the next page.

Jasper's lack of enthusiasm did nothing to dampen the excitement that Christopher felt.

He was a bundle of nerves, strange as it seemed even to

him; it was not as though he had never met Juliana before, and yet here he was, with a whole swarm of butterflies making their home inside his stomach at the thought of seeing her.

He gnawed on his lip thoughtfully, and pulled out one of the jackets he had packed earlier to exchange it for another. Only his best, he had decided. It would not do for her to see him in his second-best jacket.

"Well, I think I have everything I need," he said. "You're ready, I assume?"

Jasper shrugged. "I'll throw some things together in a while," he said. "We're not leaving for a couple of hours yet."

Christopher shook his head. "But aren't you excited? We don't want to miss the coach."

"We won't," Jasper said, turning another page of his magazine.

Christopher sighed and sat down on his cot, looking at his trunk again and trying to rack his brains for anything he may have forgotten to pick up. He ran through the events he was expecting in his mind to imagine what he would need.

His mouth twitched up into a smile at just the thought of dancing with Juliana.

It had been so long since he had had the chance to lead her in a dance. He remembered the first time they had met like it was yesterday…

Across the hall at Bath, he spotted a glimpse of yellow silk. A young lady dancing with a man, laughing with joy as she spun around in the center of the room.

Other couples made way for them as they passed through, but it was not the man that commanded the attention. If anything, he looked out of his depth.

His face was pale and strained as he strove to keep up with her. His occasional smile of joy was at his ability to make her laugh with happiness at the dance.

As they moved through the crowd, Christopher strained to catch another glimpse of her. He saw more flashes of that yellow silk, a fleeting sight of a beautiful face, hair moving with the steps of the dance.

Finally, the crowd parted in such a way that he had a full view of her. She turned in his direction as the dance dictated, and he was able to admire her in full for the first time.

She was shapely and small, the picture of a doll. Her hair hung long over her shoulders in artfully arranged curls.

The thing that Christopher noticed most of all, however, was the wide and free smile on her face. Above it, her eyes sparkled like twin stars.

In short, she was the most beautiful girl he had ever seen.

Not only that, but the most well-dressed, the happiest, the most enticing. She was like no one he had ever seen before.

At that moment, not fire or flood or earthquake could have dissuaded him from getting close to her and finding the chance to ask her name.

Christopher cut through the crowd, following her movements. He almost ran around the corners of the dance hall, brushing past those who stood to the side to converse. He had to be in the right place when the dance finished.

He had to be right in front of her.

The music came to a close and he stood, catching his breath, watching her laugh and curtsy to her partner. Then he rushed forward, but he was too late; another man stepped in and offered his hand.

Cursing his luck, Christopher followed them again. The minutes passed in agony as he attempted to keep up, trying to be as close to her as possible.

When the couple strayed into the center of the hall, he cursed and ran his fingers back over his hair and mentally begged the musicians not to stop yet.

He knew this was as clear a chance as any that he would have to meet her. She was dancing with an officer he knew, and that meant that the man would be able to offer an introduction. Without that, he would be waiting a good time longer to dance with her.

A beauty such as hers might not be allowed to rest all night, since every man in the place would wish to dance with her if he could.

At last, the music began to trail off as the young woman returned closer to the edge of the room. It was done, and there was applause and bowing all around, and Christopher took his chance.

"Captain Jeffords," he said, catching the woman's last dance partner. "Who is this young lady? Might you introduce us?"

Jeffords grimaced, unable to hold back his chagrin. Perhaps he did not want to introduce this peach to anyone else, in case she was stolen from him. However, he did it all the same.

"You have the pleasure of meeting Lady Juliana Reffern, third daughter of the Duchess of Prighton," he said.

"My lady, this is Mr. Christopher Hardwicke, a young man of noble blood who has but recently joined our camp. He is set to be a Lieutenant once his training is done."

"I am pleased to make your acquaintance, sir," Juliana said, smiling at him. "Are you an only child?"

Christopher shook his head, a flash of sadness running through him as it always did when he thought of his family. There was also a hint of shame, that he might not be able to proffer up a finer position that would be a fitting match.

"No, my lady. The Earl of Kelt is my brother. I was a second son, and our parents were lost to the sickness but a few months past."

Her whole expression softened. "I am sorry to hear it," she said. "I myself lost my father some years ago. I know how cruel such a loss can be."

Awful though it was, they had something in common. That was a lifeline, a thread of hope that Christopher clung to with all the strength of a dying man.

If they had something in common, they might be able to connect on a deeper level.

If they had something in common, he might be able to convince her to talk with him – to find other things that they shared. And if they had more things to share, perhaps their connection might begin to deepen to something more real.

Christopher gave her a sympathetic look, then deliberately brightened it to a smile. And how could he not smile in her presence?

"Might you do me the honor of this next dance? We may reminisce upon our shared sorrows."

Juliana inclined her head. "I will dance with you," she said. "But let us not talk of sorrow. It is a fine night, and young people such as we ought to be having fun."

"You have the right of it," Christopher agreed, leading her back into position.

She surprised him already. It was the same attitude which he himself might have shared, given the chance to express it. She was not held back by her sorrow nor defined by it. She was alive, and he had the sense that she knew what it was to live.

The dance was one in which couples formed a line facing one another, of which he was glad; it would give him more time to gaze upon her as they danced, and more time for conversation besides.

He wanted to drink in the image of her and follow it with information. Details that he could store up, things to connect the pair of them. He wanted to know everything about her.

"So, Mr. Hardwicke," she said, with mock seriousness. "Are you stationed nearby?"

"No," he admitted. "In fact, we are here on leave. The officers thought to bring some of us new recruits with them since they knew the season was underway."

"Then you are here just for a short while?"

"It is so."

They bowed and curtsied to one another as the music began, and walked through the graceful steps of the dance together.

"That is a shame. You shall not be able to call on me once you are returned to your barracks."

"A shame indeed," Christopher agreed. A heat had risen up his back at the idea of calling upon her. "Though I will still be in Bath tomorrow."

"I will too," Juliana informed him. "I am staying at the house of my aunt."

"And where ought I find the home of this reputable lady?"

Juliana giggled only, as they turned around one another, resuming places on opposite sides of the line to which they had started.

It was maddening. Why would she not answer? Did she not realize that his very life depended upon it?

"At least you will give me a clue as to which one of these ladies here is your aunt," Christopher suggested.

Juliana glanced over her shoulder. Christopher followed her gaze to a stout, stern-looking woman who was watching them closely.

"I do believe I have recognized her," Christopher said gravely. "And she has recognized me."

Juliana giggled again. "She is a formidable one," she said. "You ought to be careful, Mr. Hardwicke."

"So I shall, Lady Juliana," he said, grinning impishly. "In fact, I always am."

"That sounds rather dull," Juliana said, giving him a mischievous look.

That was when he knew he was under her spell, and he would never break it, not as long as he lived...

"What's so special about this trip, anyway?" Jasper asked, pulling him out of his thoughts. He sighed carelessly as he finally began to pack his trunk. "You're never this giddy usually. I'm worried I may have to fetch you a swooning couch."

Christopher ignored his barb. Nothing could dissuade him from happiness at that moment.

"This trip, I know that Juliana is waiting for me," he said. "She has given me hope that we might be betrothed by the time I return."

"Her stepfather would allow it?" Jasper snorted.

Christopher hesitated. "Well, so she has given me to believe."

Jasper laughed and shook his head. "You live in a dream world," he said. "Why should he allow her to marry only a lieutenant? Even a viscount was not good enough for her last time."

Crestfallen, Christopher had to agree with him. He made a good point. There was very little reason for him to appear an appropriate choice, particularly given Edmund's impending child.

Before very long at all, he would be so far down the line of succession at Hardwicke Hall as to have no hope of a good inheritance whatsoever.

Not that he had ever expected it to be his; but he had at least thought to be married before his brother became the Earl. In point of fact, it should have still been his father who held the position. That would have been another situation entirely.

"I shall simply have to improve my commission," Christopher declared. "Move up to Captain or Major. It's the only way."

"If a captaincy were to be available," Jasper said, shaking his head. "You have as much hope there as of finding out that you have wings and can fly."

"A little more, I think," Christopher protested. "At least becoming a higher-ranked officer is within the physical realms of possibility. And I have the funding to buy my way in when it happens."

"Possible, yet not probable."

Christopher gazed down into his trunk in dismay. It was true – all of this could be in vain. How was he going to get past this wall that had risen in front of him?

With a certainty, he felt that he would not be able to do it alone. "Say you'll help me," he said suddenly, turning back to Jasper.

"Help you?"

"Yes, help me find a commission. Captain will do. It will. If I have that, I have enough hope that she will be mine. Just say you'll help me."

"I don't see how I can," Jasper said, shrugging his shoulders. "But, alright. If you can think of a way, I will lend my assistance."

Christopher grinned, feeling hope once again. There had to be a way to find a commission, he just knew it – and with Jasper on his side, they would make it happen.

Caught up in his dreams and hopes, Christopher ignored that little knot of foreboding that briefly made its appearance in his stomach when Jasper agreed.

Read it now!

http://abbyayles.com/AmB024

SCANDALS AND SEDUCTION IN REGENCY ENGLAND

Also in this series

Last Chance for the Charming Ladies
Redeeming Love for the Haunted Ladies
Broken Hearts and Doting Earls
The Keys to a Lockridge Heart
Regency Tales of Love and Mystery
Chronicles of Regency Love
Broken Dukes and Charming Ladies
The Ladies, The Dukes and Their Secrets
Regency Tales of Graceful Roses
The Secret to the Ladies' Hearts
The Return of the Courageous Ladies
Falling for the Hartfield Ladies
Extraordinary Tales of Regency Love
Dukes' Burning Hearts
Escaping a Scandal

Regency Loves of Secrecy and Redemption
Forbidden Loves and Dashing Lords
Fateful Romances in the Most Unexpected Places
The Mysteries of a Lady's Heart
Regency Widows Redemption
The Secrets of Their Heart
Lovely Dreams of Regency Ladies
Second Chances for Broken Hearts
Trapped Ladies
Light to the Marquesses' Hearts
Falling for the Mysterious Ladies
Tales of Secrecy and Enduring Love
Fateful Twists and Unexpected Loves
Regency Wallflowers
Regency Confessions
Ladies Laced with Grace
Journals of Regency Love
A Lady's Scarred Pride
How to Survive Love
Destined Hearts in Troubled Times
Ladies Loyal to their Hearts
The Mysteries of a Lady's Heart
Secrets and Scandals
A Lady's Secret Love
Falling for the Wrong Duke

ALSO BY ABBY AYLES

The Keys to a Lockridge Heart
Melting a Duke's Winter Heart
A Loving Duke for the Shy Duchess
Freed by the Love of an Earl
The Earl's Wager for a Lady's Heart
The Lady in the Gilded Cage
A Reluctant Bride for the Baron
A Christmas Worth Remembering
A Guiding Light for the Lost Earl
The Earl Behind the Mask

Tales of Magnificent Ladies
The Odd Mystery of the Cursed Duke

A Second Chance for the Tormented Lady
Capturing the Viscount's Heart
The Lady's Patient
A Broken Heart's Redemption
The Lady The Duke And the Gentleman
Desire and Fear
A Tale of Two Sisters
What the Governess is Hiding

Betrayal and Redemption
Inconveniently Betrothed to an Earl
A Muse for the Lonely Marquess
Reforming the Rigid Duke
Stealing Away the Governess
A Healer for the Marquess's Heart
How to Train a Duke in the Ways of Love
Betrayal and Redemption
The Secret of a Lady's Heart
The Lady's Right Option

Forbidden Loves and Dashing Lords
The Lady of the Lighthouse
A Forbidden Gamble for the Duke's Heart

A Forbidden Bid for a Lady's Heart
A Forbidden Love for the Rebellious Baron
Saving His Lady from Scandal
A Lady's Forgiveness
Viscount's Hidden Truths
A Poisonous Flower for the Lady

Marriages by Mistake
The Lady's Gamble
Engaging Love
Caught in the Storm of a Duke's Heart
Marriage by Mistake
The Language of a Lady's Heart
The Governess and the Duke
Saving the Imprisoned Earl
Portrait of Love
From Denial to Desire
The Duke's Christmas Ball

The Dukes' Ladies
Entangled with the Duke
A Mysterious Governess for the Reluctant Earl
A Cinderella for the Duke

Falling for the Governess
Saving Lady Abigail
Secret Dreams of a Fearless Governess
A Daring Captain for Her Loyal Heart
Loving A Lady
Unlocking the Secrets of a Duke's Heart
The Duke's Rebellious Daughter
The Duke's Juliet

A MESSAGE FROM ABBY

Dear Reader,

Thank you for reading! I hope you enjoyed every page and I would love to hear your thoughts whether it be a review online or you contact me via my website. I am eternally grateful for you and none of this would be possible without our shared love of romance.

I pray that someday I will get to meet each of you and thank you in person, but in the meantime, all I can do is tell you how amazing you are.

As I prepare my next love story for you, keep believing in your dreams and know that mine would not be possible without you.

With Love, Abby Ayles

PS. Come join our Facebook Group if you want to interact with me and other authors from Starfall Publication on a daily basis, win FREE Giveaways and find out when new content is being released.

Join our Facebook Group

abbyayles.com/Facebook-Group

Join my newsletter for information on new books and deals plus a few free books!

You can get your books by clicking or visiting the link below

https://BookHip.com/JBWAHR

ABOUT STARFALL PUBLICATIONS

Starfall Publications has helped me and so many others extend my passion from writing to you.

The prime focus of this company has been – and always will be – *quality* and I am honored to be able to publish my books under their name.

Having said that, I would like to officially thank Starfall Publications for offering me the opportunity to be part of such a wonderful, hard-working team!

Thanks to them, my dreams – and your dreams — have come true!

Visit their website starfallpublications.com and download their 100% FREE books!

ABOUT ABBY AYLES

Abby Ayles was born in the northern city of Manchester, England, but currently lives in Charleston, South Carolina, with her husband and their three cats. She holds a Master's degree in History and Arts and worked as a history teacher in middle school.

Her greatest interest lies in the era of Regency and Victorian England and Abby shares her love and knowledge of these periods with many readers in her newsletter.

In addition to this, she has also written her first romantic novel, *The Duke's Secrets*, which is set in the era and is available for free on her website. As one reader commented, "*Abby's writing makes you travel back in time!*"

When she has time to herself, Abby enjoys going to the theatre, reading, and watching documentaries about Regency and Victorian England.

Social Media

- Facebook
- Facebook Group
- Goodreads
- Amazon
- BookBub

Printed in Great Britain
by Amazon